PASSION AND PRINCIPLE

Passion and Principle

A Novel By

Patricia McLaine

This is a novel. The families and characters whose fortunes the story follow are fictitious, as are their parts in the historical events of the time. All names are fictitious. In the course of writing a story it is possible for the names of real people to inadvertently be duplicated. Actual historical personages and events are employed within the story in accordance with recorded history between 1798 and 1871 in Ireland, England, France, Maryland, Washington, D.C., South Carolina, California, the Caribbean, and Hawaii.

ISBN: 0983785597
ISBN 13: 9780983785590

Library of Congress Control Number: 2012908622
CreateSpace, North Charleston, SC

Cover design by Stephannie Beman
Cover photos courtesy of dreamstime.com photographers:
Nejron, Petr Malyshev, and Wiltilroeotte

Dedicated to the loving memory of
My mother, Lona Corian,
My grandmother, Lona Corian,
And my maternal great, great grandparents,
The Courtneys of County Cork
Who blessed me with an Irish heart.

And to another generation thrice removed,
My grandchildren:
Oliver, Jonah, Lydia and Shaina Brassard
Justin, Chase and Autumn Jacobs
In who rests the hope of the world!

Table Of Contents

1

Born With a Veil

In the end, she sought out her beginnings, trying to understand how it all began, wondering if it was worth all the fuss and the bother, all the pain and the suffering that gleaned her but seeming morsels of wisdom and passing pleasures along the way? Each ending produced a new beginning, and each new beginning, an ending of sorts. This was how the story of her life began. The end was in the beginning—and the beginning was in the end.

Though few knew, and fewer still understood its true meaning, she was born with a veil. It was the first sign that she was to be different, an omen for those who clove to the old ways, believing the Tuatha De Danaan still dwelt beneath the hills and beyond the mists: Fairy folks and magical beings thought to inhabit the Otherworld, a welcoming world to one born with a veil, to one born with the gift to see into the hearts and the souls of many, to glimpse the future and the past. Second sight. The lass would possess miraculous and unusual powers bestowed upon a chosen few, even in Ireland. Few there might be able to fathom what was in store for her. How she could be called upon, obligated even, through various and extraordinary circumstances of her life, to live contrary to, or even above, the rules observed in an allegedly civilized society.

Her mother could see that her daughter was different from her sons, Liam and Matthew, in more ways than just gender. A golden light seemed to glow in her newborn eyes, which indicated something important had transpired in the Otherworld to set her child apart. Along with that fact, the babe had not cried, but she greeted the world with a gurgle and grin on that cold winter's morn. Only after her sister Brigid finished chanting a magical blessing had a wail of protest finally come forth, and the child accepted the full breath of life under the watchful gaze of the Blessed Mother from her likeness up on the wall.

When the babe was first placed in her mother's arms, it was agreed between her mother and her midwife sister that the veil would remain their secret, each of them making the sign of the cross to seal the promise. There seemed no need to tell Padraic that his daughter was born with wondrous powers frowned upon by Roman Catholics and Protestants alike, gifts common in women with the blood of the Clan Kelly flowing in their veins. The mark of the Old Religion was upon the child before she breathed her first breath. The *veil*. Was there not enough already to concern the child's father with the cows and the chickens, farming the land and churning the butter? It was no easy task for a tenant farmer to keep body and soul together and see to the needs of his family, since the rebellion that had broken out in Waterford and Wexford that year: The worst of it being the bloody battle on Vinegar Hill.

Over 30,000 Irishmen were hanged, imprisoned or transported, including two Kelly cousins and Thomas O'Reilly, Padraic's younger brother. Thomas, a member of the United Irishmen for the past three years, had thrown in his gun with Wolfe Tone and the other politicians, all of them promising Catholic emancipation. It was the bloodiest uprising that produced the greatest losses by far since many thousands of Roman Catholics were massacred, transported, and robbed of their lands during the terrible times of Cromwell the Butcher. Late in 1798, the British Crown called for greater restrictions all across Ireland—that reached all the way into Dingle Bay.

The last Padraic had heard his younger brother had shipped out to a penal colony somewhere in Australia, with little hope of him ever seeing young Thomas again. And yet, on that crisp November morning, Padraic's thoughts were not on his poor, exiled brother, but on the precious new life he held in his strong arms, on his living, breathing, darling baby daughter.

It was her father who insisted on calling her Mary Margaret after her mother, the name of her maternal great grandmother Kelly long before. Kathleen would be her confirmation name after her paternal great grandmother, long since departed, who had raised her father with a firm hand and a bounty of love. It was her mother who insisted that Kelly be part of each child's name and her father had no objections.

It was never her mother's intention to name a daughter after her. Their first girl, stillborn the year before, was buried in the old cemetery down the road and up the hill with just one name: Rachel. The wee babe had never uttered one cry nor taken one breath, though her mother had cried for hours, for weeks, even months, knowing from her dreams it was divinely intended she have a daughter one day, even two. Now, her sweet Mary Margaret suckled at her breast, filling her heart with a deep joy, with her the easiest birthing of them all.

It was plain that Padraic found his new daughter bonny on that crisp November morning, as the sun rose higher in a clear blue sky and a brisk breeze blew in off the bay. The sunshine filtering in through the lace curtains highlighted the rich copper of the baby's thick crown of hair, a perfect match for her mother's long tresses.

Would her new daughter have her father's green eyes or her own eyes of amber, her mother wondered: The bright amber eyes of great grandmother Kelly, also born with a veil and an abundant crown of copper-red hair?

Padraic appeared contented as he cradled his new daughter near the fire, softly singing to her an old Irish lullaby. Perhaps he was thinking of how one day she would grow tall and strong, the same as her mother, become able at churning the butter and helping out with the chores?

By that year, Liam Niall was well past four, growing taller and stronger each passing day. Though eager to help out with milking the cows, his small hands were not yet equal to the task. His inquisitive younger brother, Matthew Michael, three years the next January, was already learning how to gather the eggs from the henhouse, while being unable to resist chasing Fionn, the head rooster, about the farmyard.

Two young sons they had, fine-looking, hearty young lads of whom they were proud. And now, Padraic Desmond and Mary Margaret O'Reilly had young Mary Margaret, a bonny daughter at last.

2

The Cry of the Banshee

Her father could not bear to call her Mary Margaret those months before she turned eight. Soon after the birth of young Sean Joseph in August, her father started to call her Maggie. For on the very same day that her younger brother was born alive, their dear, darling mother had died. Mary Margaret Shannon Kelly O'Reilly's soul was carried off to heaven on the wings of angels not long after her fifth child born alive breathed his first breath and loudly cried.

"The reason your new baby brother cries so hard and so loud," her father said, "is because there is no mother to hold him to her and suckle him at her breast. The angels have taken your mother away to be with Rachel, Jesus and the Virgin Mary. The two Mary's are looking after me now, me and my five poor, motherless children," her father said and he began to weep.

"God rest her soul and God help me," he cried out, for Padraic loved his wife with all his heart and his suffering was keen with her passing.

Young Mary Margaret had feared the worst when she heard the wail of the banshee that night, along with the agonizing screams of her mother in hard labor. Her Aunt Brigid, acting as midwife, had also heard the cry of the banshee, with both of them also unsettled by the mournful howling of old Black Bart, her mother's faithful hound. The old dog kept baying at that full moon until his heart stopped and he died too. Old Black Bart was with her mother now. It was something that Maggie just knew.

Gazing out the window at the clouds drifting across the moon low in the night sky, the mist rising up off the glen suddenly assumed the ghostly images of magical beings from the Otherworld. Then, all of sudden, a huge white stag with silver antlers appeared, moving swiftly, as the Celtic White Lady of Death, *Macha*, rose up and raced toward the house. Straightaway, Maggie knew that the White Lady had come to claim her mother and take her to be with Rachel and their other ancestors, too, perhaps even with Jesus and Mother Mary.

Throughout the summer months there was this hollow feeling in her center that with all her wishing would not go away, especially when she looked at her mother and the babe growing larger in her belly. Her mother's pregnancy was not an easy one, even with her aunt's constant attention and countless herbal remedies. Her Aunt Brigid had once spoken of an herb that her mother should have taken after once again finding herself with child. Snakeroot. An herb used to hasten labor during the time of a child's delivery, and early on in a pregnancy, the herb was known to cause miscarriage.

"I will not destroy any child in my womb," her mother had shouted in anger. "Surely you know that to even think such a thought is a great sin before God. Shame on you, Brigid! For shame!"

Her father often spoke of wanting more sons to help him out on the farm. Four children seemed not many, considering the Murphy's twenty and the O'Carroll's sixteen: Twelve sons in that one family alone. Some families in Ireland had as many as twenty-two children, mostly Roman Catholics, with the Protestants a close second in terms of the number of offspring in a family. Abortion outlawed by the Crown in 1803.

Not long after the birth of Mary Margaret, Megan Caitlin arrived: Another daughter from the promise of her mother's dreams. At times, her aunt complained of her father's indifference in regard to her mother's four miscarriages and one stillbirth.

"Mary Margaret is a healthy and strong young woman," he insisted, "with a fine mind to match her rare beauty, I might add. My Mary Margaret is capable of bearing me many more fine, healthy children, for she is far from being too old for such matters."

According to her Aunt Brigid, her father's mind was closed to her repeated warnings as to the delicate condition of her mother's health in regard to bearing one child right after another. The matter seemed to disturb her aunt, who thought of herself as a capable and highly respected midwife on the peninsula. Her father apparently also chose to ignore the warnings of Dr. O'Malley, the village physician, in regard to the dangers to her mother in continuing to bear more children.

"Has Father Hennessey not said often enough from the pulpit that children are a gift from God, with coupling expressly designed for that purpose?" her father announced. "It seems to me that God does not even condone lust in the marriage bed!"

According to her aunt, her father was simply unable to leave her poor mother alone.

"From the very first moment he laid his green Irish eyes on your beautiful, comely mother, Padraic fell under the spell of the all-consuming fires of fleshly, earthly passions. With the same desires returned in equal measure by your mother, I might add. After all, your father is an exceedingly handsome man and quite virile, hear tell. Even after a long day's work on this farm, Padraic is seldom weary enough to ignore his all-consuming passion for your beautiful mother."

At times, it seemed to young Maggie that her aunt sometimes forgot that she was still a child, for she often spoke to her of things she had previously heard her discuss with her mother. And yet, on the sad, sad night of her dear, sweet mother's passing, the mournful lament of her father repeatedly resounded in Maggie's young mind:

"Whatever am I going to do now with my beautiful, wonderful, glorious Mary Margaret gone from me forevermore?"

For the two days of the wake, her mother was laid out in her white wedding gown. The frequent comments were that 'her mother looked much as she had as a young bride of sixteen.' Closely watching her as she laid there, Maggie half-expected her mother to rise up and pleasantly remark on what a fine day it was, especially considering how many of their friends and neighbors were gathering from all around the Dingle Peninsula.

Some folks brought food. Others arrived with jugs of poitin, outlawed by the Crown, but still expertly brewed in many a village and hamlet. Her father had purchased four bottles of Jameson's fine Irish whiskey through the generosity of his good friends at the tavern. Most of the other local tenant farmers were not nearly as prosperous as Padraic O'Reilly, and yet, all were doing their best on that very sad day to console him and his five now motherless children.

Folks arrived from as far away as Killarney, Tralee, Limerick, and Cork, from the Blasket Islands and Milltown Commons. Some rode on horses or donkeys, while others walked. Still others filled wagons to overflowing as mourners arrived from over the mountain in Ballyferriter where Mary Margaret Kelly O'Reilly was born on a fine day in May in 1775. All were coming to pay their respects by attending her final farewell celebration.

Father Hennessey led the Rosary. Then Padraic played upon his bagpipes, for his wife had loved to hear him play. Others had brought along fiddles, flutes, pennywhistles, banjos, mandolins, accordions and drums, as all the musicians began to play. Others simply sang along, while yet others played the bard in telling the tales of the glories of old Erin throughout the long, sad, sorrowful night.

"Sing a song at a wake and shed a tear when a child is born," her Aunt Brigid said right before she began to sing *The Streams of Bunclody:*

"Oh, were I at the moss house where the birds do increase... At the foot of Mount Leinster or some silent place... By the streams of Bunclody where all pleasures meet... And all I would ask is one kiss from you sweet..."

All the children sat listening to the many sad songs and the many fine tales until their eyes finally closed and they slept where they lay. Later that evening, a warm breeze blew in off the bay, unusual for that late in the season. A million stars seemed to light up the night sky, as the moon cast its faint glow on the shimmering waters of the bay. Then her Aunt Brigid played the Kelly harp that had been in the family for well over a hundred years. As she serenaded everyone there, she wept for her dear, sweet, younger sister, who was leaving on her heavenly journey surrounded by the hopes and the prayers of her loved ones on that truly sad summer's eve.

Not everyone was able to fit into the small chapel on the next morning as Father Hennessey said Mass in the Church. The majority stayed outside to quietly celebrate the journey of Mary Margaret Shannon Kelly O'Reilly to the Otherworld. Many were generous in their praise of her easy going ways, for Mary Margaret had never been one to complain. She was known to possess the voice of an angel whenever she sang, and the patience of a saint with her family, especially her children. Everyone was going to miss her beautiful, sweet and giving spirit.

As the day grew longer, Maggie started to wonder if the keening was ever going to end. She thought her mother must be alarmed by the terrible noises that everyone was making. Her dear mother had always enjoyed the more gentle sounds: The lapping of the waves against the shore, the whispering of the wind through the mountain pass, and the many merry songs that the family sang together in the evening after supper.

After the last shovel of earth fell upon her mother's grave, her father left with the other men to spend time in the tavern.

"I wonder if there is enough whiskey in the whole of Ireland to ease the pain in your father's heart on this sad, sad day," her Aunt Brigid said.

Pain that her father had said was sure to be his lot for all the rest of his days.

While Liam and Matthew tended to the animals, six year-old Megan left with their cousin, Sarah, who carried young Sean Joseph in her arms in a woolen blanket. Sarah was still nursing Caitlin, her six-month-old daughter, so Padraic was pleased that his new son would be fed and cared for by a blood relation. In exchange for the benefit of her mother's milk, Sarah would receive fresh eggs, cow's milk, and butter every week.

Young Megan was pleased to be trusted with the care of her new baby brother. She promised to rock him and hold him each and every day. Hearing his sweet baby sounds made her wonder how many children she might have herself one day, and yet, the death of her mother with the birth of her brother was a worrisome matter indeed. Nonetheless, while standing beside her mother's grave on that very day, Megan had sincerely promised to take very good care of her brother.

It was on that particular evening that young Maggie finally learned of her *veil*.

"To my knowledge, there was only one other child so born in County Kerry, and that was well before my time. Your grandmother, my mother, assisted in delivering the child. Naturally, my mother was a midwife trained in the ways of the Old Religion the same as I have been. Throughout the long ages, Kelly women have been priestesses and midwives, including my grandmother, your very own great grandmother Mary Margaret Kelly herself," her aunt said in a tone of some pride. "By all the saints, you are her namesake, with the special mark of the old ways upon you. I swear it, my child! For you, Maggie, you were born with a veil!"

In a tone of continued excitement, her Aunt Brigid then said, "You will be the first of your generation to learn everything I already know about herbs for good and herbs for ill, of incantations, blessings and curses, the nature of the sun, the moon, the stars, and the seven sacred planets and their effects upon all mankind. You, Maggie, will learn all about the ancient Celtic deities and the nature spirits that dwell within each tree, each plant, and each and every blade of grass upon the whole earth."

"The whole earth?" Maggie repeated, suddenly feeling thunderstruck.

"There is a unity in nature that you will learn to experience for yourself, my dear. There are rituals I will teach you. Rituals that you must honor and preserve at any and all costs, regardless of what anyone else might say to you, say about you, or say against you, including Father Hennessey!" she said in a tone of disdain while looking directly into Maggie's startled eyes.

"Our *priest*?" Maggie whispered, and her amber eyes opened wider.

Her aunt went on to explain the importance of the sacred oak tree, and how different herbs were best gathered at specific times of the morning or evening to produce the greatest good and the better chance of a cure or a curse. The great importance of hazelnuts was impressed upon her. The wisdom seeds of the old Druids would not only make her healthy and wise, but better equipped to perform her magical deeds, especially during certain times and in certain seasons. Solemn rituals were to be performed at the times of the new and full moons. These rituals were her sacred duty.

"Everything you are about to learn you must faithfully commit to memory. This is to be our secret, yours and mine," her aunt said, "perhaps forevermore."

"Forevermore?" Maggie whispered.

"I have watched you closely since you first entered this world, my child. You were born with the gift of second sight, with miraculous and glorious powers that will enable you to help others and to heal them as well. Have you not noticed how your touch soothes the cows in the barn during a thunderstorm and in times of great distress, besides greatly increasing the number of eggs in the henhouse?"

"My touch does that?" Maggie said in a whisper, "Truly?" she added, feeling astonished by her aunt's unexpected disclosure.

"Your touch is miraculous!" her aunt said, adding an authoritative nod of her head. "And now that your mother, my dear, sweet, wonderful sister, is gone forever, it is time for you to learn the old ways, the ancient ways of the Druids," her aunt said, fixing her with a stony stare as her green eyes faintly reflected the flames of the peat upon the hearth.

After she made the sign of the cross, and as if in a mild trance, Maggie added more peat to the fire. Her heart was pounding inside her chest, and she wondered if her aunt might not be perhaps a touch mad from her recent bout with grief, and yet, there was an element of truth in what she had to say. It was something that she could sense in her center. Maggie had always known that she was different, partly from the way that the other children treated her. Her mother had said often enough that she was different, except that she secretly wished to be the exactly same as all the other girls.

"Why me?" Maggie inquired, taking in a sudden breath and smoothing her apron to keep her hands from trembling. Then, all at once, it seemed to her that her aunt had already told her these things, perhaps in one of her many vivid dreams. Was the beautiful, auburn-haired lady in the flowing white gown so often appearing in her dreams her very own great grandmother Kelly?

"None of us knows exactly what the Lord of the Otherworld has in store for us," her Aunt Brigid said in hushed tones, "Though some know more than others," she added with a wink and a nod as she steadily stared into her eyes without blinking.

"But what you are telling me, Aunt Brigid, is it not a *sin?*" she said, remembering what Father Hennessey had said during some of his more serious sermons.

"The new gods and the old gods are not that much different when it comes to living in this world. It's the spirit that matters, not the name by which it is known, though names and words do have power and meaning when spoken at the right time and in the right manner. And some words cannot be taken back, though later you might wish that some of your words could be. I will teach you about that, my dear, about how to trust your instincts, about the great knowledge and the power and the terrible price to be paid for disobedience. I will teach you of many wondrous and secret things known to only a chosen few in this world, for *to know* such secrets is a great responsibility too grave for some to bear. But for you, young Maggie, to know such things is your absolute and total *DESTINY!*"

For reasons beyond her, everything that her Aunt Brigid had said up until then suddenly made sense to her in her *center*. Was it because of the veil, Maggie wondered? She sat very still and paid very close attention to every word that her aunt had to say.

"There are many languages on this earth, Gaelic being only one. Not all speak English or Irish like Master Roberts teaches you at the hedge school. Later, you may even learn Latin and Greek. You have a fine mind the same as your mother's. But unlike my dear, sweet sister, you will learn to use your mind in strange and amazing ways, ways even perhaps more important than reading and writing. You will learn the secrets practiced by those who invented reading and writing, mark my word, my child! The veil bestows sacred powers and grave responsibilities that you must bear for the rest of your days. There may be times during your life that you have to break a rule or two, mark my word, my dear, sweet niece. Mark my word!"

The "teaching" was to be their secret. Her brothers and sister were not born with "the gift." Others might not be able to either understand or believe, such as Father Hennessey, their parish priest, and the Reverend Brown, the Protestant preacher of the Church of Ireland. Many true believers still lived in Ireland, more than folks might ever suspect, especially among those who dwelled in the hills and in the mountains, practicing the rituals in secret, carrying good luck charms for their own protection and welfare. Many there were still known to converse with the fairies, knocking on the wood of an old oak tree for luck, whispering beneath the tree's branches to seek favors or bestow gifts in gratitude. There was still a great deal that Maggie had to learn.

The tradition was passed on to the girls instead of the boys in their family after great, great grandmother O'Connor, also a Kelly by birth, produced only daughters from her womb. In olden times, the eldest son was the one chosen to learn the old ways, and that was true until long after Saint Patrick and the acceptance of the Catholic Church in County Kerry. The teachings had been in the family for hundreds, or even thousands of years, her aunt explained, with the exact date lost somewhere in the Mists of Time.

"Who am I to deny the ancient traditions?" her aunt inquired. "It is important that the truth be preserved and that the work continue for the sake of our lineage. And that is true, whether you one day bring daughters or sons into this world, young Mary Margaret. One day you must pass on the teachings to one of your descendants and teach your chosen one as I shall most diligently teach you."

"But why *me?*" Maggie inquired, feeling suddenly overwhelmed.

"I've had two stillbirths and six miscarriages. Lost all my young, I did. I've been a widow for five years now, since my Ulliam died of the fever. I'm as celibate as a nun and that's the absolute truth," she said, quickly making the sign of the cross.

"But you could still remarry and have children, Aunt Brigid," Maggie said, remembering how her mother and her aunt had often spoken of the possibility of her aunt having children sometime in the future.

"I am older than your mother by twelve years. There will be no children for me."

"Mother was thirty-one in May."

"Aye," her aunt said, sorrowfully turning to face the fire. "Such a waste … such a good mother she was to you children, and how she loved and adored your father. She died giving Padraic another son." Tears rolled down her face. "Now, he has his three healthy sons, but no wife to care for them. Your mother is gone to be with Rachel and the other unborn young."

Suddenly, sadness welled up from deep inside Maggie, as a soft glow began to fill the entire room. "I know you heard the banshee, Aunt Brigid, and old Black Bart howling at the moon. They were mourning my mother before she died. I know you heard them too."

"Aye," her aunt said. "How could anyone miss that terrible, horrible howling, especially of that banshee?" She sat on the stool beside the roughly hewn kitchen table. "He's joined his mistress, old Black Bart. He is young again the same as her. Old Black Bart is running with Mary Margaret through the green, green meadows of the Summerland."

"He didn't want to stay here without her," Maggie said as she began to sob.

"I miss her greatly, my dearest, loveliest, sweetest sister and greatest friend in all this world. Our brothers flew away with the Wild Geese, off soldiering in France and America. I'm alone now, Maggie. Kevin Kelly hung in the rebellion. Daniel transported halfway round the world with your Uncle Thomas. I pray that the men are all together. But we will never see them again, never again in our beloved Ireland. I'm alone now, my Maggie, all alone in this big world," and she stood.

"You have me, Aunt Brigid," she said, standing and slipping her arms around her aunt's waist as she rested her head against her ample bosom, tears spilling from her sad amber eyes.

"That I have," her Aunt Brigid said, warmly embracing her niece. "We have each other. I shall do everything within my powers to be a mother to you and the other children, as my sister would have and expect of me. I just wish I had been able to save her ... that I had known what more to do."

Together, they wept.

"You did your best, Aunt. It was simply not meant to be," Maggie said in a tone of voice beyond her seven years, somehow knowing in her center that what she had said was true.

All at once, an enormous wave of love enveloped her. Instantly, the room brightened. The fire flamed higher, and warmth infused the entire room mixed with the sweet scent of lavender. Her mother had loved lavender. Only that morning, Maggie had placed a fresh sprig of lavender in her mother's coffin as her final farewell gift.

"There's a special light in your eyes, my child. You, Maggie, you were born *knowing*," her aunt said. "You're an old soul back from the Otherworld with a special calling in this world. You're on a very special mission, very special, indeed."

The scent of lavender grew stronger as the room filled with a soft, glowing light.

"She's here," Maggie said, deeply inhaling. "She has come to say good-bye to us."

"Aye, that she has," her Aunt Brigid said, as she continued to softly sob.

The two of them stood there together, basking in the golden glow, until the scent faded away, leaving only the musty aroma of the smoldering peat of the fire.

After falling into a deep sleep, Maggie at once found herself in a dark green glen filled with beautiful flowers surrounded by a grove of stately oaks cloaked in the bright green leaves of summer. Beneath the tall trees, dense patches of lavender and heather bloomed in profusion.

On a pond of deep blue water, inside a golden boat was Black Bart looking much as he had as a puppy, wagging his tail. Her mother was beside him wearing a gown of the purest white, with a soft smile on her beautiful face, and her long, copper hair glistening in the vibrant light.

Reaching over the side of the boat, her mother's hand lightly touched the water to send out concentric circles in every direction across the entire surface of the pond.

"I love you, my dear Mary Margaret," her mother said without speaking.

Feeling the love moving toward, around, and through her, Maggie said, "I love you, too, Mother," as tears spilled from her eyes onto the pillow.

"I will always be with you. I will always be in your heart. I will do whatever I can to guide you and the other children. You have my solemn promise, my sweet, sweet lass."

"I wish you had stayed a bit longer," Maggie whispered, yearning to reach out and touch her beautiful mother and be comforted in her loving arms yet one more time.

As her mother started to fade from view, Maggie heard her say, "Please take care of him," not knowing if her mother had meant young Sean Joseph or her poor grief-stricken father. Nonetheless, she promised to try to help take care of them both.

Early the next morning, there was a sprig of fresh lavender on her pillow still damp with the morning dew. The gift from her mother in the Otherworld filled Maggie's room with the sweet scent of lavender and her heart with a keen, aching joy.

3

The Way of the Druids

By the time she was nine, it was plain that Maggie would grow to be as tall as her mother. Her hair was the same deep auburn and her eyes the same golden brown. Her father said that her eyes were like two bright stones of amber. One day, in a shop window on Green Street, he showed her a beautiful necklace made out of amber. From that time on, Maggie fancied herself as a lady one day, wearing a fine dress of gold silk and a necklace of ambers to match her eyes. At times, the dream seemed real enough. It was only one dream of many conjured up in her bed at night as she lay awake pretending.

Her younger sister had little time to help out with the chores, since Megan cared for young Sean Joseph, who was constantly running around getting into everything. Megan had tried to gather the eggs for market, but Fionn the rooster pecked at her ankles, for young Sean tended to torment the feisty cock. For that reason, Maggie assumed the task of gathering the eggs and feeding the chickens. Her father said she seemed to have a special way with all the animals.

"It is plainly your gift. The firstborn daughter of a Kelly woman is sure to become known as one of the witches of Kerry," her father quipped one day, adding a wink. "Do not quote me on that, however, if you know what I mean? It's nothing more than an old superstition, if the absolute truth be known."

Her father's comment and the look on his face made her wonder if perhaps he knew more than she or her aunt had ever suspected. On occasion, her father was known to tell the tales of Bruscus Ceallaigh (Kelly), who her mother always claimed as a distant relation. The story went that Bruscus was once a Druid high priest and mighty chieftain in the ancient province of Munster. He was buried under an ogham stone of indeterminate age and origin. Some of those who simply touched the stone instantly received second sight; others an ability to converse with the fairies and other magical beings in the Otherworld. On occasion, her father was known to recount such tales after imbibing a few pints with his friends at the pub.

According to local legend, toward the end of his rather long and illustrious life, Bruscus Ceallaigh lived in a cave filled with gold and countless treasures somewhere in the vicinity of Mount Brandon. The cave was said to be massive and lined with brilliant quartz crystal, the same as many of the other smaller caves beneath the high cliffs of the Dingle peninsula. Smugglers sometimes used these caves to conceal their goods from the prying eyes of the Crown. There were also those who claimed that the cave of Bruscus Ceallaigh had long ago vanished into the Mists of Time where it still remained valiantly guarded by the Tuatha De Danaan.

Both Liam and Matthew had acquired uncommon skills in milking the cows and churning the butter. Their father was quick to lend praise to each of his children, who had not only lightened his load on the farm but increased his sense of pride and joy. At times, their father could be strict and demanding, with each child keenly aware of his underlying gentleness and strength, along with his boundless capacity for love.

Lately, not only the O'Reilly family, but every tenant farmer on the peninsula was required to work harder and for much longer hours. For Lord Chadwick had once again raised the rents on the land.

"It does no good complaining to Percival Pratt, the new land agent," Padraic explained to his family at supper, rolling his eyes and shaking his head with a woebegone expression on his face.

"What does he look like, this Percival Pratt?" Maggie inquired. "I wasn't here when he came for the rent this month."

"He's short and stout, a ruddy-faced Englishman who spends the better part of each day in the pub," Liam said, grinning and shaking his head.

"Every tenant farmer on this peninsula is in the same sorry state since pitiless Percy assumed his post," their father angrily added.

"One cannot take out of a sack more than the full of it," their aunt commented. "It seems to me that all any of us can do is deal with the merciless, heartless bloke, and the ruthless demands of his elegant, pot-bellied lordship in his fancy waistcoat shipped all the way from London!"

And no more was said on the matter on that evening.

On warm days, with the skies perfectly clear, Maggie and her Aunt Brigid would make their way out into the green meadows and woodlands to gather herbs for cooking, for healing, and for magical means. Charms were often fashioned to dispel evil and attract the good. Some of the herbs helped to keep the family healthy and strong throughout the long winter.

Angels or fairies were often petitioned, depending on the herb, sometimes mentally, if not whispered or spoken right out loud. Maggie was quick to memorize the old Druid incantations, applying each of them with unusual skill and clarity, in her aunt's fair-minded opinion. She was taught that the angels were somewhat similar to fairies, though of a different order in nature. Angels were higher up on the ladder and tended to be more reliable and willing to help any mortal with a serious need. However, only those specifically called upon were allowed to intercede in any mortal matter. That was Holy Universal Law, according to her Aunt Brigid.

"It's the same with all the saints and prophets," her aunt explained, "Not one of them is allowed to meddle in mortal affairs unless called upon by name with a specific purpose in mind, unless the Lord of the

Otherworld Himself happens to intervene, mind you. Burning candles and incense is both good and wise. Reciting the rosary is as important at home as it is in the Church, especially in seeking assistance from the Virgin Mother, Jesus, or some archangel such as Michael or Gabriel. Even St. Catherine, the Patron Saint of Ventry, has to be petitioned, except for the fact that she can be downright busy seeing after all the local fishermen.

"In the woods and the meadows, near a fairy ring or a sacred oak, the name of a Celtic deity may prove extremely useful or beneficial at times, such as *Lugh* or the *Goddess Dana*, a close kin of the Virgin Mary's, hear tell," her aunt said, smiling. "The invocation of the sun, the moon, the seven sacred planets, four elements and even the four directions may be extremely useful if repeated aloud while performing some sacred rituals."

During the springtime, Maggie and her aunt transplanted several herbs near the house. Some primarily for the purpose of cooking were planted in pots near a low window. Dried herbs were placed over most of the windows and doors to ward off evil spirits and elemental mischief-makers.

"You must not breathe a word of this to anyone," her aunt said, "Not a word should you repeat to Father Hennessey in the confessional, for it has not been that long since witches were burned at the stake or hung from some tree. It is rather fortunate for our kind that the Church has finally finished with the wicked, disgusting witch hunts and inquisitions," she said, quickly making the sign of the cross and shaking her head.

"Herbs must be gathered at the right time of the sun and the moon to do the greatest good. Appeasing nature spirits always assists us in the preparation of all medicines, potions and poultices. You remember that well, Maggie dear! Kindly remember!"

Fairies, gnomes and lesser elementals cared for different portions of each plant, Maggie was quick to learn. The Hierarchy of Nature was beginning to make itself known to her. Enchanting helpers from the Otherworld had started to become visible to her even during the daylight hours, some playful, others a touch mischievous. That made it clear to her why some folks preferred to maintain a safe distance from their kind at all times.

Her aunt made her a special charm to protect her from the lesser, or demonic, spirits that might try to do her harm. It was also necessary for her to protect herself from some members of the Kelly clan, in addition to a few of the Desmonds: Those who had cursed the O'Reillys in the past. Other members of the family may have intentionally, or even accidentally, committed a grievous wrong. Maggie was taught to use her mind to dispel evil, whether intentionally or accidentally directed her way.

Her aunt was pleased with how quickly she had learned to identify the leaves and scents of different plants, along with the manner in which she remembered every incantation. The name of each nature spirit and the time of day best suited for planting and harvest was written in her diary. Every herb and its root were drawn next to its name in Latin, Gaelic and English. All the knowledge stored in her aunt's head was being carefully written down for further study. Writing things down had been sanctioned to both Maggie and her aunt in identical dreams on the very same night that included an appearance of her great grandmother Kelly.

Some herbs were dried out in the shed, with others hung from the rafters in the barn, in addition to those stored in jars to last throughout the long winter. Mr. McCarthy, the owner of the apothecary in Dingle, preferred the herbs of Brigid Mahoney to those he found in Killarney or Tralee. Payment was always done in trade. Her aunt had confided that Mr. McCarthy also conversed with the fairies and also attended Mass each Sunday, the same as Maggie and the rest of her family.

In the evening after supper, her father would often recount the tales of old Erin and its once glorious high kings. His many stories included tales of Queen Macha Mong Ruad, with her flaming red hair, as well as the legends of Tain Bo Cuailgne about Cuchulain, who was highly favored by the old gods. There were also tales of Cormac McArt, the son of Conn of the Hundred Battles. Their father was especially fond of stories of Fionn MacCumail, the king who had once resided in a grand palace on the Hill of Allen in Kildare. Liam and Matthew preferred the tales of Fionn, the leader of the Fian, the ancient warriors who had once upon a time fulfilled the mandates of the High King in fighting Ireland's glorious battles during the times of old. Padraic could keep his children spellbound by the fire nearly every evening.

On occasion, their father's stories involved the times of the Viking invasions. How the Vikings had raped and pillaged up and down the entire coast of Ireland and that was long before the ports of Dublin, Waterford, Wexford, and Limerick were finally established.

"After the Vikings, it was the English who arrived with their own special brand of plunder," her father said in a tone of bitterness, "and they ended the reign of our once proud high kings. The last of them, Rory O'Connor," he solemnly added, "It is said … was a distant cousin on the Kelly side of the family."

The stories that Maggie secretly preferred were those told by her Aunt Brigid on their long walks over the hills and through the dales, the glorious tales of the Tuatha De Danaan and of magical King Dagda. Her aunt was named after King Dagda's daughter, Brigid, the goddess of poetry, though most thought her named after St. Bridget, St. Patrick's successor. Either way was fine with her aunt, since St. Bridget was supposedly fathered, or at least raised by, a Druid priest. The sites of all St. Bridget's monasteries were previously sacred to the Druids.

It was the mixing of the old gods with the new gods again, Maggie soon learned, as her studies continued in the wondrous ways of the Druids.

4

Hedge School

Even though it was no longer necessary for young Roman Catholics to hide behind hedges in fear for their mortal lives while learning how to read and write, a tenant farmer could hardly afford to pay for private schooling for his youngsters, especially for the education of a daughter. So the hedge schools continued in practice for those with a serious need and a strong desire to learn.

Years earlier, her oldest brother Liam was assigned as the hedge school lookout, eagle eye that he was by age six in detecting the prospects of Protestant intrusion heading down the road or over some hill. More than once, his class was forced to scatter to protect life and limb. Presently, that same teacher, Master Roberts, well remembered the old days of beatings for those who even attempted to provide young Roman Catholics with simply a rudimentary education. He was once thrown out of a village in Cork and told to never return. In some parts of Ireland, Catholic teachers were murdered or thrown into a rat-infested prison to never again see the light of day. However, by 1800, greater tolerance emerged after the Act of Union. Roman Catholics were now educated the same as Protestants, a modern advancement in a country where Protestants tended to still treat Catholics in a less than exemplary manner.

In spite of the fact that the new school in Dingle had refused to employ Master Roberts, he was a very fine teacher indeed. Kind and patient, though routinely unkempt, he was eager to share his knowledge with his poorer students, mostly those from tenant farms where the children worked as hard as the parents. A generous parishioner had granted him the use of an old barn to keep his students out of the weather. An old wood-burning stove also donated. Maggie and Megan were fond of Master Roberts, except Maggie secretly wished that he would take the time to comb his hair.

During the past year, Liam had grown taller and stronger. For that reason, he now worked more closely with their father. Now the older boys helped to deliver eggs, chickens, milk and butter to the market in Dingle and to other townships around the peninsula. In fact, Liam was starting to think of himself as something of an overseer on the farm. That was apparently why he had insisted on taking the wagon to Ballyferriter alone on that day. Megan was feeling a touch under the weather, so Matthew was the only one to attend the hedge school with Maggie on that day.

That was the first time that Aidan McKenna rode over the mountain on a borrowed pony to attend that particular hedge school. Aidan was younger than Matthew but much taller and larger for a lad not yet twelve. Aidan had a fine face and deep dimples when he smiled. Parts of his dark curly hair fell down into his eyes. It seemed that everyone had noticed Aidan as he sat on the bench in the back that day, especially Maggie.

The very first time she looked into his dark brown eyes a bolt of pure lightning shot straight through her, quickly racing from the top of her head down to her ten tingling toes. Vivid scenes and characters from early Irish folklore streamed through her mind, tales of the Tuatha De Danaan and King Dagda, of Queen Mauve and other legendary heroes. Visions of crystal encrusted caves loomed within her mind's eye, as brilliant flashes of lightning filled an ominous, dark sky. Suddenly, there was a clash of broadswords with cloaked riders astride sweaty, restive horses. A screeching hawk circled in the smoke-filled skies, as a white bearded wizard raised his staff and intoned a magical chant to still the raging winds and halt the blinding torrents of rains.

In an instant, Maggie was transported through time and space into an era filled with chivalry and romance from long before the invasions of the English or the Vikings. Surely this boy was the son of some noble chieftain who had made his way to Dingle to seek her hand. That thought brought color into her cheeks and her heart began to race even faster inside her chest.

Aidan stared at her long and hard. It was obvious that he was completely taken by Maggie. The other children seated near him began to snicker. His immediate thought: He should be feeling self-conscious and stupid, but he decided to ignore the others. Truly, he was fully captivated by her beautiful face, her golden eyes, and her long, brilliant red hair. Surely she was the girl from his dreams, the one encountered as he rode upon the white steed, and later, as he swam naked in the deep pool beneath the thundering spray of the waterfall. Surely he was now meeting in the flesh that very same beautiful maiden!

At the end of the class, Maggie stood before Aidan with her upturned face and questioning eyes as she openly stared right into his face. He appeared dumbfounded. Not one word escaped from his partly opened lips.

"My name is Mary Margaret Kathleen Kelly O'Reilly," she said. "But everyone calls me Maggie." Her mouth felt strangely dry as she spoke to him, and, in spite of everything, she returned the steady gaze of his beautiful, dark brown eyes. "Have we met somewhere before?"

"Only in my dreams," he said, appearing to swallow with difficulty as he openly stared back at her.

That was the moment she knew that he loved her.

Trying her best not to smile, she heard Matthew remark, "Aidan is from Ballyferriter. His father sails the high seas, don't you remember? Most of his family attended mother's wake."

"Were you there?" she enquired, searching his face and deeply inhaling the musty scent of him, for in her heart she knew that she had always known him.

"No, I'm very sorry for that. I was sick in bed with a fever. My mother made me stay at home." He took in a deep breath and glanced down at the floor. "I was sorry to hear of your mother's passing." Again, he looked straight into her eyes. "Your mother was noted by everyone for her rare beauty and you look very much like her."

"The spitting image," Matthew said. "My Da says that Maggie looks much the same as our mother did when she was a young lass. My mother grew up with your mother in Ballyferriter."

There was an awkward silence.

"When you grow older, do you intend to be a smuggler like your father?" Matthew smugly inquired, as a taunting grin slowly spread across his face.

"Whatever do you mean?" Aidan said in seemingly feigned innocence, as a silly smirk captured his face. He appeared to cautiously glance about to see if anyone else might be listening.

The three of them were now there alone in the darkening barn.

"Everyone knows about the wrecking on Inch Beach. About the silly cows with lanterns about their necks to appear as anchored boats to unsuspecting English captains, so their vessels might be lured onto the rocks and their cargo captured." Matthew narrowed in eyes in closer scrutiny. "Everyone knows that your father works for his sovereign Lord Mayor smuggling brandies and wines from France and Spain to sell to the local gentry. Is that what you plan to do when you grow up, Aidan McKenna? Be a smuggler the same as your father, Kevin, who sails the high seas and sneaks about like a thief in the night?"

Suddenly, Aidan stiffened and his face flushed. "I am a cabin boy on the *Cornelia*, a merchant ship," he said, his eyes fixed on Matthew's, except that it seemed difficult for him to turn his eyes away from Maggie. "I love sailing the high seas," he said, turning directly back to her with renewed intensity in his dark brown eyes.

Aidan was much taller than Matthew, more the height of Liam, age fourteen.

"I am sure that you love sailing the high seas," Matthew said in a mocking manner. "A merchant *smuggling brigantine* is what you are sailing with your father. Isn't that right, Aidan?" He glared at him and stood his ground, jutting out his jaw as though he was ready for a fight.

"Is smuggling not dangerous?" Maggie softly inquired.

"Perhaps, but a bit more profitable than farming, I'd say," his tone had softened. "It seems to me that you should wear fine silk when you grow up to be a lady. That is what I'd smuggle for you … bolts of bright silk and fine lace to be made into fine gowns for you to wear, perhaps to some fancy balls."

"Oh, really?" Matthew said. "Maggie will not even be ten until November. She's a long way from wearing fine silk and lace gowns, if ever she does, for a fact. Tenant farm girls don't usually wear fine silk and lace gowns, now, do they?"

"I will be a fine lady one day, Matthew," Maggie said, turning to her brother. "I shall wear silk and lace, fine gowns. It is something I just *know*."

"Sure you do," he said, quickly turning back to Aidan. "Bit of a witch, Maggie is. It runs in our family. Sees things, she does, spirits, ghosts walking across the meadow, even our dead mother. Talks to fairies, my sister." He rolled his eyes and audibly sighed.

"I am a priestess, not a witch. There's a big difference. I am a druidess returned from the Otherworld. That is what Aunt Brigid says."

"Aunt Brigid is a bit daft, Maggie. You've got to know that much. You can hardly believe anything that she tells you." Suddenly, he grabbed a hold of her hand and tugged on her. "Time to go now. Time for our supper."

"Will I see you again at the school?" Maggie inquired of Aidan.

"You just try and keep me away. You will see me again soon enough, Miss Mary Margaret Kathleen Kelly O'Reilly. Aidan Brendan McKenna is my name. Please don't let me keep you from your supper."

Immediately, Aidan turned and ran out of the barn to climb onto the pony. Then, off he rode in the general direction of Ballyferriter, trotting at a steady gait until he reached the old oak tree near the sacred well. There he stopped and turned to her, smiling. After waving at her, off he rode on up the mountain path.

From that day forward, Maggie knew that her life was going to be different. Nothing was ever going to be the same. Aidan had returned to be with her again, perhaps forever.

5

The Midwife

It started out with the calving of her favorite cow the summer that Maggie was still eleven. When her father realized that the cow was bleeding badly and in serious trouble, he sent Liam to the house to fetch his sister and bring her straightaway to the barn.

Darkness still covered the land as a sleepy-eyed Maggie stood in her nightgown in the semi-lit stall near two flickering kerosene lamps. She had only seen one calf born before and never so much blood. The arrival of puppies and kittens were often witnessed, but never a cow in serious trouble delivering its very first calf. Matters seemed grave. Her heart went out to the poor, tormented creature.

"Colleen is having a rough time of it, Maggie. Could you not put your hands on her?" her father pleaded, worry plain all over his face.

In obedience, Maggie knelt down and placed both her hands on the side of the laboring cow. At her gentle touch, Colleen lifted her head, her big brown eyes appearing to plead as a mooing groan came forth.

Tightly closing her eyes, Maggie instantly focused on her center and started to slowly breathe in and out, silently petitioning the goddess Dana, Aine of Knockaine, the fairy queen in charge of cattle, and St. Francis of Assisi. Then she began repeating *Hail Marys* out loud to seek the assistance of Mother Mary, knowing how her father could not afford to lose one cow or its calf with times being what they were.

Another heifer would mean more calves on the farm, more milk and more butter. Another bull might be used for breeding or become meat in the marketplace. Maggie tried to not attach herself to the males, although Cuchulainn had been a great asset to her father for years, living up to his legendary name by impregnating one cow after another every year without a single failure to date.

The bleeding miraculously stopped. After several failed attempts, a newborn calf was standing on its four wobbly legs, with Colleen the better for it. The cow welcomed her first calf to the herd, gratefully, another heifer.

"Good job, Maggie. Now, you go back to bed and get some sleep," her father said.

Maggie obeyed, visiting with her mother and the elders in a welcoming dream near the sacred grove in the brilliant soft light of the Summerland.

At the age of fourteen, Maggie became a midwife's apprentice to her aunt in helping to deliver the children of mostly poor Catholics, the wives and daughters of tenant farmers all around the peninsula.

It was not long before the news spread to most of the locals, including the Protestant gentry, that young Maggie O'Reilly had a magical touch in healing both the new mothers and their offspring. The rumor was that she had extraordinary knowledge of curative herbs that improved upon the quantity and quality of a mother's milk, with yet others that regulated the menses. The latter was accomplished with the aid of false unicorn root. Soon, Maggie realized the herbs in her satchel, especially those unavailable through the local apothecary, should remain her secret, with the ingredients disclosed to only a chosen few. Otherwise, fewer shillings might find their way into her purse.

The infertile also started to reach out to her, the childless willing to do anything to produce an heir. That seemed to be the only way for many women to fulfill an earthly purpose. Chaste berry, licorice and red clover sipped in a tea at daybreak and sunset helped a few of the women to conceive. Warm poultices applied to the abdomen sometimes increased the chance of a conception or prevented a miscarriage. Other herbs relieved menstrual discomfort. Wild yam, ginger, sage or basil eased their morning sickness. Cinnamon and motherwort was known to increase the ardor in a woman. A few husbands hoped to rekindle the passion in a wife of some years where desire had faded, if not altogether vanished. Charms were fashioned for those who believed in the old ways: Amulets for fruitfulness or preventative measures.

From the very beginning, Maggie relished her role as midwife, both the joy and the drama, and the occasional despair. It felt good to her to serve the needs of the women while adding coins to the family coffer. It seemed a blessing to her all around.

The first of the gentry to seek out Maggie's services in the birth of her first child was Jennifer Pratt, the wife of Percival, the dreaded land agent. Maggie was extremely pleased at being approached for the responsible task, although she tried her best to avoid 'pitiless Percy' whenever possible. Jennifer seemed agreeable enough.

Needless to say, their house was large and one of the finest in town, with five servants, three for the house and two to attend to the horses and carriage. It was an extremely handsome house right in the center of Dingle Town.

"It is the *Ps* that have it in the Pratt family," Brigid commented one evening right after supper.

"Whatever do you mean, Aunt?" Liam inquired, adding more peat to the fire.

Maggie glanced up from where she was washing the dishes and said, "They have named their first son, a fine lad, I might add, Peter Percival Pratt."

Her Aunt Brigid smiled, scraping another plate before handing it to Maggie. "There is Prudence Pratt, Percival's aunt, the comely lady in the fine house on Goat Street."

"Prudence Pratt," Matthew repeated, puckering up his lips. "Well, that is three: Peter, Percival and Prudence," he said, grinning.

"Phillip is Percival's father, the older brother of Prudence. Phillip married Penelope. His grandmother was named Philomena and his grandfather, Pierce Pratt."

"Phillip and Philomena do not have the same sound to them," Megan said with a frown.

"Still," her aunt said, "It starts with a *P*. The eldest brother is named Paul."

"The brother of Percival or Prudence?" Liam inquired.

"Prudence, naturally. Her second eldest brother is named Patrick, after the Irish side of the family. Philomena was born a Brosnan, so pitiless Percy has Irish blood in his veins, though it doesn't show much, if you ask me."

"Except for his drinking," Liam said. "Irishmen tend to be hearty drinkers, Aunt Brigid."

"Englishmen do their fair share, Liam," Maggie said. "On most days, the tavern is filled with more Protestant Englishmen than Irish Catholics, for a certainty. Are they not the ones with the pennies to spare for a pint?"

"Is that the end of the *P*s, then, Aunt?" Matthew inquired.

"Her younger sister is named Pamela. And there you have it!" Brigid said with a grin.

"Prudence, Percival, Peter, Penelope, Pierce and Patrick!" Megan said and she started to giggle.

"Phillip and Philomena," Liam added.

"Do not forget Paul and Pamela," Brigid added and she laughed out loud.

"If they have a daughter next, they plan to name her Priscilla," Maggie said. "Priscilla Pratt she shall be," and she chuckled as she nodded in agreement.

"What did I tell you?" Aunt Brigid then said, with her tone and her smile triumphant, "In the Pratt family, it's the *P*s that have it!"

6

Sailing the High Seas

For two long months, Aidan was off sailing the Atlantic through the English Channel all the way into the Bay of Biscay. Recently, he was promoted from apprentice seaman to midshipman under his father, Kevin McKenna, first mate to Captain Sean O'Shea. The crew was sailing the regal, two-masted, square-rigged brigantine the Irish crew fondly called *Queen Maeve,* although the fine vessel, built by Irishmen at the Ritchie and MacLaine shipping yards in Belfast, was christened the *Cornelia.* Thankfully, the unsuspecting British had yet to discover that the ship was being used for the primary purpose of smuggling.

The near blind entry into Dingle Harbor provided considerable refuge for all sea-going vessels, and the high sea cliffs assured a level of protection from the fierce winter gales, besides the prying eyes of the Coast Guard spies sent out to keep a close watch by King George III and the Crown. Nearly everyone on the peninsula, and more especially the sovereign Lord Mayor Stewart Gregory himself, were well aware of the fine ship's main purpose. The rumor was that the sovereign himself had hand-picked the crew to secure goods from France, Spain and Portugal, in exchange for woolen, fine Irish linen and lace. The crew was made up of able seamen clever enough to deal with the shrewd officials in most foreign ports. One man spoke French, two Spanish, and another Portuguese because of his mother.

The past July, Aidan had sailed off to France with the purpose of securing wines and brandies, silks and laces to peddle to the local gentry. He had also promised to return with bolts of pure white silk and white lace to be made into a wedding gown for his Maggie. After all, had not her mother and his own married at the age of sixteen? Was it not an excellent time for them to marry?

In response, Maggie had explained that there was plenty of time to marry and bring up a family, for she was not yet even fifteen.

By that September, Maggie started to walk the long way to Dunshean, with its ancient promontory fort, to gaze out into the bay toward the open Atlantic. She hoped to catch sight of the wind-filled sails of the *Cornelia,* for she was beginning to deeply miss Aidan. She longed for his wonderful kisses, to gaze upon his handsome face, to experience his strength and playfulness, his teasing, pleasing ways. She wanted him to come home again before the cold winter weather set in.

That month, Aidan would be turning seventeen. From a bolt of the local white linen given to her by Miss Prudence Pratt, the aunt of Percival and Jennifer, she had sewn Aidan a handsome shirt. The linen was an expression of Miss Pratt's gratitude for her apparent excellent care of her niece, the new mother, and her first great nephew, the newborn child. Young Peter Percival had arrived somewhat rapidly, since his mother seemed expressly designed to bear children with her broad hips and ample bosom.

Miss Pratt was also kind enough to teach Maggie how to embroider Aidan's monogram in dark blue on one shirt pocket: A.B.M. Aidan Brendan McKenna. Blue was his favorite color. In truth, Maggie had loved Aidan from the first day they met at the hedge school. She loved the sound of his name. His birthday was on the following Friday. If the ship arrived in time, he could wear his new shirt to Church on the next Sunday.

"I am named after St. Aidan, don't you know?" he had said to her one day the prior June. "A fine monk and a grand man was he. St. Aidan became a Bishop, as you may well already know with all your many studies."

"Now, don't you forget St. Brendan of Birr, the chief prophet of Ireland? St. Brendan the Navigator was supposed to have discovered America long before Christopher Columbus."

"Am I not a sailor, the same as St. Brendan? And yet, he had no grand ship like the *Cornelia,* but only a curragh, poor man. Brendan was a monk, too, mind you."

"Well, you are no monk and no saint a'tall. And not nearly as grand as St. Aidan or St. Brendan," she said, laughing. "So don't you go getting airs and puffing yourself up like some rooster about to crow."

That was when he grabbed her and pulled her behind the beehive hut, kissing her with a fervor she loved, pressing his body hard into hers. Both of them were soon prone on the grass, arms and legs intertwined. His hand stroked her long, silky hair, his outstretched fingers lightly touched her flushed cheek and welcoming lips. He loved the touch and taste of any part of her as he breathed in her sweet lavender scent. Gazing into her lovely amber eyes, he felt he glimpsed eternity. He loved to watch the way she seemed to enjoy watching him, with wonder in her glorious golden eyes. Everything about her was pleasing to him with nothing left out.

"I love you," he said, "with all my heart and all my being!"

"Not with all of your mind and your soul?" she teased.

"That too. With all of me I love you." He kissed her again, tasting deeply, as his hand slid down onto her backsides to press her more firmly into him. "I want you, Maggie, madly, I do. How long must I wait to have all of you?"

"Longer," she said, smiling that beguiling smile of hers, and then she turned her golden gaze toward the heavens. "I am only fourteen, Aidan." Now she looked at him with her smiling eyes. "You know that Father Hennessey says that fornicating is a sin when you are not yet married."

"That is only because priests are not allowed to fuck," he said, lying back and propping his head in his hands as he broadly grinned. "What a sorry lot, those poor, celibate priests. I've been thinking of becoming Protestant. They're not so deadset against fucking. Their preachers fornicate, marry, and even raise a family."

"You'll be watching your language, if you please. You have the mouth of a sailor for a certainty! Are you thinking of becoming a Protestant preacher, praise God?"

"Hardly! I'm a sailor, my bonny lass." He slipped his hand onto her covered breast, as her glorious amber eyes steadily gazed up at him. "You know how babies are made, being a midwife and all, helping all the new mothers the first time. Or those having fifteen like Abigail McCarthy! Pure Roman Catholics those McCarthy's!"

"Another good reason to keep you waiting," she said, removing his hand from her breast with a quick glance of disdain. "I have no intention of bearing you fifteen children in all my days!"

"Ten, then?"

"If you'll be having the half of them. I will be no man's breeding mare or milk cow!"

"Planting the seed is the fun of it. With all you know about herbs, you should be able to take care of not being with child. You have said as much, seeing as how you helped those Protestant girls and that whore over in Killarney."

"What I do with my herbs is none of your business. I will be telling you no more of my secrets or else you'll go telling the entire crew of the *Cornelia* … about your virgin midwife and her wicked herbs that increase the ardor in a woman or a man, if need be."

"Do they now? Have you been giving me your herbs and casting a spell over me with your charms to make me mad about you and horny as your bull Cuchulainn in the spring?" He ran his finger over her forearm and deeply inhaled her sweet lavender scent.

"It is your memories of the Otherworld and of our other times that make you mad for me," she said, kissing him quickly and gazing into his dark brown eyes. She had often told him how very much she loved his dark brown eyes.

"Am I to believe you are still a virgin, then?" he teased.

Maggie said nothing, only nodding and avoiding his gaze.

"What about when I am away at sea, with young Fergus following you about all moony-eyed? The poor, ugly chap is half mad for you, as are half the lads in Dingle, if not on the whole peninsula, what with your rare beauty and your flirty ways. My cousin Niall, he gets tongue-tied every time he sees you, he does, with your sweet voice and your fine Irish dancing. There is much about you to charm a man's senses, considering the whole of it, Miss Mary Margaret Kathleen Kelly O'Reilly!"

"What about my red hair? The men in the village say they will catch no fish if a redheaded woman crosses their path on the morning they plan to fish. They absolutely refuse to go fishing on such a day! Imagine that?"

"They stay all day in the pub instead, no doubt. I'm no fisherman, Maggie. I'm a midshipman on the *Cornelia!* I love your red hair, every strand of it!" As he reached out to smooth her hair, deep feelings of love welled up from deep inside him. Briefly, he considered how very much he wanted her. How very deeply he loved her. He sighed and kissed her again, feeling the heat grow even stronger in his groin.

"I only have eyes for you, Aidan McKenna," she whispered, kissing him with increased passion. "I suppose you are not a virgin, then, though we have known each other these many years, since I was nine and you eleven. I remember the first time you kissed me beside that fairy ring. It was the fairies helped me tempt you," she said, grinning. "Have you not saved yourself for me, Aidan?" She stared steadily into his brown eyes and instantly appeared to know the answer.

He glanced away, trying his best to guard his facial expression, knowing that she could read his mind if she could only capture his eyes. At that moment, silence seemed to him his best and only real defense.

"Well, just don't you go getting some horrible disease from some French whore that you can pass on to me. I am not the least bit interested in dying, or becoming sick near unto death because of some wretched harlot willing to spread her legs for a sixpence!" She got up in a huff and turned to glare at him, as she quickly smoothed out her dress with both her hands.

Aidan silently watched her.

"You had better come to me clean when the time comes, or there will be no fucking for ye with me!" she said, tossing her head and looking away.

He loved the way that her hair sometimes bounce on her shoulders, shining like copper in the midday sun, framing a face that constantly intruded into his every thought and dream. How could he keep secrets from his sweet druidess? Maggie could see right through him. His silence had said more than he intended. It was his father who said a man needed experience so as not to look a fool in the marriage bed. The whore cared not that he loved his Maggie, but only for the coins in her dish.

The pain and grave dangers of childbirth had already been fully impressed upon Maggie; first, by her Aunt Brigid, and later, by the birthing mothers in their traumas and travails. There were already six deliveries in which she had assisted; two others with her as the midwife in charge. During her second assisted delivery in Ballyferriter, a girl of sixteen had hemorrhaged and died with the birth of her first child. Her premature son had lived but three days. Her husband of twenty was forced to bury them, side by side, on a hill near the sea. Maggie and her aunt had attended the wake and services in the small Church of Ireland. They had done everything within their power to console the grief stricken family.

Remembering that sad time, Maggie had no desire to bear children anytime soon. Her aunt had lectured her often enough, reminding her of her mother's significant fertility, her many miscarriages and one stillbirth. There was no need to remind her of her mother's early death with the birth of Sean Joseph. That was something Maggie was unlikely to ever forget.

"I do not mean to frighten you, lass. You are built to bear children, but please, Maggie, not until the time is right and after your wedding day, her Aunt Brigid pleaded. "There are enough hardships in this world without creating more through your reckless, youthful passion. Keep him waiting and wanting you. It has never hurt a man yet, but only serves to increase his gratitude when he finally does get to bed you."

Maggie had always listened to her aunt. However, she had never resisted Aidan's kisses or the many pleasures he had given to her with his hands and his mouth. Sometimes he set her on fire and made her yearn to join with him. And yet, every time, she remembered young Sarah so cold in her grave, with her tiny son nearby in the smallest coffin she had ever seen. Remembering helped Maggie to control her ardor behind the barn or out in the ruins, with both of them half-naked, their hearts racing and their blood on fire. Aidan never pushed her, for he had also grown up with young Sarah and her poor bereft husband.

Once Aidan had said, "The thought of losing you in such a manner would surely drive me mad. If such a thing ever happened, I would probably soon die too from being unable to go on living without you."

7

A Bounty of Books

Besides her generous gift of the local white linen, for taking good care of her niece and her new great nephew prior to and during the time of his birth, Prudence Pratt was starting to lend books to Maggie from her vast library inherited from her late Irish grandfather, Martin Brosnan of Dublin. Prudence said that her grandfather was "a grand old man who was well aware of the fact that his favorite granddaughter would treasure and care for his books better than anyone else in the family."

The library, with its countless shelves filled from ceiling to floor with old and new books neatly arranged, held a tremendous fascination for young Maggie. All those volumes of varying sizes from the largest to the smallest made her wonder what sort of information, stories or madcap adventures might be written on so many pages. Was there enough time in a lifetime to read that many books, she wondered? How could anyone remember so many stories from so many different times and places? Was it possible to read all those books if the fine woman on Goat Street live to be a hundred years?

On the day she picked up the bolt of white linen, Maggie boldly inquired, "Would you consider me awfully rude if I were to ask you to one day perhaps lend me just one of your many fine books to read on my farm on the outskirts of town?"

"Well ..." Prudence hesitated and looked surprised.

Unable to restrain herself any longer, Maggie blurted out, "I promise to guard any book you might lend me with my very own life, Miss Pratt," and she crossed her heart with her index finger and touched the end of her nose. It was something she often did at home to prove she was telling the truth.

Instantly, a warm smile formed on Miss Pratt's lovely face and her green eyes appeared to sparkle.

"I solemnly promise to return any book you might lend to me in the very same condition in which it was entrusted to my care. I promise you that, Miss Pratt, I completely and genuinely promise you," Maggie said, curtsying and holding her breath, with the bolt of linen tightly pressed against her chest in order to try to still the rapid beating of her heart.

Without her knowing it, Prudence Pratt was already decidedly impressed with the young midwife, Maggie O'Reilly, with her openness, her strong streak of independence, and her fully uncommon candor. In the back of her mind, Prudence had already been thinking of mentoring young Maggie. No other young peasant girl in the area had impressed her up until that time. Maggie O'Reilly had qualities above and beyond all the others. In addition to that, she was beautiful, highly intelligent, and her character seemed more than worthy of further development and refinement.

"Do you like to read novels?" Prudence inquired.

"What be novels?" was her stunned reply.

"Fiction. Stories made up in someone's imagination. I assume that you can read?"

"Aye, Miss Pratt. I can count and write, too."

The first book that Prudence selected from a shelf was a newer volume titled *Sense and Sensibility*. "You might enjoy reading this novel. The author is an English woman, Miss Jane Austen. She's one of my favorite authors. You do know how to read English?"

"Aye, ma'am. Gaelic, too, and a bit of Greek and Latin, but not much."

"Greek and Latin?" she said in a tone of some surprise while she held out the book to Maggie.

In a moment of great excitement, Maggie put down the linen and grasped the book in her trembling hands. It was a thrill for her just to hold the book. For that reason, she was beyond excited that Miss Pratt would actually lend her one of her precious books from her precious library. Any book would have been fine, even an old one. But this was a brand new book. *Saints be praised!* Miss Pratt was entrusting her with a brand new book with fully clean pages with no smudges on them at all. *Beggars must not be choosers*, Maggie thought, even though she had secretly fancied reading one of the older books, perhaps some poetry or a bit of history. Master Roberts had always spoken highly of William Shakespeare and John Milton, even though they were Englishmen.

"How many days may I keep the book?"

"As long as it takes you to read it," Miss Pratt said and her eyes were smiling brightly.

At first, Maggie skipped along, and then, she nearly ran all the way home, with her bolt of linen under one arm and the book tightly held in her other hand. Her heart was filled with joy to nearly overflowing.

Right after supper, she sat near the fire and silently read to herself, savoring every word and every descriptive phrase by lamplight, by fire-light, and finally by candlelight. She was delighted with the way that each character seemed to leap off the page right into her mind. The vivid settings and the interesting dialogue involved the society of the English living in the countryside. The story was filled with deception and intrigue, but more importantly, with love. The romance in the novel made her heart leap with joy as she turned every new page eager to discover what was going to happen next.

The author resided somewhere far across the Irish Channel in England. Maggie was fascinated with the language, with the proper conduct of either the plain or the beautiful ladies, with both the odd and the handsome gentlemen, in addition to those men disposed to turn an aspect of the truth to their advantage. Throughout the day and every evening, Maggie could hardly wait to return to the captivating story. How was Elinor ever going to find true happiness with the man she loved, Edward Ferrars, and what of the actions of the dashing Mr. Willoughby? How could he possibly marry a woman for money when the woman he loved was the lovely and genuinely devastated Marianne Dashwood?

Maggie returned the book after only keeping it for three days.

Seated in the fine parlor on Goat Street, Maggie and Miss Pratt animatedly exchanged their thoughts on Miss Jane Austen's enchanting story of *Sense and Sensibility*. Both women were quick to condemn the cavalier Willoughby for his dastardly behavior, as a result of the loss of his fortune. Both of them were thrilled that Colonel Brandon had finally won Miss Marianne's heart. The marriage of Elinor and Edward was a true blessing, with both of them extremely pleased that a woman had written such a fine, enchanting and thoroughly enjoyable romantic tale.

"My cousin, Lieutenant Darcy Brosnan, promised to send me a copy of her next book for Christmas. It is called *Pride and Prejudice*. I will lend the book to you as soon as I finish reading it and we will discuss what we both think of that story, as well. Do you agree?"

"Aye! That would make me most happy, indeed," Maggie said, adding a contented sigh, for she was beyond thrilled with her sudden, unexpected and remarkable good fortune.

On that day she left Prudence's house with another novel: *Charlotte Temple* written by another woman, an American by the name of Susanna Rowson. Apparently, it was a tragic romantic tale concerning a young woman's journey from England to the American colonies during the time of the American Revolutionary War.

"I shall be happy indeed to read any stories that have anything at all to do with America," Maggie said.

Over the next several weeks, Maggie made several trips to the home of Miss Prudence Pratt for extended periods of time as their visits also increased in frequency. During their many long conversations, Maggie was to learn that few of the local women appeared to share Miss Pratt's views on the rapidly changing mores of the time in regard to the role of women in a modern society.

Seated in a winged back chair in the library, her very favorite room in the very fine house, Maggie read an article that Prudence had given to her that was published in the *Massachusetts Magazine* of 1790 and written by Judith Sargent Murray: *On the Equality of the Sexes*. She weighed every word as she read from the now yellowing paper.

"It's about time that women spoke up and had their say, if you ask me," Maggie said in a strong tone of conviction as she placed the article back on the table top.

That remark appeared to convince the fine lady on Goat Street that from that day forward young Maggie O'Reilly should address her as "Prudence" and not as "Miss Pratt." After all, did they not share the same interests in matters of learning and in the reading of books? Did they not hold the same views on issues regarding the role of women in a modern society?

After another two weeks, Maggie left Prudence's library with a satchel filled with books: Shakespeare's *Hamlet* and *Twelfth Night*, William Blake's *The Marriage of Heaven and Hell*, William Wordsworth's *Intimations of Immortality,* and Sir Walter Scott's novel, *Lady of the Lake*. All the books were interesting, fascinating, entertaining and highly informative, in Maggie's opinion.

On most evenings after supper on the O'Reilly Farm, Maggie started to read from a selected book to the members of her family. Seated near a blazing fire of peat, her family gathered to hear her read of the *Life and Strange and Surprising Adventures of Robinson Crusoe* by Daniel Defoe. The book was filled with tales that her family had never heard before, some rather hard to believe. Her father was quick to decide that the account was mostly blarney, but he appeared to enjoy the tale all the same.

When Maggie returned any book, normally with the intent of borrowing another, Prudence would invite her into the parlor for a chat to discuss the book she had returned while enjoying a cup of tea. The two of them were starting to spend longer and longer periods of time together, with each of them secretly pleased by that fact, while also surprised by the genuine friendship developing on equal grounds between them, regardless of the difference in station, age, or formal education. The relationship was pleasant for each of them; though at times Maggie thought that she had died and gone to heaven with Prudence Pratt as her special guardian angel.

At night while her family was fast asleep, Maggie continued to read a book by the light of two candles. Amazing new worlds and great and grand vistas opened before her. She was being presented with bold new concepts and radical notions she had never before even dared to imagine. Her mind was being stimulated as she gained knowledge and new insights with every new book she read and every new page she turned. Within her heart, Maggie was convinced that her dearly departed mother was responsible for bringing Prudence Pratt into her life to provide her with the refinement necessary for her to become a proper lady. How else could she have possibly secured the friendship and trust of such a truly fine woman?

Prudence was sixteen years her senior; and according to the local gossip, Prudence was a spinster and considered an old maid. The rumor in the village was that Prudence was once in love with her second cousin, an avowed member of the United Irishmen. Their marriage bonds were posted months before the Great Rebellion that had broken out in 1798, the same year that Maggie was born. As fate would have it, the young man ended up being condemned and transported far from Ireland's green shores. During those times, Maggie had already learned that many idealistic young Irishmen in favor of Catholic emancipation had perished. It was said that Prudence had never recovered and still clung to the Catholic faith of her mother, the only member of her family to never convert to the Protestant religion.

After several months passed by, Maggie gained the full confidence and trust of Prudence Elizabeth Pratt. In fact, she became her dearest friend and most valued companion. Furthermore, it was young Maggie O'Reilly who finally assisted Prudence Pratt in fully unburdening her soul.

8

Guidance on Goat Street

No tradition of any incident involving a goat in the history of Dingle accounted for the name of the street. It was claimed that the name was a mistranslation of the Gaelic, *Sráid na nGabhar*, *Gabhar* meaning *goat*. A similar word pronounced or spelled *gamhair* or *gour* meant *wintry stream*. Goat Street, elevated and sloping, during heavy rainfall in winter streams of water gushed down on both sides. This appears to be the true meaning for the name.

In spite of that fact, for Maggie O'Reilly, whether filled with gushing streams or completely dry, frequent trips to the house on Goat Street were among the most important times in her young life. Having the permission and freedom to borrow and read each and every book in Prudence Pratt's vast library was like finding a leprechaun's pot of gold at the end of some magnificent rainbow.

Chaucer's *Canterbury Tales* proved a bit of a stretch with its old English, but Prudence was patient and obliging in interpreting the words and phrases, many humorous, some bawdy that evoked gales of laughter from both of them. The English translation of Voltaire's *Candide* was another challenge, especially with its French morality, whereas Jonathan Swift's *Gulliver's Travels* was particularly enjoyed by Liam, Matthew and Sean.

The family was eager to listen to each and every chapter read aloud in the evening near the warmth of the fire.

The plays and sonnets of William Shakespeare were greatly enjoyed with all the humor, vicissitudes, romance and intrigue. It was a royal Elizabethan education for Maggie and her family, especially when her siblings began to help her read from the books. As Prudence had so generously taught her, Maggie was teaching her family, bringing greater knowledge and enjoyment to them all. At times, the reading of a book kept her father away from the tavern in the evening. Many of the stories were highly entertaining. Secretly, Padraic was proud of his daughter's willingness and eagerness to share in her great good fortune.

Her cousin Sarah, her husband Tom and their three children started to come around in the evening to hear a book being read. Everyone was impressed that Maggie could read and understand the English language. The meanings of different words were patiently explained. Nearly daily some new word appeared, with all the others delighted to improve upon their knowledge in the same manner as their now privileged young cousin.

On Sunday afternoons, the neighbors started to come to the house as well, those who had heard of Maggie's advantage in her ability to borrow a great many fine books from Miss Pratt. Throughout the summer months the number of people that gathered increased, forcing the group outdoors. Master Roberts sometimes read, with everyone eager to hear another story, especially when the books were written by Americans of Irish descent. Everyone in the village had at least one relative, if not several, living in America. In America people from different countries seemed to live side by side, though not always in perfect harmony, it was said. Still, America seemed a land of unlimited resources with huge ranges of mountains and far-reaching hills and plains, places high and low, sustained by the many immigrants in places nothing at all like Ireland. It was said that there were deserts in America where savage Indians stole the children much the same as the wee folk sometimes did in Ireland. Savages were known to burn the homesteads and kill the pioneers, with some known to take a scalp for a trophy.

There seemed no end to the books, poems and essays that Maggie O'Reilly could read to any group assembled. Some were written by Englishmen, Irishmen, Frenchmen, Germans, Italians and Americans, all printed in English on the subjects of philosophy, politics, science and mathematics, history and biography. On some Sunday afternoons, Maggie read the novels of Samuel Richardson or Sir Walter Scott, with some books viewed with misgiving or censored outright by the Church or the Crown. And yet, the library on Goat Street was a treasure house of information and knowledge beyond Maggie's wildest dreams and expectations. Her mind was continually being opened to brand new vistas and strange and unusual concepts that filled her heart and her soul with hope for her very own future.

One Sunday afternoon, Maggie read: *A Modest Proposal* by Jonathan Swift: *For Preventing the Children of Poor People in Ireland From Being A burden to their Parents or Country, and for Making Them Beneficial to the Public,* with most of those present shocked or wholly outraged, thinking the man serious in writing his essay in 1729:

"I have been assured by a very knowing American of my acquaintance in London, that a young healthy child well nursed is at a year old a most delicious, nourishing, and wholesome food, whether stewed, roasted, baked or boiled," Maggie read aloud.

"They shall, on the contrary, contribute to the feeding, and partly to the clothing, of many thousands ... There is likewise another great advantage in my scheme, that it will prevent those voluntary abortions, and that horrid practice of women murdering their bastard children, alas! Too frequent among us! Sacrificing the poor innocent babes I doubt more to avoid the expense than the shame, which would move tears and pity in the most savage and inhuman breast."

In a tone of total sarcasm, Jonathan Swift had suggested that his scheme might help to control the Irish population and provide an income to the breeders to feed their families, with breeding farms to be established. A Dubliner and Dean of St. Patrick's Cathedral, Swift was among the foremost satirists of the times, his proposal nothing more than a commentary on the deplorable conditions in Ireland and England among the starving lower classes, especially the Catholics in Ireland, with some families with more than twenty offspring.

On several occasions Maggie and Prudence had engaged in somewhat heated discussions with regard to Ireland's overpopulation. One afternoon in May of 1814, a lively conversation was underway on that very subject, while enjoying English ginger biscuits and Earl Grey tea Prudence had poured into delicate cups with pink rose blossoms and fine gold plating: The new china was a surprise birthday gift for Prudence the past March from her aunt and uncle in London.

"I do tend to feel quite grand eating off of these fine plates and sipping tea from a cup as delicate as this," Maggie said. "Which is exactly how things shall be in my parlor when I too have a fine home one day, perchance a touch larger than yours," she teased, laughing at her own suggestion.

"I am convinced that your vision of your future is most correct," Prudence responded with a smile.

Their conversation in favor of birth control suddenly ceased as the maid entered the room. Was Ona listening from the hallway, Maggie wondered? Servants tended to spy. Irish Catholic women never mentioned the matter of birth control. Ona was the same age as Maggie, a peasant girl from Lispole, and perhaps jealous of her friendship with Prudence. One time, Ona had purposely spilled tea on Maggie's clean dress, and her ill-intended act had not escaped the notice of her mistress. Her position was only maintained because Maggie had interceded on her behalf. The job of a household servant to the gentry was not easy to come by. Ona was Catholic, the same as Prudence, which was Maggie's primary consideration in coming to the maid's defense.

"But how can you be so kind and considerate on her behalf?" Prudence fumed. "I don't understand why you even bother with a lass who is so ill disposed toward you and so lacking in character as to purposely soil your frock."

"Ona is jealous of our friendship, Prudence. She will overcome her feelings in time and prove worth her weight in gold to you one day."

Since Ona was a plump lass, Prudence looked at her askance. "Her weight in gold, indeed?" she said and laughed out loud.

"It may take several years for you to fully appreciate my meaning."

"I will only keep her on because I trust your judgment and your extremely accurate insights!"

And they both laughed together.

After securing her solemn promise to keep the matter a secret, Maggie confided in Prudence that she was born with a veil. In turn, Prudence confided in her how she often had dreams that actually came to pass in the world. And, on occasion, her late grandfather, Martin Brosnan, came to her in her dreams to provide her with certain warnings and insights. Her grandfather had also appeared to her at different times in broad daylight.

"It is good to know I am not the only one," Maggie said, as she began to tell her about her own dreams that involved her mother and her late grandparents, especially her great grandmother Kelly.

In some of Prudence's dreams her beloved Rory O'Callaghan visited with her. He had held her to him on many a night, especially after he first entered the Otherworld. Prudence had already revealed the loss of her baby daughter, Juliet, who Rory also often cradled in his arms in her dreams, singing the wee babe an Irish lullaby. On rare occasions, Rory had whispered to Prudence near St. Michael's Well where her dearly departed grandfather had spoken her name out loud several times.

"It is my confirmation of life beyond this veil of tears," Prudence solemnly said.

"Life is eternal, as you well know. Your loved ones have proven that much to you. There are times that all I need to do is ask before falling asleep, and my mother and the elders bring me with them to visit in the glorious beauty of the Summerland."

Prudence's green eyes appeared to be filled with a special light as she spoke. Maggie loved the way that Prudence could sweep up her long dark hair in such a stylish manner. Her skin was milky white, but more recently, to her great consternation, a nasty rash had appeared on her chest. Maggie mixed several herbs together with butter and advised Prudence to apply the mixture to her chest in the morning and the evening before retiring. Others herbs eased her discomfort during her monthly menses, with chamomile tea and honey before bed each night to help Prudence to sleep.

At different times, Maggie provided her with her intuitive insights in order to help Prudence avoid embarrassing situations in terms of acquiring certain properties around the peninsula. In one instance, her advice was to purchase what appeared to be worthless land that she felt would prove highly profitable to Prudence in the distant future. Prudence was also advised to sign legal papers at certain times in terms of the positions of the sun and the moon. At yet other times, the two of them performed secret rituals near St. Michael's Well.

More recently, Prudence and Maggie were experimenting with throwing the rune stones, primarily when Ona and the other servants were elsewhere. Maggie had become well versed in the mystical, prophetic meanings of the stones. Prudence confided that she practiced throwing the runes while alone in her room, with her favorite cluster of crystals on the table near her. Each month her Kerry crystals were placed in a clear glass bowl of sea water overnight for the purpose of purification under the brilliant light of the full moon.

When Jennifer Pratt was once again with child, Maggie O'Reilly's services were immediately enlisted. Jennifer was pleasant enough in terms of following her advice in regards to what was best for her health and the health of her unborn child, with it instantly clear to Maggie that Jennifer disapproved of the close friendship of her midwife with her husband's blood aunt.

"It is beyond me why you invite her to tea so often, Aunt Prudence, in addition to lending her so many of Grandfather Brosnan's valuable books. After all, Maggie O'Reilly is only a midwife. She is nothing more than the daughter of a tenant dairy farmer and a peasant lass. Percival and I would also like to read the books and one day have them ourselves to further the education of our children."

"Peter is still far too young to read, Jennifer. And the books belong to me," Prudence said. "It is my privilege to do with my books as I please. However, do feel free to borrow a book any time you like. I shall be happy to lend you as many books as you want to read as long as you treat them with respect and return the books to me after a respectable period of time."

"The point is, Aunt, that you treat Maggie O'Reilly like a member of the family, a younger sister, or perhaps, even a daughter. Certainly not like one of lowly station hired to perform a service," Jennifer said with a whine in her voice. "I hope you realize that Maggie O'Reilly is simply a motherless Irish peasant lass, who has been raised by a widowed tenant farmer with no social standing whatsoever on the Dingle Peninsula or in

County Kerry. Padraic O'Reilly is simply a tenant dairy farmer and nothing else, nothing else at all!"

"Maggie is a fine midwife, is she not?" Prudence said in a tone of reserve, as she quickly turned from Jennifer to gaze out a window.

"Her gift for healing is above average, I admit that! I wouldn't entrust myself or my unborn child to anyone else, except perhaps for her aunt, Brigid Mahoney, the woman who trained her."

Jennifer had no knowledge of the tragic loss of Prudence's only child which had already been revealed to Maggie in trust and confidence. In 1798, Prudence's only child, a daughter, was born prematurely only a month after Rory was transported by the Crown to Barbados. The authorities had refused to allow them to exchange their wedding vows, perchance a lesser cruelty inflicted upon Roman Catholics in those days. After all, Prudence had escaped being burned alive in her house or being hung from a tree, with her long hair a noose for her infant: The fate of many other women. Such were the crimes committed against Catholics during the hideous times of Oliver Cromwell.

Their bonds were posted in the Church that May. Her pregnancy concealed until after the Battle at Vinegar Hill in June. It was in June that Prudence left for London to stay with her Uncle Henry and Aunt Georgina Pratt where she planned to stay until her child was born. Then she hoped to return to Ireland in relative safety.

In June of 1798, one hundred loyalists were killed in a barn in Scullabogue. After the fierce battle on Vinegar Hill, seventy Protestant prisoners were spiked to death by the United Irishmen on a bridge near Wexford town in an act of revenge. The British Army repaid these atrocities tenfold. Their mopping-up exercises nothing less than universal rape, plunder, and murder, similar to the unbridled carnage of Cromwell and his army of thugs a century before. Retribution for the rebel leaders was swift and uncompromising: Four Wexford commanders were immediately executed, their heads spiked outside the town. Father John Murphy was captured, stripped, flogged, hanged and beheaded, his corpse burned in a barrel, his head spiked opposite the Catholic Church. The troops forced the local Catholics to open their windows to let in the "holy smoke" from the priest's funeral pyre. Nearly 25,000 Catholic rebels were slain, along with 600 soldiers of the Crown. The land was laid waste, homes, farms and businesses burned to the ground, with Rory O'Callaghan imprisoned with hundreds of other men. Two months passed before the final judgment. The ship with Rory and 150 other men sailed for Barbados, only to be lost in a terrible gale with no survivors.

In March of 1799, baby Juliet died two days before Prudence's seventeenth birthday. At that time, Maggie was four months old, Juliet not yet three months, with her lungs not fully developed. After the two losses, Prudence suffered a nervous collapse and stayed in London for two more years. Finally, she returned to Dingle where she and Rory had planned to live out their lives and raise a family. No other man since had captured her attention, let alone her heart.

"Except perhaps for Daniel O'Connell," Prudence said one day as her eyes filled with light. "Who happens to be a married Kerryman in possession of regal, handsome bearings, fine oratorical skills and a great sense of humor in our Munster courts, not to mention his determination to emancipate every Catholic in Ireland, if not in the entire world!"

"I have heard he is a fine man, indeed," Maggie replied.

Prudence sighed. "O'Connell was altogether useless to the United Irishmen and my Rory back in 1798. He was deadset against using violence to secure our independence." She pensively paused to reflect. "I met him last year at the great house Derrynane at an affair hosted by his uncle, Maurice Hunting Cap O'Connell, one of our county's finest smugglers, hear tell, as you must well know."

"Is that a fact now?" Maggie said, remembering Aidan had spoken of Hunting Cap as a serious contender of his father's and the rest of the crew of the *Cornelia*.

"The year that you were born, my dear lass, Daniel O'Connell was the first Irish Catholic admitted to the bar in Ireland. He is indeed a valiant barrister, and I have heard tell, has spread the seed of his loin not only across County Kerry, but across the whole of Ireland!" Prudence made a pretense of bristling before she started to laugh.

"Is that a fact now?" Maggie said, grinning. "Randy fellow, is he?"

"It is said that his bastards are nearly everywhere." She smiled. "The fact is, Barrister O'Connell was ever so charming and attentive to me that afternoon, with his wife Mary busy keeping the other women occupied at the other end of the drawing room."

"Is that a fact? Well, I can see where he might be enchanted with the likes of you. You are comely, intelligent and highly refined, with much to offer a man in the way of companionship, but a married man such as the likes of him would only be trouble, Prudence. You would be wise indeed to keep a safe distance from that one."

"I am sure you are right," she said, her mood suddenly appearing to change as she sat in a winged-back chair beside the fire. "Did I tell you that my young cousin will be here by August?"

"Which cousin is that?"

"Darcy Brosnan, my mother's eldest brother's youngest son, if you can follow that. We were born on the same day eight years apart, with me the eldest, of course. His father is Irish, his mother English and Scot, Brianna McGregor. Brianna is a beautiful woman. My Uncle Gareth, his father, met her through her brother while he was studying at Cambridge. Darcy is quite the dashing soldier, tall and quite handsome, with a wicked smile and dancing blue Irish eyes."

"Dancing blue eyes?" Maggie said. "I shall look forward to gazing into his blue Irish eyes."

"You shall gaze into them soon enough, indeed! Darcy is currently serving with the 87th Foot of the Royal Irish Fusiliers under Arthur Wellesley, who was only recently commissioned as the Duke of Wellington for his valiant efforts in fighting Napoleon in this seemingly endless war. Darcy fought on the front lines in Portugal and Spain the last few years. In fact, he took a bullet in his leg and says that he tends to be gimpy on some days, though I seriously doubt that the bullet has hampered his fine dancing in the least."

"Dance, can he?"

Prudence smiled and nodded. "Darcy is exceedingly charming and exceedingly graceful."

"Hard to do an Irish jig with a bullet in your leg, I would imagine."

"The letters he writes to me are quite wonderful. He wrote to me often during the long campaigns, more eloquently in the times of triumph, of course. I have saved all of his letters, which I feel are quite worthy of print. When I read them I can almost see his handsome face smiling right there in front of me. Odd, is it not?"

"Not so terribly odd, considering your many dreams. If you can see the dead, you should be able to see the living at a distance just as easily.

He's an important part of our history, your cousin. He must be quite dashing indeed and fully brave."

"Dashing, brave, handsome, charming, and determined to seek his fortune in America when he finishes with his military service, which should be soon enough, it seems to me."

"Now, wouldn't we all like to go to America to make our fortunes? I, for one, would love to go to America, for a certainty."

Suddenly, Prudence appeared to watch her more closely as a sly smile spread over her face. "My cousin might well fancy you."

"Fancy me? Why, I'm as good as betrothed to my Aidan. Surely you know that much."

"You are not yet married to Aidan."

"I will not be sixteen for another half year. Aidan knows that there will be no wedding until I am closer to seventeen. If he had his way, we would be married by Christmas."

"Perchance a more worthy candidate will steal your heart away from your young smuggler. A man who can provide you with the sort of life-style that you truly desire and deserve."

All at once, a chill ran through Maggie's entire body, which instantly made her unsure of how to respond to her remark.

"I shall be having a ball while Darcy is here visiting, and I shall invite everyone that is important, including *you*, my dear lass. You will come to my ball, won't you, Maggie dear?" Prudence teased.

"Me ... at a ball? Now wouldn't that be something!" she said, and her body suddenly filled with a giddiness from the top of her head down to her toes. "It is something I have always known would happen to me one day. In my dreams, I have seen myself dancing ... in a long, green silk gown at a ball!"

9

In Search of Rainbows

Watching the *Cornelia* glide safely into Dingle Harbor, among the many smaller fishing boats anchored and moored, was a glorious sight for young Maggie. The tall sails were trimmed and skillfully tied to secure its place near the dock, with the crew smiling and waving to everyone on shore, apparently pleased to be home after two months at sea to secure cargo in Brest and Port Louise. The crew had been forced to deal with the devious French merchants, in addition to the shrewd Spaniards of San Sebastian and Santander.

The summer season was best for the long hauls across the Atlantic to the Bay of Biscay. The crew acquired cargo declared illegal by the Crown, products to sell at a profit after returning to Ireland. In the summer there was less chance of a gale that might blow the ship off course and place the crew in significant danger. It was the easiest time for the captain and crew to deal with the French fleet with Napoleon exiled on Elba and no longer trying to conquer the entire civilized world, with also less need to fear mad King George III and his ruling Regent. Before Boney's abdication, there was always the chance of being fired upon by the British or the French, being blown right out of the water, for a fact. At times, French colors were flown. Other times, a "plague standard" was hoisted.

Different flags were flown in various longitudes, with an able seaman with good eyesight often stationed in the lookout.

Standing off to one side of the crowd in her new lavender cotton dress, with her clean hair tied back with a lavender ribbon, Maggie had decided it was best to separate herself from the others. A group started to gather at the harbor as soon as the white sails were spotted entering the Bay. The crowd included many Protestants with their invested interests, in addition to the ruddy-faced sovereign Lord Mayor Stewart Gregory himself. Guinness and whiskey would soon flow at the *Ye Rose Tavern*, with the captain and crew entertained grandly with music, dancing and good food to celebrate their safe passage and return. Most of the valuable cargo had already been hidden away in the caves beneath the cliffs before the ship even reached the harbor.

All of a sudden, Maggie could see Aidan waving and hanging out over the bow, his bright smile still there as the gangplank finally lowered. Crewmembers were shouting out in Gaelic and English, with those on shore plainly glad to have them safely home again.

In the mad rush of the crew to disembark, Aidan shrugged and restrained himself. He waved at his mother, already in his father's arms, and nodded at each of the other members of his family. Then he ran down the gangplank to hug his mom and acknowledge each of his seven siblings in turn. His youngest brother, Michael, picked up his duffle bag and tossed it over his shoulder before starting up the road toward the tavern.

Soon, Aidan was standing before her.

There she was, his Maggie, smiling her sweet smile and rushing straight into his outstretched arms. He fully welcomed the soft warmth of her next to him, rubbing his freshly shaven face in her long red hair, breathing in her sweet scent, languishing in her kiss as the scent of lavender filled his head and instantly reminded him of what he had missed so much for so very, very long.

"It's grand to be home again and find you here waiting for me. Mighty grand, indeed!" he said in a rush of emotion, his arms wrapped around her and hers wrapped around him, as she gazed up at him with her beautiful golden eyes brimming full of tears. The sight and taste and smell of her were all he seemed to think about for the past two months.

He wanted to hold her every single minute of every day of every month of every year, for years and years, until she was a part of him and him a part of her, perhaps forever.

One pint of Guinness was all Aidan required, after filling his belly with food far tastier than any eaten for weeks. He listened to the music for nearly an hour, and he danced with his lovely Maggie. It seemed only right for him to pay his respects to all the folks for their especially warm welcome home.

Soon the two of them left the smoke-filled tavern and walked out into the bright afternoon sunlight. The clear blue skies held only the hint of a cloudburst as they started down the hill toward a grassy knoll with a bench where they stopped.

Aidan held out a small bag, nodding at her to sit. Then he removed two small boxes, each one tied with a ribbon. He handed her one box without saying a word.

Maggie smiled and stared down at the box. Then, she carefully opened the gift and her face instantly filled with pleasure. She removed a small French compact of hand-painted porcelain from the box, white with lavender flowers. Inside the compact was a small mirror.

"So fancy, Aidan!" she said, quickly taking note of herself in the mirror. "Thank you so very much for your kind generosity. It is a lovely gift, so very elegant and so grand."

"Like you," he said, sitting down beside her and quickly stealing a kiss. "You are elegant and grand, Mary Margaret." He handed her the other box, feeling keenly happy as he watched her beautiful face.

"For me? You're spoiling me, now," she said, quickly opening the box where she found two tortoise shell combs encrusted with tiny pearls. "More elegance!" she said, pulling back her hair to insert a comb in one side. "Like this?" she inquired, adding a toss of her hair. "Is this how the fine French ladies wear combs in their hair?"

"Perhaps," he said, gazing deeply into her eyes. "Wear them anyway you like or not at all," he added, as emotion welled up from deep inside him. "I wish I could give you the world, Maggie O'Reilly, the whole, bloody world!"

"You'll be watching your language, if you please," she said, holding up her compact to inspect the comb in her hair. "That is no way for you to speak in front of a fine lady, now, is it?"

"Forgive me, fine lady. The last thing in this world I would want to do is to offend the likes of you." He smiled and stood, watching her return the gifts to the bag. Then, he reached for her hands and pulled her up to him, kissing her before he once again gazed into her beautiful amber eyes.

"Sailing into the bay just now there was a fine-looking rainbow that ended near our special place. It could still be there. Shall we now go in search of rainbows?"

Her eyes seemed to drink him in, two liquid pools of sunlight that filled his heart with a deep sense of joy. "To perhaps find a grumpy old leprechaun with a hidden pot of gold," she teased.

"Aye! I am feeling particularly lucky today. More than usual, I'd say."

"Are you now?" She stood on tiptoe to kiss his lips. "Then, we should stop by the farm before searching for hidden treasures. I'm feeling lucky myself, if the truth be known. Perhaps Da will lend us Lancelot to take us straightaway to our castle."

Padraic helped Aidan saddle up Lancelot. No questions asked. Over the years, her father had grown fond of Aidan. It was plain to Padraic that Aidan loved his daughter and that she loved him right back. He knew all about the white silk and the lace from France to be made into her wedding gown. Aidan seemed downright impatient to marry his daughter of fifteen, too young yet to marry, in Padraic's honest opinion.

During his moments of quiet reflection, often with a pint in his hand, Padraic wondered if his Maggie might not be able to do far better than Aidan in terms of securing herself a husband. Perhaps she could meet a chap more educated and more refined, with some gold lining his pockets. After all, Maggie could read and write in Gaelic and in English. He also realized that she could do far worse than by marrying young Aidan, considering the other young scalawags hanging out all about the town.

Aidan McKenna was a fine-looking young man, tall, healthy and strong. He had good teeth and seemed honest enough, aside from the fact that he was a smuggler. The real danger, it seemed to Padraic, was the chance of young Aidan being captured, imprisoned or hanged by the Crown, not a good thing for a husband of one of his daughters, or for any grandchildren born to their union. And yet, with the sovereign Lord Mayor secretly running operations, the likelihood of such an occurrence seemed remote, praise God, even with the British Coast Guard inspecting the harbors and coves with more regularity of late. Perchance the Lord Mayor was lining their pockets with coins or filling their bellies with French brandy to insure a blind search. Clever, the sovereign Lord Mayor, and Padraic hoped that he stayed that way as long as young Aidan was involved in his wicked schemes.

At the tavern, Padraic often boasted about "his Maggie," about how she had helped to support the family with her vast knowledge of herbs and skillful midwifery. By that time many folks around the peninsula had heard all about her reading so many books and of her close friendship with Miss Prudence Pratt. There were times Padraic wondered if his dearly departed wife might truly be looking after her namesake from where she was over in the Otherworld.

On that day, Padraic O'Reilly had also seen the rainbow high above the bay, perhaps the sure sign of a blessing for them all.

Slowly making their way on Lancelot toward the distant ruins, the rainbow all but disappeared. Then, to their mutual excitement and amazement, the complete rainbow again filled the blue sky with its full and glorious brilliance. The rainbow was suspended in the very same place where Aidan claimed to have seen it sailing in on the ship. He swore it was the very same rainbow, sometimes faint, other times brilliant, gracefully curving high up into the blue summer sky.

"It's a sign," Aidan said, "A rainbow just for us and for none others."

Intermittent light showers enhanced the full spectrum of faintly shimmering colors poised in an arc from the sea to the land high above the cliffs. As the pony appeared to move closer to the grand illusive ploy of nature, the rainbow again nearly disappeared. Perchance the rainbow was stealing more deeply into the rain now lightly falling toward the sea, in its eternal and capricious mystery, a subtle spectacle of beauty beyond sight and touch, curving into invisible realms of extraordinary magic, perhaps hidden deeply within the very Mists of Time.

"It is leaving us," Maggie said in a tone of disappointment, reaching out to try to grasp the disappearing colors. She slid from the horse and carefully crept forward to peer over the edge of the cliff, looking up and out to perhaps once again glimpse at least a fragment of its misty magnificence.

"I fear your leprechaun has hidden his pot of gold in the rocks far beneath these cliffs, with the crashing sea as added protection against scheming mortals in search of treasure."

"Clever rascal," Aidan said, anchoring the hoses' reins on a boulder and Lancelot began to graze upon the rich, damp, green vegetation.

The sea stretched far out and away to the distant shore, with Skellig Michael periodically appearing from behind a misty veil before disappearing once again. For some odd reason, the rain was not falling directly on or about them, but stayed a distance off shore.

Maggie turned to Aidan. "So how does it feel to be back on Ireland's green shores after so much time away at sea and in distant lands?"

"It is always good to be home again," he said, quickly squatting to touch the ground. "As you know, I love our Emerald Isle ... with a passion."

"I thought it was me that you love with a passion," she said, sitting on a rock near what had been their summer trysting place for several years. "Do you still plan to rebuild our castle one day?" she inquired, glancing all around her at the uneven piles of aging gray and black stones that dotted the rugged landscape outside the inner, more defined ruins of the ancient fortress.

Many such ruins existed, not only near Dingle but along the entire coast of Ireland. This was *their place.* All around them were the crumbling remnants of a once grand stone edifice with its faintly outlined inner courtyard, its true grandeur lost somewhere in antiquity and relegated to a long ago time the same as so many other long forgotten rainbows.

Stories and legends still thrived about those who once dwelled there, and in which century, perhaps thousands of years ago. Knights and ladies, of that Maggie was certain, chieftains and queens from the time of Erin's own that remained within its sacred island boundaries, living in obedience to the laws of Nature administered through its Druid high priests and priestesses. These people existed during a long ago time, when, as yet, no arrogant, malevolent foreigner had dared to invade the rocky shores of the green gem in the great sea, in order to rape and plunder the vast treasures of its people and its rich land once thought to exist at the very rim of the world.

"I do love you with a passion," Aidan said, pulling her up into his arms so that his lips might blend with hers in a kiss not intended for the eyes of others.

"And I love you," she whispered, kissing him back. "But what about my castle, my lord?" she inquired, as he gently guided her to the place where they would soon recline on a patch of wild shamrocks intermingled with a throng of tiny purple violets.

"A castle it shall be, according to your own design and plan. But are there enough stones on this peninsula to build so grand a structure as you might require?"

Kneeling in the sheltered place, he reached for her hands to pull her down to him.

Maggie knelt and slipped her hands beneath his shirt. "I care not for castles, my lord, as long as your heart is in my hands," and she moved her hands over his chest to sense the faster beating of his heart. "There it is," she said, deeply inhaling the scent of him. "Is it mine, then?" she said, looking into his dark brown eyes she felt she had loved forever.

"Yours and yours alone," he said, pulling her to him for a kiss.

Soon, both of them were lying on the damp shamrocks that bloomed near the darkening pile of ancient stones that patiently kept their secret, along with the secrets of the ages.

In a moment of practicality, Maggie stopped. "I fear my new dress will be stained green and become quite muddy with all this rain."

"It is a lovely dress. Should you not perhaps remove it?" he inquired, "to protect the dress, of course?" Looking steadily into her eyes, he carefully untied the sash and unbuttoned each button between a series of wet, probing kisses.

All at once, Maggie pushed his shirt up over his head and helped him to take it off, her heart beating a touch faster. "You wouldn't want to stain your shirt," she said, her eyes glistening as she kissed his shoulder, his neck, his cheek and his lips.

"Up you go," he said, lifting off her dress, which he carefully placed on the rock next to his shirt. "What about your unmentionables? You might stain them as well," he said, with both of them now breathing faster as the heat of passion rose higher.

From early that morning, upon first catching sight of the ship's white sails, Maggie knew that this would be the day that she would give herself to Aidan completely. Every moment he was gone she had missed him more and more and had yearned for his touch. Alone in her bed at night, she made love to him in her heart, with her body, with her mind, and even with her soul, as she remembered the passion that Aidan aroused in her whenever he looked at her, let alone when he touched her in a meaningful manner. She relished his kisses, his tongue filling her mouth in a pleasing way, as his hands moved over her warm flesh to awaken her greater need to join with him. There were times when Aidan seemed to be a part of her very own heart, mind, and soul.

The last time the two of them were together like this in this place, it had taken every ounce of her being not to allow him to enter her. It was not easy for her and seemed even harder for him to control his need and his deep frustration. It was plain to her how much he wanted her. With both of them fully naked, he was no doubt convinced that the time had finally come to consummate their love. But it was the time of the full moon. Maggie knew better than to fully give in to her passions and tempt the fates with the goddess smiling down upon them from high up in the night sky, with the stars her constant and faithful companions.

But now, it was not the time of the full moon, with both of them again fully naked.

Aidan kissed her neck, his mouth moving to her breast to tantalize her nipple and awaken her to her greater needs, to his needs, to their need to be together. His hands and mouth hungrily moved over her, giving her intense pleasure, for Maggie was not some unfeeling French whore taking his sixpence for the simple purpose of his release. He loved Maggie with all his heart. It was Maggie he wanted to be his ever-loving wife with whom to share his life. Knowing and fully understanding his feelings, she opened to Aidan, giving herself to him completely on that afternoon.

At first, the pain was keen. Maggie cried out, trying to muffle the shrill sound against his shoulder as tears suddenly spilled from both her eyes. Tensing, she braced herself to endure yet more pain, as he entered her yet more fully, moving into her deeper and deeper and deeper.

Suddenly, Aidan stopped.

"I don't want to hurt you," he said, turning to look into her eyes. "I love you. I don't want to hurt you," he went on, trying to control the urge to force himself inside her. "You are plainly my virgin," he said, kissing her lips before he again looked into her beautiful eyes.

"Yours alone. Your virgin, forever and ever."

With that, Maggie tightened her arms around him and pushed up hard to accept him more fully into her, knowing it was something she simply had to do, for Aidan understood that she was his virgin—his and his alone.

Now fully inside her, Aidan began to carefully take his time, moving slowly, gently, kissing her lips, his warm breath in her ear as he whispered to her of his love. Soon both of them moved more easily, more swiftly, together and in unison.

As the pain faded, the pleasure began. Aidan was gentle, giving as much as he received, though Maggie prayed that next time it would be easier. It was plain that he was holding back until it seemed that he was unable to hold back any longer.

Aidan cried out, shuddering in release in the loving arms of his Maggie.

After a brief period of time, the two young lovers once again breathed together in unity, moving in the heat of passion beneath a vanishing rainbow, blanketed by a lightly falling rain, carefree and secure at last in expressing an ageless, timeless love within the enchanted castle of their dreams.

10

An Ounce of Prevention

After measuring and combining several herbs, water was added to the pot. Over the flame everything eventually boiled down into a condensed mix: chamomile, blackberry, raspberry, mistletoe, motherwort, pennyroyal, yarrow, and snakeroot. Lots of snakeroot. Cinnamon and honey improved upon the taste. The mixture cooled and was then reheated and further distilled, with more water added from the well. Maggie was to consume a specific portion three times a day for three days, so no child might grow in her womb, since she had foolishly given in to her youthful passion with young Aidan. The mixture was to be preserved in case of her further folly, with instructions to follow each and every time she so erred.

"You must promise me," her Aunt Brigid demanded, boldly staring into her eyes. "Now that you have let him have his way with you, there is sure to be more of the same. You must use the herbs each time without fail. You must give me your solemn promise this very minute ... do you hear me, young miss?"

"I hear you and I promise," Maggie said, relenting. "It hurt, Aunt. You never told me that it would hurt. You said it would feel good, wonderful even."

"Well, giving birth hurts a whole lot more, as you must well already know. I do not want you to get pregnant, Maggie. Marry the lad if it suits you, though you are far too young to marry, in my opinion." She narrowed her eyes and scowled. "Do you hear me, young miss?" The look on her aunt's face was almost frightening.

"Aye! I hear you!" Maggie said, looking down at the floor.

"Avoid the full moon, two days before and after, and no fruit will grow in your womb. Do you hear what I am telling you, lass? Do you hear me, Maggie? Do you?"

"Aye, I hear you!" she said, now daring to look into her aunt's cold, green eyes.

"The full moon is when the passions increase the most. You know how we tell those eager to have children to engage at the time of the full moon. Most of the time, it works like a charm, especially for the young and the fertile."

"I remember. Sadie O'Flaherty had twins after engaging thrice with the full moon in her sign. She was lucky not to have triplets."

Her aunt watched her for a very long moment. "It will feel better next time," she said, appearing to suppress a grin. "It gets easier as it goes. Didn't it feel any good to you at all?"

"It was better the second time. I put lavender light around us, the same as I do with the mothers in birthing. Lavender for pain is what you taught me."

"Hungry lad is he?" her aunt said. "I am not surprised from the looks of him. Lover boy, your Aidan, the handsome, young devil!"

Together they laughed.

"He is. My Aidan is my bonny white knight in shining armor. I love him, Aunt. I love Aidan with all my heart and all my soul."

"It is easy enough to see that he loves you too. It seems to me that you will be sewing up your white silk into a wedding gown err long."

Maggie stirred the herbs again and thoughtfully said, "Perhaps with this potion, there will be no need to sew my gown too soon. I hope next time it feels as good as you say it can. I would like to be broken in and have a better time of it by my wedding night."

After quickly glancing at her, her aunt made the sign of the cross and said, "Lavender, huh? You are your mother's daughter, all right. A woman of passion is what you are, Mary Margaret! You will have no need of lavender soon enough with the fire of passion strong in your belly ... you will be using red on *that one*. Perhaps you already have without knowing it."

Brigid laughed as Maggie narrowed her eyes.

"Poor Aidan is doomed to love you forever, my young Druidess. But he will be liking it... of that you can be certain."

Aunt Brigid was right. The loving improved with the passing of time and the frequency of their encounters. The fire of passion burned brighter without any need of lavender light. The pleasure grew greater as the two young lovers grew stronger and more constant in their desire, eager to be together as often as possible.

Maggie quickly learned to surrender to the rhythm of his thighs, as thrill after thrill coursed through her, especially when he held her close in his arms, moving in and out, bringing her to a fever pitch. His touch, his kiss, his strong body had ignited a flame that burned brighter within the safety of his loving arms. She loved the sense of him, the smoothness of his skin, the scent of him, his sound and his taste. She loved all of Aidan all the time.

One day, after redressing and heading back down the road, Aidan turned to her with a serious look on his face and said, "You will not be telling Father Hennessey, will you? It seems to me that every time we make love you feel the need to confess it to the priest, telling him how you have sinned. It never feels like sin to me, and I know for a fact that it doesn't feel like sin to you from the way you moan and groan. I would say it feels quite grand to you. It certainly does to me."

"Is that right, now?"

"Making love to you feels right divine when I am hard and hot inside you and the glory comes. I shout for joy and all the angels do rejoice in my love for you. What harm can we do to God and his angels by being together, I ask you? What harm?"

"You make fornicating sound downright respectable, Aidan McKenna. You and your blarney! Why else would a respectable young lady like me give in to the likes of your persistent and ardent advances? I know for a certainty that you didn't write the Ten Commandments and you don't obey them much, either, as far as I can tell."

"Well, if I did write them... there would have to be eleven."

"Eleven? And what might that be?"

"Thou shalt make love to your sweetheart seven times a week, no, seven times seven, and twice on Sunday. What else would you have a man do on a day of rest with his love?" He laughed at his own clever suggestion.

"You are an incorrigible, renegade smuggler, Aidan! May God have mercy on your soul!"

And she ran down the road, laughing, with Aidan close behind her.

Megan was sitting on her bed with a strange look on her face as she watched her closely. Maggie guessed that her sister had noticed the grass stains on her jumper and the mud on her shoes. Her hair was mussed a touch, since she had forgotten to take a comb along in her pocket that day.

"Have you been down at the ruins with Aidan again? The two of you seem to go down there often enough, I daresay," Megan said, narrowing her bright green eyes.

"Is that a fact, now? Keeping score, are you?" Maggie picked up a brush and tried to run it through her long hair. She stopped and pulled out a twig of heather.

"There's more on the other side," her sister said with a smirk. "You let him, didn't you? You *let* Aidan."

"Let him?" Maggie replied, trying to sound detached, since that afternoon was more special than all the rest. Certain grand feelings had made her feel downright peaceful afterwards, thrilling feelings, if the truth be known.

"You let Aidan *diddle your dew*, didn't you, Maggie?" Megan said, trying to capture her eyes, but she turned away. "You let Aidan *do it to you*, didn't you, Maggie? I know that you did! You let Aidan McKenna *diddle your dew!*"

"Diddle my dew?" Maggie huffed, feeling color rush into her face. "Whatever would the likes of you know about such things?" She turned away and sucked in her breath, trying hard not to smile. "Whatever would the likes of you know about ... *diddling?*" and without meaning to, she burst out laughing, for there was little she could keep from her mischievous sister.

Megan started to laugh. Soon she was holding her stomach and rolled from the bed to the floor in a fit of hysterics.

"Oh, Maggie! I just knew it had to be true. Aidan McKenna has *diddled your dew!*"

11

Invited to a Ball

With Aidan at home, there was little time for Maggie to spend with Prudence. Several books needed to be returned. Prudence understood that it might take her a year or more to read all six volumes of Gibbon's *Decline and Fall of the Roman Empire*. In and of itself, the first book was an enormous undertaking. Her understanding of the written English language had greatly improved. Both Maggie and Prudence had considered the project a good one, with its scholarly yet fascinating tales of emperors and kingdoms, philosophers and poets, the conquering and domination of the Romans all over the ancient world. Maggie had made up her mind to learn as much as she possibly could about the world before and beyond Ireland. Praise God that the Romans never conquered Ireland. And praise God that Prudence Pratt owned a storehouse of knowledge upon the printed page.

Recently, Maggie had discovered her need to exercise caution in speaking of the books, especially around those unable to read and perhaps unwilling to be educated. She was learning to use discretion in speaking of her own good fortune, which was also necessary with regard to her knowledge of the various herbs.

The book she was currently reading to her family was the *Swiss Family Robinson*. Next, she planned to read them *Rip Van Winkle* by an American author named Washington Irving: It was the story of a man who wakes up after sleeping for twenty years.

Even though Prudence trusted her with any book for an unlimited period of time, Maggie decided to write her a note to explain her absence, which she asked Sean to deliver.

Her younger brother was eager to see inside the big house on Goat Street, thinking every room must be filled with books, and yet, there were no books near the front door as he tried to see past the servant. Sean approved of the dark red front door with its shiny brass knocker of a boar's head.

"The ugly, fat lass with the pockmarked face was very rude to me," Sean said to Maggie.

"That's Ona. She can be highly protective of Prudence."

"I made her promise to deliver your note to her mistress straightaway."

"Good lad. You did the right thing."

In less than a week's time, Aidan would set sail for France. Captain O'Shea was determined to secure yet another shipment before the weather turned bad. There seemed enough time before having to spend the cold winter weather delivering goods to Killarney, Tralee, Limerick and villages in County Cork. During the winter, the crew spent their time honing various crafts: masonry, carpentry, shoe cobbling, cooking and tailoring. On occasion, Aidan tended bar at the *Wayfarer* in Ballyferriter in the winter. He was happy for a pint to wet his whistle after closing.

After this next trip, the ship was going to anchor first in Cork Harbor before returning to Dingle Bay. There was talk of a consignment that Aidan had refused to discuss. One evening, outside the *Ye Rose Tavern* after an apparent meeting with the Lord Mayor, Maggie had overhead Aidan and his father discussing guns and ammunitions. That sort of shipment sounded more dangerous to her than a cargo of brandies, wine, and bolts of silk. Smugglers caught by the Crown with guns were likely to soon be dancing at the end of a rope hanging from the yardarm.

With Napoleon still imprisoned on the island of Elba, it seemed to Maggie that her father and the other men had to realize that the French

Emperor could not possibly fulfill his promise to help Ireland gain its freedom from the Crown. That was the faint hope in the hearts of most Irish Catholics during the Emperor's reign. There were times Maggie wished that she was born a boy, so she might help the others fight for Ireland's freedom. Self-rule was what she also hoped and prayed for, having heard about the issue often enough since she was a babe in the cradle. America had succeeded in freeing itself from the Crown with the assistance of many Irishmen. Her secret hope was that America would also win its Second War for Independence from the British.

A cousin of Aidan's who lived in Boston, Massachusetts had written of the war taking place on the Canadian border. It seemed that the British were raiding towns up and down the north Atlantic seaboard in their attempt to keep Canada from becoming part of America. There was no doubt in Maggie's mind that the Irish were once again fighting against the Crown, for the young nation had been brave enough to declare war on the most powerful country in the world. The same as her father, she greatly admired the Americans for their spunk.

With Aidan leaving once more in August, there seemed no chance for him to return before his birthday. On September 18, 1814, Aidan would turn eighteen, something that would happen only once in his lifetime: turning eighteen on the eighteenth. For that reason, Maggie decided to give him his birthday presents early. He seemed to truly like the brown woolen jumper she had knitted herself. At Moriarity's Emporium in Dingle, she had found a dapper tweed cap for him to wear in matching shades of brown.

"You must take your things with you on your voyage to keep you warm," Maggie insisted.

"I am to wear this fine jumper and this fine tweed cap at sea in a gale? Are you quite daft, my darling?"

"Wear them anywhere and anytime you please," she said in defense.

"I will wear them on your sixteenth birthday right here in November." He kissed her cheek. "Would that suit you, Maggie?"

"Not before?" she said in a sulk. "That is long after your eighteenth birthday."

He put the cap on his head and grinned. "Perhaps November is the proper time to plan our spring wedding. Your father has given me his consent."

And yet, Maggie had confided to her father and her aunt that she hoped to wait another year to marry, especially considering all the many young mothers she cared for, the crying babies and screaming toddlers that were everywhere. Maggie had no desire to marry anytime soon.

That spring, Prudence had started to play the piano for Maggie. She explained how she and her young cousin Darcy often played piano duets together. As her birthday gifts that year, Darcy had sent Prudence the sheet music of both Beethoven's *First Symphony in C Major* and *Fifth Symphony* and the music for the *Magic Flute* by Mozart, Darcy's favorite composer. Another birthday gift for his "favorite cousin" was a copy of Jane Austen's latest novel, *Mansfield Dark*.

Maggie wondered how Jane Austen's latest novel compared with *Pride and Prejudice*. Both she and Prudence had fallen in love with the character of Mr. Darcy, and were impressed that a man of his station and bearing was able to rise above the flaws of arrogance and conceit and prove himself a man of substance. In truth, Maggie had fallen in love with nearly every character in that book, but more especially, Mr. Darcy.

It was in June that Prudence suggested that Maggie sit beside her at the piano to learn how to play. Prudence promised to assume the role of teacher, since she still had all the piano instruction books from her childhood, which she gave to Maggie to study. In the evening at home on the farm, Maggie studied hard to learn the notes and the hand movements so she could play the piano.

"You must come to the house more often in order to practice," Prudence said.

At first, the difference in their hands distressed her. Prudence had hands without blemishes or redness, with her fingernails clean and neatly trimmed. Prudence had the elegant hands of a lady, while Maggie needed to dig in the woodlands and meadows for herbs and in the garden for sprouts and potatoes. Her hands were red from so much contact with the soil and from so much work in the house. Calendula was the herb she selected, which was crushed and mixed with heavy cream. Each night before going to bed, Maggie rubbed the mixture into her hands, using a pair of old socks to cover her hands throughout the night. To her great delight, within a few weeks her hands improved and were no longer rough and red. Maggie's hands were starting to resemble the hands of a lady.

Playing the piano soothed her. After all, her father played the bagpipes and Liam the fiddle. Matthew and Sean played mandolin and banjo, and her Aunt Brigid played the Kelly harp like an angel from heaven. Maggie made up her mind to faithfully practice, since the piano seemed a right and proper instrument for a lady.

Since Prudence had often spoken of how well Darcy played the piano, Maggie began to wonder if he could be anything like 'Mr. Darcy' in the novel, *Pride and Prejudice*. Was he haughty, perhaps? A touch arrogant? Since he was a soldier, he had to be daring, perhaps even reckless to the point of courting danger, she thought. Then again, he had given Prudence the romantic novels of Miss Jane Austen and the music of Beethoven and Mozart. For a man of the sword, he appeared to be cultured and refined. Surely, Darcy Brosnan must be a most extraordinary gentleman.

With the tears still wet upon her cheeks, Maggie watched the *Cornelia* sail out of Dingle Harbor into the wider expanse of Dingle Bay. The taste of his farewell kiss still lingered on her lips, as the great, white, square-rigged sails unfurled in a strong breeze and the stately brigantine sailed for the open Atlantic in the best of all possible weather.

Slowly making her way up the hill, Maggie dabbed at her eyes and her nose with her handkerchief. Before long, she was once more comfortably seated in Prudence's exquisite parlor and began to feel more quiet inside herself again.

Prudence poured and held out a pretty saucer with a steaming cup of tea, which Maggie accepted. "Darcy will be here next week," she said, now presenting her with a platter of crisp ginger biscuits.

"Next week?" Maggie repeated, selecting a biscuit, for the tangy taste of ginger was her favorite. Prudence ordered the biscuits regularly from London.

"He's coming by coach by way of Tralee and is stopping over to visit the parents of a comrade. Apparently, Darcy is taking them gifts from his friend, something special for the man's sister, who his friend wants Darcy to meet. No doubt in an attempt to play matchmaker. The sister is supposedly a beauty."

"I think not," Maggie said, suddenly finding herself distracted by a series of images that raced through her mind in sequence.

"You think she is not a beauty?" Prudence said in a tone of surprise.

"She may well be, however," Maggie said, hesitating, "She is not the one that your cousin shall fancy—or marry, for a fact."

"My guess is—you are the one that Darcy shall fancy."

Maggie blushed and sat up straighter. "Me?"

"Just a hunch," Prudence said, looking at her directly.

Maggie felt a sudden need to turn away from her gaze.

"Next week I shall have a ball," Prudence announced in a merry voice.

"A ball?" Maggie said, suddenly feeling giddy.

"I shall teach you some dances, and you shall teach me, though I already know the Irish jig. My mother taught me when I was a child. You will allow me to teach you some proper dances, will you not, Maggie? Perhaps the minuet?"

"If you insist," she said, placing her cup and saucer on the table in a sudden unexpected rush of anxiety.

"I have a gown for you to wear," Prudence said, smiling.

"A green one?" Maggie blurted out, for the dress had instantly popped into her mind—the emerald green dress of her dreams.

"An Irish green," Prudence said. "I haven't worn the dress in years. No one around here has even seen it. It looks brand new, and I am sure it will fit you perfectly."

"It will," Maggie said, suddenly feeling faint. "You are truly inviting me to your ball?"

"I am truly inviting you to my ball." Prudence said and she smiled.

At once, the two of them suddenly got up and rushed over to the piano in order to play a duet.

12

Cinderella

In all his days, Padraic O'Reilly had never expected to see his young Maggie looking so beautiful and grand in a long silk gown with her hair up in curls held in place by two pearl encrusted combs. She looked like a lady, she did, and as fine as any lady he had ever seen in his life. He thought she probably looked much the same as her mother might have in that long, emerald green gown off the shoulders like the fancy ladies in Dublin and London were wearing.

Each day in every way his daughter looked more like her mother—*his Mary Margaret*—which was why he decided to give her the gold heart locket that had belonged to her mother and her grandmother before her. It was a Kelly locket. It only seemed right that Maggie should wear it to her very first fancy ball in Dingle Town.

The three boys fought over hitching up the wagon, yelling in loud, strident voices about who would do the honor of driving their sister to the ball.

"I will be the one driving her," their father said. "After all, it is time for me to meet this fine lady on Goat Street with all these many books." That was the main reason that Padraic had shaved and bathed and dressed in his Sunday best. "I can hardly expect a lady in a silk gown to walk or ride a horse, now, can I? Especially when she happens to be my very own eldest daughter."

"Could Cinderella not use a coachman?" Liam inquired, grinning. "I would say, being the eldest and all, that I should be the one to escort my sister. I am twenty, after all, with her not yet sixteen, and Aidan did ask me to look after her while he's gone. I am tall like you, Da, and strong enough to protect her from those ruffians hanging about outside the *Ye Rose Tavern*."

"And who will be protecting her from *you*?" Padraic said, smiling, pleased that Maggie had mended the hole in his jacket so that no one would know it was ever torn. Though, at the moment, he was having trouble getting his tie on just right.

"Your moustache needs a trim," Matthew said, holding out a pair of scissors. "And you need to trim the hairs sticking out of your nose, Da. They're disgusting, I'd say." He quickly glanced away. "How about a footman? I could be the footman for *her majesty's* carriage ride to the ball."

The three boys burst out laughing and jabbed at each other.

"No footman, no coachman. Just me, her father ... the best protector of 'em all!"

Padraic checked himself out in the glass and summarily approved of his appearance, thinking, *a bit worn about the edges, but not a bad-looking bloke all around.* His hair was still black as coal, the same as his moustache. His body was hard and lean with not an ounce of flab on him.

"Cinderella is ready for the ball," Megan announced and she curtsied.

Making her grand entrance, Maggie held a small tapestry bag in one hand, a recent gift from Prudence, inside was the compact from Aidan, a small comb, and a lace handkerchief that once belonged to her great grandmother Kelly and was carried by her on her wedding day.

"Is she not the most beautiful lass in the whole of Ireland?" her Aunt Brigid's voice cracked as though she was about to cry. "You will be acting the proper lady this evening," she said to Maggie in a sterner tone. "You will be making us all proud ... that I know for a certainty."

"Assuredly," Maggie said, curtsying, and she nervously laughed as she quickly noted the expressions on her father and all three of her brothers. She thought perhaps she no longer looked like a tenant farm girl, but more like Cinderella ready for the ball. Prudence was her fairy godmother.

"You look like an Irish princess," Megan said. "Does she not?" she inquired, turning to her brothers who now openly stared, yet nodded together in unison.

"Like a fairy princess," Sean said, "One back from the Otherworld to attend a fine ball here in Dingle Town on this very evening."

"You might be right," their aunt said with a wry smile, as she watched her nephews falling all over themselves, as though Maggie was not even their sister. They were pushing and shoving in trying to help her up onto the seat of the wagon next to their father.

"Lucky for you there's no rain this fine evening," Sean said, carefully adjusting the folds of her gown, an expression of adoration on his handsome, young face.

After nodding to Brigid and each of his children in turn, Padraic flicked the pony and the wagon lurched forward to soon turn onto the dirt road into town.

"Dance one for me," Megan called out. "One day I shall go to a ball," she half-whispered.

"Sure you will," Liam said without much conviction.

"Maggie is paving the way to glory for us all," Matthew said. "I say she's a beauty, even if she is my sister. She looks so much like our mother once did."

"We can surely hope that she will make things better for all of us," Megan said, as the wagon rounded the bend out of sight.

Back inside the house, their Aunt Brigid was stirring the pot with supper nearly ready. Megan gazed at herself in the glass, pinching her cheeks and chewing on her lips to bring up some color. Then she frowned.

All at once, her three brothers glanced at one another and sprang to the wall to fetch their musical instruments. In minutes, all three O'Reilly boys were playing a wild *Saint Anne's Reel,* as Matthew sped up on the banjo, with Sean on the harmonica.

Gaiety filled the house, which forced Megan to smile. Then she and her aunt broke into an Irish jig next to the kitchen table.

Fine carriages lined both sides of Goat Street with a large number of guests arriving. A footman helped Maggie down, as her father self-consciously stood next to the wagon with his hat in his hands. He furtively glanced about in every direction in search of a friendly face, relieved to see Dr. O'Malley with his missus on his arm entering the house through the red door.

Prudence appeared in the open doorway, smiling and waving at Maggie.

Padraic's heart was filled with pride as he watched his daughter gracefully ascend the stairs. He thought the lovely woman in lavender silk must be Prudence Pratt: Delicate pearls around her graceful neck, her dark hair up on her head in curls. Just the sight of her held him fast. There had been rumors that she was comely. Padraic was surprised they had never met before with both of them Catholics and living on the same Peninsula all these years.

Prudence was beautiful. It was hard for him to take his eyes away from her, for she made him feel strangely like a much younger man.

"Who is that man?" Prudence inquired, nodding toward her father who stood with his hat in his hand as he openly stared.

"That is my father," Maggie said. "It is said I resemble my mother. My eldest brother, Liam, is tall with green eyes and dark hair the same as Da."

"Surely you look like your mother," her voice suddenly sounded strangely tense, but Prudence instantly collected herself and smiled at Padraic before ushering Maggie into the house. "Your father is quite handsome," she whispered.

"My mother always said … he was the handsomest man in the whole of Ireland."

"Is that right?" Her green eyes appeared to sparkle.

Glancing back again, Maggie could see that her father was driving the wagon in the direction of the tavern. After turning around, she was surprised to find the house filled with so many people. At once, Prudence began to introduce her to one guest after another, as though she was one of them. Together, they climbed two flights of stairs up to the third floor of the house.

The ballroom looked amazing. Small groups chatted here and there. The candelabras were filled with flickering candles that cast shadows on the wine red flocked wallpaper. At the far end of the highly polished pine floor, musicians were starting to play a lively tune.

To Maggie's great surprise, everyone treated her with tremendous kindness as they made their way toward a table draped with white linen. On the table was a silver punch bowl surrounded by dainty crystal cups. A servant stood behind the table in readiness.

"Two, please," Prudence said to the serving girl.

The servant then handed one cup of punch to Maggie and the other to Prudence.

That was when Maggie noticed the Pratts seated directly across the room. Percy nodded at her in a perfunctory manner, instantly looking the other way; Jennifer smiled and waved. Jennifer had gotten her figure back quickly after the birth of Priscilla and looked lovely in a yellow silk gown. Her blonde hair was up, with diamonds around her neck and hanging from her ears that sparkled in the candlelight.

The sovereign Lord Mayor Stewart Gregory was near the far wall of the ballroom with his group of Protestant co-conspirators, with all the wives merrily chatting. Father Hennessey stood against one wall, with the Reverend Brown on the opposite side of the room. All the Pratts in County Kerry were Protestant, except for Prudence, which was of no concern to her.

The same could not be said of her nephew, Percival, often known to quip, 'You may very well end up burning in hell by remaining a Papist, Aunt Prudence.' With her replying in good humor, 'I shall pray for your soul, Percy dear, even when I am not attending Mass.'

Everyone of note in Dingle and all the other townships seemed to be attending the ball hosted by Miss Prudence Pratt. With that sudden realization, Maggie understood what an honor it truly was for her to have been invited.

"Welcome to your first ball, Maggie dear," Prudence said, holding up her punch cup in a toast. "May it be the first of many, for you look truly beautiful in the vibrant green of Erin."

Their cups gently clicked and the punch was sipped.

"How can I ever thank you enough for letting me wear this beautiful gown? Liam called me Cinderella, and I truly feel like Cinderella with you my fairy godmother."

"The dress is yours to keep. The color suits you far better than it does me."

"The gown is mine?" Maggie said in a tone of astonishment. "You are so very generous, Prudence, thank you so much for the dress and for inviting me here this evening. You are truly good and truly giving."

"Truly good and truly giving pretty much sums her up," a deep male voice remarked from directly behind her.

Twirling around, Maggie found a tall gentleman in the bright red dress uniform of the British Crown standing behind her. There was a captivating smile on his handsome face as he drained his punch cup dry.

"*Good* and *giving* perfectly describe my favorite cousin," he said, handing the cup to the servant with a nod, with the cup promptly refilled and handed back to him.

Never before had Maggie seen eyes that shade of blue, the dark and shimmering blue of the Irish Sea. His darkening blond hair had streaks of light gold. There was a deep cleft in his strong chin. The man standing before her appeared to be dashing, indeed.

"Mary Margaret O'Reilly, may I introduce to you my very favorite cousin, Lieutenant Darcy Donal Brosnan, born and bred in Dublin, as the son of a contrary Irishman who happens to not only be the most handsome of men, but my favorite uncle."

Darcy smiled and nodded at Prudence before he turned directly to Maggie, his steady gaze causing a tingling sensation in her solar plexus.

"His mother, Brianna, is most charming and most beautiful," Prudence said, "She was born in Inverness to a Scottish father and English mother. Presbyterian, I fear, as are all her children. Uncle Gareth accommodates her beauty at every opportunity."

"Mary Margaret," Darcy softly said, his eyes appearing to search hers for some sign.

"Please call me Maggie, Lieutenant Brosnan. Everyone else calls me Maggie."

"I shall be delighted to call you Maggie, if you promise to call me Darcy."

"Darcy," she said and she curtsied.

"Your eyes are like ambers ... brilliant, golden ambers, amazing and quite lovely."

"So my father says," she said, feeling the color rising into her cheeks.

"For the past several years, Darcy has been occupied with routing the French troops of the onetime Emperor Napoleon, with his regiment under the direct command of the Duke of Wellington. Darcy was assigned as a special guard at the signing of the Treaty of Fontainebleau when Boney abdicated last spring."

"My!" Maggie said.

Darcy nodded, his blue eyes refusing to move away from her amber eyes.

"In fact, it is highly possible that it was Darcy who made Napoleon see the wisdom of his surrender," Prudence teased.

Darcy feigned a look of total disbelieve.

"I am duly impressed," Maggie said, going along with the joke.

"My dear Maggie, do not allow my beautiful cousin to pull the wool over your magnificent eyes with her grand flattery and falsifying praise as to my great and glorious accomplishments, which I fear are not the least of what she suggests; my shortcomings in matters of diplomacy being too numerous to mention. I made but a small contribution as a foot soldier to the defeat of the once formidable emperor, because my commander happens to be a brilliant strategist and highly protective of his men."

"The Duke was born in Ireland, though an Englishman," Prudence said.

"Well, all the same," Maggie now directed her remarks to Darcy, "your bravery is obvious from the uniform you so proudly wear and from the many campaigns in which you have so valiantly fought. You are to be congratulated, Lieutenant Brosnan," she said, lowering her eyes and coyly smiling, having gleaned much insight with regard to her present behavior from the novels of Miss Jane Austen.

"Your vote of confidence is greatly appreciated."

"I have so much enjoyed the books you have given to Prudence, who has kindly lent them to me in turn, as well as many other books that once belonged to your grandfather. But the stories I enjoy the most are those more lately written by Miss Jane Austen."

"I, too, greatly enjoy her novels. It is a shame that more people have not recognized her brilliance in romantic storytelling."

"I couldn't agree with you more," Maggie said, thinking to herself, *so far so good*.

"She lives up to everything that you have told me about her, cousin," Darcy remarked to Prudence. "Maggie is a lovely Irish lass, indeed." Again, he turned to Maggie. "The letters that Prudence writes to me are forever welcome in faraway places while carrying a musket. She has written to me of your interest in history and literature, an interest we all seem to share." Darcy raised his punch cup and said, "To beauty and to literature," and he drank.

"To literature," Maggie said, sipping.

"And to handsome Irish Fusiliers with dancing blue eyes," Prudence said.

The music started to play.

"I hear you're a voracious reader, but instead of reading to me, as you do to members of your family, educating them in the language of their long time conqueror, would you do me the honor of a dance?" he inquired, extending his arm to Maggie.

Momentarily forced to catch her breath, she placed her cup on the table and her hand on Darcy's arm. "Why, yes, Lieutenant, I would be delighted."

"*Darcy*," he whispered.

"Darcy," she repeated.

And they walked onto the floor to join the line of dancers.

While seeing to the entertainment of her other guests, Prudence watched Darcy and Maggie dancing, as a subtle sense of triumph began to well up from deep inside her. She knew her young cousin very well. As the bee to the flower, so was Darcy drawn to young Maggie, no doubt attracted by her innocence as much as by her rare Irish beauty. *And so he should be*, Prudence thought. For Maggie O'Reilly was indeed the most beautiful young woman at the ball.

Let all the haughty locals and my boring relations look down their noses as much as they dared, she thought to herself, for in her opinion, the beautiful, intelligent, young Catholic girl had every right to win over Darcy heart, mind, body, and soul. In the opinion of Prudence, Maggie was more exquisite than any other young woman in Ireland, or even in the British Commonwealth.

In forming such a union, Prudence could see Maggie rise to her rightful place among the best of them in Dingle, if not in the whole of Ireland.

Then, Prudence could continue to foster the young woman she had come to look upon as a dear friend, or perhaps even as a daughter. And Maggie could become all she had ever dreamt of becoming and ever longed to be.

And, if Prudence Elizabeth Pratt had her way in the destinies of Darcy Donal Brosnan and Mary Margaret O'Reilly—that was precisely how things were going to be.

13

High Tea in Dingle

The invitation to bring along her father to tea on Sunday afternoon was an unexpected turn of events in the life of young Maggie. Never before had she been invited to high tea, although Prudence had spoken of attending such affairs in London. The occasion had the mark of the Otherworld upon it, in Maggie's opinion, considering how Prudence and her father were drawn to each other on the prior evening. Their connection was magical, of that she was certain. Perhaps her mother and Rory had conjured up something from beyond the *veil*. Perhaps not. All the same, it seemed like a strange twist of fate to her.

The invitation caught Padraic fully unawares, seeing as how the local gentry had never invited him to such an affair in all his forty-one years. A long life already lived, allowing that he was never slightly wounded, incarcerated for an hour or a day, let alone hanged because of the Kerry skirmishes engaged in during his youth in his well-meaning though ineffective attempts to oppose the British Crown. Albeit, he had concealed ammunition and guns in the barn and the far beehive hut up the hill more than once. Something Maggie thought best not to mention, silence being golden under such circumstances, in her honest opinion.

That Sunday, on the way home in the wagon after attending Mass, Maggie suggested that her father have a cup of tea after the midday meal to be poured from her aunt's fine shamrock and heather Kelly teapot. Her Aunt Brigid was in on the plan to make sure that her father could handle a delicate cup with a touch of grace. After all, it had taken some convincing to get him to spend time away from the tavern in a fine Dingle parlor of a Sunday afternoon in the company of educated and refined ladies and gentlemen.

Her father was about to refuse when Maggie said, "It's a shame you had no time to meet Prudence with all the comings and goings. She very much wanted to meet you, Da."

That had won him over, seeing as how nervous he was on the previous evening. Perhaps it was best not to mention how attractive Prudence found him after just one look, which had revealed to Maggie that this was not a simple passing pattern but one fraught with the mark of *Destiny*.

On the way home, the family had spoken of Maggie's continued good fortune in regard to her friendship with Miss Pratt. All of them at least, except Liam, who was invited to the Malone's for Sunday supper. He had met the whole family at St. James, the brand new Church of Ireland. Donal Malone's great, great grandparents converted over a hundred years ago, mainly to keep their land and protect the family business. Since the O'Reilly's, as Roman Catholics, held fast to their faith, there was serious doubt regarding the courtship of young Kathleen Sharon by their Liam Niall.

Liam's face often flushed and he often acted tongue-tied around young Kathleen, the lass who had captured his heart for the past two years. The young couple had walked a few steps behind her parents, the owners of a fine mercantile shop on Main Street, but well in front of all the younger children. The sky was blue as they all walked up the hill toward the comfortable house with its fine view of the bay. A lovely family, the Malone's, all twelve children appeared to show proper respect to their parents and one living grandmother. Donal was said to have a bad temper that helped to keep his five sons in line.

"Is Liam planning to marry Kathleen?" Maggie inquired as she climbed down from the wagon.

"Marry a Protestant?" her father snapped. "I should hope not. I have worries enough already and am frankly amazed that he is even invited to sup with them."

"Trying to convert him, they are," her Aunt Brigid said in a tone of disdain.

"Mr. Malone recently spoke to Liam about taking goods to market in our wagon over the mountain to Ballyferriter. He will be paying him, of course," Matthew said.

"Is that right?" Padraic replied as he started to unhitch the pony.

"Kathleen is your age," Megan said to Maggie. "Sixteen come September. Everyone knows she is sweet on Liam, and he is sweet on her as well. That is plain to see."

"Makes him goofy, she does," her aunt said, narrowing her eyes. "Makes a fool of him, that one, such a flirt, that Kathleen."

"They have the mark of the Otherworld upon them," Maggie said, "Star-crossed lovers they are, meeting here again. I hope some good comes of it, but I have serious doubts."

"Star-crossed lovers, indeed!" Padraic said, casting a doubtful glance at his daughter.

"He says he wants to marry her," Matthew said, removing the harness from Lancelot.

"I need Liam right here," their father said, "Not serving the local merchants with *my* horse and *my* wagon."

"It is Triona that you fancy," Megan said to Matthew, and she made a face.

Matthew quickly turned away and proceeded to lead the horse out to pasture.

"Triona Malone is only thirteen," Maggie said. "Though I thought there might be something there. Pretty she is, rather smart too. Another Protestant! I doubt they will take Liam into the family unless he converts … Matthew neither."

"There shall be *no converting* in this family," Padraic grumbled and he stomped into the house. "And there will be no more talk of the Malones, if you please. It is time to eat our meal." He sat at the table, displeasure all over his face. "In peace!" he shouted, again mumbling, "In peace."

"Why cannot *I go* to high tea?" Megan pouted, clearing away the dishes.

"Thou shalt not covet thy sister's good fortune," her Aunt Brigid chastised.

"I be not coveting a cup of tea," Megan whined. "I want to be a lady, too, sit in a fine parlor ... not just *hear* tell of it. I want to listen to the music of Mozart and Beethoven played on a piano by Miss Pratt, if not by my very own sister." Megan smiled at Maggie, who wistfully returned her gaze.

"You are not invited," her aunt said.

Megan sighed and plopped into the rocking chair with a thud, her face in an instant sulk. "Could I not have a cup of tea, then, too?"

"May I have a cup of tea, please?" Maggie corrected.

"What's the difference, then? Am I not good enough to have a cup of tea with the likes of you and my very own father?"

"It is a matter of asking for the tea in proper English," Maggie explained. "I have tried to teach you, Megan. If you want to be a fine lady, then you must learn to speak English grammar correctly. Your manner of speech betrays your station."

"Is that right?" Megan stuck out her tongue at her sister. *"May I have a cup of tea, please?"* she caustically inquired, defiance in her bright green eyes as she stood and mockingly curtsied, though she was pleased to see her aunt was pouring tea into another cup.

"I'm to have a tin cup? How am I to learn to be a proper lady drinking from a tin cup?"

Her Aunt Brigid held out the cup. "Here you go, my lady. Drink your tea and watch your manners. Wanting to be a lady is one thing... acting the part is another."

"The tea is yours to drink, regardless of how you ask for it," Padraic said from the doorway. "Though I should think, at a tea party, no one would need to *ask* for a cup of tea." He sat and stared at the delicate cup on the table. "It seems to me there will be no whiskey or ale at this shindig." He flashed Maggie a devilish grin and winked, "Though I daresay, the tavern is not far for the walking, which is a very good thing indeed, if you ask me."

"Surely there will be no whiskey at high tea, Da," Maggie said in a tone of dismay. "You are not invited to a drinking party."

Her father reached over and gently patted her hand. "Did I not say as much?" He picked up his tea and daintily sipped, winking and grinning at Brigid as he noted the close scrutiny of both his daughters. "I trust I shall not embarrass you with my clumsy ways. I promise not to eat too many of her fancy scones and crumpets with jam. Blackberry jam, you say?"

"Aye! The cooks are baking special cakes and pies for high tea this afternoon. And there shall be ham and mutton cakes as well."

"Not nearly as tasty as your aunt's mutton pie, which was particularly good today, Brigid," Padraic said with a smile.

"Why, thank you, Padraic." Brigid looked pleased.

"High tea or low, I will do my best to behave in a gentlemanly fashion to make you proud, Maggie, that much I can promise you."

"I am sure you will do right fine, Padraic," her Aunt Brigid said. "It seems to me that this family is moving up in the world right fast these days," and she poured him another cup of tea.

Never had Padraic O'Reilly expected to be in the very same stylish parlor of a Sunday afternoon with Lord and Lady Charles Chadwick. His lordship's Beatrice, who had to be sixty, was plump though pleasant-looking, with an ample bosom that expanded with her every breath. Lady Chadwick had done more than her share in serving the needs of the poorest of the poor around the peninsula. She was a fine Christian woman by anyone's standards, considering the fact that she was Protestant English.

Lord Chadwick was looking the wear and tear of his years, his skin blotchy, his hair white, his prominent white handlebar moustache neatly trimmed not far above his ample belly. His lordship was more generous and pleasant by far than his new land agent, Percival Pratt. Pitiless Percy was short and stout, early thirties, with a large nose squashed across the middle of his face above a muddy brown moustache and bushy brown beard. The only time his mouth was detected was when he spoke. Padraic thought him in serious need of a skillful barber.

"This is my father, Mr. Padraic Desmond O'Reilly," Maggie said to Prudence, adding a curtsy, with a somewhat smug grin on her face.

Ona took Padraic's hat and curtsied.

Prudence coyly smiled up at her father.

"This is Miss Prudence Elizabeth Pratt, Da, the lady who has so kindly lent me so very many of her precious books. Some of the books have been read to my family, treasures of knowledge that teach us all how to better understand the many ways of the world beyond Ireland's green shores."

"Which world is that?" Percival smugly inquired, wedging himself into the small group in the entryway.

"The greater world before and beyond Ireland," Maggie courteously replied; though just being around Percy still made her feel ill at ease.

Her father stood taller, reserve on his face, as short Percy displayed a degree of annoyance.

"I believe you already know my father, Mr. Padraic O'Reilly," she said to Percy. "Have I not seen you at our farm quite often to collect Lord Chadwick's rents?" and she turned to her father and said, "Mr. Percival Pratt, Father. I have had the distinct honor and privilege of attending to the birth of his two fine children, Peter and Priscilla. His wife, Jennifer, is in the parlor near the piano with Lieutenant Brosnan, Prudence's cousin. Darcy is the gentleman I was telling you about, though out of uniform today. At the ball, Darcy looked quite dashing in his military dress redcoat."

Darcy nodded and smiled at her, causing her stomach to suddenly flutter, which surprised her.

Padraic nodded, his eyes still fixed on Percy. "We have met often enough, I daresay."

"More often than you care to, perhaps?" Percy discourteously replied, "Since you have been late in meeting your obligations for your twenty acres a time or two. Prime land you have. You wouldn't want to lose it, now, would you, O'Reilly ... fine grazing land for those dairy cows and your breeding bull, Cuchulainn."

"Only a day or two late, now and again," Padraic said, as his face slightly colored.

"Frankly, I'm surprised to find you here," Percy said in a goading tone, "Dropping your daughter off for the afternoon, are you?"

"Mr. O'Reilly is invited to tea, Percival," Prudence pointedly said. "Is there a reason I should consult you with regard to my guest list?"

Percy flushed.

Darcy and Jennifer joined the small group in the hallway, one on either side, as Jennifer slipped her arm through her husband's in a mild display of affection.

"It's a true pleasure to see you again so soon," Darcy said to Maggie, "I look forward to getting much better acquainted." Then he turned to Padraic. "Am I to assume that this gentleman is your father?"

"That you are, sir," Padraic said, standing taller, "Padraic O'Reilly at your service."

"Lieutenant Darcy Brosnan is Prudence's cousin and has only recently returned from fighting the Emperor Napoleon under the command of the Duke of Wellington," Maggie said in a tone of some pride.

"So you are one of Wellington's invincibles!" Padraic said in good humor, vigorously shaking Darcy's extended hand.

"It seems that is how we are generally known," Darcy said, appearing somewhat uneasy. "Though on the battlefield, we are less than *invincible* and as susceptible to canon ball or musket round as any other man. I have lost my share of comrades and friends over the years. Some buried in Portugal and Spain, others in England, Scotland or here in Ireland. War is nasty business, Mr. O'Reilly, though it is preferable to play the role of the victor to that of the vanquished. My commander is extraordinary in looking after the welfare of his men."

Padraic nodded. "I have heard great praise for your Duke of Wellington."

"Indeed!" Percy pompously chimed in.

"Am I correct in assuming that you have taken a bullet in your leg, Lieutenant?" Padraic glanced down at Darcy's leg and looked back into his eyes.

"Unusual perception seems to run in your family," he said, glancing at Maggie. "As a matter of record, I took a bullet in my right leg at Salamanca on July 22, 1812, a day I shall regrettably never forget. The French are formidable fighters. We were pretty much matched toe to toe and lost 5,000 men in that battle. The French lost 7,000, with an equal number taken prisoner. I am not sure how many we have lost fighting Napoleon these many years, far too many to suit me. But we couldn't very well let Napoleon conquer the world, now, could we?"

"The British certainly couldn't," Padraic dryly responded, casting a wary look at his daughter. "Although it seems to me that the British win most of their wars with significant help from the Irish, and tend to lose wars to the Irish as well." Her father chuckled. "But then, that was in America well before your time. If the truth be known, a few of the

O'Reilly's helped to fight in the first American War for Independence from Great Britain, and I would be willing to wager that the new generation of Irish are fighting for them again, though I have yet to receive letters of confirmation to that effect."

Instantly, Darcy's blue eyes registered amusement.

"Is that right?" Percy said in a sullen tone. "The government has just sent a large number of Wellington's invincibles to America to fight that upstart of a nation which was bold enough to declare war against the Crown back in 1812. What cheek those Americans have, waging a war against the most powerful and richest nation in the world!"

"The American economy is supposedly in ruin," Lord Chadwick loudly remarked from across the room. "This President Madison is apparently a spineless chap. They call him a *gnome* in the London *Times* … Little Jimmie. Imagine a runt of a man running a country the size of America!"

Percy stood taller, a look of distress on his face as he said, "There is great disorganization within their government, it is said."

"The London *Times* announced that the Crown is ready to chastise the savages by sending over Wellington's troops no longer required in France or Belgium," Lord Chadwick grumbled as he walked over to join the group in the hallway. "I should think 15,000 muskets and bayonets might force the foolhardy Americans back into submission to the Crown, where they damn well belong!"

"Perhaps not," Padraic said, hesitating only briefly under the withering gaze of his lordship.

"It is said they plan to burn Washington to the ground in retaliation for the burning of our Parliament building in Canada," Percy added in a tone of triumph. "That was in the newspapers."

"Several of our companies left for America some time ago," Darcy said, "Soldiers, sailors and marines, frigates and warships, all of them led by Vice Admiral Sir Alexander Cochrane, a man known to despise the Americans, since the Yankee clipper privateers captured so many British merchant ships, taking the crews and cargos these past several years," Darcy said in defense.

"The Americans don't seem to enjoy having their men impressed into the British Navy," Lord Chadwick wryly remarked. "That is apparently the big fuss with this war."

"No country is keen on having their men impressed into the service of the Crown," Padraic said in some heat. "I have had cousins impressed, one hung for trying to escape when I was but a lad. It is bad business, your lordship. The Americans have a right to object to their men being kidnapped."

There was a long pause of awkward silence.

"Did you know that the White House, as the President's mansion in Washington is called, was designed by an Irishman?" Darcy said in an effort at lightening the mood. "James Hoban from Kilkenny was educated at Trinity. I hope our invincibles don't burn down the presidential residence. It would be a loss of pure Irish talent in the young nation."

"And a terrible shame," Prudence added, as her eyes scanned her many guests.

"Is that right?" Percy said. "I didn't know it was designed by one of ours."

"After our own Irish Parliament building," Prudence said.

"Then, it would be a shame to destroy it," Percy conceded.

"For reasons purely my own, I doubt the Americans will lose this war," Darcy directed his remark to Lord Chadwick. "Do you really think that so vast a nation, with so scattered and diversified a population, will be brought into submission by the Crown with only 15,000 men, your lordship? The Duke was quick to decline the command, claiming that it was a tremendous mistake for Great Britain to even try."

"Is that right?" Lord Chadwick said in a tone of surprise.

"There is still much work in France and Belgium that requires my commander's expertise."

"I suppose it is difficult to know exactly what will happen in America," Percy said, "Though I don't suppose it matters one way or the other. I have relatives living there. But, in my opinion, it was a drastic mistake for the Americans to declare war upon Great Britain."

"Independence means a great deal to the Americans," Darcy said. "They are unlikely to relinquish liberty and abide by the dictates of any king, including those of Spain or France, which is just my opinion, of course."

"The British Navy and Army are forces with which to reckon," Percy asserted. "You can be sure of that, Darcy," he said, narrowing his eyes to mere slits.

"I have spent the past six years fighting for the Crown. We are called Irish Fusiliers, though few in my regiment are actually Irish. It is well known in Europe that Irishmen are fierce and courageous fighters," Darcy said, "As for me, I am only half Irish, with English and Scot blood from my mother. She, of course, grants Rob Roy full credit for my courage in battle," and he smiled.

Everyone laughed in good humor.

"Perchance the Americans will remain free with the Irish fighting for them again," Padraic said with a wink, "General Washington's Continental Army was one-third Irish, with Scots and Englishmen tossed in for good measure." He laughed. "The Irish fight on all sides in all wars, it seems to me. Anything to get them out of Ireland, so that they are unable to fight the Crown on their native land to secure our independence!"

The men in the room, mostly loyalists, blanched, regarding Padraic with suspicious eyes.

At once, Prudence stood taller and pursed her lips, appearing both pleased and alarmed by Padraic's treasonous remarks. There was scorn on the face of Lord Chadwick, his pale blue eyes coldly fixed on her father.

"Father, might you not fancy a cup of tea?" Maggie inquired, carefully slipping her arm though his.

"I have heard marvelous things about your blackberry jam," Padraic said to Prudence, flashing her his most charming smile. "Might I not sample some of that jam on this fine Sunday afternoon?"

"Certainly," Prudence replied, taking her father's other arm, "This way, Padraic. There are all sorts of delicious morsels for you to enjoy on this fine Sunday."

"Is that right?" he said, smiling.

"High tea is served," Ona announced, bobbing a curtsy.

With Maggie on one arm and Prudence on the other, Padraic O'Reilly proceeded toward a sumptuous display of food on the dining room table. All the other guests followed close behind them to enjoy an afternoon's repast of high tea in the seaside town of Dingle.

14

The Rescue of Marie Antoinette

"It was the Irish Brigade intended Dingle as a refuge for the Queen of France, through the generosity of Count Rice and old Black Tom, his father," Darcy excitedly said, perched on the edge of his chair.

All the other guests had already left. Only the four of them remained, as the sun sank lower behind the mountains in the west, the sky filled with varying shades of orange and red streaked with black.

"Marie Antoinette!" Maggie exclaimed. "How dashing! How bold! How daring!"

"How Irish," Prudence dryly quipped.

Everyone laughed.

"All the way from Paris, France to Dingle, Ireland. Imagine!" Darcy said, blankly staring off. "I was but a babe when the Irishmen plotted to steal a beautiful monarch imprisoned in a Paris tower by angry revolutionaries' intent upon spilling her blood, which finally did happen when I was the age of three."

"No chance of you saving her," Prudence said, "Though I daresay that you would have volunteered for the dangerous plot. The Irish in your blood insurance enough for you to risk life and limb when called to arms for a so-called noble purpose, perhaps for any crown?"

Safe enough talk with the dyed-in-the-wool Protestants gone, Maggie thought. Those still present were far more Irish than the rest and now breathing easier on their own.

"Please do not discount my Scottish blood. I am descended from a MacGregor that I am proud to have as an ancestor, regardless of the pre-disposed opinion of my late English grandfather."

"A bit of an outlaw, Rob Roy," Prudence teased.

"A grand, brave and notorious one, or so my mother claims, but you know the Scots." Darcy said, laughing, with his eyes again on Maggie as they had been for most of the afternoon.

"It was the Irish established the Kingdom of Scotland," Padraic boasted. "When the old chieftains went off a plundering and conquering, completely unaware they would one day return at the command of an English king, as Presbyterians, and be given the land of Roman Catholics, without any compensation to the latter, I might add," his tone goaded as his green eyes narrowed.

"So I have heard," Darcy cheerfully said. "Our blood is not that different. The Irish traveled the world, with an Irish monk at every royal court for centuries, teaching the royals how to read and write, with our earliest Irish ancestors among the very most learned of scholars."

"An Irish claim for a certainty," Maggie said, smiling, "Though I have heard tell it is true enough. Our Kerry is where the old bards and historians memorized the genealogy of the clans as an oral tradition. They were actually treated the same as the chieftains. No one dared to ask them to leave, feeding them as long as they wished to enjoy the hospitality of the host, at times to their ruination."

"Nervy lot, the old bards," Padraic said, "Threw their weight around a bit, hear tell."

"Kerry is where the old Druids claimed that the soul comes at the hour of death to enter the Otherworld," Prudence said. "On the days when the mists and fog roll in, clinging to our hills and rugged shoreline, I find that altogether believable."

Padraic appeared to study Prudence a moment before he turned to Maggie. All afternoon, she was aware of her father watching her, and alternately, watching Prudence. In turn, she had watched her father's every move. Never before had the two of them been together of a Sunday afternoon in such fine surroundings with such genteel companions.

"It seems to me that those of us here in Kerry get to the Otherworld faster than the rest," Padraic said, "And, it also seems to me that the time has come for Maggie and myself to take our leave and no longer impose upon your generous hospitality," he said to Prudence, immediately standing.

In an instant, Prudence was on her feet. "Will you and Maggie not stay and have supper with us? After all, there is only Darcy and me. Heaven only knows there is plenty of food here. Then we can hear more of the tragic fate of the late Queen of France and the courageous plot of our Irish rogues to bring her safely to Dingle."

Now, Maggie stood and turned to face her father. Light filled his eyes as he looked at Prudence, the same sort of light she had noted in Darcy's eyes as he looked at her. From the very first moment, Darcy's vivid blue eyes had conveyed to her a sense of the Otherworld. It was as though his soul looked directly into her soul from somewhere deep inside him. It was a soul she thought she had perhaps known forever.

"Will you not both please stay?" Darcy said, rising. "So we might better enjoy the pleasure of your company?"

"Well, now, if it really won't be too much of a bother," Padraic said, unable to suppress his dimpled grin.

"It is no bother at all," Prudence said. "I will tell the cook to serve us some supper right away. It has been some time since we enjoyed high tea."

"It was the Wild Geese devised the plan to rescue Marie Antoinette from the Temple Prison," Padraic said, "to bring her to the French port by a relay of horses, an armed Irishman accompanying her and refreshing at every station. An alternate plan involved sailing a boat down the River Seine. Regardless of the plan, the queen was to be taken to a merchant ship owned by the Count anchored off Le Harve. That ship was to bring her to a house in readiness for Her Highness at Upper Main Street and Green Street here in Dingle," he said, his energy clear and high as it always was in telling a tale that he loved, his eyes reflecting the flickering flames of the candles on the table.

"Walking distance from this *very house*," Maggie said in astonishment.

"That is what I have heard," Darcy said, "The plan was in place through the scheming of Black Tom, as he was called."

"Black Tom and Count Rice put up the funds for the gallant attempt," Padraic said, carefully sipping wine from a Waterford goblet like a proper Irish gentleman.

"All of that and still no rescue," Prudence said in a tone of disappointment.

"The men made it all the way to her cell in the tower," Padraic said and he dramatically paused.

"No doubt, by bribing and killing a few French guards," Darcy put in, "Necessary to free her, of course. And to think that she refused."

"Of course, she did," Maggie whispered.

"*Of course?*" Darcy said, looking at her with surprise on his face.

"Now, if you ask me, the queen lost her head when she refused Black Tom's ship to escape to safety here in Dingle," Padraic said. "In August of 1792, Marie Antoinette sealed her fate and her ultimate date with the guillotine."

"No wonder she lost her head," Prudence said in alarm. "If she were a sensible woman, she would have accepted their valiant help and escaped. Whatever could have possessed her?"

"It was her fate that she faced," Maggie calmly said, sensing the flow of the Otherworld beginning to move through her, "Her special appointment with destiny."

"It was her destiny to die?" Padraic said, scowling.

"It was, Da. Marie Antoinette entered the Otherworld proudly, you see. How could she abandon her husband and children in their great suffering and brand herself as a coward? The queen knew it was her time. She died proudly, she did, with dignity and great courage."

"You have queer notions, Maggie," her father said, "Queer notions, indeed."

"Perhaps not," Darcy said, slowly turning to face Padraic. "It is said at the end, the queen apologized to her executioner for stepping on his foot."

"Merciful heavens!" Prudence exclaimed.

"In being taken from her quarters, she is known to have said, 'Courage! I have shown it for years; think you I shall lose it at the moment when my sufferings are to end?'" Darcy said and he respectfully bowed his head.

Padraic shook his head and turned to his daughter. "You always think it's someone's time to die. I suppose you think it was your mother's time in giving birth to Sean Joseph?"

"Did you not hear the cry of the banshee that night and Old Black Bart howling at the moon until he died, too? Could you not read the signs, Da? Sadly, it was my mother's time," she said with quiet conviction.

"That is easy enough for you to say. Easy to say a person should have died when they are dead, in fact. No one can change anything after the last breath escapes our lips, and that is a fact," Padraic said, looking at Maggie.

"There is wisdom in her words, Mr. O'Reilly," Darcy said. "I have witnessed it on the battlefield and in the field hospitals. Soldiers say, 'It is time to go.' No man seems to say, it is time to die, but only that it is time to take their leave before taking their very last breath."

"No one dies. Living is forever. Dying is like taking off that lovely uniform you wore at the ball," Maggie said to Darcy, "and putting on the trousers and waistcoat you wear today. It is not that much different, honest and truly."

"How do you know that, Maggie? How do you really know?" her father implored, "I suppose you can see into the Otherworld the same as all the other Kelly women. That you have *the gift?* It is not that I have entirely failed to notice that fact."

"Your Maggie knows many things," Prudence softly said to him. "She is a very special lass, Padraic, a very special lass, indeed."

"That she is," he said, glancing at Maggie as his eyes misted over.

"I wonder if Marie Antoinette had any second thoughts about Ireland as she knelt before the guillotine to come face to face with the Angel of Death?" Prudence said.

"None at all," Maggie said. "The queen was ready to be reunited with her husband and her children, free of all pain and suffering, in the magnificence of the Summerland."

15

Prince Charming

On the first day of September, with the skies fully clear, Darcy Brosnan rode out to the O'Reilly Farm on a spirited dapple-gray mare. In his free hand, he was holding the reins of a saddled chestnut mare that trotted along at his side.

Surprised by his sudden and unexpected appearance, Maggie stood in the garden and wiped her dirty hands on her dirty white apron. Her long hair was tucked up in a badly stained bonnet.

"Greetings, Darcy! Wherever did the likes of you find two such fine-looking horses on a glorious day such as this?" she inquired, shielding her eyes from the sun.

"The horses are on loan from a distant relation who says they can use some exercise."

"And who might that be?"

"Pitiless Percy is how I have heard he is known around about these parts," Darcy said, grinning, and he dismounted, leading the horses to the water trough.

"I see," Maggie said, pumping water into the trough, as she petted the neck of the dapple-gray and said, "Daphne and I have met before. Jennifer sometimes rides her. She is a gentle sort."

The horse nudged her, demanding attention, as she continued to stroke the mare's long neck.

"Percy thought I was saddling up Ginger here for Prudence to ride, but she declined, knowing it was my intention to take you horseback riding on this very fine day."

"You briefly mentioned the matter on Sunday. Am I to assume that you are here to invite me to go horseback riding, Lieutenant Brosnan?"

"Precisely that, Miss O'Reilly."

Glancing down at her muddy dress, Maggie thought that she must look a fright. Darcy had on tidy brown riding pants, knee high brown leather boots, a green linen shirt, and a paisley scarf tied around his neck. On his head was a brown tweed cap that looked strangely familiar.

"That is a fine cap you are wearing. Moriarity's Emporium?"

"Aye," he replied. "Prudence insisted I wear it in order to shade my eyes from the sun."

"Prudence has a preference for men wearing hats." Maggie was forced to wonder about Prudence's role in releasing her from her chores on that day. Her aunt and father might not be in full and total agreement.

"Would you care to walk instead, perhaps? We could walk through the hills, if you would prefer."

Darcy's eyes seemed far bluer than the autumn skies, which made her wonder how she actually felt about the tall, handsome lieutenant with his tousled hair covered by the same cap she had given to Aidan for his birthday. Twenty-four-years seemed not that young to still be single, and here he was at her farm, uninvited, with two fine horses to ride on a lovely September day.

"Hello, Lieutenant," her father called out, waving from beside the barn.

"Hello, Mr. O'Reilly," Darcy called back.

Until then, Maggie had failed to notice her father and Matthew standing over there with curiosity all over their faces. Liam and Sean had left with the wagon to make a delivery to Lord Chadwick's estate.

"You do know how to ride a horse?" Darcy inquired.

"I have never ridden a horse as fine as these, and none as frisky as, Ginger, you say?" She patted the mare's neck to sense its nature and the two of them nodded together. Then she turned to Darcy and she nodded to him.

Darcy seemed amused as Matthew walked over to where they were standing.

"Matthew O'Reilly," he said to Darcy. "I'm Maggie's older brother, though not the eldest," and he wiped his hand on pants before extending his hand to Darcy.

"It is a pleasure to meet you, Matthew," Darcy said, shaking his hand.

"So you are Lieutenant Darcy Brosnan. My father spoke highly of you only this morning at breakfast."

"Kind words, I trust."

"Matthew Michael is two years older than me and much taller, as you can see. He's a fine chap," Maggie said.

"Call me, Darcy," he said to Matthew.

"I hear you've been off fighting in Spain and Portugal with the Irish Fusiliers, fighting for the Crown. What was it like fighting Napoleon's army under the Duke of Wellington? I heard tell that he can be a mean bastard, but is still highly respected by his men. He executes men for looting, hear tell. Is that a fact, now?"

Darcy nodded. "He is respected, but not necessarily loved. However, he goes to great lengths to protect those under his command with far fewer casualties as the result."

"So then, you are one of Wellington's invincibles and took a bullet in your leg, according to my Da!" Matthew said, staring down at Darcy's legs with questions in his eyes. "Salamanca, Spain sounds pretty exotic to me ... on the other side of the world, I'd say."

"It was two years ago," Darcy said, lightly touching his right thigh. "It still gives me trouble when it rains or the weather turns cold and nasty."

"Kindly excuse me, gentlemen," Maggie said. "I shall go freshen up for our ride and leave you two, so that you can tell Matthew about fighting the French." She turned to her brother. "Try not to talk his leg off, Matthew. I will only be a little while," and she hurried into the house.

Running to her room and tossing her dirty cap aside, Maggie poured water from the kettle into the basin to wash her face and hands. She selected a clean green linen dress. Standing before the mirror, she ran a brush through her long, tangled hair, and was forced to wonder how Darcy could find the least thing about her attractive. That was what he deserved for showing up out of the blue, she thought. With her face clean, her cheeks pink from the sun, she pulled her hair up into a clean bonnet that tied under her chin and returned to the living room.

"He's a looker, that one," her Aunt Brigid said, peering out from behind a lace curtain, "A fine gentleman … handsome and tall just like your Da!"

Briefly glancing out the window, Maggie could see her father, Darcy and Matthew standing near the horses as she said to her aunt, "Talking about war, no doubt, about fighting the French who were supposed to be our allies, fighting the emperor who was supposed to free Ireland from the Crown." Shaking her head in disgust, Maggie said, "I have heard Da talking with the other men and my brothers about such things."

"Not likely is it," Megan said from her place at the loom. "Probably never was," she stood and stole a glance out the window before winking at Maggie. "Nice one, he is!"

"Such a grand day to go horseback riding just like the gentry on their fine estates, over the hills and through the dales. Next, he may invite you to a fox hunt!" her aunt said, laughing. "Nothing wrong with that one that I can see from here. He's a fine specimen, even though he is only half Irish. He just might be worth your charming, Maggie, my dear."

"Cinderella's prince charming has come to take her to his castle," Megan teased. "Did he not bring along a glass slipper to try on your dainty foot?" she started laughing as she watched Maggie wash the mud from between her toes and pull on a pair of clean socks and a pair of leather shoes that had seen a far better day.

"He brought along two fine horses instead of a slipper," Maggie said, pinching color into her cheeks.

"Did you not say that he danced with you all evening on Saturday?" her aunt said from where she was slicing potatoes into the cast iron pot.

"When you go to a ball, you must dance with someone, Aunt. Darcy was kind enough to dance with me, and with a few of the other young ladies, including Prudence, of course. He spent most of his time with me, however. I also danced with the mayor, don't you forget. Maggie O'Reilly danced with the sovereign Lord Mayor Stewart Gregory in the home of Miss Prudence Pratt. An almighty Protestant danced with a lowly Catholic lass, though I seriously doubt that he knew who I was, since we barely spoke a word to each other."

"He thought you were a fairy princess who magically appeared at the ball!" her Aunt Brigid teased all smiles.

"That ruddy faced old smuggler!" Megan groaned, "Lecherous and lewd he is. Leers at the youngest of the lasses, unfaithful to his wife, he is. Whoring he goes to that brothel near Ballyferriter used by the sailors. If you ask me, he is always drunk as a skunk, uncouth and generally disgusting."

"And how would the likes of you know such things about our mayor?" her aunt inquired in feigned innocence, "You being only fourteen and all."

"I have heard such talk at this very table about that old geezer … and about the whore house, too. I am not deaf, dumb or blind, Aunt."

The two girls laughed as their aunt shook her head.

"You will not be engaging in that sort of talk in front of your father or you are likely to get a beating behind the barn." She tried to scowl. "Big ears you have. You two don't miss a trick, now, do you?"

"Not hardly," Megan said.

"He was being *kind*, you say, dancing with you? Being kind?" her aunt said to Maggie.

Frowning at her sad, old shoes, Maggie glanced out at Darcy's fine leather boots. "Ugly shoes. Hardly shoes to be worn by a lady to go horseback riding."

"He was not being kind," her aunt said. "Look at him! Darcy Brosnan has come a courting with a fine horse for you to ride. I would be willing to bet you that Pitiless Percy would not be pleased to know that his horse was intended for his wife's midwife, the poor daughter of a tenant dairy farmer!"

"Courting?" Maggie stood up straighter and frowned.

"*Courting!*" her aunt said.

"But, Aunt Brigid, Darcy is from a fine family in Dublin. His Irish father converted for the sake of his mother. Why would Darcy Brosnan court me? I'm a Catholic and as good as betrothed to my Aidan. All Darcy could ever want from me is my friendship."

"*Friendship?*" her Aunt Brigid said, laughing. "Mark my word, Mary Margaret O'Reilly, that handsome bloke with a horse for you to ride upon has come out here a courting."

"Poor Aidan," Megan teased. "He is about to lose you to one of the Crown's Protestant redcoats, one of Wellington's invincibles, no less. A man who could well hang Aidan by the neck until he is quite dead from catching him for being a smuggler."

16

Castles and Kings

The horses grazed not far from the crumbling remnants of Rahanane Castle and its ring fort, providing an excellent view of Ventry Bay. The clear blue skies offered a fine spectacle of the sea lapping against the distant shore near The Kells. The emerald green mountains of County Kerry, the McGillycuddy Reeks, often cloaked in clouds or misty rain, were now towering in the distance in regal splendor.

Darcy sounded much the same to her as her teacher, Master Roberts, as he said, "Rahanane Castle was built centuries ago, the exact date unknown. It was the seat of the former Knights of Kerry responsible for the FitzGerald lineage through the Norman invasion of 1169. One leader, Maurice, son of Gerald and the Welsh princess Nesta, became known as Maurice Fitzgerald. Strange as it seems, it was from that one man that all the Geraldines in Ireland have descended."

"*Fitz* is like *Mc* or *Mac*," Maggie said. "All once meant *son of,* but that no longer seems to be the case."

"John Fitzgerald, his grandson, was the first to settle in County Kerry. Tragically, he and his son, Maurice, died in an ambush at the battle of *Callan* in 1261, fighting the McCarthy Mór. King Henry III granted a charter, with the title of Lord of the Decies and Desmond, his sons became known as the Knight of Kerry, the Knight of Glin, and the White Knight, distinctions that no longer existed by the end of the 16th century."

"My father claims to be descended from the Desmonds. Desmond is his middle name, but perhaps not through marriage." Maggie smiled. "How is it that you know so much about our history here in Dingle?" she inquired, turning to gaze out to sea, since talk of far other times always put her in touch with the Otherworld. Often she vividly glimpsed fragments of the past within her own mind. At times, Maggie could see the near physical forms of the departed, much more than mere ghostly images. She had learned to read the *Faerie Light, Leabhar n Beatha f,* where patterns exist eternally, known to some as the Mists of Time. The patterns were easily accessible to one born *knowing,* or to those with sufficient courage to embrace the timeless ways of the Druids.

"Knowing that the town of Dingle was burned thrice to the ground by an angry lord or mob of some kind, it is amazing we are all still here." Maggie began to search through a patch of shamrocks. "No extra luck today, it seems," she said, shaking her head as she turned to Darcy.

"I have never found one with four leaves. Do they actually exist?"

"You will find one if Dana sees fit to bless you. I have already found four."

"Four? You must be lucky, indeed."

"Lucky enough. How is it that you know so much about our Kerry when you hail from Dublin?"

"From Prudence and my father, who is fascinated with the history of our country. He was the first in our family to wed outside his bloodline. On my father's side I have cousins in Kerry, others in Cork, also Catholics. They live simple lives, raising sheep, growing flax for the linen industry here in Dingle, fishing, not at all an easy life, I would imagine. One cousin has a small dairy herd like yours not far from Tralee. I will be visiting with Thomas Brosnan after I leave here. He and his wife Mary do rather well with their fifteen children."

"Fifteen! Very good Catholics," she said in a tone of derision, her mind suddenly filled to overflowing with questions to ask him. "So there are Brosnans who are still tenant farmers?"

"My poor relations. The few who joined the military no longer remain within Ireland's green shores, but are scattered throughout Europe, Australia and America."

"Wild Geese," Maggie said, looking up in time to catch sight of a formation of geese flying south. "Da says the Wild Geese have flown away for 125 years. I have uncles and cousins in that flock." She watched the graceful birds in flight formation. "It seems there will soon be a change in the weather."

"Wild geese," Darcy said, looking up and noticing the birds. "Most flew away to escape execution, never realizing false promises were made and they would never again see Ireland, though some responded to the call of adventure, I would suppose. It is normal and manly to want to see the world beyond the rocky shores of our beautiful Ireland."

"Whatever the reason, it was each man's fate to go. I, too, would like to see the world, which is not easy for us lasses. I would love to see America," she said, again glancing toward the sky. "But that flock doesn't seem to be headed in that direction, so I will not be catching a ride with them."

"They're probably headed for Africa. I'm not sure where flocks hereabouts migrate for the winter, since I am not much of a birdwatcher," he said, standing, his expression pensive as he turned to her. "Do you really want to see America, Maggie?"

"More than anywhere else in the world. It is the land of opportunity, a continent of unlimited resources with wild game and fine land, and it is larger by far than the whole of Ireland."

Darcy laughed. "Much larger by far."

"You can only get there by a ship sailing across the sea."

"My father's brother, my Uncle Shane, lives in America in a place called Maryland not far from the Atlantic Ocean that is accessible through a bay known as the Chesapeake. He lives near a large city originally settled by an English Catholic named Lord Baltimore."

"Baltimore," she softly repeated.

"The Catholics in England escaped persecution back in 1627, less than 200 years ago."

"Your Uncle Shane is a Catholic?"

Darcy nodded. "Shane wasn't searching for religious freedom. He ran off in search of adventure at the age of twelve, signing on with a merchant ship and lying about his age and his name. He told the captain he was a poor, forsaken, orphan lad."

"Poor and forsaken?"

"It seems my grandfather could be rather strict and was likely to give him a good thrashing if he misbehaved. Shane was the rebellious type and quite stubborn, hear tell, always wagering with the other children and taking away their treasures. He had a small trunk filled with things he had won playing cards. It seemed all he could ever talk about was joining the military or going to America to make his fortune. If he hadn't known how to read and write, I doubt my family would have ever learned of his whereabouts."

"He must have worried his parents a great deal."

"He didn't write for five years. My grandparents thought he was impressed into the Royal Navy or sold into slavery, if he wasn't already dead."

"How long ago did your uncle run away?"

"Forty years ago ... well before I was born."

"Forty years?"

"Uncle Shane is in his fifties now. He fought in the first American War for Independence that started in 1775 and ended in 1783. More than likely, he is fighting the Crown again in the present conflict."

"You know my Da's thoughts on that subject. He thinks it unlikely that Ireland shall anytime soon gain its freedom, so he says the Irish might as well fight for their freedom in America."

"He might be right. I hope they do win this war, and frankly, I don't see how they can lose." He paused. "I trust I am safe in expressing my treasonous thoughts to you?"

"Strange ... coming from one of Wellington's invincibles."

"I was glad to be busy fighting Napoleon when the troops were called up for America. Since I was long overdue for a leave, I wasn't pressed into joining up with General Ross. He and the men no doubt have arrived there by now. Ross is Irish, but eager to even the score for the destruction of the Parliament building in York." He reflectively paused. "Robert Ross is a fine commander, calculating and shrewd, with a sworn allegiance to His Majesty King George III, mad though he may be. His Regent is a disaster and rather disgusting. I'm not fond of the royals. Perhaps it is the blood of the Scots and Irish in my veins." Darcy chuckled.

"It is my guess that you want to go to America with no allegiance to the Crown," Maggie said, feeling drawn to the man's dash, wit and charm, even his seeming inconsistencies.

"True," he said, looking at her with his dazzling blue eyes. "Though I shall probably only admit that to you and Prudence. I'm counting on the two of you to keep my secret. After all, I am a quarter English, with my father 100 percent Irish. When my time in the King's service is done, I shall endeavor to make my fortune in America the same as my Uncle Shane, perhaps next year."

"Hardly the same as your uncle. You are a bit over twelve, Darcy."

He smiled. "Uncle Shane writes to me of his tobacco plantation near the Gunpowder River. He says there is money to be made in tobacco. The land is cheap for those willing to work hard. His African slaves do most of the hard labor. He also employs a few of the local Indians."

"Indians?" Maggie sat up straighter. "I have read about Indians." She thoughtfully paused. "Your uncle employs dark-skinned natives with long braided hair that wear deerskins and live in wigwams?"

"On his plantation, he says they live in log cabins and a long house not far from the river. There are many different tribes in America, some warlike, others quite peaceful. Uncle Shane deals with the Piscataway, a tribe that is scattered and peaceful."

"Out west, the tribes are fierce and sometimes kill the settlers."

"Not the Piscataway. On Uncle Shane's plantation it is mostly the African slaves that do the planting and harvesting of the tobacco."

"So your uncle owns slaves?" she said and that thought troubled her deeply.

"If any of them die, or the children are too young to work, he says he buys more."

"Some of the slaves are children?"

"They breed just like anyone else."

"Does he buy slaves as children?"

"Well, boys do grow up to be men."

"Who sells him these Africans slaves?"

"Mainly the Dutch and Portuguese, sometimes Spaniards. There are people in England who have African slaves as well. In America, owning and buying slaves is common practice."

"The Greeks and Romans brought their captives back as their slaves, but that was a long time ago. Selling people doesn't seem right at all to me, Darcy. What sort of men engage in such a repulsive trade? I would never want to be a slave, would you?"

"New laws in Great Britain and America forbid the selling or buying of more new Africans, but laws are often broken." He appeared to struggle with the concept. "Some farmers sell their slaves, I would imagine. They are black-skinned, primitive tribesmen and women sold into bondage by other African tribes."

"And that makes it right?" The idea of buying or selling children seemed outrageous to her. "Do you know anything about growing tobacco, Darcy?" she inquired, preferring to change the subject as a distinct heaviness suddenly settled in over her. Someone from the Otherworld appeared to be closing in and making her feel uncomfortable.

"My uncle has agreed to teach me all that I need to know. I hear you have a way with herbs. Tobacco is an herb. Smoking has become quite fashionable. Your aunt and your father seem to enjoy sharing a pipe."

"I don't know much about tobacco," she said, though she had grown plants from seeds without much luck.

"I shall learn," Darcy said. "Up until now my entire adult life has been spent as a foot soldier. I have no doubt killed enough men to last me for the rest of my days." He paused. "I am terribly sorry, Maggie. I didn't mean to say anything that might offend you."

"Saying what is on your mind is fine with me, Darcy. I should think you have fought in enough battles. Growing tobacco in America sounds peaceful, once the Americans have routed the bloody English again," she said, smiling.

There was gentleness in his eyes in the manner he was watching her. "There will always be babies. Perhaps you can be a midwife in America."

"There is no end of such work, it seems to me," she said, walking over to her horse.

"Is a midwife with flaming red hair also a milkmaid, the same as Queen Mauve?" Darcy teased.

"I am fond of the cows, but the lads do that work. I feed chickens and gather eggs. I am glad we have no pigs, for I cannot bear the stench of them. I know how to milk and churn butter, but with my father and my three brothers such work does not fall to me."

"I know nothing of cows."

"I would imagine not." She softly laughed and petted Ginger's long nose.

"My grandmother had a farm and I fed the chickens a time or two. I gathered eggs for breakfast at least twice."

"You spoke Gaelic at the ball. Did your parents teach you Gaelic?"

"Only a few words and phrases. With me, you must speak English. I was educated at Eaton and both my parents speak English."

"I was surprised to see you Irish dancing, and even more surprised to see Percy doing an Irish jig. What a sight!"

"You should see my mother do the Highland fling and the two of them dancing together. The Scots dance quite a bit, too."

"It is the Irish in 'em," she said.

"Time to move on. The sun is lowering beyond yonder hills." Darcy picked up the reins of his horse.

"Do you still want to see my ancestor's ogham stone?"

"I wouldn't want to miss it, actually."

Darcy helped Maggie up onto her horse before climbing onto his. Then, off they cantered in an easterly direction toward the Short Strand at *Emlagh East*.

"Why is it that you have no wife, Darcy? Has no bonny lass yet managed to steal your heart?"

"Soldiering leaves little time for the pursuit of romance," Darcy said.

"No sweetheart in all your days seems strange for a man as handsome as you."

After looking at her askance, he said, "Sally stole my heart when I was sixteen. I was mad for her."

"But you did not marry her. Was she not fair?"

"Exceedingly fair."

"Well, then?"

"She eloped with a lieutenant, an Englishman in the King's Cavalry, a true redcoat."

"How rude."

"Rude indeed. I thought I would never get over her."

"So you decided to become a lieutenant to win her back and wear a redcoat like you wore at the ball, the same as the man who stole away your Sally?"

"By the time I joined the regiment, Sally had given birth to her second child and moved to London with her captain."

"Her captain? Sally was English?"

"English."

"You should have chosen an Irish lass. You cannot trust those English girls. I have heard tell they all run fickle."

"And Irish girls are never fickle?" Darcy was laughing.

Ignoring his remark, Maggie turned and pointed. "There is my ogham, the grave of Bruscus maqi Caliaci, an old form of Ceallaigh, Kelly in English. It is my mother's maiden name. I am Mary Margaret Kathleen Kelly O'Reilly."

"I see," he said, helping her down from her horse, his eyes steady on hers so she could sense his longing and the lightness of his breath.

That afternoon, each time Darcy had helped her off her horse it seemed that she weighed nearly nothing. The two of them stood face to face, eyes locked in more than a passing glance. His face moved closer to hers. He had not immediately stepped back as before, but looked as though he was about to kiss her when she stepped back, her heart racing as her trembling hands smoothed out her dress.

Turning to face the ogham, Maggie was unable to dismiss the sense of his breath on her cheek. Her heart was still pounding, as she thought of his lips, so full and inviting, his bright eyes the deep blue of the Irish Sea. Darcy was inquisitive yet caring, a gentleman charmer with an educated turn of mind. Never before had she kept company with such a man, except while reading a novel, or more recently, in one of her more vivid dreams.

Darcy turned to his horse and opened his saddlebag. He removed something and turned back to her. He was holding out a book. "Before you introduce me to your ancestor, kindly allow me to give you a copy of Miss Jane Austen's latest novel, *Mansfield Dark*."

Stunned, Maggie simply stared, not knowing exactly what to say or do. He was watching her closely with his dancing blue eyes.

"During the past several months, Prudence has written to me often and mentioned you in many of her letters. That is why I purchased three copies of this book, so you might have one for your own library."

"My library? But I ..." Her heart was pounding even faster.

"You do want the book, don't you?" Darcy inquired, suddenly appearing confused.

"Of course, I do," Maggie said, taking the book into her trembling hands. "It is just that no one has ever given me a book before." Tears filled her eyes. "Thank you, Darcy. You are too kind."

"You are most welcome, Mary Margaret Kathleen Kelly O'Reilly. I thought you should have your own copy, so now you do."

Holding the book tightly against her chest, she said, "You are too generous. I shall be eternally grateful to you for your great kindness."

"It is only a book, Maggie, one small book."

"But a very special book. You know how fond I am of Miss Austen's novels."

"As am I. I shall endeavor to send you *Sense and Sensibility* and *Pride and Prejudice*, so you will have them for your library as well. I may be able to secure copies in Dublin or London before I return to my garrison in a fortnight. Before that I shall be spending time at the country estate of my parents' at Glendalough in Wicklow."

"It must be very lovely there."

"No more so than the Lakes of Killarney and the McGillycuddy Reeks." He glanced at the towering mountains in the distance.

"I have never seen the lakes. Prudence says that I should see the Ring of Kerry ... that it is beautiful beyond words to describe."

"Aye, you should. I heard the *Teezeley Weezeleys* whilst I was there, calling *hello* from the mountain."

"The wee folk?" she said in surprise.

"I am joking, of course. It is an echo of your own voice that comes back to you from the mountain. No one can actually hear the *Teezeley Weezeleys.*"

Watching him, Maggie silently attuned to her center, feeling the energy emanating from the ogham stone. She thought Darcy might not understand, nor even believe, if she tried to explain to him what she could feel in that place. Her Aunt Brigid was right. Few there were who understood the invisible. Fewer still were those able to see the magical beings of the Otherworld, and even fewer those open to learning the ancient ways of the Druids. The Catholic priests had nearly completely destroyed the ancient truths, keeping only that which seemed acceptable to them. For Maggie, the Church had only a portion of the truth and not the whole of it.

"Tell me about your ancestor," Darcy said, more closely inspecting the markings on the side of the stone. "Kelly is written here, you say?"

Upon closer examination, she touched the strange writings and said, "The man buried here was once a great and glorious Druid High Priest, a Celtic High King of olden times, all wise, all knowing, magical and amazing beyond the comprehension of most mortals."

"How do you know this?" he inquired, a quizzical expression on his face. "The stone is timeless, granted, ancient, but how might anyone know who is buried here or much of anything about them?"

"His name is here," she said, lightly running her fingers over the etchings, "Written in the ancient symbols passed down through the tradition of the Druids, specifically the Ancient Order of the Druids of the Clan Ceallaigh."

"Kelly," he said with his smile wistful.

"For thousands and thousands and thousands of years."

"That many thousands?" Darcy smiled, and again appeared to study the markings before he turned to her with his eyes filled with questions. "You say it's a family secret?"

"Aye," Maggie said, turning to place the book in her saddlebag. When she turned back, the expression on Darcy's face seemed to indicate that she was taking herself much too seriously.

"A Celtic chieftain without a castle?" Darcy said, turning his gaze toward the sea.

"He has a castle now … made of light and crystal off there in the mists. It is said that he shall return one day, perhaps to be a king again. It is his choice, you see, to be whatever he will be."

"I see," he said. "Are you a Pagan or a Roman Catholic, Maggie?"

"I am a Pagan Catholic. Mostly, I'm just me. I am certainly not a Presbyterian."

"No," Darcy said, laughing, and he helped her back up into the saddle.

What Darcy could not understand, nor was he prepared to see, was that Maggie could sense the energy of olden times moving in and through her in that place. An energy that granted her extraordinary memories and clear visions of ancient holy stone circles, grand and glorious castles, noble and benevolent Irish High Kings that existed yet within the gathering mist beyond the sacred shores of the Emerald Isle in that southwestern point near the sea.

17

Fond Farewells

It was Liam who insisted on driving Maggie into town for her luncheon on Goat Street that day. Darcy was leaving. He planned to spend the night with his cousin not far from Tralee before he boarded a coach for Dublin on the next day.

"I plan to come back through here and give you a ride home," Liam said, stopping the wagon directly in front of the house. "Should there be any delay in making Mr. Malone's deliveries to Ballyferriter, either wait up, or else start walking. I will look for you along the way."

"Either way, thank you kindly for bringing me here, Liam," Maggie said, getting down from the wagon. "I am much obliged."

"Are you, now? Well, you take care with that lieutenant. Aidan asked me to keep an eye on you. Intends to marry you, he does, come spring. With the white silk you already have for your wedding gown, you are as good as betrothed. Just you remember that, Mary Margaret."

"So Aidan says," she replied, straightening out her skirt. "It seems to me that I am the one to make that decision. I am in no rush to marry Aidan McKenna or anyone else, for that matter."

"All the same, it is plain to me that Darcy fancies you. I am not so sure that Aidan would be happy to know of him, should I so decide to tell him."

Bristling, Maggie replied, "You will not be doing that. You will be keeping your mouth shut or I will be forced to turn you into a toad at the next full moon," she said with smirk.

Liam laughed. "Is that what you would do to me, Maggie?"

Her answer was simply an impish grin.

"Well, I'll think about it. It is plain to me that the lieutenant is sweet on you, and I am not so sure that you are not sweet on him, as well."

"Liam Niall!"

"Don't you go playing coy with me, young miss! I saw the way you looked at him when he brought you home on pitiless Percy's fine chest-nut mare."

Guilt started to creep in, but Maggie still maintained her silence.

"Go on and have your fancy meal with the fine Miss Pratt and all your fond farewells with your handsome lieutenant, who fights for the Crown. But don't you go getting airs and forgetting that you are already promised." He flicked the horse and the wagon lurched forward.

He stopped at the corner and waved. "Good day to you, my sister," Liam called out.

"Good day!"

The dining room table was set with Prudence's new Tara shamrock china and Waterford goblets. Sliced ham, steamed greens and boiled potatoes were served with mutton pies tender enough to cut with a fork. Lemonade filled the goblets. The weather was cooling. Dark storm clouds were gathering in the west.

"I'm so glad you could join us today, Maggie. Darcy could not bear to leave without saying good-bye to you," Prudence said, her eyes quickly moving from Maggie to Darcy and back again. She reached for the bread and tore apart a piece.

"Maggie has promised to write to me," Darcy said. "Often, I hope." His smile was brilliant.

"Very good," Prudence said, nodding for Ona to refill all the glasses. "I'm sure she will be an excellent correspondent."

"To be perfectly honest, I have written no letters that have ever left Ireland, as I have not yet myself, of course. I shall require your patient assistance," she said to Prudence, "and I shall hope that Darcy is able to read my handwriting."

"It can't possibly be as bad as all that," he said.

"I have not the least bit of confidence in my penmanship, having only attended the hedge school and practiced at home. In your agreement to write to me, you are giving me a wonderful opportunity to refine my skills through our mutual correspondence."

"Truly," Prudence said, looking pleased.

"I promise to be patient. For that reason, I expect you to write me many letters so as to better improve upon your skills," he smiled as he chewed.

"I shall see to it that she does," Prudence said. "And I will help you, if you wish."

"Oh, please, Prudence. I am counting on you."

"And, in turn, I trust you will have no difficulty in deciphering my military code," Darcy said while cutting himself another bite of ham.

"You will be writing to me in a secret code?" she said in astonishment, "In an entirely different language? Now, that shall be most perplexing, Darcy!"

Darcy and Prudence burst out laughing.

"Now, you have her going," Prudence chastised.

"Something like the writing on your ogham stone, perhaps? Might that do?"

"You are pulling my leg. I have seen the letters you have written to Prudence. Your handwriting is … quite lovely."

"Not bad for a military man in a hurry to complete a sentence without proper punctuation," Prudence said. "In his haste, there are times I can almost hear the canons firing, smell the gunpowder, and see the smoke rising up off the page."

"Is that right?" Darcy laughed. "I thought I had protected you from the horrors of war." He turned to Maggie. "I seem to have failed with Prudence, but I shall endeavor to keep you out of all battles as much as possible. Though I hear it is possible for me to be sent to America." His expression sobered. "Though it seems that war might well be over before the ship arrives."

"But you don't want to fight in America," Maggie said in a tone of alarm.

"I do not."

"We shall light candles for you in the Church and pray that is not your fate," Prudence said. "I thought there was a chance of you being sent to India for your remaining service."

"India?" Maggie said. "They have elephants in India … those creatures with big ears and long noses!"

"Trunks," he corrected. "They do have elephants. Tigers, too."

"Tigers?" Maggie blinked. "Actual tigers?"

"And horrible snakes and creepy, crawling things," Prudence said, "Gigantic cobras that live in dark caves, or in the baskets of strange men wearing turbans who play upon a small flute to make the snake rise up and dance."

"Dancing snakes? My word! I am glad St. Patrick drove the snakes out of Ireland."

They all laughed.

"Perchance I could teach a cobra an Irish jig while playing upon a bagpipe, and thereby secure my fortune?" Darcy laughed, his eyes briefly lingering on Maggie.

"Surely they will not send you all the way to India," Maggie said in protest. "For if such were the case, then how would you ever receive my letters."

"Just make sure that you write to me. I shall look forward to hearing about life in Dingle on your farm, about the children you deliver, your family, and, of course, the books you have shared with Prudence."

"Darcy's term of service is up next year, unless he signs on for longer," Prudence said, "Which makes me doubt that his regiment will be sending him all the way to India!"

"Small chance," he confessed. "Besides, who knows how long Napoleon will stay away from his beloved France? I have heard that many in his country still hold the exiled emperor in high esteem and long for his speedy return."

Prudence stood, motioning for Ona to clear the table. "We will take our tea in the parlor," she said before turning to Darcy. "Percy will be sending over the carriage soon. I will leave you two alone for a moment. I need to check on something," and she left the dining room.

Darcy helped Maggie with her chair. "Shall we?" he said, extending his arm, and they strolled toward the parlor. "I shall miss my cousin's ever so pleasant companionship and fine hospitality. Prudence has made my stay beyond enjoyable. We have always gotten on so very well. Prudence is very dear to me."

"There is no way that I can possibly repay her many kindnesses to me. I am indeed grateful for her friendship. It means a great deal to me."

"She feels the same about you, I can assure you," he said, moving closer to look down into her eyes. "I am going to miss your lovely presence and your beautiful amber eyes. I have never seen eyes like yours before."

He moved closer.

Her breathing quickened. Maggie could feel herself drawn to him. The magnetism was there from the first time she looked into his blue eyes on the evening that she danced the night away with the handsome lieutenant in his bright redcoat. The attraction was powerful, even stronger than on the day they had ridden horses to the ogham stone.

Darcy kissed her, softly, sweetly, and then he gazed into her eyes with longing.

"I don't know what to say," she whispered, secretly longing for him to take her fully into his arms and kiss her again.

"Say that you'll miss me," he whispered and his words caught.

"I will miss you," she whispered, meaning every word, remembering how cleverly she had avoided his kisses until that moment. And yet, alone in her bed at night, she had wondered what it would be like to kiss his lips, be held in his arms, as profound feelings for Darcy coursed through her.

Now taking her completely into his arms, Darcy kissed her again, long and deep, making her feel that she might faint if he let her go.

All at once, she broke free of him, stepping back, as she said, "We can't. We mustn't."

"Why mustn't we?" His face was flushed and filled with the longing of a man who plainly wanted a woman and she knew that she was that woman.

She wanted him too, and yet, the image of Aidan suddenly filled her mind, along with her brother's words of warning. *What am I to do,* she wondered? Never before had Maggie found herself in such a dilemma, wanting a man that she felt she had no right to want.

Ona cleared her throat and entered the parlor carrying a tray with a pot of tea, a stack of plates, and cups and saucers, which she placed on a table. Prudence walked in right behind her with a platter of blueberry tarts topped with gobs of freshly whipped O'Reilly cream.

"Time for tea," Prudence said. "I trust these tarts taste as good as they look."

"Aye, ma'am," Ona said, smiling as she poured tea into three separate cups.

Darcy motioned for Maggie to sit beside him. "Please," he said, pulling himself together in a gentlemanly fashion with his face less flushed.

Obedient, Maggie sat beside him, her heart now beating in a nearly normal manner as she reached for a cup of tea.

Prudence seemed to be watching her closely. She also appeared to know that something had happened between them as she spoke directly to Darcy, "We shall miss you very much."

"Not half as much as I shall miss you and Maggie," he said, his eyes quickly moving from Prudence to Maggie as he raised a cup of tea to his lips to drink.

"I daresay you have a very good reason to return to Dingle sometime soon."

Struggling with the emotions welling up inside her, Maggie demurely cast her eyes at the colorful carpet and could feel herself blushing as she remembered his kiss.

"I daresay, Prudence my dear, I have several excellent reasons to return to County Kerry and the quaint and charming Dingle Peninsula at my earliest opportunity."

18

Autumn Winds

Earlier than usual that autumn, fierce winds blew in off the bay, with more gale warnings than was customary across the North Atlantic and English Channel all the way into the Bay of Biscay. The brigantine *Cornelia* and its crew had not returned to port by late September, which was a source of concern for many, and especially worrisome for young Maggie, from having overheard whispers of guns and ammunition. Her long walks to Dunshean in search of white sails became far less frequent because of the unremitting autumn winds.

"No sense in you getting blown out to sea," her father contended, "You would be of no use to Aidan or to us then, and I could not bear to lose you," he said, hugging her and kissing the side of her head.

"Where might Aidan and the crew be after all this time?" Maggie moaned.

"No doubt in some port, swigging down ale and humping Frenchies for a sixpence," her father said, laughing, and he winked at the boys. "Getting practice and keeping warm, he is, in order to make you a skillful husband."

"Da!" Megan said in protest.

Brigid cuffed Padraic on the side of his head and said, "Worrying her, you are," and she scowled as she tossed more peat on the fire. Then she turned to Maggie and said, "Don't you pay any mind to your father. He's been at the tavern for more than a few pints this day."

"He means well enough," Maggie said, stirring the stew as she forced a smile.

"Let us hope that Aidan doesn't give you a wedding gift of the clap," Liam said, laughing. "Two men got infected last trip. Careless, those French whores, adding a bit extra for the price of a pop."

"You will be watching your language in front of your sisters," Padraic said.

"Maggie is a midwife, Da. She knows all about such things. You cannot keep anything from Maggie," and he winked at his sister.

Padraic glanced at Maggie before he turned to Megan and Brigid. "I guess there is no keeping secrets from the women in this household."

"No secrets at all," Sean said. "I have heard that scrubbing doesn't help."

Everyone in the room suddenly fell silent and looked askance at eight-year old Sean.

"No, scrubbing doesn't help, but it can't hurt, either," Maggie said, patting him on the head. "When you grow up to be a man you must practice cleanliness and discretion in such matters to insure your continued good health and to make sure that you contaminate no one with whom you engage in such activities."

Liam and Matthew looked at each other and burst out laughing.

"With whom you engage in such activities?" Liam repeated. "You've been reading too many novels by Miss Jane Austen. She's no doubt still a virgin."

Padraic smiled and he winked at young Sean. "You listen to your sister, the good midwife, who can teach you a few things that it is good for a man to know," and he sat down at the table to have his supper, nodding for the others to join him.

"We will be needing more peat, if these winds keep blowing so fierce and strong," Brigid said, "Time to trade out more butter and chickens to Finnegan. The sooner the better, I say."

"Aye," Padraic said. "I shall see to it within a fortnight. There should be enough for now."

"We will be needing more blankets for the horses and cows," Sean said, sitting near the fire. "There are not enough blankets to go around, especially if the winter is as bad as it might be."

"They will be fine," Padraic said. "Stop worrying about the cows and eat your mutton stew."

"Will we still be getting the sheep?" Liam inquired. "Trading a calf for the four lambs?"

"Aye," Padraic said. "Wool for the spinning wheel and mutton for the table, getting a black one as well, hear tell."

"Baa, baa, black sheep," Megan said. "How can we ever kill and eat him—or her?" She looked distressed. "Why not just use its wool without having to dye it. That might be a very good thing."

"Baa, baa, black sheep?" Sean said. "That's a nursery rhyme."

Everyone smiled and ate their stew.

"McGill said he would teach me more about shearing," Matthew said. "But he keeps talking to me about his daughter, Maureen, the ugliest lass I've ever seen." He made a face and laughed.

Everyone laughed, with all the boys nodding in agreement.

"She is not that bad," Sean said.

"Then, you have her," Matthew countered. "I can tell you for sure that she is not the lass for me to marry ... or even to bed, for that matter."

"Give her to you gladly, he would," Megan said, "Along with four sheep and two cows for a dowry." She laughed. "Maybe even a nice house, Matthew."

Everyone laughed, except Maggie, who was staring into space with a basket of bread in her hands. "What if they have all been hanged or thrown into some horrible rat-infested prison in England or France?" She handed the basket to her father as her eyes filled with tears.

"Not likely," Liam said, helping himself to the bread. "They have papers onboard that show the *Cornelia* is a genuine merchant ship."

"But they are smugglers," Sean said. "Perhaps I shall be a smuggler someday ... sail the high seas plundering the rich like Aidan."

"And visiting French whores," Liam said, nudging him.

Sean glanced at Maggie. "Not me. I do not want some terrible French disease."

Everyone looked at each other and laughed out loud.

"The clap is not necessarily a French disease," Matthew said. "I would have to say it is worldwide in its distribution."

"Leastwise, wherever sailors have been," Liam added.

"A pirate, then?" Megan said to Sean. "Pirates are different from smugglers ... much more ferocious and terrible. Pirates kill people and set them adrift in a dingy, or leave them on some God forsaken island to fend for themselves."

Padraic cast a disapproving glance at Megan. "You will be a dairy farmer and the better for it," he said to Sean. "No pirate, no smuggler. At least the crew trades potatoes, linen and wool for their bounty, so they are not likely to be imprisoned or hanged as smugglers or pirates!"

"Farmers don't get hanged anymore," Megan said. "But I have heard tell that they used to be hanged right here on the peninsula. Had their lands taken away, especially from Catholics like we are. Too bad our family didn't convert. Then we could be landholders like the other Protestants."

Everyone turned to Megan with expressions that ranged from scorn to amusement. Brigid chuckled and nudged Maggie, who was trying not to laugh.

"You would make a good whore," Matthew said.

"Watch what you say to your sister," Padraic said, seemingly unsure of his actual position.

"Our family stood firm in their beliefs," Brigid said, "Though at times I am not exactly sure why." After glancing up at Mother Mary on the wall, she quickly made the sign of the cross.

"More than likely, it was the Irish more than the Catholic in us," Maggie said. "The Protestants never punished anyone strictly for being Irish. The British wanted to do away with the lot of us, take the land, with all of us dead and buried. It seems to me that they tried to exterminate the Irish."

Padraic turned to her. "You may have a point. One day you may end up as a politician like our O'Connell, fighting for Catholic emancipation. That would not surprise me in the least, Maggie, knowing who you are, my daughter."

"God help us!" Liam said, "A woman politician? I doubt that will ever happen, Da."

"It shall happen one day, you shall see," Maggie said.

"That is rubbish," Liam responded.

"Might happen," Matthew said. "Besides, the way Maggie's life has been going the past year that could be how she ends up. You had better be nice to your sister and show her proper respect, for one day she may be the one who decides your fate."

They all turned to Maggie, who dipped her bread in her stew and took a bite.

"Did you happen to see the letter beside your bed?" Sean inquired. "Have you read it yet?"

"Letter?" Maggie sat up straight. "I received a letter and no one told me?" She narrowed her eyes but a smile suddenly filled her face.

"You were away at the Gleeson's with the birthing of their new daughter," Liam said. "Eight pounds, you said."

"The letter came all the way from England," Sean said.

"Has prince charming written Cinderella a letter?" Megan teased.

Padraic laughed. "Good sign, if you ask me. For, should your young smuggler die in some shipwreck, I am quite sure that young Darcy would be more than happy to ask for your hand. He is smitten, that is plain enough for me to see."

Brigid nodded in agreement.

Maggie stood and ran for her room with everyone at the table still laughing.

19

A Letter from London

The very first letter that Maggie O'Reilly ever received was there on the table beside her bed. It was written on off-white linen paper in a graceful, legible hand. She was already familiar with his script, since Prudence had insisted that she read his letters to her to make sure that she could read his handwriting.

Lt. Darcy Donal Brosnan was written on the back above an address in London, England. Her mouth was dry, her hands trembling, as she carefully unfolded the paper. Her heart raced and she tried her best to breathe, evenly and deeply.

In the upper right-hand corner of the first page: *September 7, 1814.*

Briefly, Maggie stopped. She closed her eyes tight and held her breath. Then she turned up the lamp and began to read:

My Dear Mary Margaret,

I have decided to address you by your christened name, although on occasion I may still call you Maggie. The pet name bestowed by your father suits your effervescent nature. Kindly forgive my impatience in writing to you so soon after my departure. I am only recently arrived at my parents' country home at Glendalough in County Wicklow. I had nearly forgotten how beautiful it is here, as is most of our beloved Ireland. Prudence and you must join me here on holiday sometime. The house has eight bedrooms with enough fire-places to dispel the morning and evening chills. It has been many years since my family enjoyed the pleasure of Prudence's company in these surroundings. Contemplative it is, nearly to the point of making one believe in those nature spirits you claim that exist for a fact.

Since you have never been here, Glendalough is south of Dublin and sur-rounded by forested mountains not far from the Avonmore River. Two inviting lakes are nestled in a restful valley that heals body, mind and soul. I went canoeing early yesterday to get some exercise and enjoy the solitude alone. At first, the only sound besides my oar cutting through the blue water of the lake was the singing of a single exquisite yellow bird that flew directly in front of me. I cannot remember seeing that kind of bird here before—a cheerful yellow that lifted my spirits with its sweet morning song.

You said seeking solitude is part of my nature, since I am Pisces, accord-ing to the signs in the heavens, the same as Prudence, for we share the same birthday. Natural mystics, you said, though perhaps that part is deeply hid-den in me and awaiting someone like yourself to bring it to the surface.

Like me, Prudence values time spent with nature, as well as being alone to enjoy the words on the page of a fine book, or to perhaps play Mozart or Beethoven on the piano. There is a piano here, another in our home in Dublin. I enjoy playing and find it healing, especially after the terrible horrors of war, the cries of the wounded and the dying. I wrote to Prudence yesterday and shall post your letter with hers. That way they should arrive on the same day, so neither of you feels slighted by a lack of my correspondence.

Prudence was her usual kind and loving self whilst I was there. She made my visit truly memorable. I have many happy memories of my time in Dingle, the most meaningful being my time spent with you, Mary Margaret. Dancing at the glorious ball, especially our spirited Irish dancing, since we were well applauded by the assemblage. It was as if we were called upon to entertain without compensation. Nonetheless, the pleasure of your company was more than payment in full measure for our brief dancing exhibition on that evening.

I must confess, from the first I was captivated by your amber eyes, so like two precious jewels, as well as the crowning glory of your red hair, also worthy of much praise. My mother's hair is the same as yours. I fear red hair is a weakness for the men of my family. Queen Mauve being a prime example. We all love Queen Mauve, even us Protestants!

You are certainly a breath of fresh Irish air, delightful in every way possible, charming without any effort, I might add. I shall always treasure the brief time allotted to us by Grace to share. I confess that I eagerly look forward to spending more time in your company. I shall endeavor not to count the minutes, yet cannot help but count the days until we are blessed to meet again.

Maggie stopped reading, stunned by the beauty of his eloquent and flattering words and phrases. After taking a deep breath, she let it out slowly and returned to the first two pages to read them over again, and then she turned the page and read:

The name of this place in Gaelic is Gleann Dá Locha, 'the valley of the two lakes,' as you must already know. I am trying, Mary Margaret. I pray for your patience on my behalf in remembering my Irish roots and Gaelic, which is not an easy language. But is any language? I still know very little Spanish or French.

It was here that St. Kevin founded a monastery in the 6th century, one of your fellow Roman Catholics, a right serious monk, hear tell. I doubt St. Kevin was any sort of Pagan, but one never really knows the secret thoughts of any priest or monk, I daresay. During its time, this was a center famous for scholarship throughout Europe. In 1398, the settlement was destroyed by the British, who else? Just joking, for you cannot see the smile on my face. Many different nationalities have destroyed and plundered throughout the centuries, as I am sure you know through your considerable reading of history. The cathedral and a few buildings gratefully survived. One day you must let me to show you all of it. I know you would love it as much as I do, perhaps because it is a truly special part of our Emerald Isle.

On the next page was written: *September 16, 1814, London.*

Kindly forgive my tardiness in completing your letter, but my siblings, parents, aunts, uncles and cousins made themselves unmerciful nuisances in demanding my company for the rest of my time at Glendalough. I had not seen many of them for a long time, and being together was surely good fun. Frolic and feast we did in abundance: cricket on the lawn for hours. The most fun enjoyed with the lads was balancing on a log on the lake where several of my young nephews did their best to drown me, without success, as you can see, for I am again writing you this letter.

I am currently in London in the home of my delightful maternal grandmother, Eunice Longfellow MacGregor, a stubborn, opinionated, Presbyterian Englishwoman, who married an equally stubborn and opinionated Presbyterian Scotsman, Brian MacGregor of Edinburgh on June 17, 1736, when she was but 16. Grandmother MacGregor is now 94 years, nearly deaf and partly blind in one eye. Even with such infirmities in one of such advanced years, she still beats me at chess and Chinese checkers, although you have to watch her, because she tends to cheat. Grandmother still enjoys her fine Scotch whiskey of an evening and warmed apricot brandy before retirement. Longevity runs in her family. Her mother lived to the ripe old age of 102.

I am busy seeing friends from Eaton and my regiment. I promised myself that I would finish this letter and send it off to you. I fear Prudence has already received her letter. I apologize for the delay. Hers was posted in Glendalough. My intentions were of the best, but alas, kindly forgive me, Maggie. I feel the need to appeal to your frivolous side. The best place to write me back is at my garrison south of London. One good thing about the British Army is that mail eventually finds me. I shall write the address below and count on receiving letters from you regularly.

My wishes and hopes for you are of the very best. Kindly give my regards to Bruscus Ceallaigh and the rest of your ancestors, as well as your father, Padraic O'Reilly, your brothers, Liam, Matthew, and Sean, to dear Aunt Brigid, and to your sweet sister, Megan. I have in mind a very good friend who I think might well fancy your pretty sister, though perhaps we should let her grow up a bit first. His name is Kevin Gallagher. He is a full-blooded Irishman and no saint at all, but a jolly fine fellow and a handsome devil reared in Cork near the coast before he joined up with the King's Army and was assigned to my regiment.

Until next time, I faithfully remain,
Very fondly yours,
Darcy.

When Maggie looked up, her entire family was huddled together just inside her bedroom door.

"Good one is it?" her aunt inquired. "He has fine penmanship?"

Maggie simply nodded, amused to see all the nosey parkers standing there together.

"Not being insulting is he?" her father ventured. "Making any sort of indecent proposals? He is being respectful, is he?"

"Most respectful, Da."

"Are you going to read it to us?" Megan inquired. "Like you do the books?"

"Sometimes there are letters in the books as well," Matthew said, looking sheepish.

"Are you going to read it to us?" Sean asked, grinning shamelessly.

"I imagine it's too personal. Right?" her aunt inquired, nervously wiping her hands on her apron with an expectant look on her face.

"Well ..." Maggie said, staring down at the letter in her hands. After all, Darcy had mentioned each of them by name.

"Is it too *personal*?" Megan enquired, flirtatiously batting her eyes. "Is it a love letter he has written to you ... a mushy, gooey one?" Giggling, she covered her mouth with her hands.

"Not a love letter, exactly," Maggie said, and yet, he had signed it *Very fondly yours.*

"Perhaps you wouldn't want to read it to us," her father said, chewing on his pipe as he cast a lingering glance her way.

"Well ..."

"Oh, come on, Maggie," Matthew said. "What harm could it do? You are the only one in the family to ever receive a letter from London ... any letter at all that I can think of, for that matter."

"It is my first letter," she said.

"I got a letter once," her Aunt Brigid proudly said, "From a cousin in Cork."

"Which cousin?" Padraic inquired.

"Shannon. Asking for money, short and sweet ... a few lines on one page."

"Did you write back to her?" Megan asked.

"Merciful heavens! I pretended not to even receive it. Never heard from her again, praise the Lord. How was I going to give money to the likes of her? What money?"

"I don't imagine I would have written back, either," Padraic said, puffing on his pipe.

All eyes once again turned to Maggie.

"All right," she said, reluctantly sighing.

They all smiled at once.

"But just because I read you this letter does not mean that I will read you all of Darcy's letters ...should there be more."

"Of course not," her aunt said. "Just this one, don't you think? I brewed a pot of tea."

The family gathered around the kitchen table with steaming cups of tea, the same as on the evenings that Maggie read a book. There were expectant faces all around the table as Maggie again carefully unfolded her letter.

"He only wrote on one side," her aunt said in amazement. "And it's a long letter."

"Just one side," Maggie said, and after taking in a deep breath, she read aloud, "September 7, 1814."

Everyone watched and waited.

After another deep breath, she smiled at her family and read:

"My Dear Mary Margaret ..."

20

Perilous Times

The second week of October, the brigantine *Cornelia* finally made its way back into Dingle Harbor heavily laden with goods to be hidden away in attics and caves. The saddest part was that two crew members had not returned from the long, arduous journey.

A young seaman of twenty, Kerill O'Farrell, was killed in a brothel in the French port of Cherbourg in a violent dispute over his favorite whore: Madeleine. She was a dark haired beauty of fifteen. Stabbed, he was, ten times, perhaps to make sure he was dead? His body was left in an alley and found by his shipmates not far from a favorite tavern.

Aidan was the one to discover Kerrill's body in a pool of blood. Aidan's father, first mate Kevin McKenna, made the arrangements for his burial in the seaman's cemetery at St. Trinity's. Then, sailing back across the Atlantic, two crewmembers came down with a serious fever. At first, the captain feared the worst: cholera. There was an outbreak in Port Louise where the ship was anchored.

Seaman Brian Houlihan, forty, died after three days at sea. He was well liked by the men and received a proper wake and burial from the ship. With the two men gone, a shroud seemed to hang over the ship.

The nasty weather kept the men busy, with sudden squalls producing heavy downbursts and huge swells that rose up out of the sea.

The other seaman to come down with the fever was a lad of fourteen, Austin Courtney of Ballybeg. Thankfully, he recovered, but remained overly fearful after Brian was food for the fishes. Since joining the crew, the two men had formed a close kinship. Brian was an orphan lad. Being short of hands placed considerable strain on the other men, with little rest to be had during the rest of the voyage. Everyone was relieved to once again be back in Ireland.

After another four days, three of the other men came down with the fever, including Aidan's father, who was seriously ill for three long weeks. Herbs were prepared according to instructions received in a dream in which Maggie's mother and great grandmother Kelly appeared in white gowns with a rosy glow all around them. The recipe was shared with the other women, since the herbs were apparently blessed by their loved ones in the Otherworld.

Rags were boiled in water with the herbs and applied to the chests and backs to relieve congestion. Special charms were used to petition *Aine of Knockaine* to increase the life force, *Lugh* for healing, with *Hail Marys* said for good measure. Candles were burned in the Church and on altars at home. Brigid helped prepare the charms, with both her and Maggie grateful for the fine cloth and trinkets received in payment. The kitchen buzzed with her father's blessing, for no good deed went unnoticed by those over in the Otherworld.

Weeks before Aidan returned, at Prudence's persuasive insistence, Maggie had sat down to write her first letter to Darcy. Prudence had presented her with a gift of fine stationery from London. Otherwise, Maggie might never have practiced on the front and back of one piece of paper by constantly rewriting words and phrases. Finally satisfied, she removed a fresh sheet of paper from the box.

Dear Darcy she wrote, not *My Dear Darcy,* after some thought. He was certainly not *her dear Darcy.* She had decided to write to him in the same manner she might write to anyone else; with no intention of letting him know that he might be dear to her. By that time, Aidan could have well been lost at sea. And yet, with every new sentence she wrote to Darcy, Aidan had intruded into her thoughts and mind. That was why she decided to write of perhaps meaningless things and subdue her feelings. Nonetheless, she still remembered his kiss and how he had swept her into his strong arms. Those memories were not easy for Maggie to cast aside.

One night, panic gripped her during one of her vivid dreams. She was watching the *Cornelia* being assaulted by strong winds and high waves. Lately, several fishermen were lost at sea. Plainly, all was not well with the *Cornelia* and its crew. Her disturbing dreams left her little room for doubt in that respect.

For that reason, to Darcy she wrote:

Liam and Matthew have made my father nervous since you left. They keep talking about joining the military to seek adventure. Father says there would be no adventure if they got themselves killed, which is more than likely considering your many fallen comrades. I shall not blame you if they join up, of course, but you may truly have to contend with my father.

Sometimes I think Da secretly regrets not having flown away with the wild geese himself. But he could not bear to leave my mother, and she could not bear the thought of him leaving, so there you have it. If my father had not stayed in Ireland, none of us would have been born and there would have been no one to raise us up in this trying world.

On a lighter note, Maggie now wrote:

We have 20 new baby chicks with the latest hatchlings. Our young rooster, Dermot, has recently come of age. He is named after an important hero of Irish legend, a king of Leinster who stole away the betrothed of another chieftain, Finn MacCool. For that reason, I expect the young cock of the walk to be something of a rascal in the henhouse. It is said that a name determines one's character. What are your thoughts on this matter?

Dipping her pen into the inkwell again, she wrote:

I trust you are feeling well and thoroughly enjoyed your games of chess and checkers with Grandmother MacGregor. If you simply allow her to beat you, she is sure to know, of course, as most women are able to discern tomfoolery in the men they treasure.

139

She stopped, in her mind she could see Darcy with his aging grandmother, somehow knowing he would adore her letter regardless of whatever she might write to him.

I must close now. One of my mother's has gone into labor, so it is time to assist Delores in the delivery of her fifth child. The O'Brennans hope for another boy, since three of their four are girls. I shall tell you the gender and name of the child when next I write to you. Until then, I remain,

Yours very sincerely,

Mary Margaret Kathleen Kelly O'Reilly.

The thought of mentioning Aidan to Darcy had crossed her mind, but Prudence had forbidden her to write of him. Prudence said there was no need for one man to know of the other. She seemed pleased with her letter, however, only saying that it might have been longer.

"Would you not be happier married to a man of substance?" Prudence had inquired on that day, "Your smuggler could end up imprisoned or hanged."

"Aidan could become a farmer like Da," she cautiously replied. "I know Da would give us an acre or more and help us to build our own place."

"Will Aidan go with you to America? Darcy shall be going to America."

It seemed that Prudence was constantly speaking of Darcy and acted uncomfortable if she even mentioned Aidan. In walking back home one day, Maggie tried her best to attune to her center, but was clearly unable to discern her own path ahead. Many times she could see the path that someone else might take, who the person might marry and how many children might be the result. For herself, no matter how hard she tried, her destiny remained clouded, though she could see herself living in America one day.

Aidan's father, Kevin McKenna, was seriously weakened by his illness. Therefore, Aidan assumed his father's duties at home, and in part, with the crew. He was reporting directly to Captain O'Shea who needed to hire more men than those recently lost. Consequently, there was little time for Maggie and Aidan to be together and make love near the old ring fort amid the forgotten shamrocks.

One night in December, they made love in the loft of the barn.

"How about a Christmas wedding?" Aidan inquired. "We could be husband and wife to celebrate the New Year."

"Perhaps in another year we could marry and go to America," she replied.

"And why would we ever do that?" he asked, running his hand over the smooth skin of her backsides in his eagerness to once again make love.

"To have a fresh start and make our fortunes."

"Our fortune is to be made right here ... with me as captain of the *Cornelia,* bringing back fine goods from Spain and France to sell to the local gentry. As I advance in rank, I will receive more of the bounty." He tenderly kissed her. "Did I not promise you silks and lace when I was but a lad?"

"You did," she said, running her fingertips over his lips while gazing into his dark brown eyes. She kissed him in response to her deep and profound feelings.

"Have I not done as much already, with us not yet married? Soon there will be enough profit to build us a fine stone house on a hill with a view of the sea. Then you can watch for the sails of the ship without traipsing all the way to Dunshean. Do you not think I might make a fine sea captain one day, my Maggie?"

"Aye," she said, as a sudden heaviness fully enveloped her. "You would be gone for months and months with me sick with grief from not knowing where or even how you were. Is that the life you want for me, Aidan?"

"You will be taking good care of our young, being a fine mother and fine midwife to the others. You will grow herbs and vegetables and do all your healing around Ballyferriter where your mother and her kin grew up as well. You will have a fine life, Maggie, a very fine life indeed."

21

Runaways

In a matter of days, the news was all around the peninsula. The fair Protestant maiden, Kathleen Sharon Malone, sixteen, of Dingle, had run off with a sailor in the British Royal Navy, Lieutenant Kenneth McDougall, age twenty-two. Kathleen had met the young seaman in August in England while assisting her cousin with her six small children under the age of eight. Her cousin had just given birth to twin girls in Manchester and was sorely in need of her assistance.

According to the rumors, the young lieutenant had survived the burning and sinking of the *HMS Reindeer,* an 18-gun British brig-sloop. The ship had engaged in many battles patrolling England's proud shores to protect its citizens from the treacherous Americans since the beginning of the War in 1812. It was reported in the news-papers that "of the *Reindeer's* crew of 98 men and 20 boys, her com-mander, purser, and 23 petty officers, seamen, and marines were killed; 42 wounded, 27 dangerously and severely." The damage was inflicted by the *USS Wasp,* an American warship-sloop, in the western part of the English Channel in June. The news had secretly pleased many Irishmen, for the *Wasp* had captured or destroyed fifteen ships of the British Royal Navy.

Lucky indeed was Kenneth to escape with his life, miraculously avoiding capture by the triumphant Americans, along with another shipmate in a dinghy. The men rescued at the last opportunity by an English fishing vessel out of Plymouth, the homeport of his once prized *Reindeer*.

In a short letter to her parents, Kathleen wrote that she and her sailor had eloped to Gretna Green, Scotland. Kenneth had decided not to seek his parent's approval, since so recently he had nearly lost his life. He loved Kathleen and she loved him. She wanted to be with him forever. The McDougall estate was in East Lothian near Edinburgh, his family business was bookbinding. Perhaps Kenneth would join his father in the trade, but they were also thinking of immigrating to America to seek their fortune.

All the Malones were fully distraught, especially Kathleen's mother. Her father refused to sanction the union of his Episcopalian daughter to a Presbyterian of Scottish and English descent. There was no mention of marriage in her first writing of the midshipman, but she had run off and married him just the same.

Liam was devastated.

"I cannot believe she has done this to me," he said to Maggie in the barn. "He must have cast a spell over her ... given her a love potion." He poured more grain into the bin than was needful. "I thought that she loved me."

"Did she tell you that she loved you?"

"Not in so many words."

"She never said that she loved you?"

"We kissed ... lots of times." he said, leaning back against the wall.

"Just kissed?" she said, closely observing her handsome brother who looked more like their father every day. He was tall and strong with the same dark hair and the same green eyes, "Nothing more than kisses?"

"I happen to be a gentleman!"

"Perhaps that was your problem."

"What kind of talk is that?" He stood taller and squared his shoulders.

Trying not to laugh, Maggie inquired, "You kissed her often, then?"

Annoyed, Liam said, "Lots of times. I loved her, Maggie. I loved her."

"It doesn't sound as though there was much passion between you."

"I thought I would marry her." He sighed. "Then, there would be plenty of passion. I was even thinking of converting to please her family."

"You really did love her, then, didn't you? I am sorry that she ran off and left you and her family in such distress. It was a selfish thing for her to do. But if Kathleen really loves this sailor then she did the right thing."

"How can you say that?" he cried out. "I thought that she loved me!"

"She never said that she loved you, Liam. Kissed you, but it seems a lass can kiss many a lad without being in love, and without feeling any real passion. The sailor ignited her passion. Her sister said she had only known him a month."

"Two years I spent with her. Two years!"

"Did you tell her how much you loved her?"

"I don't want to talk about it. There is nothing to be done now," he said, striding off across a field and on up the hill.

"Supper is nearly ready. It will soon be time to eat."

"I am not hungry. I won't be needing any supper tonight," and he walked on toward the top of the hill.

"And just where might you be going?"

"To America," he yelled back.

Dear Family, I am leaving Ireland and do not know if I am ever coming back, Liam wrote on one piece of her fine stationary in a handwriting difficult to read, with ink splotches all over the paper.

I don't want to spend my entire life in Dingle. I want to see the world like Darcy Brosnan and Kenneth McDougall. I will let you know where I am once I have decided where I am going. I don't know how long it will take me, nor where you will be able to find me. For, you see, I am going far away, probably to America. I shall miss you all dearly.

Love, Liam.

Tears filled her eyes as she stared at the paper. During the entire month, Liam was moody and distant, beyond being distracted, since he had learned of Kathleen and her sailor.

Wherever has he gone? Maggie wondered. Whatever will he do to take care of himself once he gets there? And how shall our father ever manage on this farm without him?

Only a short time passed before Padraic started to mourn the loss of his son as though Liam had died. Many Irish families mourned their loved ones, for large numbers had left Ireland for America and other faraway lands for many centuries. The truth was that the majority never returned, not knowing how to read or write, lost they seemed to their families and friends, dead and gone forever.

"I will forgive him, if he comes home," her father said in the beginning, remembering Liam once ran away for a day at the age of twelve. That happened not long after their mother's death. Even then, Liam said he was going to seek his fortune in America.

"He will come back," Matthew said after a week, "As soon as he gets really hungry."

"He will not be getting hungry," Maggie said. "Liam is big and strong. He is able to earn his keep. He knows how to read and write, and Liam is no dimwit, either."

"I will forgive him for abandoning us without a proper farewell," Padraic said as Christmas drew near, with snow falling upon the highlands.

Mostly after supper, their father would sit and stare into the fire, puffing on his pipe, tears running down his face as he rocked back and forth in the chair made by Grandfather O'Reilly. Sometimes her father was near keening, worrying his family with his excessive discontent. Her father did not appear to listen as she read of the birth of Jesus from the newly engraved Bible with pictures, a gift from Prudence. In fact, her father seemed to not hear any of the Christmas stories that year.

More often than was perhaps needful, Padraic visited the grave of his dead wife, even on days when cold winds howled under brooding skies he would stand by the headstone and speak to her in Gaelic. Prayed to her, it seemed, asked her to keep Liam safe and watch over him, to wrap the errant boy in her love. Their father was convinced that his dead wife was the only one able to bring Liam to his senses and home again.

The workload on the farm increased for Matthew and Sean, who were young though hearty and willing to work.

Young Sean sorely missed Liam, his big brother protector, as he inquired one evening after supper, "Why did Liam not take his fiddle? Surely he could play the fiddle on a ship or in America to cheer himself."

"It is your father's fiddle, an O'Reilly fiddle," their aunt said in a tone of annoyance.

"He could have it," Padraic said. "I told him the fiddle is his when I die."

"You are not dead yet," Megan said.

"Why could he not tell me of his troubles?" Padraic lamented, rocking back and forth in the chair. "There are thousands of lasses to love the likes of him in Ireland. Kathleen Malone betrayed him, she did. You can never trust those Protestants girls, not one of them," he said, narrowing his eyes at Matthew in an attempt to make a point.

"There are Catholic lasses far bonnier than Kathleen," Matthew said. "Like Carleen at Puck's Fair back in September. She fancied him, flirted, she did, and she was prettier by far than Kathleen and Catholic as well."

"She should fancy him. Our Liam is handsome the same as our father," Maggie said. "Mother always said you are the handsomest man in all Ireland."

Her father nodded, a faint smile capturing his eyes. "Your mother was the most beautiful woman in the world, and there she is young and beautiful in the cold, cold ground waiting for me to lie down beside her." He grimaced and motioned for Matthew to add more peat to the fire.

"You will not be joining her anytime soon," Maggie said, "You are not so old and you are still handsome, Da."

He cast a begrudging smile at her before he turned to stare at the wall.

"What about Prudence?" Maggie inquired, noting the light in his eyes as he turned to face her.

Everyone turned to look at Maggie, and then noted their father's response to her impertinent question.

"What about her?" he asked, knocking his pipe against the hearth.

"Prudence is right fond of you, Da."

Everyone reacted in shock or amusement. Megan started to giggle. Sean's eyes grew wider. Matthew wiggled his eyebrows in jest.

"Is that a fact?" Padraic said, straightening up. Then he picked up a twig to relight his pipe. "She is a fine lady, Miss Pratt." He pensively nodded and handed the pipe to Brigid.

"And?" Maggie said, feeling especially bold at that moment, "Prudence thinks you are a fine man."

"Does she now?" he said, taking the pipe back for a puff.

"She should," Brigid said. "There have always been devilishly handsome men in the O'Reilly family," she added, laughing and nodding at the boys.

"I am an old man," Padraic said, pursing his lips and scowling.

"Not too old," Megan said. "You are only forty-two. Peggy's father is near sixty and her mother is fifty-two. Now that's old."

"Young enough for her, I say. And you are in need of female companionship," Matthew said, "Womanly charms and womanly wiles?" Again, he wiggled his eyebrows in humor.

"Womanly wiles?" Padraic said and he smiled.

"The Widow O'Meara fancies you," Sean said.

"The Widow O'Meara has three young children, think well of that," Brigid said, pouring hot tea into all the cups, "She was married to a fisherman lost at sea in that terrible storm last year. Such a pity!"

"She has two young sons and a daughter," Padraic said.

"You know?" Megan sat up straighter. "Have you gone courting without telling us?"

"Thought about it more than once. Pretty woman … she smiles at me in church. Young she is, twenty-eight." He nodded and turned toward the fire.

"You know her age?" Maggie said, suddenly feeling surprised and annoyed. "She is sickly, Da. Why would you even give her a second thought? I have treated her often enough with my herbs. She is puny and frail," she added in a tone of thorough disdain.

"She is a woman, not a horse," Sean called out. "Women needn't be as strong as horses."

"Is that right?" Maggie said, cuffing him. "Well, you just think twice before you marry some sickly female, or she will die on you and leave you with children to rear up alone. Keep that in mind, will you, young Sean?"

"I will check her teeth," he said.

"And her haunches," Matthew added, trying not to laugh, "Best to check them, as well."

"Haunches, indeed!" Brigid said, cuffing Matthew before he could duck.

"Her hips?" Megan said, smiling.

"Especially her haunches," Padraic said with a wink. "For female companionship, womanly charms and womanly wiles," he added, laughing for the first time since Liam had left.

"Father!" Megan said in feigned disgrace.

"Eileen has bad lungs and her heart gives her trouble. Scarlet fever she had as a child," Maggie said. "What about Prudence? She is pretty, healthy, not sickly, and she has no children. She owns land and is a fine Catholic just the right age for you, two years younger than mother, four years older than Eileen."

Padraic again took his pipe from Brigid, knocking it against the fireplace to add more tobacco. After holding the twig to the fire, he raised the flame to his pipe, watching Maggie out of the corner of his eye as he puffed and turned to her. "I have nothing to offer Prudence Pratt, not that I am not drawn to the woman. I am for a fact. She is handsome, intelligent, cultured and refined, the finest woman I have been privileged to sup with, the only one of her class with the kindness to invite me into her parlor for entertainment and conversation with the gentry. I am a dairy and chicken farmer, better off than most, but a tenant farmer with nothing to offer to such a fine, lovely lady."

"That is a fact," Brigid said, casting a stern glance at Maggie. "Whatever would Prudence Pratt do with the likes of your father? She is wealthy and educated. Your father could not afford to buy her even one of those fancy frocks from London she wears ... you say she has a private dressmaker!"

"They are closely connected through the Otherworld," Maggie said, knowing in her heart that it was true, that her father and Prudence were supposed to be together.

"That doesn't help me much in this world!" Padraic said. "You said that about Liam and Kathleen, who ran off and broke my son's heart. I do not need that kind of help from the Otherworld. That shameless girl cost me my son!"

"Sometimes it is not easy to understand the way of destiny, Da. Some things take years and only then can we understand the true reasons."

He turned back to the hearth. "I am also connected to your mother in the Otherworld. I loved her with all my heart and all my soul and I still miss her keenly." He turned to Sean whose face was now sad. "It was not your fault, Sean. I will not have you blame yourself for your mother's death."

"If I hadn't been born, she never would have died," he said.

"That is not true, Sean," Maggie said. "Don't you even think such thoughts! Our mother's death was not your doing."

"I wish I had known her for a little while, even for a day or two."

Everyone in the room solemnly glanced at each other.

"I wish you had, too, Sean," Maggie said. "She watches over you from the Otherworld, watches over us all, even Da. We all miss her. We all loved her dearly."

"Your mother was my life ... other than the lot of you," Padraic said, standing to look at each child in turn. "I will always miss my sweet Mary Margaret. She does watch over us all." His eyes filled with tears as grief once again claimed him. "And now I have lost my eldest, my firstborn, my Liam. He is gone from here and has left me behind forever."

"Stop your grieving," Brigid said, patting his shoulder and filling his cup. "Drink some tea. Liam may be gone, but he is strong, your son, with a fine head on his broad shoulders. He is a grown man and he will do fine. I really think so, don't you, Maggie?" she inquired.

Silently attuning to her center, Maggie said, "I feel no real harm has come to him. We will hear from him again, see him again, perhaps."

"I feel that, too, Maggie," Megan said. "I feel really good about Liam, like I am going to see him again one day sometime somewhere."

"I don't!" Padraic snapped. "I shall never see my son again. Never!"

"He is heartbroken over a Protestant who ran off with another Protestant," Brigid said in a tone of disgust. "I am sure it will prove best for all of them in the long run."

"The widow O'Meara lives in Lispole," Matthew said, "In a small house with a broken window and a bent hinge on the front door."

"That she has ... a broken hinge," Padraic said, picking up his cup of tea.

Suddenly, everyone in the room turned to look at him, watching him rock back and forth in his chair, all of them concerned about the sorry state of his mind.

"She watches you at Church," Sean said. "I think she fancies you, Da. I like Mark, the one who's seven, but Brian is a bully."

"Is that right?" Padraic said. "Needs a firm hand, does he?"

"Cathleen is a spoiled brat," Megan said, "An eight-year old trouble-maker who spits at folk for no good reason. She should be acting much better."

"A rude and undisciplined child," Brigid muttered.

"The widow reminds me of mother," Matthew said.

"Her coloring is similar, but her hair is not as red. Maggie has our mother's hair. Besides, the widow is peaked and puny," Megan grumbled, "Not nearly as beautiful as our mother."

"Not at all," Maggie said, as an odd feeling suddenly washed through her.

Her father had a strange look on his face which made her think of them being together, her father and Eileen, husband and wife, in the same bed he had once shared with her mother. That thought instantly made her very, very sad.

Suddenly, Maggie sensed how disappointed Prudence would be if her father were to marry the Widow O'Meara. How disappointed she and her brothers and sister would be if he was to truly wed Eileen. That thought caused large goose bumps to cover her entire body in what Maggie considered to be an appalling confirmation of the truth.

22

Troubled Hearts

The fourth letter Maggie received from Darcy arrived on the same morning as a lightly falling spring snow. Most of the day, the sun played hide-and-seek, with white and gray clouds racing by overhead. The sky turned light, and then, darker, with wispy patches of white or gray, and occasional thin streaks of black added for artistry.

Sean Joseph said that Prudence requested the pleasure of her company for afternoon tea to give her Darcy's letter. Over the past few months, three other letters had arrived on Goat Street from Lt. Darcy Brosnan addressed to Miss Mary Margaret O'Reilly. Darcy had also sent her the novels of Miss Jane Austen, *Pride and Prejudice* and *Sense* and *Sensibility,* as promised, wrapped in bright red paper at Christmastime. Maggie was thrilled to have her very own copy of each book, which she enjoyed rereading.

With her chores done and the skies presently clear, Maggie bundled up in her brown tweed woolen coat that had once belonged to her mother, adding a green plaid scarf around her neck. She then pulled on her sturdy old boots before starting up the road to town.

In the afternoon stillness, she relished the sound of snow crunching beneath her feet, a tune of nature in a wintry mood. A red fox scurried across the meadow, leaving a trail to mark its path.

"Just you be staying out of our henhouse," Maggie called out, noting how her breath seemed to hang in the air as she walked right through it.

The fox was not headed toward their henhouse. *Praise the Lord,* she thought. Lancelot trotted near the bottom of the hill, tossing his noble head, with the newly acquired mare, Grace, trotting right behind him. Her father had said that it was an act of grace that the mare could still stand on her four legs, since 'the old gray mare was not what she used to be.' Perhaps Lancelot's youthful vigor had revived her. The mare was sweet natured and did her fair share of the work. Lancelot seemed better for the companionship, since Annabel their late mule entered the Otherworld suddenly in December.

The snowdrifts along the side of the road reached over a meter from the constancy of the wind blowing in off the bay, the road covered with only a light powdering. Snow seldom stayed long in the lowlands, but on that day the countryside of frosted, fluffy white reminded her of the cakes Prudence might serve that afternoon: "Special cakes to share with her special friend," she said.

After being inside the stuffy house for the better part of the day, with the windows and shutters closed tight, the crisp air seemed to clear her head. Peat had constantly burned in the fireplace and in the cook stove. By mid-morning, Matthew and her father had hitched up the wagon and loaded chickens, butter, cream and eggs to make their rounds. Her Aunt Brigid was still churning butter when she left the house, with Megan practicing writing down words and phrases from a book.

That morning at breakfast her father had spoken of adding more thatch to the roof in the spring. But that was not the main topic of conversation Maggie now vividly remembered:

"I plan to marry Eileen O'Meara come May," Da said in a strong voice that startled the lot of them.

Those around the table quickly glanced at each other in a relative state of shock.

"We will marry in the Church, since we are both Roman Catholic. We have both been widowed for some time now."

All were silent as their father appeared to be avoiding their eyes. Instead, he stared at his porridge and picked up a spoon to eat.

"She will be sleeping with you, then, in your bed?" Sean inquired, breaking the silence.

A smile slowly spread across their father's face. "When a man and woman marry, they usually sleep in the same bed, Sean."

"Unless they are angry with each other," Megan said for no apparent reason.

Everyone snickered.

"Aye," he said. "That is always possible in a marriage."

Brigid stood. "I will move back into my place well before the wedding," she said, spooning porridge into her bowl. "You will need my room for all those children."

Everyone at the table turned to look at their aunt. No one wanted her to go.

Padraic narrowed his eyes and nodded. "You will have chickens, a milk cow, and a lamb for starters," he said in a monotone.

"Thank you kindly, Padraic," their aunt replied, and tears suddenly spilled from her eyes.

"I will help you to clean the cottage and fix it up," Matthew said, for he was always very fond of his aunt. "I will do anything that needs doing, paint and clean, whatever you say. You just let me know, all right, Aunt Brigid?"

"Aye, Matthew," she said, sitting back down at the table with relief on her face.

"Me, too," Megan and Sean said together.

"You cannot see out of those windows," Megan added. "They need a good cleaning."

"One is broken," Sean said. "Matthew and I can fix it for you."

"Of course, you can," Maggie said to her brothers. "You can count on me to help you out with your garden. I am quite good with potatoes and sprouts now, as you well know."

"That you are. Your help will be quite welcome," her aunt said, including them all with a sweep of her eyes.

And that was the end of that.

It deeply saddened Maggie to think that, after the nine years since her mother's death, her aunt would be required to move back into her small cottage up the hill. All of them would miss her, perhaps her father the most. Maggie seriously doubted that the widow could cook a proper meal. The woman was skin and bones with a chronic cough. Whatever possessed her father to want to marry such a woman? Surely she had no dowry and nothing whatever to add to the comforts of the family with her three rude, obnoxious brats as part of the bargain.

Walking along, Maggie tried her best to dismiss her deep feelings of disappointment. After all, she was looking forward to reading Darcy's letter and wondered where it was posted from this time. Each letter had arrived from a different place. The three in the box under her bed were reread so many times she nearly had each one memorized.

During the past few days, news had reached Dingle of the escape of Napoleon from the Island of Elba. That had to mean an assignment to a new regiment for Darcy under the Duke of Wellington. Napoleon had returned to Paris as a hearty hailed hero and forced King Louis XVIII into exile. Everyone in Europe was convinced that the Emperor was busy reassembling his vast army to once again march forth to conquer the entire civilized world.

Her father was prompt to appraise Napoleon's position as exceedingly good for the Irish Catholics, but no good at all for the Protestant English, who, in his estimation, held even greater designs on conquering the world. Padraic was openly pleased with the Crown's failure to bring America back into submission. The peace treaty signed in Belgium granted the young nation nearly everything it required of Great Britain.

Major General Andrew Jackson, a full-blooded Irishman, and his rabble of men from all walks of life, including African slaves and bloody pirates, had given Wellington's invincibles a thorough thrashing at the Battle of New Orleans, with some of the British apparently lucky to escape with their lives. With America winning its Second War for Independence, greater respect was generated abroad for the young nation. There were to be no further impressments of Americans into service in His Majesty's Navy and no more blocking of American merchant ships carrying goods to ports in Europe, which Darcy had noted with great pleasure in his last letter.

Hot-spiced cider or chocolate was sure to be waiting for her, Maggie thought, along with warm gingerbread or pecan pie. Sean and Matthew had reportedly consumed large portions of gingerbread topped with freshly whipped O'Reilly cream in Prudence's kitchen early that morning. Since their Sunday invitation to high tea, Prudence Pratt had made a point to purchase all her dairy products and fresh chickens from the O'Reilly Farm.

During the past two weeks, Maggie was forced to cope with complications in two different pregnancies, in addition to the deliveries of two newborns, one in Milltown, the other in Ballybeg. Her reputation as a midwife had spread even faster after Nellie MacBride nearly died with the birth of her daughter the past November. It seemed that Nellie and her child would both be lost and Maggie had rescued them from the very portal to the Otherworld. A banshee had wailed at the moon that night, but through her prayers and many chants, both Nellie and the babe were spared.

Felix, Nellie's husband, had worried from the start. An even dozen youngsters seemed more than enough to suit him. Felix was a fisherman and had nearly drowned twice during the past two years. He was afraid to tempt the fates any further. A third time might be the charm to cross him over. Leastwise, that was what he boasted of often enough at the tavern. The other fishermen were quick to agree, since past experience was the proof of the pudding. Felix had fished near twenty-five years, and for Felix MacBride, an omen was an omen.

The brisk walk into town had provided Maggie with plenty of time to think. She was pleased that Kevin McKenna had at least partially recovered his strength. He suffered two relapses of the terrible fever. Aidan had experienced more illness than usual since Christmas, considering his normally robust nature. He had asked Maggie to stay away when he was sick. Not even Dr. O'Malley could ascertain the exact nature of the illness. Herbs were ministered, with everything written down for Riona, Aidan's mother, regarding the inhalations and poultices, before Maggie realized that his mother could neither read nor write. Riona quickly forgot the name of each herb after being told repeatedly. Maggie thought the woman's mind was definitely starting to slip.

She missed seeing Aidan. He still knew nothing of her correspondence with Lieutenant Brosnan, and Darcy knew nothing at all of Aidan. The situation was starting to make her feel ill at ease, though she tried not to think much about it. After falling into her bed at night, at times she was unable to fall asleep from sheer exhaustion. In truth, she found it impossible to stop thinking about the two different men in her life, each one attractive in his own way. At times, she struggled with her undeniable longing for each of them, for Aidan, and other times, for Darcy, who had also awakened a deep passion within her. Her attraction to each man seemed equal in measure. At least she no longer suffered from guilt because of her longings. She no longer felt the need to run to the confessional about her acts with Aidan in the ruins or out in the barn. Her love for Aidan had created a sense of the sacred within her heart, her mind, her body, and her soul.

Stranger still to Maggie was the fact that she had come to terms with her secret longing for Darcy. The content of her letters to him were kept casual, though there were times she yearned to reveal her feelings as being equal to his own. In her heart, she could never betray Aidan. She guessed that her feelings for Darcy would remain her secret, perhaps until her dying day.

Seated in the cheerful parlor, the sweet hot chocolate tasted perfect on such a wintry day. Once again, light snow was starting to fall outside, wetter than before, attaching itself to the windows, shrubs, trees and rooftops. The warm gingerbread tasted good to her with its sweetened whipped cream as she sat near a blazing fire. After all, it was O'Reilly whipped cream.

"I hope the long walk was not too tiring for you," Prudence said. "I have missed you for nearly a month it seems." She sipped her hot chocolate and inquired, "How is your father? Matthew and Sean seem to deliver everything that I want or need these days."

"Da is fine," Maggie said, not knowing what else to say at that particular moment.

The month of May seemed way too soon for her father's wedding, considering how her life was likely to change as a direct result. How grand her life had become since her meeting with Prudence. Their friendship was very important to her, besides all the books, her wonderful ball, and her patient lessons in teaching her how to play the piano. Prudence had indicated that she was progressing nicely in her ability to play.

In August, Prudence had begun to attend Mass at the same time at the Church as her family. Pleasantries were often exchanged, although her father generally remained aloof whenever Prudence tried to speak to him. That was usually when Eileen and her children were present. The mere thought of her father marrying "that woman" suddenly made her shudder, which caused her to pull her shawl more securely around her.

"Are you cold, dear?" Prudence inquired. "Shall we add more peat to the fire?"

"No, Prudence, I am fine. I hope you don't mind if I wait until I'm home again to read Darcy's letter."

"As you wish," Prudence said, with a gentleness in her eyes that made her wonder how she could ever tell her of her father's intended marriage plans.

"My letter probably contains much the same news as yours," Maggie said. "It bears the same postmark, military perhaps, to keep us from knowing exactly where the soldiers are right now."

"Possibly." Prudence poured more hot chocolate into the cups. "And yet, perchance Darcy writes to you of entirely different matters." The smile in her eyes was teasing.

"Perhaps." Maggie could feel herself blushing, for his letters had become increasingly personal. She preferred to read his letters alone in her room, with only portions shared with Prudence and her family.

"I am not exactly sure what to think of Darcy and his regiment with Napoleon back on his throne," Prudence said. "Surely, the Emperor is reassembling his army to war against the British who are intent on recapturing him. Our armies cannot afford to remain idle while a scoundrel of his ambition and determination is planning an attack."

"Perhaps Darcy did not know of Napoleon's escape at the time he wrote to us. It seems to me that he has been fighting Napoleon most of his life, and now, he will no doubt be fighting him again."

"There is no mention in my letter from the third week of February, which seems to be when your letter was written. The Duke needs to make preparations to confront Napoleon to save England and the rest of Europe." Her expression showed concern.

"A vast army will be needed, and there shall, no doubt, be many losses. Napoleon is brilliant, but my sense is that he shall be defeated," Maggie said. "And yet, the battle will be terrible for all concerned."

"Kings of many different countries fear Napoleon. And yet, perhaps by combining their forces they will indeed win. I pray you are right, Maggie. So many men, women and children have been lost because of this tyrant who has burned countless villages and produced widows and orphans in great numbers. He must be stopped."

"We must pray for Darcy, for if the Duke of Wellington goes to war again against Napoleon Bonaparte, so goes Lieutenant Darcy Donal Brosnan."

Prudence solemnly nodded. "We shall pray and light candles for Darcy and for all his brave comrades who might join together to fight the formidable French." She paused. "Has there been any word yet from your brother, Liam?"

Maggie shook her head. "I fear my father already thinks him dead. His grief has made him bitter with no forgiveness in his heart for my brother. I know that Liam will write to us one day. I am not sure why he hasn't already done so. No word at Christmas. I hope he has not joined the British, for I couldn't bear the thought of losing Liam and Darcy." She raised her hands to her face as tears suddenly spilled from her eyes.

"It seems to me that Liam must already be in America. I cannot imagine a young Irishman like him joining the British, except against his will."

"It is my hope that Liam is in America," Maggie said, regaining control of her emotions, "Especially since the Americans won their war. But Liam left well before that news reached Ireland."

"Your brother is probably off on a new adventure. Perhaps he joined up with a merchant ship out of Cobh. Has Liam any experience at all with sailing?"

"None, I fear. Cows, horses and sheep have been Liam's lot. He can kill a chicken and knows some cooking. Perhaps he has worked in a ship's kitchen or tended the animals for slaughter. He was saving his money to marry Kathleen. What little he might have had."

"Surely Liam lives!"

"He so admired Darcy and did speak of America. We have relatives in Boston and New York. But Liam should not worry our father so. He should write to us of his whereabouts."

"I hope Padraic finds it within his heart to forgive him," Prudence said. "Having a child leave him like that cannot be easy in any way for your father."

"No," she said, as an image of Eileen O'Meara suddenly filled her mind.

"I couldn't help but notice that your father spends time with the Widow O'Meara."

Suddenly, Maggie was nearly holding her breath.

"I saw them out last Sunday while I was taking food and clothing to the Riordans. Those tenant farmers can barely feed their fourteen children, so I do what I can to help out."

"You have helped so many, Prudence, in so many different ways."

"Is your father courting Eileen O'Meara?" she asked point blank.

"Aye," she replied, slowly meeting her gaze.

All at once, Prudence placed her empty cup on the table and got to her feet, vigorously rubbing her arms with her back to the fire. "She has three children, does she not?" she inquired, with a hint of pain suddenly filling her lovely green eyes.

"Aye."

"Her husband drowned," she flatly said.

Maggie nodded. "I fear my father plans to marry her. It is what he told us at breakfast this morning."

"Is that right?" Prudence drew herself up, pursing her lips and narrowing her eyes. Then she took in a deep breath. "Eileen O'Meara is extremely lucky to marry a man as handsome, charming and honorable as your father." She turned her back and looked down into the fire, but Maggie thought she had seen tears forming in her eyes.

For the past few months, Maggie had tried to find it in her heart to like Eileen O'Meara, but she could not. Neither had she any affection whatsoever for her three children. It was Prudence she had wanted her father to marry. Invisible threads seemed to bind them one to the other the same as the gossamer threads between Prudence and herself. Was Prudence not so like the mother she had always wanted and hoped for? Was Prudence not as beautiful as her own mother, both inside and out? In her way, Prudence was like her angel in the flesh, with her mother her angel in spirit.

And yet, seeing Prudence Elizabeth Pratt before her in her fine blue plaid taffeta gown just newly arrived from London, with her dark hair up in a fashionable chignon, how foolish, Maggie thought to herself, for her to even dream of having such a fine woman as her mother. Prudence was born into a cultured, educated and refined family as a member of the upper class. Her father was born into a proud but humble family of poor Irish tenant farmers forced to work from dawn to dusk to make ends meet. That was regardless of the fact that the O'Reillys and the Kellys were directly descended from the blood of Ireland's once proud High Kings and all-wise Druid High Priests.

In that brief moment, her future looked bleak to her indeed.

Suddenly, Maggie O'Reilly realized that all her wanting and all her learning, all her loving and all her yearning had done little to guarantee the ultimate success of her very own destiny.

23

The Fires of Beltaine

As the sun lowered beyond the crest of the mountains, the great double bonfires were set ablaze on top of the hill. Two enormous pillars of fire reached high into the night skies and could be seen from miles around in a timeless celebration of greeting the return of mighty Bel, god of light, the *Shining One,* back to Ireland in a yearly pagan festival. Each day now held the promise of becoming longer and brighter as the sun warmed the earth, enabling the farmers to plant and harvest their crops in order to fatten the livestock and nourish the people throughout the land.

The annual Fires of Beltaine, an ancient ritual of the Druids, still flamed yearly in County Kerry on the last day of April, oftentimes in secret on the Dingle Peninsula. In olden times, identical bonfires blazed from mountains and hilltops throughout Erin, weaving a magical web of light across the land in a mysterious pattern in the night skies that brought hope and joy into the hearts of many after enduring a long, confining winter.

On the next day, the children danced around a Maypole decorated with flowers and colorful ribbons in a joyous salute to the warming of the season. Perchance the local priests and preachers had gleaned sufficient wisdom to abstain from condemning those who engaged in an

innocent festival in order to guarantee the attendance of their superstitious parishioners at Sunday services. The festival was harmless enough,
though in olden times, all had reveled in the sensuous delights of love
and the wonders of the procreative mystery. Rather than the unmarried
the unloving were pitied. Young and old alike gathered flowers, weaving garlands of hawthorn, marigold and rowan. A husband was guaranteed the affections of a wife on such a night, or of another woman
should she be disinclined. Though not just the married took delight
in the preferential pleasures of the flesh on the night of the Fires of
Beltaine.

The Province of Munster was the last stronghold of the Old Religion
in Ireland, holding out for another 150 years beyond the advent of St.
Patrick in fully embracing Christianity. Even then, conversion often
occurred with marked restraint and resistance on the part of many. Nearly
all the ancient pagan holidays were adopted by the new priests who added
a Christian flavoring, perhaps to ensure the transfer of power from the old
gods to the new Divine Trinity of the Church.

Beltaine was a fertility festival, welcoming the green back to the
trees and shrubs that would again blossom forth in renewal. It was a
festival of purification, with the cattle being run through the flames to
receive a blessing from the Druid high priests and high priestesses. More
especially, it was a time when mortals could more freely conversed with
the Divine. Magical beings from the Otherworld, from the lesser to the
greater, often made themselves known. The fairies ventured out of their
rings and subterranean realms at Beltaine, perchance to impishly play
with mortals, or on occasion, grant a special wish masked in the grand
and glorious mysteries of Nature.

For Maggie and her Aunt Brigid, the ritual of Beltaine was carried
out a week earlier on the night of the full Scorpio moon opposite the sun
in Taurus, the sign of the Bull of Fertility. The Scorpio moon ruled death
and rebirth, generation and regeneration, the deeper and truer meanings
of the sacred in terms of procreation and sexuality.

After an extended plea on the part of Maggie, Prudence was allowed
to join the other women in the circle around the great bonfires. According
to tradition, the full moon was the time to invoke the magical powers and
the blessings of Bel, god of light, as his eternal bride, Dana, mother of
the gods, reflected his brilliance in the nighttime skies. This ritual was

performed yearly, as Beltaine was honored by the ancestors, the wise men and women of olden times, the Druid high priests and high priestesses.

Accordingly, atop their secret hill not far from a dwindling sacred grove, eight women gathered in blue and white robes to form a circle and light the double bonfires. Intoning sacred incantations in Gaelic, the women acted out the rituals to welcome the warmth and fertility back to the once cold earth of Ireland.

After completing their appointed tasks, each woman planned to leave for home. Prudence hid her horse and buggy in the woods, having driven herself to secure the secrecy of a ritual condoned by neither Catholics nor Protestants. Brigid accepted a buggy ride to her newly refurbished cottage. Maggie declined, for she secretly planned to linger in the sacred grove to meet Aidan and fulfill her sacred task as a representative of the goddess on that special night of the year.

Aidan was borrowing a horse, for the *Cornelia* was due to set sail for France at dawn. That was in spite of the British being involved in massive preparations to engage Napoleon in a great battle. Crossing the Atlantic would be fraught with more danger than usual. British colors would make the ship a sitting duck for the French, with French colors arousing equal fury in the British, if not in the whole of Europe.

On that night, Darcy in his dashing redcoat was not foremost in her mind. Rather, it was Aidan, perchance her first love and her only true love, though of that she could not be absolutely certain. Still, Aidan had been her only love in the flesh. It was to Aidan to whom she had completely given herself near the ruins after riding upon Lancelot in search of rainbows. On that day and on countless other days, she had given herself to Aidan. Never could she deny her love for him, nor did she plan to deny him anything on that night. That was so regardless of being in short supply on snakeroot and penny royal with the moon full in the sign of her birth. Maggie would give herself to Aidan again completely on the sacred Eve of Beltaine.

It was not because she was lacking in feelings for Darcy. She cared for him more than she thought was prudent. Darcy often appeared in her nightly dreams. His letters were always filled with news of amazing places and remarkable people. In one letter, Darcy had asked her to ride with him again along the cliffs of the Dingle Peninsula to visit the ogham of her ancestors. He solemnly promised to return to her after the great battle. He had even boldly suggested that she accompany him to America, with no mention of marriage, of course. It seemed to her that a man such as Darcy would never marry the daughter of a tenant farmer without any dowry. And what if Darcy happened to die in the battle about to determine the fate of the entire civilized world?

In his last letter, Darcy had written of the troop movements out of England. He was pleased to be back in his regiment and confident that the Emperor Napoleon would finally come face to face with the great Duke of Wellington. The two famous military commanders had never before directly engaged each other in battle. The Duke was looking forward to his date with destiny in fighting his brilliant and clever opponent. Clearly, Lieutenant Darcy Brosnan was looking forward to experiencing the same.

Alone in the woods, under the bright light of the moon, Maggie silently prayed for Darcy and the Duke and for all the brave men about to march forth into battle, knowing in her heart that the outcome was up to higher powers, the fate of everyone up to the patterns of Destiny.

The bonfires burned less brightly as she sat upon a log and watched the sparks ascending to the heavens, praying that the gods might honor their humble offering. She also prayed to Bel, Dana, and all the deities for Aidan's safe crossing of the Atlantic Ocean.

Softly, she prayed aloud, "Hail Mary, full of grace, the Lord is with you, blessed art thou among women, and blessed is the fruit of thy womb … Holy Mary, Mother of God, pray for us sinners now and at the hour of our death. Amen."

Tiny lights danced and spiraled out of the various fairy rings, along with a multitude of lights that rose up out of every mound and well on that Eve of Beltaine. Deep within her center, Maggie knew that something truly extraordinary was about to happen. Then, she heard the sound of the hoof beats of a horse coming up the hill, along with a horse's labored breathing.

Silhouetted in the moonlight, with his back to the diminishing flames of the fire, Aidan called out, "Maggie, are you here?" as he searched the woods with his penetrating, dark brown eyes. "Where are you?" he whispered more loudly.

Entering the clearing in her long blue robe, her long, auburn hair cascading down her back and over her shoulders, Maggie noted the expression on his face. It seemed that Aidan thought he had discovered the moon goddess herself in the woods. "It's me," was all she said.

He stopped as though transfixed. "You are beautiful," he said, wonder on his handsome face.

"And so are you beautiful, my Aidan."

"In the light of the fire and the moon in that gown ... you are utterly magnificent. Are you sure you are not a princess, priestess, or the goddess, in fact?"

"I would like to think I am all of those in your eyes and your heart." She walked over to him, her arms soon around his neck as she kissed his lips. Then she leaned back to gaze more deeply and directly into his eyes. "This night your eyes are filled with moonlight, my prince."

"And yours with firelight, my angel. I love you, Maggie, more than you can ever know."

He kissed her, tasting the sweetness forever in his thoughts. Her warmth blended with his as the passion welled up inside both of them.

"Come," she said, taking his hand, pulling him toward the sacred grove. "I have prepared a bed of leaves covered with a blanket, a bed on which to rededicate our love on this night ... on this special Eve of Beltaine."

"I wasn't here last year, remember? I was away in Spain."

"And soon you will be in Spain again. Come, my love. Come be with me!"

Stepping into the wood near the blanket, she turned and dropped her robe, standing before him in her full nakedness. The light of the bonfires and moonlight shimmered through the trees to illuminate her fair flesh with an otherworldly luminescence.

Silently, she soon was gazing upon his sumptuous nakedness bathed in the dwindling light of the fire and the brilliance of the moon. Tall, strong and handsome, Aidan emanated the strength and beauty of youth, with adoration in his eyes on a night designated for the delights and raptures of sensual love.

Instantly, Maggie was in his arms, flesh to flesh, body to body, god to goddess, both of them soon prone on the blanket over a bed of leaves. Arms and legs intertwined, touching, feeling, sensing in fullness, kisses that soon flamed from hungry warmth to searing heat as tongues tasted and blended, keen to join so two might be as one. Hands and mouths and fingertips gave and received in equal measure, to and from the other, as was ordained from olden times until that night on the wondrous Eve of Beltaine.

Suddenly, the two young lovers were surrounded by whirling, brilliant lights of many colors that moved in, over, and around them. First, white, then violet, blue, green and gold, as the red of passion filled their bodies, hearts and minds. Willingly and gratefully, Aidan filled the keen warmth of his Maggie with the fullness of his love, receiving and giving as perhaps never before. Moving in and out and around his beloved goddess, priestess, princess, lover, for to Aidan on that night she was everything she could ever be to him and he was everything to her.

"When I return I want you to marry me," he said, "I want you to be my fair and bonny bride. Will you marry me ... will you please, please marry me, Maggie? You have got me on both knees," he said, smiling down at her in great tenderness.

Staring up into his dark, sparkling eyes that reflected the remnants of the dying bonfires, Maggie nodded. "Aye, Aidan McKenna. I shall be your bonny bride. It is something I have perhaps always known would happen from the first day we met at the hedge school."

"You will make your wedding gown, you must promise me," he said, running his fingers through her long hair and gazing into the beautiful amber eyes he loved.

"I promise you, my love."

Again, the loving began anew. Hands, mouths and bodies moved with joy and pleasure one for the other, giving and receiving in equal measure.

She was unsure in terms of the time of night or the approach of the morning light when she first heard the white wolf howling up at the full moon and the soft, low wail of a mournful, sorrowful banshee. But she had heard them both for a fact. At once, Maggie knew in her center that both the howl and the cry were ominous portents that she could not bear to consider on that moonlight night within the safety of Aidan's strong and loving arms.

Gazing up at the great moon in the sky, she noted that clouds now hid the great face, but she was convinced that she had seen the goddess smiling down at her, promising her comfort and protection in what she might have to face in the days directly ahead. On that night, Maggie was keenly aware that all the memories, emotions, smells, tastes, sights and sounds of that one Eve of Beltaine would remain in her heart and her soul for all the rest of her days.

24

May Madness

Mid-May, the simple wedding took place in the Catholic Church with few in attendance. Most of the children wore long faces dressed in their Sunday best, except for the children of the widow: Brian, Cathleen and Mark. They had to know that they were bettering themselves by moving out the small shack in Lispole and into the O'Reilly farmhouse on twenty acres.

Padraic continued to prosper even without Liam's assistance. With no word yet, Matthew assumed all of Liam's responsibilities, albeit he was also apprehensive about his father's marriage. At nineteen, he was courting Jennifer O'Connor, sixteen, from Ballyferriter. He tended to blush when anyone even asked him about his relationship with the pretty, young Catholic girl.

The young O'Meara girl, Cathleen, age nine, moved into Sean's room. After a great deal of pleading and bargaining, Sean moved in with Matthew. Brian and Mark were in Brigid's old room, which left Maggie and Megan to themselves as usual. Brian the bully was eleven. Young Mark, seven, was docile and seldom spoke. He looked nothing at all like his siblings. Maggie thought his father might not have been the widow's late husband, a fisherman often away at sea. The rumor in the village was that Eileen once had eyes for Arthur, the baker's son. He was a handsome chap years younger than her who left town soon after Mark's birth. After meeting the baker's youngest son, Kenneth, Maggie found a marked resemblance. Her suspicions were shared with her aunt, knowing how her father would never pay any mind to local gossip. On the other hand, Maggie and her Aunt Brigid shared a great many secrets.

"How are things with the new Mrs. O'Reilly?" Prudence enquired one afternoon while sharing a pot of tea with Maggie, glancing out the window with marked restraint around her eyes.

"Well, it has only been a week. We are all trying to adjust to having four new persons in the house ... a bit crowded, if you ask me," Maggie replied, selecting a ginger biscuit and taking a bite. "I have two expectant mothers that require my attention, one due this week. Agnes can be quite a nuisance, so I'll be glad when it's over and done with." She drank tea from her cup. "I've spent three evenings helping my Aunt Brigid with her potato patch. I miss her cooking. My poor father!"

"Truly?" Prudence said, appearing to smirk. "It is unfortunate that your new stepmother cannot cook when there is no servant." She selected a ginger biscuit. "It seems to me that you have missed Brigid ever since she moved out of the house. I am quite fond of her, actually. She is teaching me about the old ways."

"Well, you are very good at keeping secrets," Maggie said, thoughtfully pausing. "Aunt Brigid has been a mother to us all, so naturally all of us miss her daily presence in our lives."

"I am not sure of the reason that we have not received another letter from Darcy," Prudence said. "Massive troops seem to be crossing the English Channel. At least that is what his mother writes to me."

"There will be a terrible, horrible battle."

"Perhaps we should write to him again at his last address, though his mind may be on more important matters than writing letters to us. It makes me honestly glad that I am a woman."

"As am I. I shall write to Darcy this evening, if some woman in labor does not prove a distraction and demand my attention." She selected another ginger biscuit. "When the war is over, Darcy plans to go to America and raise tobacco with his Uncle Shane."

"Shane Brosnan. I know. He has said as much to me." Prudence paused. "Darcy would like you to go with him, of course. He has mentioned that to me more than once in his letters ... as his wife, naturally."

With that disclosure, Maggie nearly dropped her cup. "As his wife?" she exclaimed, and suddenly her hands began to tremble as a truly strange sensation coursed through her entire body.

"As his wife!" Prudence said with something of a flourish, standing to smooth out her skirt. "Please forgive me for revealing his most serious intentions. Darcy should propose to you himself. He has never asked me to speak to you on his behalf. But you have to know from all the attention he has showered on you ... with all his many letters," she hesitated, "I have known for some time now that my handsome cousin is hopelessly in love with you." Her bright green eyes appeared to expect an equally joyous response to her unexpected and surprising revelation.

Stunned, Maggie blankly stared past her.

"Can you honestly say that you do not have feelings for Darcy? I have seen how you look at him. Tell me that you love him, Mary Margaret ... that you want to marry him." Her expression was fully serious. "Then you will be my cousin and I will take you shopping in Dublin and London so my dressmaker may design proper gowns for your trousseau. Gowns for the lady you truly are and have always been in your heart!"

Beginning to tremble deep inside, Maggie could not believe how pleased Prudence seemed at the prospects of her marriage to Darcy, an educated gentleman far above her. She was already a week late with her menses, since her time with Aidan on the Eve of Beltaine. The night of the fertility ritual performed for the goddess when she had pledged her eternal love to Aidan. The night she promised Aidan that she would be his wife.

Prudence appeared impatient.

With significant difficulty, Maggie found her voice, "I am promised to Aidan. We are to be married when his ship returns. At the present time I am sewing my wedding gown with my Aunt Brigid's assistance."

Prudence turned pale.

By then, trembling inside and out, Maggie was trying her best to regain her composure.

Prudence seemed to be trembling as well, her face now turning a slight shade of pink.

Not in her wildest imaginings had Maggie thought that Darcy might propose to her. She dared not to think such a thought. Until that day, her intended nuptials with Aidan were only shared with her aunt. First, the gown had to be made. There was her father's wedding, besides her suspicion of conception on the night she had promised Aidan to marry him.

"But you have been writing letters to Darcy!" Prudence said, as she began to pace back and forth in front of Maggie. "You have expressed your feelings to him! I know that you have! You must have!"

"I am very fond of Darcy ..."

"You have been leading him on ... letting him think that you had feelings for him when all along you were planning to marry your stupid, ignorant smuggler!" Prudence shrieked, her face now fully flushed, her fists clenched as she stared at her with accusation on her face.

"That is not true ..." Maggie said, knowing that in her dreams she had experienced wild, sexual encounters with Darcy. At times, she had even dared to imagine herself as his wife, sailing with him on a ship to America. But she had never planned to betray Aidan. Never. The man she had always trusted who had loved her in the Otherworld more than once. How could she possibly love Darcy too? How? If Darcy had actually proposed to her, things might have been different. But it was much too late for that now.

"I have been trying my best to help you, Maggie," Prudence suddenly sounded strangely detached, with her face still partially flushed. "I have been loaning you books to improve upon your mind, your knowledge of the world, teaching you the manners of the upper class to help you rise above the station into which you were born, and now, you are going to ruin your life by marrying a smuggler, a common criminal who might well one day be hanged and leave you all alone! I cannot believe that this is your choice!" Prudence raged, "Not after all I have done for you. I have tried to do everything within my power to create a wonderful future for you! How can you do this, Maggie? How can you?" she cried, tears now streaming down her face as she appeared to struggle to regain her self-control.

"I am so sorry, Prudence, so very sorry. I don't know what else to say," Maggie cried, immediately sensing the enormous the pain she had caused to both Prudence and herself. Unwittingly, she had betrayed the best friend she had ever had, a woman she loved and admired above all the others.

"You're sorry?" Prudence shrieked. "You have no idea how sorry you are going to be, Mary Margaret. You have no idea what a miserable life you have sentenced yourself to by marrying Aidan McKenna. You are going to be very, very sorry indeed!" And she turned her back on her.

Never before had Maggie seen Prudence so angry or so very deeply disappointed. She was shocked by her unexpected behavior and unsure of exactly what to do or how to act next.

"Perhaps you have some idea of how miserable you are going to be now that your father has married the promiscuous, sickly Eileen O'Meara and taken on her three miserable brats. You will soon be witnessing first-hand the life you have chosen for yourself. Is that want you want, Maggie? Her life?" she shouted, turning to her with tears streaming down her face.

"I don't know what to say to you, Prudence," Maggie said, standing and gathering up her shawl, "Except to say that I am sorry." She could not stop her own tears from flowing. "Darcy never asked me to marry him. He should have told me of his feelings—not you." Thankfully, calmness was starting to return to her center.

"You will write to Darcy of your intended marriage. You will write to him, correct?" her tone was cold and demanding. "It is the least that you can do!"

"Aye," Maggie said, filled with anguish as her tears continued to flow.

"You will tell Darcy that you are marrying a smuggler. Right? You will tell him that!"

She had just returned the last two books she had borrowed and read. She thought it best to leave the new ones where they were on the table.

"Go, Maggie! Leave my house at once!" Prudence screamed at her.

Silent, Maggie walked out the front door of the fine house on Goat Street into a lightly falling spring rain. The angels are crying too, she thought, as she slowly made her way down the hill—as well they should on such a day as this!

25

Waterloo

During the entire month of June, the weather was stormy. Powerful gales raged across the Atlantic and all around Ireland during the first two weeks of the month. It was late for such erratic weather. Temperatures so far below normal could not be favorable for waging a major battle, Maggie thought, nor for the crossing of the Atlantic for the *Cornelia* and its crew. The sovereign Lord Mayor had already expressed his concern, her father said, while enjoying a pint at the tavern. The ship was long overdue with its highly valuable cargo.

The ship's cargo was of no special concern to Maggie, except for the life of one midshipman: Aidan McKenna. Early that month she had experienced repeated nightmares of the ship being tossed about in a great storm. Huge waves had washed over the deck, taking the seamen out into the churning, turbulent, dark water. In her last dream, the ship had come apart on some rocks, with the entire crew drowned. Their desperate cries had filled her head and her heart with inconsolable sorrow.

The most vivid of her dreams had occurred on June 5, 1815, as the wind howling outside the house resembled the mournful wail of a banshee. Tossing and turning in her bed, Maggie had seen the ship in the darkness tossed about like a cork on the raging sea. The wind had howled even louder as enormous waves rose and fell in the terrible tempest. Suddenly, the ship broke apart and swiftly sank. The desperate cries of the men for help filled her head as she fervently prayed, knowing in her center that all of them were truly lost in the terrible, unyielding storm.

She had heard Aidan's sad cry, her name upon his lips as the sea swallowed him up, pulling him down, down, down into its swirling depths of darkness. The sea had taken her love away, with its vast graveyard as his final resting place.

Nearly at once, there was a bright glow in her room. Aidan was standing there with water running off his body. He smiled his beautiful smile at her, but he looked strangely different. He seemed cold and gray as he reached out to her with both his hands.

Without a moment's delay, Aidan was in her bed beside her, touching her, kissing her, holding her, making love to her in the manner he always had, but the sense of his flesh was not the same. He was cold, clammy, damp, and yet, the passion was still there: the great passion that had always existed between them. Feeling the thrust of him deep inside her, plunging with urgency, she could sense his final release as she too cried out, waves of pleasure pulsating through her, filling her body and her head with pure bliss.

"Call him after me," Aidan whispered. "Call him Aidan, my beloved, for surely one day we two shall meet again."

Maggie wept.

Then she slept soundly until the morning's first light.

Before fully awakening, she briefly visited with her mother near the deep blue pond and sacred grove. The elders had gathered there in the misty light, and, for a brief moment, she caught sight of Aidan, handsome as ever, smiling at her from the boat out on the pond. Rickets, the hound he had loved in his childhood, was beside him. The two of them were together again in the rosy glow of the Summerland.

Morning light filtered through the windows. A bit of seaweed and a fresh sprig of lavender was on her pillow, gifts from those she had loved the most, together now, beyond the veil of the Otherworld.

During that June, many shipwrecks were reported in the North Atlantic and the English Channel. The *Cornelia* and its cargo and crew numbered among them. Maggie had known in her heart and soul that

Aidan would never return. Even though she now carried his son in her belly, she was determined not to destroy the child. She had promised to raise him with his father's name. For a time, she told no one, thinking that it was no one else's bloody business.

News of the victory of the Duke of Wellington and his allies' (Prussian, Dutch, Belgian and German) over the Emperor Napoleon and his troops at the Battle of Waterloo arrived first by carrier pigeon in London. Then the news reached the rest of the European capitals. The Austrians and Russians had arrived after Napoleon was already defeated.

All the newspapers reported heavy casualties: one in four British soldiers was dead: 15,000 total. The Prussians lost 7,000 men and the French 25,000, with 8,000 taken as prisoners of war along with 250 guns. There was no count of those permanently maimed or blinded by the slaughter. Some entire regiments were lost, the remnants severely damaged, with the majority of the men under the age of twenty.

By the end of June, the newspapers reported that the French Emperor was defeated and had once again abdicated his throne. Boney was exiled on the island of St. Helena in the Atlantic Ocean west of Africa, an island half the size of Elba. No more Napoleon to worry the British Commonwealth about conquering the world. But what had happened to the wounded? In particular, what had happened to an Irish Fusilier named Lt. Darcy Donal Brosnan?

At the outset, no one in Ireland was able to determine whether Darcy was dead or alive. Prudence had left for England, with the only deliveries now made to the servants. Finally, a tearful Ona told Matthew that Darcy was reported as dead on an early list of casualties.

Every night, Maggie now prayed for Aidan and Darcy. The two men she had loved were apparently dead and gone forever, leaving her with only her very fond memories.

26

Unrequited Love

Even her Aunt Brigid had obstinately insisted on the marriage, which seemed entirely unfair to Maggie. She had at least expected her aunt's support with regard to her future happiness.

"But I do not love him!" Maggie cried out. "I hardly even like him, for that matter."

"Love is not important in your delicate condition," her aunt said in a chastising tone. "A father for your child is the important thing. Your respectability in the community is no small matter with the locals, not to mention Father Hennessey and the Church. Without a proper husband, you will be considered a fallen woman! It is not the way it was with the Druid high priestesses in times of old. Those women could do as they pleased. Choose a husband or not when with child, but times have long since changed, my dear niece."

Scowling, Maggie said, "I am a modern woman. Modern women do not need to be married because of being with child. After all, this is 1815!"

"Modern, are you? You must be the first modern midwife in the whole of Ireland!" With her hands on her hips, her Aunt Brigid towered over her. "All the same, Niall has fancied you all your life. Leastwise, that is what he tells us. He has always loved you. And Aidan was his first cousin, a blood McKenna. They even look the same, sort of."

"Are you blind, Aunt?" Maggie shrieked.

"Well, at least the child will have his name. I should think you would take that into consideration for the sake of the child."

"Oh, horse pucky!" Maggie flared, pulling weeds from the potato patch near the cottage which she now resentfully tossed onto the pile. "Niall is much slighter than Aidan, inches shorter and not nearly as strong. His hair is light and fully unruly, his eyes not as dark." Her eyes filled with tears. "I don't see why I have to marry a man I cannot love!"

"Because you are with child, my bonny lass. You neglected to come to me soon enough to use snakeroot and penny royal with no harm. You did not use your herbs, as you should have ... an ounce of prevention would have saved you from all this."

"I will not destroy Aidan's child. I could never forgive myself. It is our blood, his and mine, that lives on in my child."

There was tenderness in her aunt's eyes. "I suspect it was on that full moon at Beltaine when you played priestess to your Aidan in the grove. The goddess had her hand in this," she crossed herself while shaking her head, "And I pray she knows what she is doing with your life!"

Turning to pull more weeds, Maggie realized that no one could possibly understand how trapped she was feeling, and yet, her aunt had made a point.

"That is what I thought!" Brigid groaned. "Fertility rites! Does it every time! You know how we tell the infertile to use the time." She sighed. "The goddess gave you a gift all right, with no thought of the fate of the father. A poor child who shall never see Aidan's handsome face or know his touch. It is a shame, Mary Margaret, pitiful, with the Almighty's blessings on you and your child from me," and she crossed herself again.

"A son," Maggie said, gazing out across the green glen.

"A son?"

Noting the compassion on her aunt's face, Maggie added, "Aidan wants me to name him after him ... Aidan. He told me in a dream. I think it was the night that he drowned. Aidan Brendan the same as him." She frowned. "I hope he looks like his father. I need a handsome, charming son to raise up. We need more handsome, charming men in this world, that is a certainty," she said, dabbing at her tears with the back of her hand and smudging her face with dirt.

Her aunt sighed. "I imagine he drowned during one of those terrible storms, lost with the *Cornelia* and its crew." She knelt to pull more weeds from the softly hoed earth. "A shame it is," she said, absently crossing herself again and shaking her head with a woebegone look on her face.

"In my dream I saw jagged rocks. I heard screams and could feel their fear as the sea took them from everyone who loves them." She tried to dispel the sad vision that still filled her mind.

Again, Brigid crossed herself. "At least if you marry Niall, there will be another Aidan McKenna, except that might not thrill him one bit." She laughed. "I dreamed you had a boy with dark curly hair like your Aidan."

"Good," Maggie said, her eyes now filling with happier tears. She cried for him often enough it seemed, remembering how Aidan looked in the Otherworld. He and her mother were friends now. Often, she could sense his presence, but never again as on the night of her dream. At times, Aidan's love seemed to envelope her. Love survived in the world of spirit. The day that her mother died her love had enfolded Maggie in the sweet, sweet glow of the Summerland.

It was true that Niall looked a bit like Aidan, but he was not nearly as handsome. Maggie had never known Niall in the Otherworld, or in some other lifetime. He was a complete stranger to her. The worst part of it was that she felt no passion or attraction to him whatsoever. How could she marry a man without passion? That was unimaginable to Maggie.

How did Niall truly feel about her carrying his cousin's child in her belly, knowing they had been together? How many times was none of his bloody business! How could Niall take her to wife just to make her 'respectable' and be a proper parent to his cousin's offspring? Who was this man who wanted her as his wife? Was he a saint, free of all desire, or perhaps a lunatic? That seemed more probable to Maggie.

Niall acted self-conscious, afraid to even touch her. He had none of Aidan's playfulness. Should he so choose to punish or abuse her, she had decided to poison him. A pinch of some herbs would do the trick. Then she could be a merry widow and find a man who stirred her passion, a man with spunk, perhaps a man like Darcy. Surely he was buried somewhere near Waterloo as one of the many heroes of the fierce battle. His letters had stopped in May. She had never written to him of Aidan. That no longer seemed necessary.

Some herbs might render Niall impotent, especially during her pregnancy. After all, she had helped other women with that matter. She could not bear the thought of him even touching her anytime soon. If he raped her, she would poison him on the very next day. Her aunt might even help. Perhaps poisonous toadstools in a tasty Irish stew would do the trick.

Niall was not an ugly man. It was just that Maggie never would have chosen him as a husband. In marrying her, he seemed to be trying to do right by Aidan. But what about doing right by her? He had to know she had no feelings for him. None whatsoever.

Father Hennessey was the most difficult of them all.

"Young woman, you have *sinned,* conducted yourself in an immoral and unseemly manner by breaking the commandments of God and the Church," he said in his most self-righteous tone.

In her eyes, the priest was only a mortal man in a long black robe with a large gold crucifix fixed around his neck. He had no secret knowledge of Druid rituals. She was convinced that Francis Hennessey would never have made the cut as a Druid high priest. He seemed to have no mind of his own, simply did whatever he was told. He had not even the power to stop a thunderstorm from ruining a summer afternoon's wedding: no magical powers whatsoever in his blind obedience to the Church.

"If loving be my sin, then I have sinned," she said. "I have no regrets in regard to my love for Aidan McKenna. What you call immoral put this babe in my belly by the grace of God. I carry my child proudly, I do. I loved Aidan with all my heart, my mind and my soul. He asked me to marry him, gave me the silk for my wedding gown. We planned to marry when he returned, but he drowned at sea. I saw it all in my dreams, Father Hennessey. All of them lost forever. Aidan and I were promised to each other in the sacred grove before God, all the angels, and the goddess in the moon as well."

"There is no goddess in the moon!" he bellowed. "You speak blasphemy! You talk like a Pagan, Mary Margaret, not a proper Roman Catholic brought up in the Church. You have sinned, my child. You have sinned!" he shouted as his spittle showered her face.

"If such loving be a sin, Father, I want no part of your religion or of any religion that condemns such love. What happened is between Aidan and myself and the Lord of the Otherworld. I have no need of earthly priests to tell me what is right for me and my child. I know what is right in my heart, and you will not change my mind with all your threatening, yelling and screaming. I won't go to hell for my sins, for there is no such place. It is hellfire you frighten your parishioners with, but you will not frighten me with your nonsense. Hell is right here, right this minute, with you and your God forsaken screaming!"

Glaring into his bloodshot eyes, Maggie was sure that the priest had spent several hours in the tavern earlier that day. She had received the full benefit of his whiskey breath.

"It is only right and proper that you marry Niall McKenna, who has generously accepted the responsibility of rearing his cousin's child. That is noble sentiment for a young man who professes love for you. And you had best consider your father's wishes, with your stubborn ways, Mary Margaret, and raise your child a Roman Catholic. No more pagan talk. No more I say!" he shouted, gratefully retaining his spittle that time.

What else could she expect from a Catholic priest who thought he knew the Lord's plans for her better than she knew them herself? Her father was nearly as bad, though she knew he was trying his best to look out for her. Did not even her aunt want her child to have a father, since Aidan was food for the fishes? Eileen had even pushed her, the widow of a fisherman, though to Maggie the woman appeared more like the walking dead herself.

Remembering how Aidan had teased her about Niall being moonstruck over her, perhaps it was true in spite of her long, red hair. Had he perhaps overcome his superstitious fear, she wondered? How many men would be willing to marry her when she was with child? The thought of leaving Eileen and her three children was fine with her. All of them had started to get on her nerves.

Sassy Cathleen and Brian the bully had put worms in her porridge and dirt in her shoes. Brian was downright reprehensible. There had already been more than enough of Cathleen's temper tantrums. And as for her dowry, her father planned to provide them with three acres on which to build a house. The men from both families had pledged to help out with the building. Matthew and Sean were already piling up rocks. Additional gifts were to be a horse, cow, and ten chickens with the livestock shared the first year. There was a promise of milk, butter, chickens and eggs, and beef at a slaughter. The garden was to be shared, since Maggie was particularly good with the potatoes. The assistance from the nature spirits was her best kept secret.

Early on the August day of her wedding, Maggie walked to the ruins where she and Aidan were frequently together. The shamrocks and wild violets covered the place where they first shared their love one day in search of rainbows, finding the purest of gold in each other's loving arms.

"I have not yet felt any movement," she said aloud. "He is fine, our son. I have stopped eating things that might harm him, with no plans to reach the size of our barn."

Facing the brisk breeze off the sea, tears coursed down her cheeks. She could see Aidan's smiling face in the sunlight as she remembered his playfulness, his strength, and his loving kindness when he held her. How serious he could be at times. How he always tended to respond to her every want and need.

How well she remembered the first time Aidan arrived at the hedge school from across the mountain on a borrowed pony. From that moment on, Maggie realized that she had known him before, especially his dimpled smile, his dark tousled hair, and his beautiful brown eyes. Aidan promised her silk from France and had more than fulfilled his promises. He had given her many beautiful things to remind her of him, perhaps most poignantly, the child in her womb.

On the day of her wedding to Niall, she could not bear to wear the white silk and lace given to her by Aidan. Another dress was sewn from the local white linen, part of the bolt from Prudence from which Aidan's shirt was made several years ago.

Maggie was wearing a simple dress because of simple feelings in marrying a man she would never love as she had once loved the first. Aidan was the man she knew in her heart she was destined to love forever.

27

A Fateful Meeting

The drop in the temperature arrived early that fall, forcing an untimely harvest. Because of the excessive rainfall, the potatoes and sprouts were not as plentiful, with all of them stored in a beehive hut by September to protect them from the cold. It was an early winter for County Kerry, more severe than in many years.

The original plan was for Maggie and Niall to live with his family in Ballyferriter until their house could be built in Dingle. Even though his mother's name, Letitia, translated as *joy*, the woman created no joy for herself or anyone else. In a brief time, Maggie found her new mother-in-law ill-tempered and a constant complainer who added whiskey to her morning tea. That fact was accidentally discovered when Maggie drank from the wrong cup one morning. The whiskey had turned her stomach, since she tended to avoid strong drink.

Letitia could be pleasant enough early in the morning when only slightly tipsy, but by the afternoon, she grew intolerable. Niall's father was a fisherman more often at the pub than out fishing. He refused to even look upon Maggie on any morning he planned to fish. Her red hair was sure to bring him no luck at all. Both of Niall's parents continuously reeked of whiskey and tobacco, which made Maggie wonder what she had gotten herself into by marrying into a family that was nothing at all like Aidan's.

By October, Maggie and Niall moved in with her Aunt Brigid. The cottage was warm and cozy smelling of herbs and warm peat and possessed a tidiness not to be found at the home of the McKenna's. Immediately, Niall appreciated her aunt's cooking and found her domestic skills "somewhat superior to those of his well-intentioned though errant mother." Brigid was happy to have Maggie near in order to keep a close watch on her. The babe had become highly active and tended to wake Maggie up at night. Sharing time with her aunt meant a lot to her as her seventeenth birthday drew near.

All Hallows Eve arrived, the time when the souls of the departed leave their graves or their place in the Otherworld to visit those in the land of the living, not that spirits ever resided in the cold ground. A sacred ritual was planned to guarantee peace to the departed for yet another year, including Aidan and Darcy. Maggie considered Aidan to be her true husband, even though he now resided in the land of the shades.

To date, there were no sexual advances from Niall. He seemed respectful of her needs. Two years older than Aidan, he had looked up to his taller, stronger cousin and had also voiced his admiration of Aidan's defiance of the Crown with his smuggling activities. Niall was meek and had no love at all for the sea. Whereas Aidan had refused to farm, Niall willingly relinquished fishing to work on the farm with her father. Padraic seemed fond of his new son-in-law, for from the start Niall had done well in tending to the cows.

In spite of no lovemaking, Maggie frequently had erotic dreams, most involving Aidan, though on occasion, Darcy made love to her in her dreams. Some nights, Niall only wanted to hold her, which was something she tended to allow. She sometimes wondered if Aidan and Darcy had run into each other over in the Otherworld. The two men she had loved were now tragically gone, leaving her with only sad musings of what might have been.

Since the horrible day when Prudence ordered her out of her house, Maggie had not seen her. Thankfully, Prudence Pratt still purchased produce from her father, so her family was not being punished for her mistake. Had Prudence learned of the fate of the *Cornelia,* she wondered, as she had learned of Darcy's sad fate at the Battle of Waterloo from her servant?

At her father's insistence, the circumstances of her hasty marriage to Niall were disclosed only to those in the family. Many on the peninsula were aware that Maggie and Aidan were sweethearts. In her opinion, it was going be almost impossible to conceal her condition much longer, since her belly was starting to resemble a ripening autumn pumpkin with less than three months ahead of her. Only that morning, Megan had tried to convince her that she barely showed.

Less than an hour later, Megan breathlessly burst through the cottage front door calling out, "Maggie, you must come to the house immediately! You have a visitor!" her face was fully flushed and her shawl pulled securely around her.

"A visitor?" Maggie said, reaching for her shawl. "What sort of visitor?"

Grabbing her hand, Megan pulled her toward the door and said, "Kevin Gallagher, Darcy's good friend," with her green eyes opening wider. "Come now! Come quickly!"

Both of them were soon out the door and half-running down the long hill, with Maggie holding her belly with one hand. It was a respectable distance from the cottage down to the farmhouse.

"Watch out ... there's a low spot here," Megan warned, as Maggie searched her mind for a Kevin Gallagher. The name somehow sounded familiar.

Near the bottom of the hill, a tall man was standing next to a horse. His hair was a thick, dark red, his shoulders broad and his face pleasant. His clothing was that of a gentleman as he leaned on a cane with both hands.

"Kevin Gallagher?" Maggie inquired, trying to catch her breath.

Standing taller, he released the cane with one hand and said, "Kevin Gallagher at your service. I am Darcy's friend from the regiment, Lieutenant Darcy Brosnan." His eyes narrowed as he appeared to more closely observe her. "We fought together at the Battle of Waterloo and in many battles throughout the years in Spain, Portugal and Belgium."

"I see," Maggie said, noting that he seemed to require the cane for support. "You were wounded at the Battle of Waterloo fighting against Napoleon?"

"Aye," he said, "Took two nasty hits in my right leg and a horror in my left shoulder. But I wasn't hurt anywhere nearly as bad as Darcy. For the longest time there, we thought we were going to lose him."

Suddenly feeling faint, Maggie gasped, "Darcy is alive?" Instantly feeling weak, she grabbed for her sister's arm for support.

"Just barely alive, you might say," Kevin solemnly said. "Darcy was hit in both legs, his right shoulder, left side, and in the head. We were afraid he might lose the sight in his right eye, but they were able to save all of him, luckily. It's a miracle that Darcy is still here after all his many grievous wounds. We prayed night and day. He is my very best friend, so I never wanted to lose him. Gratefully, Darcy is still with us on this earth."

"That is … wonderful," Maggie said, trying her best to pull herself together as she turned to Megan. "Perhaps we should offer Mr. Gallagher some refreshment. It is chilly and damp out here."

Megan brightened. "I have gingerbread and tea. Would you care to come in?" She smiled and her green eyes nearly glowed.

"Why, thank you, Megan. Thank you, kindly," Kevin said and he smiled.

A pot of tea was brewed as the three of them sat at the table near the fire. The wind was picking up off the bay, so Megan added more peat to the fire.

"My father took my stepmother and the children to Lispole to visit relatives. My brothers are out with the cows, so it is just us here inside the house," Megan said, partly for the benefit of her sister. "I am glad I was here to greet you, Mr. Gallagher," she added, bringing the gingerbread to the table to cut three pieces, which were placed on separate plates.

"I am exceedingly glad that you are here, to be honest, Megan. It is a long ride from Cork. I started out early this morning. My parents own an inn on the coast and are eager to put me to work. My aunt and uncle in Killarney own an inn as well. I have wanted to come and meet you for some time now," he said to Megan, "but I needed to heal a touch first."

"I see," Megan said, appearing to watch him closely.

Kevin seemed to study Megan, her pretty face and her features, before he suddenly turned to Maggie. "I must confess that I am primarily here to meet Megan," he said, instantly turning back to Megan with a highly expectant expression on his handsome face.

Seated directly across from him, Megan boldly stared into Kevin's large brown eyes. "Darcy wrote of you in his first letter to Maggie. I remember the name, Kevin Gallagher. Darcy said that you are pure Irish and he wanted you to meet me one day when I was older."

Both of them smiled at the same time, with Kevin eagerly nodding and blushing slightly.

It was then that Maggie remembered, noting the utter delight on her young sister's face. Kevin was eating his gingerbread with his eyes seldom leaving Megan. Maggie figured he had to be Darcy's age, with Megan but fifteen.

"You came all this way to meet my sister?" Maggie inquired.

"Aye," he said, blushing slightly again. "Darcy always spoke highly of the both of you, and quite often at that." Now, he turned to Maggie. "Smitten with you, he was. He never stopped talking about Mary Margaret O'Reilly and how much he loved you."

Suddenly feeling the color rise into her face, Maggie hoped that her pumpkin belly was well hidden as she leaned closer into the table. Feeling fully at a loss, she took note of the stricken look on her sister's face at the mention of Darcy's affection for her. Instantly, Kevin's declaration had made her feel strangely empty inside. It was such a shock for her to know that Darcy was still alive.

"Right before the great battle at Waterloo, Darcy received a letter from his cousin, Prudence, who lives here in Dingle. She told him that you were marrying a smuggler named Aidan McKenna."

At once, Maggie and Megan exchanged troubled glances, both of them still plainly in shock. Maggie could sense Kevin's gaze on her and her sister appeared to study him.

"Darcy was devastated, of course. The news broke his heart right before the great battle. I remember how he said it no longer mattered to him whether he lived or died, and he nearly did die."

Suddenly, tears filled and spilled from Maggie's eyes. Completely overcome, she was unable to speak and started to sob as she struggled with the powerful emotions welling up from deep down inside her.

"We thought he was dead," Megan said, wiping the tears from her cheeks with her apron as she handed a kitchen towel to Maggie.

Sitting taller, Kevin now fully turned to Megan. "Darcy told me all about you, about your long dark hair and your green Irish eyes, how pretty you are. He said he would not be surprised if I fell in love with you on the spot." His warm brown eyes were gently fixed on Megan.

Megan blushed and stood. "I had best pour you some more tea, Mr. Gallagher," she nervously said, plainly pleased by his boldness. "Did he tell you that I am nearly fifteen and a half and will not be sixteen until May?"

"He was uncertain as to your age. But he did not stretch the truth in speaking of your beauty," he said, helping himself to another slice of gingerbread. "I am telling you the whole truth, Megan O'Reilly, and the truth is that I have come a courting, fifteen years or whatever!" He quickly chewed and swallowed, glancing from Megan to Maggie. Then he winked at Maggie, who had gratefully recovered, before he turned back to Megan and inquired, "Would you have any serious objections as to my sincere intentions concerning you?"

Straightaway, Megan shook her head, for she was obviously transfixed by the striking man.

Observing their energetic exchange, Maggie had detected gossamer threads that connected them one to the other through patterns that existed in the Otherworld.

"War teaches a man fast about what's really important in this world and what is not. Many of my dearest friends and comrades died at Waterloo, as well as in various other battles. I nearly lost Darcy and a few other lads were severely wounded, their lives now frankly in ruin. I will be twenty-three in February, perhaps not terribly old, but I have been fighting the bloody French emperor and his troops since I was fifteen, long enough to know a few things. I have seen a lot of men die far sooner than they should have, in my opinion, and I am planning to leave the regiment and go to America. My Uncle Lucius, my mother's brother, lives in Charleston in the Carolinas. He has a tavern and hopes to build an inn, sort of the family business. He has asked for my help, my Uncle Lucius, promising me gainful employment as soon as the boat docks from Cobh. The fact is that I would like to take an Irish wife with me to Charleston." Again he turned to Megan with a sly but definitive nod.

Both Maggie and Megan simply stared at the man.

"Sometimes next spring, more than likely, I'll be sailing after the seas are calm. I'm no good on rough seas, no good at all." He smiled and drained the last of the tea from his cup.

The two of them were speechless.

It seemed to Maggie, from the look on her sister's face, that Megan was open to his bold and direct offer. Kevin Gallagher was handsome, intelligent and a fully straightforward fellow. Megan might never find another man like him anywhere near Dingle, especially if she truly fancied him. The local lads who had dared to seek her affections paled by comparison. Most definitely, Kevin Gallagher was another of Wellington's invincibles.

"How is Darcy?" Maggie finally had enough courage to ask.

Kevin's eyes misted over. "He was in the hospital in Belgium for four months, and then transferred near London for rehabilitation. I hear he is now at his parent's home in Dublin." He paused. "Darcy had amnesia and couldn't remember who he was or what had happened for a spell. It is not uncommon with the horrors of war, especially with the severe wounds he suffered, his head being shot and all. He lost so much blood they thought he was a goner for sure. Angels must have been watching over my friend, for a certainty."

"Angels were watching over him," Maggie said. "I am so relieved to know that Darcy is still alive. I had heard he was dead and no one ever told us anything to the contrary."

"At first, he was falsely reported dead," Kevin said.

Maggie was convinced that Kevin had noticed her ripening belly.

"So you married your smuggler?" he said, looking into her eyes.

"No," she said.

His reaction was one of puzzlement. "But you are married, are you not?" He nodded at her wedding ring.

"I am now Maggie McKenna," she said.

"McKenna was the name of your smuggler."

"Aidan died in a shipwreck," Megan said, and she blanched at the reproachful glare of her sister. "She has married his cousin, Niall. He is not a smuggler and never has been."

"I see," Kevin said and he stood. He turned to Megan and inquired, "May I take you to dinner at the *Hotel Geraldine* this evening in Dingle Town? I have a need to speak with the proprietor. I am told the chef is excellent."

Megan flushed and stood. "What time?"

"I will pick you up at six in a carriage that I am borrowing from Darcy's cousin, Prudence." He then turned to Maggie. "Is it all right if I call upon your sister?"

"It is fine with me, if it is fine with her."

"Good day until later then, Megan. I shall ask your father's permission when I have the opportunity to meet Mr. Padraic O'Reilly."

"Good day," Megan said, curtsying, and she giggled.

"Mrs. McKenna," he said to Maggie, returning his hat to his head.

Then, out the door strode Kevin Gallagher, climbing onto his horse and galloping off in the direction of Dingle Town.

28

A Child is Born

The winter was more bitter than in many years, but the severe wintry weather did little to deter Kevin Gallagher from traveling by horse or coach, or even by boat, from Cork to Dingle to court young Megan O'Reilly. He secured the permission of her father, Padraic, to follow the overpowering dictates of his heart to pursue the bonny young lass of fifteen with the purpose of marriage in mind. Naturally, that was in accordance with his daughter's wishes and her full encouragement.

By Christmastime, Kevin had brought along an emerald ring bequeathed to him by his late beloved maternal grandmother, Ina Courtney, with the express purpose of placing the ring on the finger of his Megan. During the holidays, Kevin sincerely hoped that she would finally agree to become his faithful and beloved wife.

With the two of them alone in front of a roaring fire in the O'Reilly parlor early that snowy Christmas Eve, Kevin knelt down on one knee to formally propose to young Meg, as he preferred to call her. In a state of complete and total happiness, the fair young maiden accepted his ring and his earnest proposal. She agreed to accompany Kevin Gallagher to Charleston, South Carolina, in the spring as his wife. Together, they planned a brand new life in America.

The ring fit Megan perfectly, since her hand and the hand of his grandmother were remarkably the same. It was the sign of a promise of marital bliss. Kevin had sworn that his grandparents were happily married until the very end, dying six months apart after fifty-two years of marriage. He thought they might be together still in heaven.

The holidays were happy ones for the O'Reillys, including Niall and Maggie who tried to make the best of things for the sake of her sister. Eileen came down with a respiratory infection two days after Christmas that progressed into pneumonia. Maggie and Brigid nursed her with herbs and warm poultices applied to her chest to reduce the fever and the coughing. Cough syrup was made from coltsfoot tea and wild honey. To everyone except her father, Eileen seemed eternally peaked and fragile. Her daughter, Cathleen, played at sickness, perhaps to imitate her mother, whining and constantly complaining. The thought of leaving her "wicked stepmother" and her three bratty offspring was of enormous relief to young Megan, but she did not feel the same about leaving the rest of her family.

"However am I going to get along without you?" she said to Maggie in tears on a crisp January day while visiting her at the cottage.

A menacing wind was howling up the hill and sounded much like the cry of a banshee. Peat blazed on the hearth to warm the kitchen, as tea laced with honey warmed them inside.

"I can see a bright future for you and Kevin in Charleston," Maggie said. "Your Kevin is a fine man, who absolutely adores you, as you adore him. You have done quite well for yourself, my sister, in securing yourself a handsome and capable husband. I know Kevin shall make you happy indeed."

"I am quite sure of it," Brigid said. "It seems Kevin cannot do enough for you, bringing you jewelry and fabrics, emerald green velvet to go with your eyes. I will do my best with your wedding gown, but I am not nearly as fine a seamstress as might be required for the rest of your fancy gowns, your bonnets and all your capes."

With difficulty, Maggie pulled herself out of the chair to make her way to a cupboard to get the cornbread and warm it on the stove. She placed the jug of honey on the table.

"Are you sure I am only having one child?" she said to her aunt, placing a hand on her extended belly. "He seems quiet today. Do you think he is all right?"

"He has dropped and is getting ready to breathe on his own," her aunt said as she walked over to fondly place her hand on Maggie's great belly.

"Are you sure the child is a boy?" Megan inquired. "You both seem so cocksure."

"In my dreams, Aidan told me we will have a son ... thrice he has told me!" she said, suddenly experiencing a sharp pain. "Might it not be today?" she inquired, reaching for the cupboard to steady herself as another sharp pain shot across her lower back. "It seems my labor has begun."

"If that be so, no cornbread for you, lass," her aunt said, pushing the pan toward Megan. "No more food for you on this morning. We will have enough to do with you and the rain. Listen to that wind howling! We don't want you choking on your own vomit, now, do we, young midwife?"

All of a sudden, Megan lost interest in the cornbread, watching her aunt add peat to the fire before she glanced out the window at the darkening storm.

"I will pump more water," her aunt said and she turned to Megan. "You will be helping, so you had best eat the cornbread and honey and drink your tea. You will need your strength to help with the birth of your first nephew. But you had also best not make a glutton of yourself in front of your poor, laboring sister," and she grabbed a bucket and was out the door into the blowing rain.

Megan stared at the cornbread and briefly glanced at Maggie, not knowing whether to eat, so she sipped her tea instead.

With the next stabbing pain, Maggie doubled over, turning to find her sister staring at the cornbread. "Eat, pray God," she said, laughing. "I do not want you to faint from hunger should I need your help. I always eat heartily before delivering a child from not knowing how many hours might pass until the job is done."

Brigid entered the cottage with a bucket of water. She slammed the door shut and walked to a cupboard to remove various pots and jars.

Again, Maggie doubled over in pain. "By the saints!" she cried out. "This hurts more than a little, Aunt."

"You should know as much from all the birthings," her Aunt Brigid said. "It seems to me that those pains are coming close together. Walk if

195

you can and breathe through your mouth. Put your knowledge to work and you could well be your own midwife."

"I pray not," Maggie said, beginning to pace.

Megan cut and buttered a large slice of cornbread, adding honey and taking a big bite. She chewed. "I must fortify myself," she mumbled, washing down the cornbread with her tea.

The labor pains intensified, growing stronger and more rapid, one following the other. Within an hour, Maggie was in her bed gripping the iron bars and trying her best to follow her aunt's instruction. She breathed in the manner prescribed for all women in labor, knowing such pain had been endured by countless women from the beginning of time. The pain was working its magic in her body to bring her child into the world. Her labor started a week earlier than calculated and now rapidly progressed into longer, sharper pains, one soon after the other.

According to her aunt's instruction, Megan boiled water and mixed herbs to prepare a strong tea made from black snakeroot stored in a ceramic pot.

"You can yell and scream all you like," her aunt said, taking her hand. "You need not be so brave, my child! Do not hold it all inside you. Let it out, my sweet lass!"

Beads of perspiration formed on her upper lip as Maggie cried out, "Where are you, Aidan? I am having your child!" she screamed. "Can you help me from where you are in the Otherworld? Can you bring me some angels to help with the birth of our son?" she cried out and the tears dried before they reached the pillow.

Holding her sister's hand, Megan said, "I am sure Aidan is here. He must be. It is only right that he should be, since it was him who made you this way."

"I am responsible," Maggie said. "I was careless. I have no one to blame but myself!" Another pain ripped through her that made her feel as though her back was going to break in two. Gritting her teeth, she tried not to cry out during the most intense time of her labor.

Her Aunt Brigid applied a warm, damp cloth to her brow and brought the cup to her lips. "Drink," she said. "It will ease your pain and bring your child to you that much more quickly."

With effort, Maggie drank, knowing it was snakeroot, passion flower and cinnamon with honey. After swallowing one gulp, another pain shot through her. She twisted and turned in her agony.

When any of the others members of the family approached the cottage, they were sent back to the farmhouse, all now aware that Maggie had entered her time of travail. Eileen was busy making supper, having recently recovered from her illness. Padraic had purchased a bottle of Jameson Irish whiskey and generously poured to celebrate the birth of his first grandchild. He planned to save a glass for Brigid.

After the sun set behind the western mountains, the cry of a newborn let everyone know that his lungs were healthy and strong. Her first great nephew squirmed in Brigid's strong arms, protesting the need to enter a space less comforting than that of his mother's womb, forced to breathe in the warm cottage air of an Irish winter as the storm outside slowly began to abate.

"Aidan Padraic," Maggie said, as her son was first placed in her outstretched arms.

"Your father will be pleased," Brigid said. "It is a fine name, Aidan Padraic McKenna."

The first time she looked into her newborn's eyes it was love at first sight. Seeing his dark, searching eyes, Maggie instantly knew that here was a soul she had known before somewhere, sometime. He was a soul back from the Otherworld to be with her again. As a wave of deep love washed through her, Maggie could not help but wonder, is it you, Aidan? Have you come back to be with me again? Will we be conquering new worlds together?

She stared into his wee face for the longest moment and held him close, breathing in the fresh scent of her bundle of joy sent to her from heaven. Holding her child in her arms helped her to forget about the bitter pain of her labor. All the suffering had brought her a fine, bonny lad she was convinced would be with her for all the rest of her days.

With Niall often in the cottage during the fierce winter, he would stare at the baby and watch young Aidan whether the child was awake or sleeping. He refused to hold the baby or take any part in his daily care. After all, Maggie had suggested a time or two that Aidan had returned from the Otherworld in the form of her newborn son. The mere suggestion seemed to unnerve Niall.

Even Niall's mild attempts at romancing her were rebuffed. Now his touch repulsed her and made her genuinely regret that she had married the man. He was too mild mannered to suit Maggie, too slowwitted and fully lacking in ambition. He could barely read or write and refused to learn. Aidan could read and write and loved to listen to her read a book for hours at a time.

From the first moment that Maggie learned Darcy was alive, she had pulled farther and farther away from Niall, especially after the birth of her child. All her love was now lavished on Aidan Padraic McKenna, her bonny, jolly and healthy young son.

29

Celebrating a Wedding

The early May wedding was not going to be a simple affair, but the grandest wedding in the O'Reilly family in perhaps centuries. Nearly all the rooms of the *Hotel Geraldine*, and in all the smaller inns, were booked to capacity, mainly by the relatives and friends of Mr. Kevin Gallagher. Folks arrived from not only County Cork and County Kerry, but it seemed from the whole of Ireland. Kevin was generously covering the cost, since he had recently received a sizeable inheritance from his late paternal grandfather, Kerill Gallagher.

"Imagine," Padraic said, "folks coming from all around the country to attend the wedding of my daughter, all the way from London and Edinburgh too, now, isn't that something?"

The rest of the family also thought it was "something," since Kevin Kerill Gallagher was baptized Roman Catholic to marry Megan Caitlin O'Reilly in the Church, with the majority in his family Protestant for over a hundred years. His conversion caused quite the stir, the locals craning their necks to catch a glimpse of all the fine folks gathering for the festive occasion. It was said in the pub that Padraic O'Reilly was a lucky man. A tenant farmer was marrying off his youngest daughter to a family of respectable innkeepers, not only in Ireland but in America.

Maggie thought it some kind of miracle, in spite of their connection in the Otherworld.

It was Maggie and her Aunt Brigid who finished the gown intended for Maggie to wear to marry Aidan: The pure white silk and lace he had brought to her from France. At first, Megan objected, and yet she was secretly thrilled with the fine gift from her sister, for it was a gown she could ill afford herself. Megan was not as tall as Maggie, but just as slender and fair. For her marriage vows, Megan would be resplendent in her white silk gown, with her sister as her Matron of Honor in her emerald green silk. The handsome groom would be formally attired, along with the best man, his eldest brother, Michael. There were rumors of Darcy Brosnan standing up for Kevin, since he was responsible for the meeting.

"Darcy is invited, as you know," Megan said near her big day.

Standing taller, Maggie tried to ignore the catch in her mid-section at the thought of seeing Darcy again. She had never answered his last letter. How could he know she had loved him, perhaps every bit as much as Aidan, thinking them both dead when she married Niall? Could Darcy have even wanted her knowing she carried another man's child? Was there a man alive who could love a woman who loved two men at the same time?

"Darcy should be there," Maggie said. "He should rejoice in seeing Kevin marry you, be pleased for the happiness of you both." She forced a smile. "After all, he could stay with Prudence in her fine house. She has plenty of rooms."

"He is staying with her," Megan said, cautiously venturing, "For it is in Prudence's fine ballroom we will celebrate our wedding wake. Musicians are hired. Prudence insisted on giving us a wedding cake because of Darcy's fondness for Kevin, who has always been there for him. Darcy is making a gift of the whiskey and French champagne. Ironic, is it not, since the French nearly killed him?"

"Ironic, indeed!" Maggie said, tears suddenly filling her eyes.

"You cannot consider not being there, for you are the one responsible for my happiness, because of your friendship with Prudence and Darcy and teaching me how to read and write and behave. I would have nothing without you, Maggie. I would not be marrying my Kevin."

About to burst into tears, Maggie said, "You are asking me to return to that house when it was there that I first wore the green gown and danced with Darcy at the ball feeling much like a fairy princess." Tears spilled down her face. "It was a magical evening, Megan. Many wonderful afternoons were spent in that house with Prudence."

"I am asking you to be strong for my sake. You are my sister and I love you, Maggie. I want you to share in my joy on my wedding day. I cannot do it without you." Megan took her hands. "And if you promise to keep a secret ..." her green eyes brightly widened as she paused.

Maggie nodded, pressing her lips together to stem the flow of tears.

"You promise?"

Nodding again, Maggie was growing impatient with her younger sister.

"Kevin and I have been practicing ... the waltz!"

"Or have you, now?" Maggie's expression turned into one of feigned horror, "That sinful dance where a man holds a woman in his arms near his ... manhood?"

"Not so very near. For a year at least, it has been the latest fashion in Europe. Kevin says we will waltz in America ... it being such a modern country and all. Imagine, Kevin and I waltzing at a ball in Charleston, is that not a truly scandalous thought, my sister?"

They both laughed.

"Well, I suppose I must not miss seeing you and Kevin dance the wicked, devilish waltz as husband and wife on the eve of your wedding!"

"You must promise to be there, Darcy or no Darcy." Megan said, "After all, you will have Niall there to protect you."

"Fine protection he would be from the feelings I have in my heart. He knows little of Prudence and nothing of Darcy. I will not tell him, either, and you had best not say a word!"

"I promise," Megan said, crossing her heart and touching the end of her nose with her index finger.

"Your wedding day shall be both joyous and sad for me, my dear. Here you are marrying before your sixteenth birthday and sailing off to America in a fortnight. Cobh to Charleston, you are leaving us, Megan," she said, taking both her hands in hers. "I feel joy for you and Kevin. He will make you a fine husband and you him a fine wife. Promise me that you will write to me, will you not?"

"I promise," Megan said, hugging her. "Perhaps one day you will come to Charleston. Niall wants to live in Baltimore. One day we could all be living in America! I hope to find Liam there. I truly hope I do."

"America is vast, Megan. Baltimore is nowhere near Charleston. I remember looking at the map in Prudence's library. Ireland is but a drop in the sea compared to America. It is a vast, vast country, indeed."

"Still, it would be grand to not be separated from each other by the great sea, would it not?"

"Father needs Niall here," Maggie said. "He is losing you, but at least he gets to say his farewells. You will not be breaking his heart the same as our Liam."

Picking up the wedding gown, Maggie held it up for her.

"It is so very beautiful. You are the kindest sister in the whole world to give me your gown. The silk and lace are so very fine. In my heart, I shall thank dear Aidan on my wedding day."

"And you shall be the most beautiful bride in the whole world!"

"The whole world?" Megan said, laughing.

"Well, at least in the whole of Ireland!"

Marching down the aisle on her father's arm, Megan could barely keep from crying. Proud Padraic beamed in his Sunday best, his new white linen shirt and blue silk tie special gifts to him from Kevin. Aunt Brigid had insisted that the emerald green silk gown was perfect for the late afternoon candlelit wedding. The wreath of violets and shamrocks for her hair and her bouquet held special meaning for Maggie. But she could not have been happier for her sister marrying in the Catholic Church. It was a true triumph for the O'Reilly family.

The weather was cold for May, an early planting already destroyed by frost. The bride and groom were driven to the house in the fine carriage of Miss Pratt. A large carryall transported the wedding party, which pleased Padraic no end. Eileen wore a yellow dress of the local linen, her bonnet green silk. The children's new party clothes were sewn especially for the occasion.

After helping Maggie down from the carriage, Niall said, "You go on with your fancy friends. I may come around later for some whiskey. I have some business to take care of at the tavern."

"What sort of business keeps you from your sister's wedding celebration?" Maggie inquired in surprise, pulling her shawl more closely around her.

Niall smirked. "My business! You tend to yours and I'll tend to mine," he sullenly said, turning from her to head for the tavern.

"You cannot blame him," Matthew said. "You ignore the man and he is your husband."

"Who shall dance with me? You?" Maggie inquired, secretly relieved that Niall was gone.

Matthew smiled. "I may find time to dance with you, for you look quite fair, my sister! Cinderella has arrived for another fancy ball."

"And you look more handsome than usual, Matthew."

His smile showed off his dimples.

"I will dance with you," Sean said. "You are perhaps the second fairest lass here this evening. I plan to dance with the bride at least once."

"I should hope so," Maggie said, kissing his cheek.

"I wish I were taller," Sean said, standing on his tiptoes. "I don't seem to be growing as fast as I should." He quickly scanned the rooms as they walked up the stairs to the third floor. "It is a fine house, a very fine house, indeed."

"So it is," Matthew said, and as the other family members lined up to greet the many guests, he impishly wiggled his eyebrows. "Even though I am older, you shall stand before me this day as a married Matron of Honor. Fortunate for you, I daresay," he said with a grin.

"Indeed," Maggie said, curtsying, and she took her place next to the bride.

Many guests filed by in a cheerful manner, freely exchanging pleasantries, for not many elaborate celebrations had graced Dingle that year. The sovereign Lord Mayor Stewart Gregory and his missus mingled with his conspiratorial cronies and their wives. Her father had insisted on the invitations, since Kevin wanted the local dignitaries present. In such a small town, the officials were usually included in social events to pay their respects to the young couple leaving for America. After all, Padraic Desmond O'Reilly had powerful though ancient relatives who had once held positions of great honor on the Dingle Peninsula.

When Maggie looked down the line, she could see Prudence approaching the bridal party on Darcy's arm. Darcy's limp appeared more pronounced than the two summers earlier. He now used a cane. There was a sizeable red scar near his right eye, only seemingly one of his many wounds described by Kevin. The scar did not detract from his handsome features and would probably be less noticeable with the passing of time, she thought. Darcy wore the latest London fashions: dark green leggings, a cream ruffled shirt, a waistcoat of paisley print in purples and gold, and a dark green jacket.

Dressed in a gown of deep purple silk edged in black, Prudence's necklace and earrings were of iridescent opals, which suited her, Maggie thought. All at once, she was keenly aware of how very much she had missed spending time with Prudence to discuss the characters in some romantic novel while drinking tea and sharing ginger biscuits.

"My congratulations on the marriage of your sister, a fine match, is it not?" were the first words Prudence had spoken to her since that unfortunate day that seemed long ago.

"A truly fortunate match," Maggie said. "A fairy tale romance filled with love and humor, for they are forever laughing. You are most generous for entertaining our entire family in your lovely ballroom, but then, you have always been a very generous lady."

"It is a blessing for me, as well," Prudence said, moving on to Matthew who playfully kissed her hand. "So you have another sister married now," she said to him, "with Megan and Kevin soon leaving us for America's faraway shores."

"So it seems," Matthew affably replied. "I shall miss her, but I also celebrate her good fortune in securing so fine a husband. I am quite fond of Kevin and am greatly satisfied with the match."

As Maggie turned, she found Darcy standing directly before her. He appeared to move with difficulty with each step taken. Nonetheless, her heart raced in sensing him so near.

"It seems you are married too," Darcy said, turning to glance around the room. "Is your husband here?" He turned back to her. "I had hoped to meet him."

"Had you?" Maggie said, feeling only slightly unhinged, though secretly wanting to run from the room. "He is at the tavern with his friends."

Darcy chuckled. "Typical Irishman, I see," he said, glancing down at the floor and back up into her eyes as he whispered, "However is the smuggling business these days?" his tone goading before he quickly glanced away.

Sadness welled up from deep inside her as she considered what might have been. She was surprised that her feelings for Darcy had not changed. "My husband farms with my father and cares not for smuggling. It seems that you have been ill informed."

His looked puzzled and tried to stand taller. Suddenly, he winced and faltered slightly.

Instinctively, Maggie reached out and touched his arm. "Are you all right?" she inquired, as her stomach reminded her of her need to eat something soon. Before long, it would be time for her to nurse Aidan.

"I am fine," Darcy said, "Though perhaps I should sit down for a spell."

"Of course," she said, instantly wanting to help him while managing to restrain herself.

Haltingly, Darcy moved on down the line to briefly speak with each member of her family before he made his way to a chair on the side of the room.

Instruments tuned and music soon played. The guests dispersed around the candlelit room with its highly polished floors. Toasts were made with champagne. Then a tasty supper of corned beef and cabbage was served before the wedding cake. Champagne was constantly served, along with generous rounds of whiskey.

After her father danced with Megan, he danced with her. Then, Maggie danced with each of her brothers in turn. Everyone seemed to be having a merry time. More than once, Maggie caught Darcy watching her with questions in his bright blue eyes. Perhaps he remembered how they had danced so many times at the ball.

After again dancing with young Sean, Maggie rested on a chair not far from Darcy. In the corner, her Aunt Brigid was rocking a tram back and forth while tapping her foot to the music. Sensing her breasts filled with milk, Maggie wondered if Darcy had noticed the matronly change in her figure. Events of the past year had made her feel much older than her years. And apparently, Niall had decided to remain at the tavern, which she thought was probably just as well.

Walking over to the tram to speak with her aunt, Maggie said, "It is time for me to nurse. Ona has promised to help me with my dress," and when she turned around, she found Prudence standing directly behind her.

"I must see this child I have heard so much about from his proud, proud uncles, his aunt, his great aunt, and his extremely exuberant grandfather," Prudence said, looking down at Aidan who gurgled and smiled up at her.

"He is four months," Brigid said, "and a handsome bloke already."

"He is beautiful," Prudence said. "Megan says you have named him after his father and yours, Aidan Padraic."

"I fear my sister lacks discretion," Maggie said, flushing slightly.

"Where is your husband?" Prudence inquired. "I should like to meet Aidan. I hear his child has his exact dark hair and dark eyes and not your eyes of amber."

Anxious glances were exchanged between Maggie and her aunt. It seemed that Kevin had honored her confidence and not exposed her sorry situation. Suddenly overcome with a rush of emotion, Maggie wished she could disappear. The thought of telling Prudence the truth at that moment made her feel fully unsettled and quite faint. She could see Darcy watching the two of them from across the room.

Brigid stood and faced Prudence. "Aidan perished with the *Cornelia*. Did you not see the news posted last June, the same month we heard that Darcy was lost at Waterloo?"

"I was in England in June and July," Prudence said. "We feared Darcy might be killed, so I went to the Netherlands to stay with friends." She turned to Maggie in an obvious state of confusion. "You married a McKenna. Matthew said you were married in August."

With tears now coursing down her face, Maggie picked up her son and said, "Kindly excuse me, Prudence, Aidan needs to be fed," and she hurriedly left the ballroom.

Slowly, Prudence turned to Brigid. "Whom did she marry?"

"Maggie was to marry Aidan after his voyage across the sea," Brigid said, briefly hesitating. "You know how young people are nowadays, Prudence, reckless with their passion. After Aidan was lost at sea, we thought it was best for her to marry his cousin. Niall was happy to marry her, even with her four months along." Tears spilled from her eyes. "They are living with me in my cottage near the farm."

"Does Maggie love this Niall?"

"Not much, I fear."

"Not much?" Prudence said and her eyes immediately misted over. "Good God!"

"We all thought it was for the best, you see. At least young Aidan is a McKenna."

"I see," Prudence said, suddenly remembering another time, another unwed pregnant girl, another child whose father was lost forever in the sea. "I must see to my other guests."

Significantly recovered, with her emotions again contained, Prudence circulated among the many other guests in her ballroom at an otherwise joyous occasion.

30

Sailing to America

It was late May when the O'Reilly family traveled over land by horse-drawn wagon and a borrowed carriage to the port of Cobh in County Cork. It was time to bid farewell to Megan and Kevin Gallagher, who were about to set sail for Charleston on the passenger ship *Tranquility*. Everyone prayed that the ship's crossing proved equal to its name, except that the low temperatures, brisk winds and plentiful whitecaps guaranteed only the small chance of an entirely calm passage off the coast of Ireland that day.

A large group had already gathered on the dock: men, women and children of various ages, size and appearance, all warmly dressed. Around 150 passengers were ready to board the ship, along with eighteen crew-members and the ship's physician. The deckhands were busy loading trunks and boxes into cutters to row out to the ship where items were being taken onboard. The shallowness in the harbor prevented the dock-ing of the larger ships that were always anchored some distance off shore.

Some of the young couple's furnishings and the bulk of their wed-ding gifts were shipped on a vessel heading for Charleston the prior week. Because of the unruly weather, the captain had announced that more than six weeks might be required to reach Charleston Harbor. Spring was late

that year, already delaying planting, with many of the farmers doubtful that spring would ever arrive. The fields had not yet greened for the
livestock to graze.

Fiddles and banjos were playing up and down the dock, with mer-
riment in the air. Some sang or danced a reel near the weather-beaten
building. And yet, many on the pier that day wore long, solemn faces.
Several O'Reilly's were weeping half the way to Cobh, with Brigid unable
to stem the flood. By that time all had assembled, with Kevin and Megan
about to climb into the cutter, no one was more distraught than Padraic
O'Reilly. His green eyes overflowed with tears in his great displeasure
that his youngest daughter was sailing away from him far across the sea.

"You will write to me," her father said for the umpteenth time,
openly weeping.

"Please, Da," Megan said, also crying, and she threw herself into her
father's arms and held on tight as they wept together.

Kevin was also crying, as both of his parents desperately clung to
him. Everyone knew it was farewell forever. No one was able to contain
their grief in losing the young folks to a new way of life in the faraway
land of America.

"You are making me cry even more, Da," Megan said. "You are making everyone cry. Look at what you have gone and done." She tried her
best to smile but could not.

Most of them tried to contain their grief as Megan's tears suddenly
stopped. "I promise to write to you often, Da. I promise," and her head
was once again on her father's shoulder with both of them once again
weeping.

The Gallaghers, the Courtneys, and every O'Reilly tried to be brave
and strong. Most had traveled some distance to bid Megan and Kevin
farewell. The last hours with the two of them were beyond dear to everyone present.

"I shall write," Maggie said, hugging and kissing her sister, and then
she hugged Kevin and kissed his cheek. "Dear Kevin, do take very good
care of my sister."

"I shall do my very best, I promise," Kevin said, protectively putting
his arm around Megan.

"I shall write to you, too," Matthew said, and he hugged and kissed
Megan.

"I hope you can read my handwriting," Sean said to Megan. "I shall do my best. Maggie has promised to help me." For a long moment, he clung to his sister.

"You must practice your penmanship, Sean," Megan said, gazing into his sad face.

"I shall help him," Maggie said, "but Sean needs to go to school and learn more."

"I will ... I promise," Sean said.

"Maggie will read you my letters," Megan called out to Niall, who had stayed some distance from the others.

Since seeing Darcy at her wedding, Megan had felt true pity for her sister, for she had never had any affection for Niall. Her stepmother, Eileen, was standing off to one side, coughing, with none of her children there. The seven of them had been enough to fill the wagon and the carriage, along with the three trunks now taken onboard ship.

Soon Megan and Kevin boarded a cutter with other passengers and were rowed out to the ship. Many already on deck were waving to their loved ones on shore, until the ship finally set sail for the open Atlantic.

On that day, hundreds had gathered to grieve, keening as if attending a wake, for a wake it was for the greater number. Husbands and wives, daughters and sons, aunts, uncles, cousins and friends had little chance of ever seeing them in their native Ireland again.

Standing together on the dock, all of them watched the great, white, square-rigged sails grow smaller and smaller as the ship disappeared into the distant gray mist. Soon, rain started to fall, lightly at first, and then harder, forcing everyone to seek shelter in the overcrowded tavern. After a pint or two, a loaf of bread and a bowl of stew, nearly everyone left for their various villages and farms.

The seven members of the family left behind, trying to cope with their heartfelt sorrow, were soon back in the wagon and carriage to head over the sodden Irish hills for the Dingle Peninsula and home.

31

The Year Without a Summer

The whole month of May the winds blew brisk off the bay, as well as all across the North Atlantic. The temperatures remained well below normal, not only in Ireland but in England, and seemingly, throughout the entire world. Early June, the ground was still hard and unyielding to hoe or plough, making it nearly impossible to plant crops to feed the creatures and the people. Animals sought shelter from the cold huddled together for added warmth with their kind. Peat constantly burned upon the hearth, the winter being nearly unbearably extended.

The first week of June, meager shoots of grass sprouted from the nearly useless soil, with ice and snow flurries still intermittent out of the threatening, dark skies. There was no promise of a rainbow, with the skies only an occasional pale blue, white and gray being the predominant colors. Trees bereft of foliage appeared to shiver from the freezing wind, the ancient oaks still in groves resistant at any attempt to uproot them. Even minimal effort of shrub or tree to bloom was instantly destroyed by the errant, demoniacal forces of nature. The old gods and new gods seemed greatly displeased with all the vegetation, the creatures, and with every earthly inhabitant that year.

Supplies of grains, vegetables, sprouts and potatoes grew scarce around the peninsula, which became cause for alarm. The counties in the north suffered more than those in the south, Kerry and Cork respectively, where the sea warmed so exotic flowers and shrubs generally bloomed enhanced by the Gulf Stream. Every church was filled with astonishing regularity: Farmers and merchants, peasants and gentry, Irish, Scot and English urgently prayed together for a radical change in the weather. Everyone longed to feel the force of the sun and its radiance on their faces and backs as it warmed the field to the plough, so that the animals might graze upon the now less than fruitful land of the Great Mother.

With diligence, magical rituals were performed at the time of the new and full moons, along with the tracing of unusual signs in the soil with an oak branch, with herbal mixtures sometimes sprinkled in the fields and over the animals. That year it seemed the secret fires of Beltaine had done nothing to appease Bel, the *Shining One*. Nature spirits and the various gods of the Otherworld were constantly petitioned to prepare the land for planting, with the goddess Danu called upon daily. Prayers were repeated at Mass, before meals, and on their knees every night. Special incantations were spoken aloud thrice, in English and in Gaelic, for a fortnight between the new and full moons, which appeared to only increase Niall's apprehension over the forbidden pagan practices of his strange and uncaring wife and her equally odd aunt. And yet, he too was willing to try anything to bring the warmth of the sun back to Ireland.

Seedlings in boxes and pots were placed near the fire to encourage growth. Finally, late June a few plants were set out in the ground near the cottage with a windbreak made of old cloth tied between posts. Summer had still not found its way to Erin, with prospects that the weather might never warm, which was a frightening concern for everyone throughout the land.

When Sean brought the invitation from Prudence to invite Maggie to the house for tea that afternoon, she was taken aback. Somewhat tearful, she asked her aunt to accompany her to town.

Her Aunt Brigid was quick to decline, "And who would be taking care of young Aidan, I ask you," she declared, carefully measuring out her vanishing favorite: raspberry tea. "I need to watch over these seedlings. Niall knows nothing of planting. Matthew tells me that the man is useless with the cows as well. Anything Niall does is by half or less by measure. A sorry lot he is, a man who must be told everything thrice. His mother was no doubt on the sauce while carrying him or his brain was damaged in the delivery! His father is a brawler and wife beater, hear tell. And your Niall picks a fight in the pub over apparently nothing at all."

"If he ever hits me, he's as good as a dead man," Maggie said. "Poison him, I will." She was playing with Aidan on her lap, tickling him, as he happily responded to her touch.

Brigid was watching the two of them. "A fine son you have. Aidan is a true treasure."

The babe now nursed at his mother's breast as Maggie said, "Mine was not a marriage of choice, if you remember rightly. I care nothing for his parents and near nothing for him."

"Well, at least I hope he has finally had his way with you. It is time. Niall is your husband."

"His way with me, indeed? Whatever makes you think him capable of performing such an act?"

Her aunt looked surprised. "Not quite a man, is he?" She made a face. "Can't say that I'm particularly surprised. Gave him some of your herbs, did you?"

"I did not!" Maggie said in a loud voice that startled Aidan. Soon, she was handing her son over to her aunt and removing her woolen coat from its peg. "I will not stay long enough to make him terribly hungry. I will just be gone a couple of hours."

"At least the rain has stopped," Brigid said, studying her niece. "So Niall has never consummated your marriage?" Her expression was one of amused curiosity.

"Limp as a baby. No need for herbs. No passion. He is completely unmanly. I'm amazed that his blood is the same as Aidan's, the man who wanted me always. No doubt Niall has the same blood as his drunken parents."

"I am sorry I insisted you marry him. Truly, I am."

"Not as sorry as I am for not listening to the spirits who warned me, the feelings I had on my wedding day told me I was making a horrible mistake. I should have signed on as an indentured servant and gone to America to have my son, but the past is the past."

"You would have broken your poor father's heart in two. I'm glad you didn't run off like Liam. Yet, with all those many letters that Niall has you writing to his uncle in Baltimore, perhaps you will end up in America just the same."

"If I'm lucky. The rain has stopped. I will give Prudence your best, Aunt Brigid. Please tell Aidan a story. He loves to listen to the sound of your voice."

And she was out the door walking briskly toward Dingle.

The parlor looked much the same, except for the newly purchased mahogany lamp table. The piano was just the same, though Maggie had not played on it for nearly a year. She thought she might have forgotten how to play. And yet, Prudence was as lovely as ever.

Ona entered the room. "The pot is filled with Earl Grey, your favorite, ma'am," she said, placing a platter with slices of chocolate cake and sugar cookies on the table. She appeared pleased to see her.

"Flour is hard to come by this year due to the horrible weather," Prudence said, "I still purchase eggs and dairy products from your farm," she added, handing Maggie a steaming gold embossed cup of tea on a lacy gold saucer. "The chickens are a true blessing, and at least keep us fed."

"New cups?" Maggie inquired, admiring the delicate flowers.

"A purchase in London last summer while I was there."

The fire warmed the room, with Prudence seated opposite her, making her feel as though nothing had changed. "Lovely cups," Maggie remarked.

"I suppose you've heard nothing from Megan and Kevin as yet?" Prudence inquired.

"No," she replied, "I doubt they have reached Charleston yet with all the wind and rain. My hope is that the wind pushed the ship swiftly across the Atlantic in a record's time."

"A pleasant thought! Each of them has promised to write to me. Kevin is such a delight, and the two of them are so charming together. They seem a perfect match."

"A perfect match," she softly repeated, helping herself to a cookie and savoring its sweetness, such delicacies non-existent on the farm of late.

"Would you care for a slice of cake?"

"Aye! It looks delicious. Your Margret is such an excellent cook and a fine baker, indeed."

Prudence handed her a plate with cake. "Did Megan happen to tell you of Darcy's engagement?"

At that moment, Maggie could swear her heart skipped a beat. She tried to chew. "She did not," she said, swallowing and immediately reaching for her tea to wash it down. The cake seemed lodged in her throat.

"Therese is from the town of Bath, England. Therese Winthrop. She was a nurse in the hospital where Darcy spent so many months of his recovery. She was unable to make the journey here to attend the wedding because of a fever that puzzles the doctors. She is apparently still recovering from some undiagnosed illness."

"How sad," Maggie said, trying to conceal her true feelings. "When do they plan to marry?" She had another bite of cake, while trying not to think about the unfortunate situation, all the while thinking: *Darcy is planning to marry someone. Darcy is engaged!*

"The wedding is planned for September. Leastwise, that is what Darcy wrote to me in his last letter. He only stayed here for three days, though I tried hard to talk him into staying longer. He was concerned about Therese, which is only to be expected, of course."

"Of course," Maggie repeated. "It must have been wonderful to have him here with you for three days." She gulped some tea. "Has he fully recovered from his many wounds? It has been a year since Waterloo. I see that he now walks with a cane. Does his leg bother him much? He winced when he took one step at the reception." All the questions rushed out of her at once.

"We nearly lost him," Prudence solemnly said, placing her cup on the table and raising a lace-edged handkerchief to her teary eyes. "It is a miracle that Darcy still lives."

"Last year, I heard that he was dead," Maggie whispered, "Ona told my brothers."

"He was listed as dead ... then as missing, and finally wounded. Most men in his division perished, horrible wounds made them essentially unrecognizable from all the canons and explosions, not easy to identify."

"War is horrible, bloody business."

"Indeed," Prudence said, and momentarily, she appeared to study her. "And your young man perished at sea. He was lost on the *Cornelia*."

Unable to hold back her tears any longer, Maggie said, "Aye," placing the unfinished cake on the table. "All the crew was lost in a terrible storm," she said and she began to weep.

"With you carrying his child?" the question came as a whisper.

"Aye," her voice trembled as the tears now flowed.

"I know about those things, Maggie. You know about my Rory and my sweet Juliet. Why did you not come to me?" her voice broke. "Did our friendship mean so little?" Tears coursed down her cheeks and she dabbed at her eyes.

"You ordered me out of your house, Prudence. That didn't make me feel that I could freely turn to you again in my time of need."

"I was foolish. I knew that Darcy loved you ... I thought you loved him. You acted like you did." Prudence was also crying. "I am so very sorry, Maggie, so very, very sorry."

Both of them were crying, looking at one another through their tears.

"I did love him," Maggie said. "But I never thought that Darcy would ever marry me, the daughter of a tenant dairy farmer? He wrote of taking me to America but he never mentioned marriage. He never wrote that he loved me, Prudence. Why would a gentleman like Darcy ever marry a girl like me?"

Prudence stood and went to the settee to sit beside her. Reaching out, she took Maggie into her arms. "He would have married you, Maggie. I know he would have. Please forgive my selfish, foolish anger. It was not right for me to treat you in that manner."

Pulling back, Maggie stared into her tear-filled green eyes. "When I was carrying another man's child? Aidan and I were sweethearts since we were children. How can any man love a woman enough to marry her when she is carrying another man's child even if the man is dead?"

"I think Darcy loved you that much. I never should have told him of Aidan when he was ready to go into battle. It was stupid and selfish of me. I was angry with you, but I never should have written to him of your smuggler. Darcy nearly died because of that letter. For a few moments, he didn't want to live anymore. That is what he told me when he was here at the wedding."

Her entire body began to shake and Maggie began to sob, uncontrollably.

"I am so sorry, Maggie, so terribly, terribly sorry. I ruined everything."

"No! It is my fault. I was the one who spoiled everything by being careless, and now I am married to a moron I despise. I will never love Niall. Never!" she cried out, leaping to her feet and gathering up her cloak that she quickly wrapped around her.

"You poor child, I am so very sorry that you married him."

"I thought they were dead, both of them, Aidan and Darcy. My family insisted that I marry Niall. It seemed I had no choice." Pulling her cloak more securely around her, Maggie said, "I hope Darcy and his nurse are very happy together. I wish him the very best. You will tell him that for me, won't you, Prudence?"

Prudence stood. "I shall tell him what you said."

"It is nearly time to nurse my child. He is a fine and healthy boy, my Aidan. I shall never regret bringing him into this world. I love him dearly."

"I am sure that you do. He is a handsome child."

"Thank you for the tea and the cake. It was lovely of you to invite me," Maggie said, starting for the door.

"You will come back again soon, will you not? We haven't played on the piano together for such a long time." Tears streamed down her lovely face.

"I may not even remember how to play, Prudence."

"You will remember. Perhaps you can bring Aidan with you. Ona could help to look after him. I am sure she would like that."

"Perhaps I will bring him, if summer ever comes. Good day to you, Prudence."

"Good day to you, Maggie. May the good Lord watch over and protect you always."

Out in the crisp, gray daylight, Maggie hurried down the road toward the farm where her young son was waiting.

32

A Wake for Cobh

Summer never arrived that year. The months of July and August more closely resembled early springtime, warming the air and soil only slightly. Some crops reached stunted fruition. The cows tried to graze and the chickens pecked for nourishment. Fewer insects seemed a blessing, with useful herbs scarce in the meadows and woodlands. The newspapers reported that people had frozen or starved to death in different parts of the world, especially in New England in America settled by the English.

Three newborns arrived in the month of July. Four more babies were delivered by the second week of August, three boys and four comely girls increased the local population that summer. The long, cold winter had kept the unguarded in bed, with snakeroot in short supply to hasten the deliveries. Maggie did her best for the women. Her midwifery helped with the purchase of imported cloth from England, with her husband pleased with his new shirt of light blue cotton.

Niall tried his best to warm to her, but Maggie continued to avoid his kisses and his lightest touch. There was no reason for her to search for Queen Anne's lace to forestall conception, for Niall was impotent, which only made her loathe him that much more. What use was he to her, no farm worker and no true husband? Maggie had never intended to marry a brother, knowing her own to be able men from hearing them boast of their conquests. Sean, only ten, now dreamed of nude maidens, which seemed a good sign to Maggie. She doubted Niall had ever enjoyed such nocturnal delights and surmised a childhood illness had robbed him of his manhood.

"I am serious about going to America to make my fortune," Niall said at supper one evening in August, after he had spent the better part of the day in the pub. "I have enough money for passage to Baltimore for the three of us," he said, "I have no plan to leave young Aidan here behind, I can assure you, my wife."

Wife indeed, Maggie thought. "I would surely never go anywhere without him. You must know that." She narrowed her eyes and turned away in disgust.

"I would never expect you to go anywhere without him," he sullenly responded.

"I have thought of going to America ever since Liam left. But what would I do while you work for your uncle? Such work requires great strength. Are you sure you can do it?"

"There are many jobs to be had in Baltimore, much more attractive than shoveling manure. I could work on a tobacco plantation or in the mercantile shop of Carl, my cousin, stocking shelves."

"And what of me?"

"You shall be a midwife, of course. Surely there are many babies also born in Baltimore. There have to be herbs, for America is fertile. You have read the letters. My uncle and aunt want us there, the sooner the better. I have booked passage out of Cobh on the tenth of September."

"The tenth of September!" Brigid screeched. "Is your father to lose two daughters in the same year? Saints preserve us!"

Padraic was deeply distraught at the prospect of losing his Maggie. But all the packing was accomplished within a fortnight. The three of them were ready to set sail on the brig *Pegasus* on September 10th. After passengers embarked at Liverpool, the ship would anchor at Cobh to pick up the rest of the passengers leaving for Baltimore, Maryland, in America.

"You are leaving in another week?" Prudence said, bouncing Aidan on her knee. "Is this not a rather sudden change of plans?"

"Aye, truly sudden," Maggie said, her eyes misting over at the thought of leaving everyone behind.

Prudence kissed Aidan on the forehead and hugged him. "Your father is losing another daughter and son. That cannot be easy for Padraic, both daughters leaving him in one year. Poor Padraic!" Prudence hugged Aidan again, turning his face to gaze into his brown eyes, kissing his nose and each cheek in turn.

"Young Aidan shall miss all your loving," Maggie said.

Her eyes filled with tears. "Here I am just getting to know him and he is being taken away from me. It is such a shame for the both of us," Prudence said, pulling him close, their bond strong from the first.

"My father is not at all pleased that Niall surprised us with this. But Niall is a poor milkman, his hands apparently unfit for the task. I hope he can manage to unload a boat, which requires simple brute strength. But he rarely listens and can be quite rude. He is greatly lacking in common sense. It was I who wrote the letters. I doubt that his Uncle Lucius knows anything as to his considerable limitations. I wonder if the Guinness has perhaps not dimmed his wits earlier than usual in a man."

"I am sure he has neglected to mention his shortcomings to his uncle and aunt. At least Niall seems smart enough to conceal the truth from them."

"He sings my praises, promising his uncle a fine midwife who knows herbs and how to read and write. Niall can barely scribble his name and refuses to let me teach him. He brags about Aidan, 'his son, a fine lad who will grow up to be tall and strong.'" Maggie sighed. "It is his true father he speaks of, Aidan Brendan McKenna."

Prudence placed the child on the carpet so he might crawl around. Aidan smiled up at her, perhaps to better secure her heart. Subtle traits of his father were surfacing in her son, Maggie thought. The lad was definitely a charmer, and momentarily, content to play with the wooden blocks with bright letters given to him by his Aunt Prudence, in addition to the brown teddy bear with a blue ribbon around its neck.

"You are too kind with all your fine gifts, enough clothes for him to wear for years from your dressmaker in London, in so many different sizes and colors that he will be handsomely dressed for some time to come, my young ruffian." Maggie gathered her son up into her arms. "I can hardly wait to read him the nursery rhymes from the fine book you gave to him."

"I hope you both enjoy them."

"You are coming to the wake my father insists upon, are you not? Your elegant wake for Megan and Kevin was grand indeed. Father says he can never repay you or thank you enough for what you did for Megan and Kevin."

"I shall be at your wake. How could I ever let you and Aidan go to America without a proper good-bye from me? I fear I shall never see you or your fine young son again." Tears spilled from her eyes and ran down the face of a woman that Maggie felt she was unlikely to forget for the rest of her life.

Folks began arriving from miles around, nearly every O'Reilly and every McKenna attended the wake, in addition to nearly everyone else in the town. Most of them had watched Maggie grow up, plus all the mothers and fathers with the children she had assisted in entering this world. Everyone was sad that Maggie was leaving and would no longer be in their lives.

Fiddles, bagpipes and drums played. The whiskey flowed. There was dancing and singing as her father played on his bagpipes. Brigid played the Kelly harp, singing her mournful tunes in Gaelic, which served to remind Maggie of their many good times together.

"I am mourning the three of you," Padraic said, wrapping his arms around his bonny daughter, "First Liam, then Megan, and now you, my sweet, sweet Maggie. All of you are leaving me forever. Never again shall I see my sweet children, not even as I breathe my last breath on this earth."

"You may see us again, Da," Maggie said, tears filling her eyes, for her father was still strong and seemed young for his forty-four years. He was every bit as handsome as her mother had always said, "You are still the handsomest man in all of Ireland," Maggie teased, and she kissed his cheek.

"At least I know where my Megan is," Padraic lamented. "She wrote me a nice long letter and told me of her safe arrival in Charleston with Kevin on the *Tranquility*. A fine letter my daughter wrote in a very graceful hand. I shall endeavor to improve upon my penmanship and write back to you with Brigid's help." He placed his arm around Brigid, pulling her close to him as his wife cast a disapproving glance at his sudden display of affection for his former sister-in-law.

Everyone was aware that Eileen had never fully accepted Brigid as a part of the family, though Maggie suspected her father's love for her aunt was still strong within his heart. Brigid was like a sister to him, with Eileen a woman often jealous and filled with envy. In that respect, the only thing Eileen received from Maggie was her pity.

"You shall have my full assistance any time you wish," her aunt said to her father, slurring as she downed another whiskey, puffing on their mutual pipe, with a look of triumph cast at Eileen, who still had not learned how to read or write.

"I expect you to write to me often," her father said, his arms over Maggie's shoulders, his eyes lovingly gazing into her eyes. "Only God knows where my Liam is in this great big world, perchance he is dead and gone, his bones lying on the bottom of the sea."

"Stop your worrying, Padraic," Brigid said. "Forget about Liam."

"Liam is still alive, Father," Maggie said. "It is something I just know."

"Perhaps," he said, taking in a deep breath. "This day I shall mourn all my children, knowing that I shall never again see your bonny face for the rest of my days. You shall be gone and never return to your father or to your beloved Ireland."

"I will return one day, Da. It is something I know in my bones. I will not be buried in the ground of Ireland, but burned upon an altar of stones as in olden times, my ashes scattered in Dingle Bay so my spirit might wander and embrace the whole of Ireland and my loved ones here forever."

"You are a strange lass, Mary Margaret, but I love you just the same. There is little likelihood that I shall be here to grant you your final request."

"I love you with all my heart, Da. Perchance, we should both leave our fate up to destiny."

Having apparently overheard her remarks, Father Hennessey turned to Maggie with a scowl and said, "You must be buried in the ground to await the second coming, Mary Margaret McKenna. Renounce your pagan thought of burning your body. Your body shall be needed for the resurrection of our Lord and Savior Jesus Christ when He returns at the Last Judgment." His breath reeked of whiskey as he stared into her eyes.

"I cannot imagine the Savior wanting my old, decaying bones in the Kingdom of Heaven, Father, after the worms are done with it. However, on this, the eve of my departure, I have no wish to engage in a religious discussion with the likes of you, since everything is actually in the hands of the Lord, don't you agree, Father Hennessey?"

Standing taller, she observed his bloodshot eyes and said, "The crew of the *Cornelia* perished in the sea. What pray tell me happens to good Roman Catholics at the resurrection when their body has been eaten by sharks and crabs and other fishes? Countless men, women, and children have drowned in the sea. Will the sharks and crabs spit them out at the time of the resurrection?" she inquired in a tone of defiance.

Narrowing his eyes, Father Hennessey said, "You and your smart questions, I do not recall hearing from you in the confessional of late. Perchance you would like to confess your sins before crossing the sea in such foul weather in order to insure the eternal safety of your soul?"

"I have nothing to confess or to fear for my soul. You must kindly excuse me, for I see some cousins just arriving. Thank you for coming, Father Hennessey, and may God bless you."

"God bless you," he said, turning to refill his glass with more whiskey.

It was a fine gathering. Everyone seemed to have sincere affection for Maggie and her husband. However, Niall was in a drunken stupor by ten o'clock. All planned to awaken at dawn to board the wagon and buggy to Cobh. The ship's departure was mid-afternoon. Eileen wanted to stay home because of the poor weather. Neither would Niall's family be there, though the less she saw of them, the better, she thought. Her hope was that Niall might greatly improve far away from his unpleasant relations.

Each brother, Matthew, and then Sean Joseph, spent time with Maggie to express their love and sincere affection for their sister. Late that night, her Aunt Brigid took her aside and gave her a shiny silver pentacle on a silver chain to wear throughout the voyage.

"You shall not tell Father Hennessey, no confessions, aye? It is our little secret, yours and mine. You must wear it daily for your protection."

"It is beautiful, Aunt Brigid. I shall treasure it and wear it forever."

"It will protect you while crossing the sea, so Manannan, god of the sea, our blessed Danu, and the sacred Mother Mary shall all watch over you and your young son, Aidan Padraic. I shall miss you more than I have words to say, Maggie, and I shall greatly miss young Aidan as well. That bonny lad is sure to grow up to be a handsome man, indeed. I see a bright future for young Aidan and for you. Your son shall make you proud one day, I can guarantee it."

Warmly embracing her aunt, Maggie kissed each of her cheeks. "How can I thank you enough for all you have done for me, for all the many things you have taught me? You are a fountain of wisdom and have been a wonderful mother to us all. You are the best teacher of the sacred mysteries in the entire world."

"The entire world?" Brigid chided.

"Well, at least in all of Ireland."

"You are taking your book with you with the drawings and the writings about the herbs?"

"Aye! How could I ever remember them all without you and my book to remind me?"

"You have been like a daughter to me, Maggie, one that makes me mightily proud. You shall be in my prayers each and every moment, and I promise you that for the rest of my days."

"I love you, Aunt Brigid. I shall write of things to you that you must not reveal to Da or my brothers. You have always been my confessional. It is your love that has given me courage when I needed it the most to be brave. To me, your heart is the heart of all Ireland."

"I am very proud of you, Maggie, so very proud."

Again they hugged, smiling at each other through their tears.

As Brigid walked away, her father approached her and they sat together near the fire. Reaching into his pocket, Padraic removed a small gold cross on a gold chain that had once belonged to her mother. Unclasping the chain, he placed the cross around her neck and kissed the side of her head. Then he wrapped his arms around her and held her close.

"I know that your mother wants you to have it," her father said. "You are her namesake and you look so much the same as she did when the both of us were very young and very much in love. We prayed for a daughter and you finally came to us, bringing us great joy and gladness. Never a day goes by when I don't remember your mother with the deepest of love and gratitude in my heart. I know she has somehow helped me over the years from where she is in the Otherworld." He now looked deeply into Maggie's eyes. "It was your grandmother's cross I gave to Megan, which only seemed right at the time."

"Aye, Father. Megan treasures the cross and the memory of great grandmother Kelly. One day the cross will belong to her daughter and remain in the family for generations to come."

"That will be a very good thing indeed."

Both of them stood, quietly facing each other, and her father grasped her shoulders and gazed steadily into her eyes. "Wherever do you get your courage, my daughter, losing Aidan, the man you loved most in this world, and having to marry Niall, and now, you are leaving for America? Wherever does your courage come from, Mary Margaret Kathleen Kelly O'Reilly McKenna?"

"From you and from my mother and from the Kellys, perhaps," Maggie softly said, tears streaming down her face as she recalled her despair on the night that Aidan was lost at sea. Now, she was leaving her father and her family, going off to America with a man she could never love. Suddenly, an intense sense of fear gripped her. Was she mad to sail away on the next day beneath the cold, gray September skies?

"I am so sorry that you lost your true love," her father said. "Aidan was a fine young man in spite of him being a smuggler. I was afraid you would one day lose him to a hangman's noose. Your boy looks so very much like him. Young Aidan shall keep your Aidan ever present as he grows to be a man, just as you have always reminded me of my eternal love for your beautiful, wonderful mother."

"I never want to forget Aidan, Da," she whispered, "We were together before, so it is likely we will be together again someday. All of us will be together again, including you and my beautiful mother."

It was the first time that her father had spoken of Aidan and expressed any sorrow for her loss. Briefly, Maggie tremble deep down inside, considering all she had been through in just the past year. Silently, she prayed for the courage to face a brand new future in a brand new land.

Awake in her bed late that night, Maggie remembered the sweet glow in her father's eyes that revealed the depth of his love for her. His love would surely help to sustain her. It was the first time he had called her Mary Margaret since the terrible night when young Sean Joseph was born and her dear mother had died, taking her gentle strength and beguiling smile into the Otherworld.

That night before her departure for America, her mother came to her in her dream, promising her a safe journey beyond the sacred Isle of the Blessed in the West and leaving a sprig of fresh lavender on her pillow.

33

Sorrow at Sea

The voyage started out smoothly enough, with the weather calm and the sun shining in a bright blue Irish sky. The ship was larger than most that had stopped at Cobh. The Braque, the *Pegasus,* was a three-masted, square-rigged sailing vessel larger by far than the *Tranquility,* providing for 255 passengers and a crew of twenty-two for the crossing to Baltimore.

The passengers hailed from many nations other than England and Ireland, some from Scotland, Wales, Holland, Germany and Austria, still others from Spain, Italy and France. Never before had Maggie met anyone but Darcy with Scottish blood. She found the brogue and mannerisms charming. To her, Darcy always sounded more Irish, and secretly, she regarded English accents as sounding snobbish. After 700 years of English rule, her father still called them the "foreign invaders," an outlook apparently shared by many Irishmen since Strongbow first arrived with his troops in 1167.

Highly inquisitive and eager to explore all aspects of travel on her first voyage at sea, Maggie soon learned the distinguished-looking Captain Randolph Smithers, with his dark eyes and dark wavy hair with a dash of gray, could speak twelve languages, including Hindi, Arabic and

Chinese. That was a thoroughly remarkable discovery for a young woman formerly confined to life on the Dingle Peninsula.

The ship's physician, Dr. Frederick Hoffman, hailed from an English mother and German father. His light blue eyes were filled with light and his gray haired head bald on top. He was fluent in English, French, German, Italian and Irish, with enough knowledge of Spanish to converse with those passengers onboard. Considering both the captain and the doctor, conversation seemed possible with every passenger on the ship, which she thought was splendid. The captain announced the ship was fast. He expected to reach Baltimore in less than two months, six weeks, perhaps. The prior return voyage to Liverpool required only an astonishing thirty-nine days.

The gusty, wind-filled sails made the shoreline of Ireland rapidly recede into the distance. Standing at the back of the ship, holding Aidan, who played with the long strands of her hair lifted by the wind, Maggie was feeling melancholy as she watched her homeland fade from view. She tried her best not to weep. Instead, she showed young Aidan how to wave at the vanishing island, the emerald green gem at the western edge of the sea that would always be home. She hoped to return one day, perhaps both of them would sometime return to their blessed Ireland.

The cramped accommodations in steerage were a huge disappointment for Maggie. Discolored gray curtains separated one small cubicle from those on either side. They were to sleep on thin mattresses. There was no privacy. The other women shared her qualms. Everyone tried to adjust, since no one had any other choice in the matter.

The air smelled dank. The number of people below deck produced a mustiness of human odors, which made it difficult for her to breathe. Knowing the closeness to be unhealthy, Maggie planned to often seek out the deck above and walk the length and breadth of the ship, 177 by thirty-six feet, more spacious by far than any ship in Dingle, much larger than the *Cornelia*.

She encouraged Niall to take some air. However, he complained of the dampness from the sea spray and chose to stay below. Early on the morning of their departure, Maggie had placed her mother's gold cross and her aunt's silver pentacle around her neck beneath her dress, with the lavender tucked into her pocket to keep her mother near. In her center,

Maggie felt everything would go well for her and young Aidan. Niall too, perhaps. However, nearly the moment the ship was boarded, Niall started to act even more sullen and distant, which added to her anxiety. She felt lonely and alone, except for her happy, smiling son. She already missed her aunt and her family. Weather permitting, Maggie walked the deck with young Aidan to watch the crew fulfill their many different tasks onboard the ship at sea.

To dispel her sense of loneliness, Maggie began to converse with total strangers, at first, mostly the Irish. Most of them shared her misgivings, along with her sense of adventure in going to America, the greatest adventure for them all. Never before had she met so many Irish from so many different counties and cities, mostly Protestant. After a few days, Maggie was speaking with the English too, knowing that language was mostly spoken in America. Before long, she was speaking to as many people as were willing to share her hopes and her fears. Many had relatives waiting for them. Among the Spanish, French and Italian were mostly Roman Catholics. She was unsure of how much of a Catholic she truly was and thought it best to keep such thoughts strictly to herself onboard the *Pegasus*.

Members of the crew were of interest to her. But the seamen were forbidden to fraternize with the passengers. A few officers seemed to find the young Mrs. McKenna a delight with her many questions: What was it like to spend their life at sea? Where did they hail from? Did they have a wife or sweetheart at home? How often did they write to their families? And about the grand *Pegasus* itself built in Belfast. Maggie was pleased to be on an Irish ship with its great, white, square-rigged sails, a ship named after a mythical horse with wings. For a fact, the ship seemed to fly swiftly before the wind across the Atlantic toward the distant shores of America. They were sailing toward a democratic country whose laws promised liberty and justice. Men, women, and children from many lands immigrated to America every year. Surely, America must be a land of unlimited opportunity.

By the end of the first week, Niall had found some drinking buddies who also brought along bottles of whiskey, all of them Irish. The four men spoke only Gaelic, the same as Niall, who preferred to avoid using English. They played cards and drank together in a corner with a lantern, often complaining of the wind up on deck and preferring the dim corner in the galley. On Sunday, one officer joined them, which encouraged all of the men to gamble. That troubled Maggie, considering how little they had to start a new life in a strange new land.

For their departure, Niall's relations had presented them only with bottles of liquor, nothing else. The gifts from her family had consisted of linen, lace, blankets, china, pots and pans. Prudence's gift was a fine bowl of sterling silver, so as not to break their friendship, she said. Maggie had always admired the silver on display in Prudence's fine house. The bowl was safely packed away, since Niall was quick to say, "That bowl may be sold to pay our way." Maggie did not share his opinion. All necessities were to be paid for with hard work, she told him. Without Niall's knowledge, coins and notes were also hidden away for safekeeping.

The second week of the voyage, Maggie met Cornelius Finnegan, an Irish doctor emigrating from Tralee. He was tall and slender, open and friendly, with thinning gray hair and a prominent nose beneath his light blue bespectacled eyes.

"My wife Shannon and our four youngest children are already in Baltimore. They left two months ago. I had business because of my recently deceased father in transferring land to my eldest son, Robert. He is happily married. In fact, he and his wife, Ayla, just presented me with my first grandchild, Molly Ann. The bonny lass stole my heart with just one glance."

"Aidan is my father's first grandchild," Maggie said, "which is why it is so difficult for him to let us go to America with my husband. I fear my father took my leaving badly."

"That he would," Cornelius said, glancing toward the horizon of the seemingly endless sea. "You are a midwife, you say, with knowledge of herbs?"

"I am. I hope to secure work along those lines in Baltimore."

"I may be of service through my medical practice. I could use a skilled midwife."

An unexpected change in the weather forced them below. Moving toward her cubicle to put Aidan down for his nap, Maggie happened upon a pregnant Italian woman in another cubicle who seemed to have gone into premature labor.

Dr. Finnegan was at a total loss trying to converse with the hysterical woman. In a few minutes, Dr. Hoffman arrived and asked Dr. Finnegan for assistance. The two doctors were trying to get the frantic woman to the medical quarters on another deck. Screaming in Italian, the middle-aged woman clutched at her belly, her four frightened, young children crying and carrying on inside the cubicle.

"It is her seventh child," Dr. Hoffman said, trying to get the large woman down the narrow aisle. "It does not look good. She is not due for several months."

The woman appeared to scream even louder as the doctor spoke to her in his broken Italian. "I am unfamiliar with her dialect," the doctor explained, wearily shaking his head.

Maggie said to Niall, "Please see that Aidan sleeps."

"Must I?" Niall slurred, reeking of whiskey and tobacco. He was plainly annoyed with all the crying and screaming, with Aidan now starting to fuss, too. "What business is that of yours?" he inquired in a tone of scorn.

"I may be of some assistance," she said to Niall.

He scowled, shrugged, and reluctantly took Aidan from her.

At that point, Maggie followed the doctors and the hysterical woman, along with her husband, all of them making slow progress down the narrow aisle. She noted that the woman was greatly overweight, which was good neither for her or her unborn child.

"I am a midwife," she said to the ship's doctor. "Would you like me to try to help?"

"Please, yes," Dr. Hoffman said.

In her mind, Maggie took stock of the herbs in her satchel, knowing none were capable of stopping premature labor.

The ship's doctor again spoke to the woman in Italian before he turned to Maggie and said, "She has suffered three infant mortalities during the past two years."

"Good God," Maggie said.

The woman's husband was talking to the doctor in frantic Italian, no doubt the same dialect. The doctor told him to stay behind with his daughters while they dealt with his wife who continued to moan and scream.

Finally, they reached the medical quarters on the next deck up.

233

Sadly, that night the woman died from bleeding out, losing her only male child. The husband and her sister cared for the four young girls. All of them were now crying together in Italian, except to Maggie, sorrow sounded the same as it did in Irish.

On the next day, the mother and her child were buried together at sea. Many of the passengers gathered in the lightly falling rain, as the captain spoke the service in his broken Italian. With Maggie and young Aidan wrapped up together in her woolen shawl to watch the service, she remembered other young mothers and babies back in Ireland who had also died too soon.

It was unclear whether it was his drinking or the seasickness that caused Niall to vomit into a bucket all night. For some reason, Maggie was never bothered by the motion of the ship. In fact, the rocking tended to put her to sleep. Young Aidan was a born sailor the same as his father. Perhaps it was in his blood. Many onboard suffered from seasickness, especially during stormy weather. Few seemed to have their sea legs until far into the voyage. There were simply not enough herbs to help them all, and as usual, Niall refused her assistance.

Then, one night it was more than just vomiting. Niall also had dysentery and was running a high fever that made him sweat profusely. In another day, he was fully delirious from the fever.

After entrusting Aidan to one of her new Irish friends, Maggie assisted the ship's doctor in getting Niall to the lazarette, the place onboard for contagious diseases where he was quarantined. Two of his drinking companions had come down the same symptoms: delirium and high fevers, vomiting and dysentery.

"It is typhus," Dr. Hoffman said, adding a weary shake of his head. "A flea borne illness often spread by rats, frequent stowaways on these ships. The illness may also be spread by human body lice."

After another day passed, ten men, including an officer who had played cards with Niall and the other men were all together in the lazarette. All the men were burning up with fever and starting to cry out. After a red rash appeared on their bodies, their pores began to bleed. All the men had the exact same symptoms. Typhus. All were in contact with Niall, sitting together and drinking from the same bottle.

The first man to die was Kenneth, age twenty, from Kildare. He had planned to join his brother in Baltimore.

On the next day, Niall's fever was extremely high and Dr. Hoffman called for Maggie.

"I am sorry," Niall kept saying over and over. "I am sorry, Maggie. I am so very sorry."

"You have no need to be sorry, Niall. I am sorry that you are ill. I wish there was something I could do for you."

"Your herbs? How about your herbs?" he said, his eyes now glazed and unfocussed.

Tears spilled from her eyes, as she shook her head and cried, in part for herself, fearful for her own health and the health of her young son.

"I have never been a proper husband to you," Niall said, shaking his head. "Never!" he cried out. "Do you forgive me, Maggie? Please say that you forgive me."

Knowing exactly what he meant, she said, "I forgive you, Niall," and she took his hand. "I forgive you," she repeated in a whisper.

Moments later, Niall was dead.

Six men died over a period of three days, one after the other, all of them buried at sea. The captain and the doctor did their best to contain the disease. Clothing and bedding from all the compartments was tossed overboard to rid the ship of lice or fleas transmitting the typhus. The compartments scrubbed down with soap and lye. Rats were hunted, killed and tossed into the sea. The primary problem seemed to have been the men themselves, Kenneth Godfrey and his cousin, Cecil, were both crawling with vermin. Their belongings were tossed overboard, except for money and jewelry that the doctor promised to return to their poor Irish families.

After Niall's burial at sea, Maggie was comforted by her newfound friends, especially the Irish. Sympathy was expressed by the captain, the doctor, and other members of the crew. Some said that the dreaded typhus had claimed friends and shipmates before, but never on the *Pegasus*.

When young Aidan first showed signs of a fever, Maggie held him, keening and rocking him back and forth, singing him Irish lullabies. The doctor was unsure of the exact nature of his illness, since the symptoms were not the same. And yet, Aidan had slept in the very same bed as Niall on more than one occasion. That thought frightened her and caused her to constantly rock her child in the newly scrubbed-down cubicle.

With the fever high on the third day, Maggie wrapped young Aidan in a woolen blanket and carried him up onto the deck. First, his father was claimed by the angry sea. Then, Niall was buried in the deep, dark, mysterious water. Maggie was beside herself with the thought of losing her young son. What if they all ended up in the sea, she thought? How would her father in Ireland know what had happened to them on the great *Pegasus* sailing across the Atlantic for America?

A light rain was falling out of an ominous and threatening sky, as Maggie made her way toward the bow of the ship, clutching young Aidan in her arms. If her young son was going to die, then she would die with him. All of them would be together in the great sea: father, mother and child would be with Manannan, god of the sea. That would be the end of it then. Maggie had made her decision.

With tears streaming down her face, she stared down into the dark water rapidly rushing past the bow of the great ship as it swiftly cut through the sea. The full sails were being driven forth by a great wind that was taking the ship farther and farther toward the west, with most of the passengers below deck because of the inclement weather.

At first, she thought she just might jump right in, so that the two of them might quickly drown together. Perhaps they would be knocked unconscious by the ship itself and be quite dead before they even hit the water, before anyone even noticed that they were gone.

She stopped.

Would it not be better for her to go aft of the ship, Maggie wondered? Things might be less messy that way. At least, she might be lucky to have it over and done with quickly enough, for she was simply unwilling to go on living without her young Aidan.

"How is Aidan?" a familiar voice with an Irish accent inquired from directly behind her.

Whirling around, Cornelius Finnegan was standing right behind her. The doctor was bundled up against the weather, whereas she wore only her woolen shawl. She had decided that cumbersome clothing might be bothersome and keep her from her engagement with the dark blue sea.

Cornelius reached out to touch Aidan's forehead. "His fever seems to have broken."

That was when Maggie remembered that the doctor had looked in on her while she was so distraught. Since her plans seemed to have been foiled, her sigh was one of relief.

The doctor placed his hand on young Aidan's cheek and said, "By tomorrow he should be much better," and there was tenderness in his blue eyes.

Placing her cheek against Aidan's, her child did feel nearly normal to her. "Well, I'll be!"

"He has no typhus, Maggie," Cornelius said, looking stern right before he smiled at her.

"Would you happen to be an angel, Cornelius Finnegan?" she inquired, as the rain started to fall harder on her face, "An angel direct from heaven?"

"Just a man," he said, his eyes gentle behind his round spectacles.

"Well, then, you are a man who has just performed a miracle. That's what you are."

"My dear Maggie, how would we Irish ever have survived these many centuries without believing in miracles?" The rain started to fall harder as he added, "I think it is time to go below and get out in of this weather."

"So it is," she said. "So it is."

And that was the end of that on that day.

34

Baltimore

Seated at the desk near the attic dormer window, Maggie gazed out at the gently falling rain that was darkening the cobblestones on the street three stories below. In reflecting upon the various events of the past two months, tears rolled down her cheeks, the same as the raindrops on the windowpanes. Raising a handkerchief to her eyes, she glanced at the off-white paper on the desk, picked up the quill and dipped it in the inkwell. Then, she began to write:

31 October 1816
Samhain

Dearest Father, Brothers and Aunt,
I have so very many things to tell you that it is difficult for me to know exactly where to begin. Strange as it seems, as I write to you on this Eve of Samhain, the first thing you must know is that Niall is dead. After sailing from Ireland for less than three weeks, a tragic illness robbed him of his life. Sad news you must pass on to his family.
It was on a gray day of softly falling rain, suitable to my sorrow, that Niall was buried at sea, along with five of his newfound friends, Irishmen everyone. All of them dead from the same terrible typhus, a swift and horrible disease that induces a high fever and delirium before blood seeps from the

pores. Four other young men survived, escaping death at the very portal to the Otherworld.

So here we are, young Aidan and myself, safe in the City of Baltimore in the State of Maryland in America. I could not bring myself to reside for long with Niall's unclean, ill-tempered, drunken uncle and his shrieking, disheveled, drunken aunt in their miserable quarters not far from a wharf that reeks of dead fish in what has to be the saddest part of this city. Upon discovering the extreme extent of their poverty, I could not bear to place my infant son and myself amid such squalor for fear of catching some terrible disease such as the typhus with both of us soon dead in this foreign land.

Lucius McKenna made me promise to repay the five pounds he loaned to Niall for our passage, something Niall had never disclosed to me. They obviously planned for us to be of unlimited service in improving upon their miserable lot, his uncle's letter written by a scribe to conceal the man's shameful character and his inability to write. I have already given him 3 pounds 10 pence with a promise to pay the remainder within the next three months, a small fortune for me when Niall's relations painted such a glorious picture of their circumstance, which was a true fairy tale, I fear. But fear not that we shall go hungry. Our present circumstances are quite comfortable due to Divine Providence, no doubt with the help of my dearly departed mother and great grandmother Kelly.

I had a bit of luck on the Pegasus in meeting a fine doctor, Cornelius Finnegan from Tralee, who became my guardian angel in intervening with an insufferable Englishman from Liverpool. Not long after Niall's tragic death, Mr. Reynolds, an ugly, fat man with a pockmarked face tried to get me to sign on as an indentured servant, claiming he knew people who wanted someone with my skills on a tobacco plantation five hours from Baltimore on the eastern shore of Maryland. He said I could bring along my child, thinking to get two for the price of one, no doubt.

As you may well already know, an indentured servant is bound to a master for 4 to 7 years before gaining freedom. I knew that for a fact, since I had already inquired into such matters, but the thought of being a servant held no appeal for me when I am a competent midwife who can read and write, plus I know my herbs. Why should I spend my life scrubbing floors, boiling laundry, or doing whatever else some master might require of me?

Fortunately, Dr. Finnegan told Mr. Reynolds that he planned to employ me as a midwife. After discovering the deplorable state at the McKenna's home, I instantly sought out the doctor and accepted his kind offer. My wages include room and board for Aidan and myself in this lovely house in the middle of an area known as Fells Point. So here I am with my young Aidan in the home of Cornelius and Shannon Finnegan and their four lovely children in the middle of Baltimore, nearly 65,000 souls living here, according to the doctor, the third largest city in America with an ever growing population. Never before have I been in such a city as this, though I hear London has well over a million residents now, which is hard for me to even imagine.

There are steamboats here that run with a paddlewheel, no sails at all, right on the Chesapeake Bay. A gentleman opened a foundry to build even more steamboats in Baltimore Harbor. Imagine, Da, boats without sails or oars that glide through the water. Would you not say that is modern, indeed? I live in a grand city of fantastic inventions.

In exchange for our keep and a few shillings a week, I work for the doctor and help Shannon. There is also an Irish indentured servant, Caitlin Culhane from Limerick, who does most of the cleaning, laundry and cooking, and she is not a bad cook. At the outset, Shannon wanted Caitlin to sleep in the cellar, but the attic is large, so I insisted that she stay up here with Aidan and myself unless his crying drives her daft. But you know my sweet lad, he rarely cries. With the door open, the heat rises and keeps us all warm and cozy.

Maggie paused to reflect on her fortunate situation and secured another piece of paper.

Cornelius Finnegan is a fine man ten years your elder, Da. Shannon is a pretty, plump, dark-haired woman still healthy after bearing him eight children, although two died soon after birth. The remaining six children are handsome and smart. His eldest sons are in Ireland to care for his lands and collect rents from his tenant farmers. The Finnegans are not poor, yet they are Irish and have moved to Baltimore in part because of the magical allure of America, a fine land indeed, without the Crown overtaxing the people.

Shannon and the four children arrived two months earlier on the brig Morgan out of Cork. The children living here include two boys and two girls from 8 to 14 in years. The attic has a large window through which I may gaze out upon the activities below as the horses and carriages race by. Most of my belongings are still in the trunk, for I have no real need of them yet.

In Baltimore, there are many fine shops and businesses easily reached on foot. Shannon has loaned me a tram for my Aidan, insisting the boys go with us on outings to see the ships anchored in the harbor. I am pleased to be near the water, except, because of all the many industries you often find the carcass of a dead animal in the harbor and much debris. I miss the sparkling blue sea of Dingle Bay across the road from our farm, for in spite of this being in a port, Baltimore is far inland from the sea. The Atlantic Ocean is much farther from Baltimore than Dingle is from Cork, though portions of the Chesapeake Bay are as wide as the sea and nearly as endless.

There is the Peale Museum in the city which we visited with the Finnegans on Saturday last. The building is lit by gaslights, another grand modern invention. No candles or lamps, but gaslights to illuminate the fine paintings displayed on the walls. People may stay as long as they like long into the night. By next February, the streets of Baltimore are to be illuminated by gaslights! This is the first city in America to have the modern invention! Is that not amazing? I now reside in a wondrous place called Baltimore in America, the land of the free!

I have seen my first Africans, Negroes with skin sometimes black as coal. Some are slaves for those who can afford them. Most were brought by ship from Africa where other tribes sold their own kind into bondage. I have learned the first slaves arrived with the original colonists. Since the Revolutionary War, Americans continue to buy slaves to work in the house, farm the land, raise tobacco or cotton, and even more so in the southern states. Some slaves eventually earn enough to buy their freedom, and many of the free men and women work for a wage or own a business here in Baltimore. Some former slaves even have slaves of their own, and it is truly difficult for me to understand this kind of thinking.

I agree with our Kerryman, Daniel O'Connell, that slavery is a blight upon the human soul and truly unjust. Apparently, in 1808 a law was passed in Great Britain that ruled against importing more Africans as slaves, but that law is not always upheld nor does it stop the slaves from breeding and being sold at an auction. Truly disgraceful! Children of slaves become slaves to serve the same master, which seems a true pity to me. In Baltimore there is an African Methodist Episcopal Church, but Cornelius claims they have their own religion from Africa, an ancient tribal religion I hope to learn more about one day.

Other than the typhus, we suffered from only one bad storm on the voyage that came to its conclusion without injury or serious incident. A pregnant woman was lost in premature labor, along with her only male child. I fear I utterly failed her, Aunt Brigid, leaving her husband with four girls without a mother.

Reflecting on the sad situation, Maggie noticed the rain had stopped and the sun was again illuminating the bright autumn leaves on the trees. She regretted having to write on both sides of the fine stationery, so unlike the letters of Darcy which she still often reread, thinking him most certainly married to his nurse by that time. Again, Maggie began to write:

Other than that, the Pegasus was a fine ship with an excellent crew and a handsome captain. As we prepared to sail into the Chesapeake Bay from the Atlantic Ocean, I took young Aidan up on deck so he could see America. The bay is vast. The ship sailed along the shores of Virginia with its woodlands ablaze in red, orange, yellow and gold. It was beautiful! The air was crisp as we reached Maryland and sailed past island after island, with birds flying overhead, some I had never seen before. Ducks and wild geese were also flying in formation toward the south, so winter seems to be on its way.

All manner of small vessels were all around us, as well as many fishermen, according to the first mate. By the end of the voyage, I was on a first name basis with the officers, some Irish, others English and one Spaniard. The Irish have sailed the seven seas for hundreds of years, Da, as you have always claimed. It is true.

It seems strange to be here at Samhain so far away from my beloved Ireland. Perhaps this evening Niall will visit me in spirit, or Aidan or my mother. We have so many loved ones in the Otherworld. I have seen no fairy rings nor mounds or heard of any here yet. Cornelius says the wee folk prefer the Emerald Isle, though one Scotsman claimed that they dwell in Scotland as well, and also in Wales.

"Maggie!" she heard called from downstairs. "Maggie!" again sounded more loudly.

Opening the door wide, Maggie replied, "Aye?"

"I need you down here in ten minutes," Shannon said. "Kindly finish your letter and come down and lend a hand."

"Right away," Maggie called out, hurrying back to the desk to write:

Kindly share this letter with Prudence and the others. I shall write to each one separately soon. We have a post office nearby where this letter will be taken tomorrow. It is an advantage living in a large town.

I read to the Finnegan children and help them with their penmanship. The Finnegans are Protestant, which is why they retained their land. They insist I attend the Presbyterian Church on Sunday. The Catholic Church is not far away and I have attended Mass only once. The Presbyterian preach-er's sermons are no more comforting, disconcerting, or terrifying than those of Father Hennessey. In the evening, Cornelius reads to us from the Holy Bible, so religion seems to be part of my fate in America. But it is far better than liv-ing in the filth with the drunken relations of a deceased husband and forced to endure the constant smell of dead fish.

I love you all forever. I must have read Megan's letter from Charleston 50 times. Her new home sounds glorious and the hotel shall be a huge success under Kevin's wise management. Her marriage is fortunate. I shall write to Megan next.

Please write soon and keep us in your prayers as you are always in mine.
Yours in love,
Maggie and Aidan
Baltimore – America.

35

A Christmas Surprise

By mid-December, snow dusted the rooftops, trees and shrubs with a sparkling, sticky white that glistened in the frosty light. It was a winter wonderland. Smoke curled from numerous chimneys up and down the street. Horse drawn buggies and carriages sped by over the cobblestone streets, clattering in a clip-clop, clip-clop musical rhythm that broke the monotony of a wintry day inside the warm house.

Three babies were delivered amidst the holiday planning, two hearty boys on the same day, December 18th. Maggie attended the younger mother in the delivery of her second child not far from the Finnegan's house. Cornelius donned his wig and winter cloak, as the new stable boy hitched up Chester, before he climbed into his buggy with his satchel and hurried off to the outskirts of town. The doctor delivered a fifth child to woman of thirty, her second son. The third baby turned out to be a noisy girl where the mother nearly died. Yet, the bleeding miraculously stopped. It was a merry Christmas for a family now with three children, as the two boys welcomed their highly vocal sister. The baby weighed over nine pounds with a full head of dark hair.

In a short period of time, Maggie had proven herself to be a tremendous asset to the doctor's medical practice, especially with her knowledge and use of herbs that he had found superior to his skills. Cornelius suggested that she publish her notebook of herbs and their various remedies, so that other doctors might benefit from them, perhaps throughout the world.

"Throughout the world? Surely there are others with far more knowledge of herbs than my Aunt Brigid and myself!"

"Perhaps the Chinese. I have heard they have astonishing techniques, ancient and profound." Recently, Cornelius had grown a well trimmed beard that distinguished him. "I shall write to my cousin in New York who has a friend in the publishing business. Meanwhile, copy your notebook for me, won't you, please?"

"Perhaps," Maggie replied, and yet, she had already copied her notebook as her Christmas gift to the doctor. It was already wrapped and under the tree.

On Christmas Eve morning, several letters arrived. Maggie was off to the apothecary to pick up some needed herbs. She had separate packets for the kitchen and measured out coltsfoot for a tea to be mixed with honey for Gregory and Stephen's stubborn coughs. Instructions were left with Caitlin to make another pot of tea. Gregory, fourteen, and his brother Stephen, twelve, shared a room so tended to share their illnesses. Maggie sometimes helped the boys with their studies, but not on this day.

"Are you sure he's not bothering you?" she asked Rachel in the parlor as Aidan crawled around dragging his teddy bear along with him.

Priscilla, age eight, piled blocks on top of each other, and as soon as she was finished, young Aidan knocked them all down, giggling in his triumph.

"I knew you would do that!" Priscilla bristled, immediately starting to pile the blocks up again. "How can Aidan possibly bother us?" she said to Maggie and made a face. "One day, he shall build something that I will knock down. Just you wait and see."

Aidan pulled himself up on a chair and took a bold step toward his mother before he toppled over. He frowned and fussed before he smiled.

"I think he is going to be walking soon," Priscilla said.

"Not yet," Rachel said, pulling him over to her. "He's still a baby." She hugged him.

With that, Aidan protested, fussing until she released him. Once again, he unsteadily pulled himself up on the chair.

"He will be a year in just weeks," Maggie said, lifting her son to her, kissing his face and smoothing out his dark curls. "You look more like your handsome father each day," she said, kissing each cheek before again placing her son down on the carpet.

Aidan turned to look up at the brightly decorated tree and crawled closer to better inspect it. Suddenly, the fire snapped and crackled, which startled him, as his mother tossed another log on the fire.

"Go ahead and read your letters. We'll take good care of him," Rachel said. "You have two letters over there on the table. One arrived all the way from Ireland."

Gathering up her letters, Maggie said, "This one is from my sister, Megan, in Charleston, and this one from Prudence in Dingle. Kindly forgive me, but I must read them both this very instant! It is like having two wonderful Christmas presents to open this day," she said, running for the stairs.

The door to the attic was propped open to better warm the room. Then, Maggie wrapped herself in a blanket and opened Megan's letter first:

My Dearest Sister,

First I must tell that you we have two of our very own African slaves to help us run the hotel. Imagine, your sister with a Negro slave to wait upon her hand and foot! Nearly everyone in Charleston has slaves, as does every plantation owner in South Carolina. I am sure you must be aware of that fact by this time.

The middle-aged man is called Cooper, 35 years, named by his master after a river that runs through Charleston. Fancy that! Cooper helps Kevin take the baggage to the rooms and he cleans and sweeps. The girl is called Angel, a name bestowed upon her by her former mistress, a kind woman who was very old when she died. Abigail Parker, 87 years, had many slaves on her rice plantation. At this point, we can only afford the two purchased at the local auction. No one else wanted Cooper. Twenty slaves were bought by the new owner to keep on the plantation, but Mr. Windsor also brought along *slaves from his plantation in Georgia. Many men did bid on Angel, for she is a pretty mulatto and 16, the same age as me. The local gossip is that the son of the master was her sire yet he denied this before being killed in the last war. I made Kevin bid the highest. Angel was purchased for $1,000. Do you not find that outrageous, my sister?*

I knew those evil men would abuse her, forcing her to sire one child after another. I could not bear to think of that happening to so pretty a girl. Now Angel is my personal slave and I am fond of her. I will be good to her, even though I own her to do as I please.

Maggie stopped reading and quickly sucked in her breath. She stared at the words on the paper, hardly able to believe what she had read. Her sister had a slave named Angel which seemed to delight her! A slave named Angel!

So far, Angel has been a great help to me. For you see, my dear sister, I am now with child. Our first born shall arrive in July. Perhaps I shall have a son on Liam's birthday, July 10, to resemble our father. I wish you could be here as I was with you during Aidan's birth, although Aunt Brigid did most of the work. Or rather, you did the work in producing such a fine and winning son. I am glad that our children shall be near the same age and pray that the cousins meet before they are too old to play as boys. Listen to me, assuming to have a son. We must find a way for our children to meet. You must come to Charleston, for you would love it here. It is a charming southern town on the sea.

Staring at the words again, Maggie's eyes filled with tears. So Megan was going to be a mother, which made her weep happy tears. She wished they lived closer to each other, for taking a stage coach to Charleston was likely to take forever and be most costly. It was nothing that she might afford anytime soon.

"Joyous news," she said aloud. "You shall be in my prayers each night, Megan."

For a moment, she envisioned her sister's beautiful face on her wedding day as she danced the wicked waltz with her handsome husband, Kevin. Quickly returning her eyes to the letter, she read of Charleston, of Megan's new friends, and then, she stopped short.

The church we attend is Protestant. I know Kevin was baptized, but it seems more practical for me to attend St. Michael's Episcopal Church. Uncle Loran and Aunt Carleen have been members for many years. Kevin does everything he can to please them. They refer to Pope Pius VII as a mackerel snapper and laugh each time that his uncle makes that remark.

In all honesty, Maggie had wondered how long it might take for Kevin to revert to the faith of his youth. Next, Megan wrote of James Hoban, the Irishman from County Kilkenny who designed the local courthouse. After George Washington witnessed the restoration in 1792, he asked James Hoban to design the White House. Hoban was asked to do so yet again after the British burned the place down in 1814. He had supervised the reconstruction. The new presidential residence would be completed the following year, so Maggie had suggested that the Gallaghers visit Washington to join in the celebration. It seemed a propitious time to have a family reunion in America.

Your suggestion of a trip north next summer seems impossible. Kevin says that such a trip is unlikely very soon because of all the demands he has with the new hotel. Write to me soon please. A belated happy birthday and happy Christmas to you and Aidan, my dear nephew.

Yours in love,
Megan and Kevin
Charleston, South Carolina

Next, Maggie opened the letter from Prudence and began to read:

November 28, 1816

Dear Mary Margaret,

Two days ago, Matthew brought me your letter to read. The ship with your letter must have flown like the Pegasus across the sea to inform me of your safety and good health. I was thrilled to read a letter written in your hand, but saddened to hear of Niall's tragic end from the typhus. My heart goes out to you that such a terrible thing should happen less than a month away from Ireland, a true tragedy. Perchance as tragic as the loss of your Aidan when we thought Darcy was also lost at the Battle of Waterloo.

Your life has not been easy, and yet, I am truly grateful that Providence has made us such good friends. It was a blessed time we shared that I shall always treasure. I wish you a belated happy birthday, 18 years on the 7th of November. I hope the enclosed pound notes help you to buy something pretty or useful as a gift from your good friend back in Ireland. The money is yours to do with as you wish.

Two five pound notes fell out from between the pages. Maggie gasped. The money would pay off Lucius McKenna. How dear Prudence was. However could she ever repay her immense kindness and generosity? The silver dish was still safely hidden away in her trunk.

Next, she read:

I have the most important news to tell you about Darcy ...

When her name was loudly called from downstairs: "Maggie!" and again louder, "MAGGIE!" Rachel now called out from the attic doorway, "Come quickly," she said, with her face fully flushed.

"What is it?" Maggie inquired, dropping the letter. She stood and her heart started to race. "Is it Aidan?" and she ran after Rachel down the stairs.

At the top of the second floor, Rachel stopped and turned to her and said, "Nothing is wrong. It is a gentleman. He has come to call on you."

"Call on me? A gentleman? On Christmas Eve?" Maggie began to search her mind, but could think of no one who might call on her. "Do you know him?"

"You know him. His name is Darcy Brosnan and he hails from Dublin."

Suddenly, Maggie stopped short as panic gripped her.

"You do know him, do you not? He is handsome, so I should think you would want to know him." Rachel giggled and hurried on down the stairs.

Suddenly feeling quite breathless, Maggie felt as though she could not move. Prudence had been about to give her news of Darcy in her letter. She had half a mind to run back up to the attic and read the rest of the letter before she continued on down the stairs.

"Darcy is here?" she whispered.

"Aye. He's in the parlor."

"Alone?"

"Not exactly."

Maggie froze.

"The family is also in the parlor, Maggie. After all, it is Christmas Eve."

"Darcy is here alone and he asked for me?" she said just above a whisper.

"There is no one with him, if that is what you mean."

"Are you sure he is not here to see your father?"

"He asked for Mary Margaret McKenna ... O'Reilly McKenna," she corrected. "It's all right, Maggie, I will protect you," Rachel said, giggling as she ran on down the stairs and directly into the parlor.

Slowly breathing in and breathing out and taking one step at a time, Maggie descended the stairs. Her stomach was all aflutter as she tried to breathe in order to calm herself.

Shannon walked into the entry dressed for dinner. That was when Maggie realized that she was still wearing her work clothes. She had not even bothered to change.

"There is a gentleman here to see you all the way from Ireland," Shannon said. "His name is Darcy Brosnan and he says that you are well acquainted."

Standing on the very last step, Maggie hesitated.

"He is waiting," Shannon said. "And he is a gentleman," she whispered, pulling her off the step and nudging her toward the parlor.

Gregory and Stephen were playing checkers near the window. Rachel and Priscilla were on the sofa in their pretty Christmas dresses, with Rachel smirking. Darcy had his back to her. Cornelius faced her. What perhaps surprised her the most was that Darcy was holding Aidan in his arms and showing him the ornaments high up on the Christmas tree.

"Do you like angels?" he asked Aidan, pointing to an angel ornament.

Aidan reached out, but Darcy instantly stepped back. "No touching," he said.

"We have an Irish visitor on Christmas Eve," Cornelius said all smiles. "Is that not lovely, Maggie? One only recently arrived the same as ourselves."

Darcy turned to face her.

"He says that you are good friends," Cornelius cheerfully added.

That was when Aidan grabbed Darcy's nose, which he laughingly endured, removing his hand and gently tweaking Aidan's nose in playful reprisal.

Aidan giggled.

"Aidan, it is not nice when the gentleman is trying to show you the decorations high up on the Christmas tree," Maggie scolded, relieving Darcy of her squirming, giggling son.

"Merry Christmas, Mary Margaret," Darcy said, smiling at her with his clear blue Irish eyes. "I must say that you look quite well. Your handsome son already has me fully charmed, the same as his mother, I daresay."

Instantly feeling herself blush, Maggie quickly took note of the pleasure on the face of every Finnegan in the room. "Merry Christmas to you, Darcy. You are looking quite well yourself. I was just beginning to read Prudence's letter when Rachel summoned me downstairs. Prudence was just mentioning you when I was forced to stop reading, which places me at a distinct disadvantage, perchance to tell me that you are also newly arrived in Baltimore?"

"A lovely coincidence, you reading her letter as I arrived," his expression was serious as he said, "I just received a letter from Prudence three days ago wherein I learned of the sad death of your husband at sea." He nodded to Cornelius in a manner to suggest that the matter was already discussed between them. "There were no such tragedies on the *Morgan*, though sometimes buffeted about by powerful storms, one with gale force winds, which caused many on board to be very sick, myself included."

"I suffered from no seasickness, though that was not true of all passengers onboard the *Pegasus*," Maggie said, pausing before she added, "You learned I was here from Prudence?"

"Precisely."

"I was blessed with the arrival of two letters today, another from Megan. Though you know Prudence, she sent me two five pound notes for Christmas. She is so very generous and kind."

All the Finnegans looked at each other quite pleased.

"A fine gift for you and Aidan for Christmas," Cornelius said.

"For my birthday and for my Aidan for Christmas. I miss being able to enjoy a cup of tea with Prudence in her lovely parlor," she said, turning to Darcy. "When did you arrive?"

"Not long after you and the doctor did, it seems, in late October. I am living with my Uncle Shane on his plantation a mere half day's journey on my able bodied thoroughbred, a recent gift from my generous uncle. My horse is called Wellington," he said, happily glancing around at everyone in the room.

"A fitting name," Maggie replied. "You could hardly call him Napoleon."

Everyone laughed.

"Then, I would have to shoot him," Darcy said, turning to Cornelius. "I served under the Duke in the Peninsular Wars and was severely wounded at Waterloo. Luckily, I survived."

Cornelius looked down at Darcy's boots. "I see you wear Wellingtons for riding, as well." His expression sobered. "We lost too many to that egocentric lunatic. Thank God you helped put him out of commission. We do not need another Napoleon in this world."

"May we not speak of something more cheerful than war on Christmas Eve?" Shannon gaily interrupted, taking her husband's arm. "War is a dreadful topic. Hopefully, the president's mansion will be duly restored, for the last war in America was won right here at Fort McHenry. I want no more wars in my life ... is that too much to ask?"

"Optimistic at best," Cornelius said, affectionately patting her hand.

"I pray you are granted your wish, Mrs. Finnegan, but knowing the nature of man, it seems highly unlikely," Darcy said in good humor.

Shannon exchanged woebegone looks with her husband.

"Your Uncle Shane is well?" Maggie inquired.

"I am most pleased to say that he is most well. Although he has some problem with his heart, it is difficult to keep Uncle Shane down. Perhaps you can visit the plantation and check out my uncle," Darcy said to Cornelius.

"That can be arranged whenever you chose," he amicably replied.

"I am pleased that your uncle is somewhat well," Maggie said, "though I am sure Dr. Finnegan could render him excellent service, and perhaps I can help out with my herbs." She paused. "I am truly surprised to find you here on this particular evening, Darcy."

"After I finished reading Prudence's letter and learned of where you were, I felt the need to see you as soon as I possibly could," his expression was serious as he watched her very closely. "What better time than Christmas Eve with an able horse and clear weather in which to ride? Most of the snow has already melted, with the temperature most pleasant for December."

"Your horse is outside?" Cornelius inquired. "Shall we put him in my stable?"

"I left Wellington at a stable not far from here to be watered and fed. I wasn't sure if you even had a stable."

"Your uncle's plantation ... does it have a name?" Maggie inquired.

"Marcus Manor."

"Marcus? I thought your uncle was Brosnan, the same as you?"

"The plantation has the name of the original owner. Marcus was the man my uncle won the plantation from back in 1788 when Shane was but twenty-five. He has had the place now for over twenty-eight years."

"You say he won the plantation?" Cornelius inquired.

"I guess I never told Maggie that the plantation was won in a poker game," Darcy replied.

"No, you never told me."

"It seems that this Marcus was an inveterate gambler and old when he met my uncle, besides being extremely ill, if the truth be known. He was not expected to live very long. He lost his first wife in childbirth and his second wife, along with his six children, to cholera. There was no one to leave the plantation to. At the time, my uncle was young, handsome and terribly clever. I think Marcus intentionally lost the property to him. Besides the manor house, 280 acres of land, several barns and outbuildings, the slave quarters and thirty African slaves were included in his winnings."

"My word!" Cornelius exclaimed. "Your uncle was exceedingly lucky."

"And quite clever, no doubt," Shannon added.

"The land situated near the Gunpowder River is most fertile, not far from the Chesapeake Bay. My uncle has never regretted being involved in that particular poker game."

"I should think not!" Cornelius said, turning to his wife in feigned indignation. "Think of it, Shannon, winning a tobacco plantation and all those slaves in a game!" He turned back to Darcy. "Your uncle must be some poker player!"

"I learned long ago to never wager with the man. He can be most formidable," Darcy said, chuckling, as he turned to Maggie. "How do you find Baltimore and Maryland these months since you've arrived?"

"Very fine indeed, thank you. I gather you have enjoyed your time here, as well?"

"Immensely." Darcy said, turning around to retrieve a colorfully wrapped gift from the table that he handed to Maggie. "I thought you might enjoy having your own copy."

Maggie stared at the gift, with Aidan still in her arms.

"I can take him," Rachel volunteered. "Mother gave him applesauce, so he shouldn't be too hungry. I will give him milk from a cup, if it is all right with you." Rachel fidgeted.

"Of course," Maggie said, handing over her son, "But only a little milk. He needs to nurse or I shall be most uncomfortable."

Rachel nodded.

All at once, Shannon snatched Aidan away from her daughter.

"Mother!" Rachel protested.

"Perhaps we should both see to him," she said, nodding toward the kitchen. "Tell Caitlin to warm some milk in a pan."

"Not yet, Mother," Rachel said. "I want to see Maggie's Christmas gift." She blushed as she looked from Darcy to Maggie with her eyes opened wider. "Do you mind terribly?"

Everyone was watching and waiting.

"Of course not, Rachel, but will you not all unwrap your gifts soon? There are gifts for everyone under the tree," Maggie said, feeling embarrassed.

"We don't mind waiting," Priscilla said, as her eyes darted from Maggie to the gift.

Everyone nodded.

Darcy smiled. "Please do go ahead."

After carefully untying the bow, Maggie removed the paper to find a copy of *Emma* by Jane Austen, which confirmed her suspicions. "Why, thank you, Darcy," she said, showing the book to everyone. "The novel is by my favorite author, Miss Jane Austen."

Everyone looked pleased and nodded.

"And mine," Darcy said.

"Thank you so very much, Darcy."

"You will find it charming, as are all her novels, of course. I have already read it and sent a copy to Prudence as well."

"You are too kind," Maggie said, suddenly feeling the need to inquire, "And your wife, how is she these days?"

Everyone looked surprised, including Darcy. Only the crackling of the fire could be heard.

"I have no wife ... that I know of," he replied, lowering his eyes. "I have never been married ... as you have," he said, and his eyes included everyone who had sensed his sudden lack of ease. "I should like to be married ... one day," he said, taking in an audible breath.

Standing there in stunned silence, Maggie collected herself enough to say, "Prudence said you were to be married in September."

Awkwardly glancing about, Darcy said, "Therese broke off our engagement. I think it happened before Prudence even managed to tell you that I was engaged."

"I am so very sorry," was all she could think to say, feeling the need to be kind.

"Are you?" he said, and his blue eyes twinkled in an amused manner. "Therese was a sickly sort, chronically ill, I fear. She didn't want me to always be looking after her, which was why she suggested that I go to America alone."

"So you did," Maggie said, suddenly feeling stupid. "That was a very good thing," she nervously added.

"I thought it was a very good thing," he dryly remarked. "She saved me from breaking off our engagement myself. It was better for her to do it, don't you think?" He waited for her answer in a somewhat expectant manner.

Breaking the awkward silence, Shannon said, "I hope it's all right that I have taken the liberty of asking Darcy to join us for supper. After all, it is Christmas Eve, and he is far from Marcus Manor. I have heard it is twenty-five miles north and east of here."

"Aye," Darcy said.

"We could never send an Irishman out into the night alone on Christmas Eve, now, could we, Maggie?" Cornelius inquired. "It is unlikely that Darcy would even arrive in time for Christmas morning without sleep or nourishment. You shall spend the night here and share our Christmas morning," he said in an adamant tone. "There is a spare bed in Stephen's room."

Stephen politely nodded. "That will be fine, Father."

"You are too kind," Darcy said. "I had planned to get a room at the inn."

"We will not hear of it!" Cornelius said in a tone of finality. "You are staying here. Caitlin makes a marvelous Christmas pudding I am sure you will enjoy tremendously. Sausage and eggs for breakfast, scones and marvelous tea. You will likely enjoy that, too!"

"I am sure that I will," Darcy said and he turned to Maggie.

"He must stay, of course, for supper and for breakfast," Maggie said, taking in a quick breath. "It would be delightful to have him here with us, would it not? Although I must tell you that Darcy is only half Irish," she added, turning from his soft blue stare and feeling more than a little flustered by her sudden and surprising change of circumstances. "He is also Scot and English on his mother's side."

"Thank you for your kind hospitality," Darcy said to Shannon and Cornelius, glancing at Maggie with a pleased expression. "I can think of no other place, or of no other people with whom I would like to be on such a night as this."

Feeling herself blush again, Maggie said, "I must feed Aidan before we all sit down for supper, regardless of applesauce," and taking Aidan from Shannon she said to Darcy, "Kindly excuse me. It is time to feed my son," and she hurried toward the kitchen.

"I want a Christmas surprise," Priscilla petulantly demanded.

"Soon, you shall have your Christmas surprise. Patience, my dear Priscilla."

In overhearing Cornelius offer Darcy a glass of sherry, Maggie decided that she had already enjoyed several Christmas surprises: Her wonderful letters from Megan and Prudence, a brand new novel by Miss Jane Austen, but most of all, Darcy, the very best Christmas surprise of them all.

36

A New Year in America
1817

It was the first New Year's celebration with guests invited to Marcus Manor in many years. Plans were immediately set into motion on the same day that Darcy returned from Baltimore to inform his uncle of his great good fortune in finding the beautiful, amber-eyed, red haired, young Irish widow he loved only a half day's journey away.

Pleased was his Uncle Shane to hear the good news, and eager he was to meet the winsome Mary Margaret and her young son, Aidan. Naturally, they were invited, along with everyone else, to a gala banquet and ball at Marcus Manor on New Year's Eve. Musicians were to be hired for dancing and singing. Even the field slaves, often idle during the cold weather, were to assist in the preparations inside and outside in sprucing, cleaning and polishing. The slaves were also going to share in the feast in the serving kitchens and be allotted a moderate amount of ale or whiskey to more cheerfully bring in the promising New Year.

All the Finnegans were invited to the celebration, along with their indentured servant to help attend to the children. All were encouraged to stay on for an extended holiday. Games and amusements were designed for both the adults and the children: Chinese checkers, dominoes, card games, and hikes through the woods. The waterfalls on the Gunpowder

River were often frozen in winter and best viewed in other seasons, the rugged terrain unsuitable for wagon or carriage. Nature walks were planned, weather permitting. Should fresh snow fall, horse-drawn sleighing would take place through the paths around the fallow fields or down the country lanes, with few roads suitable near the plantation. Sleds hanging from rafters in the barn were often used by the slave children in the winter, and would soon be shared with all their young guests.

In the nearby woodlands, abundant wildlife thrived: elk, deer, beaver, otter, possum, fox, skunk, wolf, squirrels, chipmunks, and an occasional mountain lion endangered the livestock. Wild fowl was plentiful: ringed-neck pheasant, dove, duck, goose, grouse and wild turkey. Early in the morning, Darcy often watched the hawks and bald eagles soaring in search of prey. The persistence hammering of a woodpecker was sometimes heard, along with the trills of chickadees, titmice, wrens, jays, nuthatches, sparrows and blackbirds, for many a feathered friend braved the winter and provided entertainment with their feeding and nesting habits.

The huge barn had a resident owl named Barnaby. The bird of prey conveniently controlled the rodent population, while four able cats patrolled the halls and rooms of the manor house. In the attic, the local bats could be a nuisance, swooping through the house late at night, at times startling Shane as he read a book in the library. The bats had caused a few slaves to run shrieking from the house. With their entry holes securely blocked, the nocturnal creatures were forced to take up residence in a deserted shed. As a result, to the utter delight of most of the children, there were often stories of vampires recounted in the slave quarters.

The Maryland black bears hibernated in winter, but in warmer weather were sometimes sited in the woods. Slaves had reported one beast lumbering near the beehives the past summer. Inside the manor house were two large black bearskin rugs, one with the head intact on the library floor, with the other bearskin headless in front of Shane's bedroom fireplace. The master enjoyed hunting and fishing, for the brooks and river overflowed with trout and a variety of other fish. The Piscataway were credited for Shane's tracking and fishing skills, with most developed after he won the plantation from the original owner.

Two Piscataway families, separated by choice from their tribe years earlier, still peacefully resided near the Gunpowder River on land that was part of the plantation. The families lived in two rough log cabins and one long house situated between the tobacco fields and the river. The elder, Yuma, *son of the chief*, was baptized by the missionaries with the Christian name of Charles, but Shane still called him Yuma. The medicine man had proven to be an asset over the years in matters of planting and harvesting tobacco. Yuma also taught his grandson, Helaku, *sunny day*, to work with curing tobacco. His daughters, Amitola, *rainbow*, and Mahala, *tenderness*, assisted the slaves with the garden in the springtime, being especially gifted in raising corn.

Every year, pelts of fox, mink, otter and beaver were presented to Shane by the Piscataway as payment for allowing them to occupy his land near a river filled with fish and allowing them to hunt to provide their families with food and clothing. Another cabin would be erected in the spring for a brave marrying a Powhatan squaw from Virginia. Shane trusted the Piscataway implicitly, and he enjoyed sharing his land with them. However, few of his neighbors agreed with him.

Late that December, white tailed deer were hunted, their skins dried, the meat mounted to roast over a pit. Ducks, geese, pheasants and wild turkeys were hunted with the help of Shane's three Golden Retrievers: King, Prince and Queenie. There would be enough game for everyone to enjoy. Two highly trusted slaves, Moses and Arthur, regularly hunted with the Piscataway, who helped them to acquire skill using a bow and arrow. On occasion, muskets were used to hunt. Few slaveholders in the area trusted a slave with a rifle except for the master of Marcus Manor.

Shane Brosnan was a fair-minded and kindly slave master and highly respected by his slaves. The opposite was true of his neighbor, Jeremiah Plunkett, who was a reprehensible sort of man. Jeremiah claimed he had religion on his side, but he was also a man known to abuse his slaves by whipping them into submission with a cat-of-nine-tails. Jeremiah also took advantage of the young girls. Besides having six children with his wife, Sarah, he had sired at least eight children that became his slaves in time. Young slaves not sold at auction were assigned to the easier chores in the household by age five. What bothered Shane the most about Jeremiah Plunkett was the fact that the man had never shown the least degree of kindness toward his illegitimate offspring and denied his part in their paternity.

One slave at the Plunkett Plantation was a young girl named Israel who often visited with the slaves at Marcus Manor. Sometimes Israel brought along her children on a visit, especially her youngest child, Salome, who was sired by her master. By the age of fourteen, Israel already had three young children. Unfortunately, her own mother had died with her birth.

The Plunketts were not invited to the New Year's Eve celebration or to any other social event at Marcus Manor. Shane had never considered himself a good Catholic, but he still could not find it within himself to condone the brutality and perversity of Jeremiah Plunkett in his treatment of his slaves. He considered the man sadistic and hypocritical, in addition to fully lacking any degree of humanity.

Early on December 30, 1816, as the sun rose over the crest of the hill to the east, Darcy and two slaves hitched up the carryall. Then, Darcy and Moses headed down the trail blazed by Indian tribes hundreds of years earlier that led directly into the city of Baltimore.

A few days earlier, a slave named Isaac had delivered the invitations and returned to the plantation on that same day to report to his master that Dr. Finnegan and his group eagerly awaited young Master Darcy's arrival to bring them to the celebration for the New Year. Their own horse and buggy would also be made in readiness for the journey to Marcus Manor.

The skies were a bright blue upon their arrival at the Finnegan house in the city to enjoy a light lunch before the return trip, which was likely to prove tedious for the children. Maggie and Caitlin kept the children busy singing and counting cows and other critters along the way. Hours later, in the diminishing light of a wintry evening, the plantation came into full view. Countless lanterns flickered along the lane leading up to the great house: Marcus Manor.

Instantly, Maggie was amazed by the magnificence of the Georgian colonial mansion with its six great white pillars, for the plantation immediately stirred a memory. Upon first entering the manor house, she noted the polished lion brass knocker and was forced to take in a deep breath.

The vivid scenes of her childhood dreams now existed in physical reality before her. Chills ran up and down her spine and both her arms, causing her to shudder. It only took a moment for Maggie to realize that this was the place where she was going to spend perhaps the rest of her life. All around her were objects that reminded her of Ireland, not those found in the home of a tenant farmer, but in the elegant parlors of the gentry. The house was much grander than the home of Prudence Pratt, perhaps even more exquisite than the mansion of Lord and Lady Chadwick. Marcus Manor was a great house furnished in both grand and exquisite taste.

Once the group entered the house through its two great doors, they were met by an imposing carpeted staircase of mahogany that ascended to a second story. From the ceiling, a Waterford crystal chandelier sparkled, its many candles flickering in the entry of highly polished pine floors. Chairs upholstered in a tartan plaid were placed on either side. On one wall was a large mirror framed by gold painted wood with a bright brass American eagle perched on top.

They were the only guests to arrive a full day early. A young, tall, lean colored man dressed in the fine clothes of a servant and wearing a white wig had opened the grand doors.

In eagerness, Darcy rushed over to open the double doors of the library as he called out, "Uncle Shane, our guests have arrived, though by now you had perhaps considered us lost somewhere between Marcus Manor and the city of Baltimore."

Out walked Shane Brosnan, the master of the plantation, a tall, striking man who seemed much younger than his fifty-odd years. His salt and pepper hair was tied back at the nape of his neck. His striking blue eyes perfectly matched Darcy's. He wore the elegant dress of the lords and ladies back in Ireland. Shane was plainly Irish, with his dancing blue eyes and deep dimples, his smile constant as Darcy made proper introductions all around.

Soon the slaves were showing them to their quarters so that they might freshen up before supper. The adults were expected in the parlor for a glass of sherry. Maggie was sharing her room with Aidan and Caitlin: The two beds had high, carved mahogany headboards and there was a crib against one wall. From the window, Maggie glimpsed a darkening view of the woods, with a bright moon rising and snow softly falling. The fire in the fireplace had warmed the room. Maggie washed and changed into a dress of brown plaid, vowing to one day own many fine dresses to wear in so elegant a house on so promising an evening.

The four young Finnegans were in adjoining rooms. Gregory and Stephen shared a manly room with two full beds, with headboards of polished maple and forest green velvet bedcovers and matching draperies at the windows. Rachel and Priscilla shared a smaller room with one bed. In their girlish excitement at being in such a grand manor house, they giggled and rolled around on the bed.

Cornelius and Shannon had the room directly across the hall with a canopy bed draped in red velvet with white lacey pillows. The fireplace crackled with warmth. Slaves were assigned to look after each person. None of the older children seemed to know how to behave with their own servant in such a grand house.

Before long, all the children and Caitlin were led to a large pantry off the kitchen with a table set with their meal. Soon after supper, the children were to go to bed. The promise: The children would share in all the festivities and be allowed to stay up past midnight on the following night. That quelled their highly vocal protests. After their supper, the household slaves looked after Caitlin and the children, singing them songs of Africa, which sounded downright magical to Maggie.

It seemed curious to her to discover that each slave had a name from the Bible, especially since Cornelius often read from the Old and the New Testaments after supper in Baltimore. The first slave was called Moses, the one who had driven the splendid carriage that brought them to Marcus Manor. It was Joseph who had opened the front doors. Isaac was in charge of taking the horses to the stable. Rebecca and Ruth served the children. Mary was assigned to help Maggie, but Mary was also her name. How many other biblical names were given to the slaves at Marcus Manor, she now began to wonder?

On New Year's Eve, the food was superb in both taste and aroma. The music was merry, the many guests amicable and appearing to enjoy themselves. And yet, after being introduced several times as the "Widow McKenna," Maggie ushered Darcy into his uncle's vast library.

"But you were married and your husband died at sea. That makes you the widow McKenna," he said when they were behind the closed library doors.

"In name only," Maggie said. "I was never really his wife." The silly pretense bothered her. However, the truth was that she had gotten pregnant after meeting Darcy and after his kiss. Those thoughts raced back and forth through her mind as she noticed him watching her closely, and she was unsure of how much Prudence had already told him.

"You have a son and your husband died. Your son is Aidan McKenna," Darcy said, narrowing his eyes. "Are you trying to tell me ... that Niall is not Aidan's father?"

Suddenly, she felt as though the house was closing in on her, making it difficult for her to breathe.

"What is it you are trying to tell me, Maggie?" Darcy inquired with his blues eyes steady upon her.

"Niall is not ... Aidan's father," she said, "And he never really was my husband. He had problems, perhaps partly my fault. We were married, and yet, we were never really married."

He sighed, nibbling on his lower lip. "I had hoped you would tell me this," he said, his expression softening. "I wanted you to be the one to tell me, Maggie."

"Aidan's father ..." she started out, tears now spilling from her eyes, "also died at sea."

"In a shipwreck," Darcy said. "Your smuggler, Aidan, the man Prudence said you were going to marry, he died in a shipwreck. Kevin told me after the wedding. He said you were with child when he came to see you and you were forced to marry his cousin after Aidan died. Niall was Aidan's cousin, is that correct?"

"You never knew before the wedding?"

"Prudence said you had married a man you could hardly tolerate. So Aidan is Aidan's son," he said. "I knew that long before Prudence wrote to tell me of Niall's death."

"We were promised, Aidan and I," she explained. "We grew up together. We met when I was nine. I did love him. It was not a wanton thing between us. Our feelings ran deep."

"You owe me no explanation," he said, suddenly flushing and quickly adding, "Although you could have written to me of him. I would not have wanted to know the whole truth, but it might have been the honest thing for you to do." He looked into her eyes with blame and hurt now on his handsome face.

Stiffening, Maggie thought his rebuff was justified, and yet, she said, "I could not bear to tell you of him, nor him of you. Aidan knew nothing, and somehow, I thought you and I might meet again. I hoped we would. I was confused after I met you by the passion I felt for you, thinking myself unworthy of either man, being torn between two such very different men, each man caring for me and me caring deeply for each of you. I know of no other way to explain myself, Darcy."

Suddenly, light seemed to fill his eyes, and he said, "Do you still have these feelings for me? Do you still care deeply for me?" He took her hands into his, now trembling slightly, and he gently pulled her to him.

"How can you even ask me such a question, Darcy? Are you so insensitive as to be unable to see what is right before your magnificent blue eyes … eyes that I shall never forget? You have haunted my dreams from the day that we met." Feeling the heat rising inside her, she yearned to be fully in his arms.

"Torment me no longer. Please say that you will marry me," Darcy said, sinking to his knees. "Please be my wife! I love you with all my heart and all my soul, Mary Margaret!"

"I love you, Darcy," she said, looking down into his eyes now filled with tears. "I shall be happy to be your wife until the very end of my days."

As tears streamed down her face, Darcy stood, pulling her into his arms, kissing her fully and deeply, appearing to drink her in, as they held onto one another, body to body, passion increasing, arms wrapped around one another in a glorious moment of fully committed love.

Near midnight, as accounted by the old grandfather clock in the hall, the master of the plantation, Shane Brosnan, announced the engagement of his nephew Lieutenant Darcy Donal Brosnan to Mary Margaret

O'Reilly McKenna of Dingle in County Kerry, Ireland. All assembled were invited to return in the spring to celebrate a wedding at Marcus Manor.

Shane ordered fine French champagne served to everyone present, and he made a toast in his distinguished Irish accent that had never lessened throughout the years:

"To Darcy and Maggie's eternal happiness, as well as to the excellent health and immeasurable prosperity of all those herein gathered, for a perfectly marvelous and absolutely wonderful New Year!"

Music played.

Everyone danced a lively reel soon followed by a graceful waltz.

Bells rang and whistles blew to welcome a new year to all gathered at Marcus Manor in the State of Maryland in the United States of America, if not in the whole world, for 1817 was here!

37

A Wedding at Marcus Manor

The doctor was not pleased to lose Maggie's excellent services as a midwife, and yet, Cornelius and Shannon could not have been happier for her in her engagement to such a fine gentleman. Maggie was marrying up, bettering herself, and the couple was deeply and completely in love. It was a marriage made in heaven with young Aidan gaining a father, Maggie an adoring husband, with the prospect of inheriting Marcus Manor from Darcy's remarkable uncle one day. Although Shane Brosnan had a slight murmur, his heart was strong enough to serve him for many years to come. Shane was an optimistic man in spite of his various wounds and grievous tragedies that resulted, in part, from his own foolishness during his former years.

There seemed to be much for Maggie to learn about Darcy's charming uncle before their April nuptials. The striking man was married twice. His first wife died with the birth of their second child. Altogether, Shane had sired six children: two having died from diphtheria in infancy. Of his grown sons, Rory, the eldest, was a casualty in the war against the Crown at the Battle at Bladensburg on August 17, 1814. There were more losses for the British under General Ross than for the ragtag, untrained, frightened American militia, with many more of them fleeing into the woods than dying on the battlefield: This happened to the amusement of the highly trained British soldiers who had only recently defeated the Emperor Napoleon.

Many British soldiers died from heatstroke while marching in their winter wool uniforms in the high August humidity of a Maryland summer. "Mighty foolish," according to Uncle Shane. The British were ignorant of the seasonal temperatures, day and night, along the Mid-Atlantic seaboard. The troops were on their way to capture Washington, from which President Madison had long since fled, as had various members of his cabinet. The unpleasant result: The British marched in more or less unobstructed.

"The bloody redcoats burned the White House and most of the public buildings, shooting, plundering and terrifying all the citizens that remained. It was revenge," said Uncle Shane, "for our burning of the parliament building in York."

"I understand," Maggie said.

"But Dolley Madison, the President's indomitable wife, she saved what she could from the mansion, including a fine portrait of our first president, George Washington, who clobbered the British in the Revolution! I fought in that war, along with plenty of other Irishmen who helped us to win it! Took a bullet in my shoulder and my right arm has never been the same since."

Touching his shoulder, Maggie said, "We will try some poultices with my herbs."

"Aye!" he said, and then he went on, "The portrait was hidden away from that bloody Ross, with whom our Darcy happens to be well acquainted, an Irishman if you can imagine ..." he dramatically stopped and hit the table with his fist, "An Irishman fighting with the bloody British against our bloody Irish in America. Can you imagine?"

"Ross is Irish," Darcy said.

"And that cocky Rear Admiral Cockburn," Shane said in a tone of disdain, "was the second-ranking naval officer in the expedition, and he dared to dine with his men on the food on the president's table before stealing whatever else seemed to suit them, and then burning the mansion until no more than a shell of its former magnificence. Imagine that?"

"I heard it was designed by an Irishman," Maggie said.

"Who else, my dear? Who else?"

Shane's younger son, Lorcan, was also present at the Battle of Baltimore, with father and son armed and ready to preserve their liberty as American citizens. No wounds were sustained, the battle waged mainly at Fort McHenry. More than 16,000 Americans were eager to fight 5,000 British soldiers and marines, including fifty British frigates and warships with canons and terrible bombs.

"It was our Baltimore merchants who made the greatest sacrifice to win the brave fight. Outraged by the burning of Washington, they scuttled their fine ships in order to block the warships from getting close enough to raze the town."

"Baltimore was claimed to be a nest of pirates," Darcy said.

"That is because our fine clipper ships captured so many British ships the three years of the war, a fine job they did, I can promise you that!" Shane boasted, and again he banged his fist on the table.

In his youth, Lorcan had fallen in love with a Piscataway girl, one of Yuma's pretty nieces. Their affections never wavered. Finally, they married when Lorcan was twenty and Dayani sixteen. Two sons were soon born: Robert and Sean. Lorcan had no interest in staying in Maryland. Since he was a lad he had read of the adventures of Lewis and Clark and yearned to settle somewhere near the Rocky Mountains.

"There was no way I could talk him out of risking his life and the lives of his wife and sons in taking a covered wagon to the frontier. I warned him about the unfriendly Indians. Still, they joined a wagon train two years ago this April, and I haven't heard a word from him since."

Both his daughters were happily married and had left home by the age of twenty. The eldest, Caroline, was married to Earl Ingram of German and Dutch descent, a ship builder in New York. They resided in a spacious home with their five children, three boys and two girls. Shane found the stage coach trip to see them quite jarring, so since then he only corresponded. He respected Earl for his ambitions and was fond of his son-in-law.

"His ancestors were among the original Dutch colonists that settled New Amsterdam in the 1600s," Shane said one evening during dinner, "Now known as New York."

His other daughter, Elizabeth, was married to Thomas Warwick, an Englishman in the printing business in Boston, Massachusetts, where they resided with their three daughters. Letters were often exchanged.

In fact, Shane's eldest granddaughter, Sally, now ten, often wrote to her grandfather. Thomas owned a fledgling newspaper in Boston. It seemed that his brother, Henry, planned to work on some canal from the Hudson River to Lake Erie to facilitate shipping to the Great Lakes. The project would create jobs for the Irish and other immigrants that continued to arrive almost daily in New York.

None of Shane's children were remotely interested in raising tobacco. That was why Shane was pleased that Darcy had a genuine interest. On top of that, the young adventurer was a foot soldier under the honorable Duke of Wellington.

"Darcy was honored with a medal from Waterloo for his service to His Majesty," Shane boasted. "Besides taking five bullets and nearly dying on us. He would have made the rank of captain if he had decided to stay on with the service."

In Shane's mind, that meant a bloody hero was planning to help him raise tobacco. His prayers were answered. Darcy had a sincere interest in running the plantation, along with the manor house recently remodeled inside and out, according to Shane's authorization and design.

"On top of that, he has the good sense to marry a full-blooded Irish lass, not only mighty pleasant to gaze upon, but a midwife who can read and write by the grace of God Almighty."

All Shane's prayers were answered that year. For on a bright spring day, a wedding would take place at Marcus Manor. The ballroom not decorated in such a manner since the weddings of his daughters. The rooms were bedecked with large bouquets of spring flowers, while a feast was prepared and musicians hired for dancing.

The cream colored silk and lace fabric for her wedding gown was a generous gift from Cornelius and Shannon. The gown was designed by a dressmaker in Baltimore. The ceremony would take place in the gazebo out in the garden now resplendent with azaleas and rhododendrons in great clusters of fuchsia, pink, red, and white. A Protestant minister would seal Maggie to Darcy. In her center, she felt theirs would be a very good life indeed.

All the Finnegans were present on that day. By then, all of them were good friends. Shane often stayed at their house in Baltimore on business trips to the city. For recent events had brought Shane a new son and a brand new daughter, fully grown, along with young Aidan. The toddler immediately bonded with his three Golden Retrievers, particularly Queenie, the bitch, who became the boy's guardian protector. The dog condoned her hair and tail being pulled without a snip, although Queenie did topple the lad over on occasion just to keep him in line. It was love at first sight between a dog and a boy.

Perchance the distance between the plantation and Baltimore had served to postpone the physical consummation of their love. In Baltimore, there were always people around, and Aidan could put a damper on romance. Never before had Maggie been forced to completely control her passion, though she often wished that things were different.

In talking with some other women, Maggie learned that her passion was greater than in those women who simply tolerated a husband without experiencing any enjoyment in the act. She had advised women willing to listen, with some beyond grateful for her advice. Their lives dramatically changed as a result, along with the lives of their husbands.

On the night of her wedding, Mary Margaret Brosnan was looking forward to being fully naked in her husband's loving arms to experience the fullness of the man she had loved for so long. She yearned to explore every inch and aspect of his strong, manly body on her wedding night.

Wearing a nightgown of soft white cotton, Maggie took down her long, auburn hair, strands falling down her back as she brushed it out and noted her freshly washed face in the mirror. The low blaze in the fireplace had dispelled the late evening chill in what was now their room as husband and wife. Seated at the dressing table in the lovely room in the elegant manor house, she felt truly blessed as she had every day since Darcy had reappeared in her life, especially since he had asked her to marry him.

In the mirror, she could see Darcy walking toward her in his dark blue dressing gown. He stood directly behind her, with one hand on her shoulder, the other hand smoothing out her hair. "I love your hair," he said. "It has the glow of rich copper silk."

"I love all of you," she said, turning to him with her heart overflowing with love.

Darcy bent down to kiss her lips, and grasping her arms, pulled her up so that he might more fully embrace her. He held her and pressed her warm, yielding body tighter into him.

"I love all of you," he whispered between wet, probing kisses, tongues blending in an increasing heat, "All of you forever and ever," he said, kissing her, stopping only to look at her with his blue eyes glazed with the heat of passion.

"I want you, Darcy, forever and ever," she whispered, running her fingers through his soft blond hair and her hands down his strong, muscular arms. "I love you and I want you, my husband. Make love to me, please. Now."

The two lovers fell upon the bed, flesh soon upon flesh, arms and legs intertwined, both dressing gowns fully discarded. Then, two strong, young bodies blended into one filled with passion that seemed beyond reason and beyond measure.

Impatiently yearning to have him inside her, Maggie loved the sense of his soft skin against hers, desperately wanting to be full of him, having fantasized about the moment until she was unable to wait any longer, she opened to him, pulling him up and over her with a deep thrill to be completely his at long last.

In her mind, it seemed it had been far too long since she had known the fullness of passion first kindled by Aidan. An integral part of her being was the passion that flowed hot in her blood, gratefully bestowed by her mother and her father in the depth of their love for each other. Love shared with her, which she now lavished on Darcy. Heatedly, he moved inside her, touching her, kissing her, filling her up and bringing her to a fever pitch.

"Oh, Darcy!" she cried out, taking a deep breath as she sensed the release of a strong warmth moving through her, feeling him shudder in the release of his life force that filled her up.

"I love you," he cried out, "I love you, Maggie," he now whispered.

Feeling the perspiration on the side of her face and the release of the tension in his arms and legs, he melted into her. It was wonderful for her to feel his weight upon her, a moment she now treasured and had genuinely longed for.

"I don't want to crush you," he whispered, kissing her cheek.

"Crush me," she pleaded, joy filling her heart as she brushed her lips across the side of his face. "I am yours," she whispered. "Yours alone."

His lips found hers again in a lingering kiss that brought her a keen sense of pleasure. She loved his strength, his sweetness, his gentle caring. Darcy was her gift from God she gratefully now received in full measure.

"You are wonderful," he said with a sigh.

Soon, they were making love again, each eager to give and receive greater pleasure.

Afterwards, she found him watching her, his fingertip tracing her lips. Opening her mouth, she sucked on his finger, turning to him to grab his hand. She smiled before she kissed his lips.

"Have you been with a great many women," she asked him. "I know I am not the first."

Silently, he watched her for a long moment. "When I was fourteen my father gave me a book, *Aristotle's Masterpiece*. From that small volume I learned the mechanics of the male and female bodies. When I was fifteen my father took me to a brothel on the outskirts of Dublin where I was taught, through direct contact, the finer aspects of the female anatomy by a lass of sixteen from Belfast. Not all that pretty, but with an ample bosom and well versed in the sins of the flesh."

She smiled. "Is that right? How nice for you."

"She was proficient in teaching young men control and certain techniques to please a woman." He paused, pulling her to him and steadily gazing into her eyes. "Since then, there have been numerous encounters with women in the profession, except in Spain, an exotic whore gave me a bad case of the clap while our loyal troops were fighting the French. After that, my urges were moderated and discretion employed in selecting a partner for such engagements."

"I should hope so," she teasingly flared, pushing him away as she leaned back against a pillow to separate her back from the ornate headboard. In an act of modesty, she pulled up the white sheet to cover her nakedness.

Reaching up, with a sly smile on his handsome face, he pulled the sheet away to gaze at her breasts. "I love your breasts," he said, pulling himself up to take a nipple into his mouth, first one, and then the other.

"I love your mouth," she said, holding him close to her.

Momentarily stopping, he looked at her. "How many men have you been with?" he asked, and the question quite frankly surprised her.

"As you have loved more than one woman ... I have loved more than one man. Each love is different, though, Darcy, as you must know; rendering each one no less important."

Abruptly, he sat up and with a sullen face pushed a pillow behind him. "I have never loved any woman as I deeply love you ... I have never before been with a woman I loved, only harlots for hire."

"Not even Sally?" she teased.

"Never Sally. She would not even kiss me."

"Her loss." She turned to him. "How about Therese ... your sickly fiancée?"

"Only kisses ... nothing more," his anger was plain to her.

"And you were going to marry her, but felt no passion for her?"

Reaching out, he took her hand and kissed her palm. "Not like the passion I feel for you."

"I had no passion for Niall, poor man, and he was my husband."

"In name only," he reminded her, which made her smile.

"The only feelings I had for him were pity. He was stupid and never wanted to be anything else. It was awful that they made me marry him. Aunt Brigid apologized before I left Ireland."

There was a long moment of silence.

"But you loved Aidan," he said in a strained tone. "You gave yourself to him after we met. That is hard for me to forget, Mary Margaret."

"I had already given myself to him before we met, Darcy. Long before."

He looked surprised. "You were only fifteen." He frowned.

"I have always had passion, Darcy. I was born from passion. My parents were madly in love when I was conceived." She paused. "They were always madly in love, my mother and my father."

"I imagine mine were, though I have never discussed the matter with them."

Thoughtfully pausing, Maggie took his hand and held it against her breast. "You will probably never forget, Darcy, for I bore Aidan a son. But you must forgive me, my husband."

At that moment, he looked as though he was studying her without really seeing her.

"I loved Aidan from the first moment we met. I gave myself to him when I was fifteen, almost a year before I met you and before I ever considered that a man as fine as you would come into my life and love me. You must understand that Aidan and I planned to marry from the time we were children."

"What about me? About us?"

It was easy enough for her to see the pain in his eyes, to know how he felt knowing she was with Aidan before she was with him. That she had loved Aidan. It was plain to her that the truth was deeply hurtful to Darcy.

"I think I loved you from the first moment I saw you in your fine red-coat, dancing all night with me at the ball. How could I resist falling in love with you? You simply have to forgive me, my husband, for if Aidan had not died ..."

He turned and quickly kissed her, stopping the flow of her words with his passion, taking her into his arms as his smooth hands moved over her soft flesh to arouse the heat inside her once again. Her passion for Darcy was easily aroused, his passion for her all consuming.

Again, they made love, several times on their wedding night. Each of them softly promised the other to forget the past in order to share in the joys the future might bring to them, separately, and together, for all the rest of their days.

38

Life on the Chesapeake

There appeared to be a major difference between sailing on Dingle Bay, on Baltimore Harbor, and on the Chesapeake Bay. During the long summer, while sailing out on the vast bay, warm breezes toyed with her long hair, sometimes blowing her hair across her face when she forgot to tie it back or to bring along a bonnet. Some days the wind appeared to caress the whole of her, with care needed less the breeze reveal her unmentionables, as Darcy took her sailing on the wide expanse of the Gunpowder River. It was peaceful sailing in the warm sunlight as she watched her handsome husband steering at the helm. Darcy was proficient in navigating his sloop, the *Maggie*, catching the wind just so, as the boat glided through the wide expanse known as the Chesapeake Bay.

Summer was much longer and warmer in Maryland than in Ireland. On a weekend in Baltimore visiting the Finnegans in September of 1817, Maggie was surprised to be able to walk down the street in the evening, under the splendid glow of the new city gaslights, without the need to wear a shawl. Indian summer it was called, with no sign of a frost to change the color of the leaves. Twilight was the best time for taking a stroll. One could sometimes catch sight of the lamplighter illuminating the various gaslights up and down the streets.

"Just think," Maggie said to her husband, "the first city in America so illuminated!" That thought gave her a sense of pride. "Not even in Dublin, Darcy."

Darcy smiled, for he had often seen gaslights in London.

Her love for her husband ran deep, in addition to her great pleasure in residing at Marcus Manor. In fact, Maggie had fallen in love with her new country. It pleased her to be near the rapidly growing city of Baltimore with its busy harbor and many industries to provide jobs to men in need of a good day's wage. More than a few of the men employed were Irish.

Was the state called Maryland for no other reason, perhaps, than that it was the Land of Mary, the Blessed Mother, reborn and reclaimed for a new generation of souls in a new country, the United States of America, a country growing larger and more powerful every day. The citizens were forced to fight for their freedom, not once, but twice, from the domination of Great Britain. That freedom tended to make any Irish heart soar on the wind like the billowing sails of the boat on the Chesapeake Bay.

The past December, the Indiana Territory was admitted to the Union, the nineteenth land and its settlers so admitted to the United States of America. The Mississippi Territory would be next, making the states and the territories an even twenty. One portion of the great continent after another was requesting admittance as another division united under the auspices of a democratic system to be governed by the people of these United States. It seemed a wondrous thing to a young woman from County Kerry that a country might grow as fast as a child in its youth, becoming more than it was before in its ever expanding growth. Maggie was proud to think of herself as an American, though her heart would always belong to Ireland.

"Now I understand more about my father's claims," Maggie said.

"What is that?" Darcy inquired.

"That you can take the man out of Ireland, but you cannot take Ireland out of the man. It is true of you as well, my husband, with you only half Irish!"

The month after the wedding, Maggie accompanied Darcy to the Bentley Shipyards in Baltimore to check on the finishing touches of his new twenty-foot sloop to be christened the *Maggie,* the first boat ever named after her, and the first she had watched being built. Darcy made many trips into town before the wedding as an excuse to see her. When the time arrived to claim his prize, Moses and Isaac joined him. Isaac would return the carriage to Marcus Manor, and Moses help him to sail to the new dock on the Gunpowder River.

"Does this carriage have a name?" Maggie asked on the ride into town.

"Not that I know of," Darcy said.

"We shall call it Napoleon," she said.

"Indeed!" Darcy scowled. "I should not like to ride inside the villainous emperor. That is a truly disgusting thought, my dear."

"Is the buggy not led by the horses in command?"

"Wellington is not one of these horses," Darcy fumed. "These are Turk and Lightning. Wellington is too fine a thoroughbred to pull a carriage. These two are better suited to the task."

"You say *Maggie,* the sloop, is a beautiful girl. Are all ships girls?"

"In a sense ... that is the practice."

"The *Pegasus* must have been a very mature woman carrying all those passengers across the Atlantic in her belly."

All ships must be female, she thought. Was the sea not the Great Mother as the Druids had always claimed?

All the Finnegans had gathered to see them off from the pier as the *Maggie* was launched on her maiden voyage on a bright June day with the skies clear. Maggie took note of the expansion of Baltimore in a moment of surprise, as she remembered once sailing out of Dingle in a packet with Aidan. Momentarily, the memory tugged at her heart, and yet, the faint hills of Maryland were a far cry from the emerald green hills of her blessed Ireland.

Moses helped Darcy to hoist the sail. The slave was tall and striking, with wide set dark eyes, chiseled features, and a strong, muscular frame. He was two years younger than Darcy. The two men often hunted together, shooting deer and other wild game to feed everyone on the plantation. Moses had no memory of Africa. He was born at

Marcus Manor, as were his parents. The stories and traditions from his native country survived only as an oral tradition. Stories told by the African elders reminded Maggie of her Aunt Brigid and her ancient Druid lore.

Uncle Shane had always made a practice of keeping his families of darkies together. He never separated husband from wife or parent from child as many plantation owners did in an attempt to maintain submission. Shane wanted to keep his workers happy, and he allowed them free time. The slave quarters at Marcus Manor were cleaner and sturdier than others, with glass windows and wood shutters and wood-burning stoves. Their slaves were better clothed and better fed, Maggie felt, and that fact eased her mind to some degree about owning slaves.

"This here's a fine boat, Marse Darcy," Moses said, "A fine boat, indeed." His smile showed off his straight white teeth. Good teeth ran in his family, and Moses never seemed to stop smiling. He had a special way with all the animals, especially the horses. He was a good man just like his daddy, Uncle John, Shane always said. The slave's gentleness with Aidan and the children had not escaped her notice or his close friendship with the Piscataway braves.

"Is this not a fine day indeed for sailing?" Darcy said at the helm. "And is this not a fine sloop, my Maggie?"

"Are you addressing your boat or me, dear?" she inquired.

"Do I not usually address you as Mary Margaret?"

Moses appeared to watch their exchange with affection in his eyes.

"So ... you are addressing your boat. Now, you converse with sailboats, Master Brosnan, is that it?" Maggie said.

Moses laughed.

Maggie smiled at him, their relationship pleasant from the start, though all the slaves treated her with kindness and proper respect.

"I was asking you about my sailboat and calling her by name," Darcy explained in good humor, "Posed the question to you. You understood my meaning. My sloop is unable to converse ... in words."

"Actions speak louder than words ... that's what the preacher man say," Moses said.

Darcy nodded. "She handles well."

"What you are saying is ... your Maggie ... your boat," she said with a smirk, "speaks to you in how she handles, is that what you're saying, Darcy?"

"That's as good a way to say it as any," he said, as the wind filled the sails, swiftly taking the boat out onto the Patapsco River in the direction of the Chesapeake. "Although it seems to me that I now have two Maggies," he said, grinning.

Moses grinned and nodded.

"I see," she said. "I shall have to think about that. You just sail your sloop and get us as near the plantation as you can. The water seems cleaner the farther we sail away from town."

"Away from those factories," Moses said, "The furnaces and chimneys dirty the water."

"You had best put on your hat," she said to Moses, turning the rim of her bonnet to better shade her face. "Just because you have dark skin does not mean the sun will not harm you."

"Yes, ma'am," he said, picking up his hat, which the wind instantly blew out into the water out of reach. Woefully, Moses shook his head.

"I will get you another hat, Moses. I'm truly sorry," Maggie said. "I think Darcy has a hat he doesn't wear. If it is all right with him, I will give you one."

Nodding, Darcy turned. "I trust you have brought us a hearty lunch, perhaps we will stop somewhere between the Back and Middle Rivers and have a picnic."

"Quite hearty. Shannon and Caitlin were kind enough to prepare fried chicken, potato salad, cornbread, sharp cheese, pickled beans, chocolate cake, ginger cookies, apples, and some lovely plums. I had one earlier. So did Moses."

The slave smiled. "Mighty sweet, those plums, Missus."

"How does our lunch sound, my Captain?"

Looking pleased, Darcy said, "It sounds delicious. I have brought along some fine champagne for this special occasion ... to celebrate my Maggie's homecoming to Marcus Manor."

"I know ... both your Maggies," she said

"Both," Moses said, grinning.

"I trust there is enough champagne for Moses to have some," she said, glancing off toward the shore to avoid her husband's gaze.

Maggie was fully aware that Moses had overheard the conversation only that morning about Great Britain abolishing the slave trade. She wondered what he thought about so many states in the North freeing their slaves born after 1780 by their twenty-eighth birthday. Moses was twenty-five. Why were their slaves not free the same as those in Pennsylvania and other northern states, she wondered? They lived not that far from Philadelphia where slavery was frowned upon and most slaves already freed.

"No sense in wasting fine champagne by breaking the bottle on the hull of this sloop, which might damage it," Darcy said in an uneasy tone. "Perhaps I am captain of my ship now, a fine title for an old foot soldier once in His Majesty's service."

"You are hardly old. You are twenty-seven. And need I remind you that you are no longer a subject of mad King George III? Have you forgotten that you live in Maryland as an American?"

A smile played on his lips as he said, "I have not forgotten, Mary Margaret."

"You shall fight no more wars for the Crown," she said in a strong voice.

"Against them … perchance," he replied and his smile slowly faded.

"I should hope not." Maggie stood to grasp the mast as she gazed out across the water, "Our country is growing in strength each and every year. I think the Crown may soon find us too formidable to ever try to conquer us again."

"You have little understanding of King George's ambition to conquer the world, or at least to maintain its territories, India for one. Canada is still loyal to the Crown, our neighbors to the North."

"Stupidity!" she snapped, removing her bonnet and tossing her hair out of her face. The bonnet was soon back on her head and tied under her chin, for the wind was brisk.

Turning the boat into a strong gust, the sail sagged. Darcy readjusted his direction and the boat once again glided in relative calm. "An apple might be nice," he said. "I should have eaten more at breakfast."

Opening the basket, Moses removed two apples and handed them to Maggie.

"Thank you," she said, handing one to Darcy. "You must eat for strength, my captain." She turned to Moses and said, "Help yourself, Moses. There are several apples."

Darcy bit into his apple and Maggie daintily managed a bite.

The slave hesitated. "I'm not feeling hungry just yet. Thank you kindly, Missus."

It was a still way to the Back and Middle Rivers where there was an open spot near Cedar Point. The anchor was dropped and lunch was served on the boat. Darcy uncorked the champagne and the cork flew into the water. Two glasses were poured, with one handed to Maggie, who reached into the basket to pull out a tin cup. She held out the cup for her husband to pour.

"For Moses ... please," she said, gazing directly into his eyes.

After he hesitated only briefly, with Moses watching him closely, Darcy filled the cup halfway. Then, Maggie handed the cup to a stunned Moses who seemed to have briefly forgotten how to smile.

"You must help us toast our new sailboat," she said.

Staring at the cup, Moses said, "I ain't never drunk champagne before."

"I have never drank champagne," she corrected in her attempt to improve the grammar of all the slaves, which at times seemed to her a daunting task.

"Yes, ma'am," he said, puzzled, and he stared at the champagne in the cup.

Lifting his glass in a toast, Darcy said, "To my new sailboat, the *Maggie*, may she sail upon calm seas under clear skies and always be safe for her passengers."

"To Maggie," she said, sipping.

After one sip, Moses looked startled. "Now, that has a bite!"

Darcy and Maggie laughed.

"Like my Maggie," Darcy said, hugging her and kissing her forehead.

"I sees what you mean," Moses said, taking another swallow and grimacing only slightly. "She sure seems like some kind of sparkly woman to me."

And everyone laughed.

Several days later, Maggie persuaded Darcy to accompany her on a walk through the woods toward the river. Crossing a creek, she inquired, "What is the name of this creek, Darcy?"

"I do not know that it has a name."

"Well, it needs a name. Shall we call it Kerry Creek, Dingle Creek or Dublin Creek?" Surveying the creek, she narrowed her eyes. "I doubt Uncle Shane will mind if we give the creek a name, unless he has already named it."

"Kerry Creek it shall be. Dingle or Dublin is not a suitable name for a creek, in my opinion."

"What about the pond near the fields ... what shall we call that?" Taking a breath, she admired the richness of the place that was now her home, the magnificent trees and rolling hills, the special beauty of Maryland.

"It shall be Dublin Pond," Darcy said with a nod and he laughed. "Do you also have a name for the well?"

"It is Maggie's Well, of course. You should have figured that one out yourself."

Darcy stopped and pulled her to him, wrapping his arms around her and gazing into her eyes before he kissed her. "I am awfully glad that I married you. Do you know that, Mrs. Brosnan?"

"I am awfully glad that I married you, too, for I wouldn't have a well or a boat named after me."

Again, they walked on into the woods, with their arms around each other.

"And we wouldn't be having a son next year, either," Maggie said.

At once, Darcy stopped and turned to her. "You are with child?"

Smiling, she said, "I know it's a boy. Mother told me so in a dream. We are going to have lots of children, Darcy. Will that be all right with you?"

Grabbing her, he twirled her around, and then, he carefully put her down. Overjoyed, he called out across the river, "It's wonderful. I'm going to be a father! Darcy Brosnan is going to be a father!"

All along, Maggie had thought that Darcy might be pleased.

39

Generations

For Maggie, the years seemed to fly by like the leaves in an autumn breeze that marked the passing of the seasons in shades of green, yellow, red, orange, gold, and russet. Fourteen months after their April wedding, Dermot Desmond arrived. Their son was hearty and highly vocal, named after Darcy's favorite uncle and her father's ancient family roots, the knightly Desmonds of County Kerry. His dark hair and dark eyes were similar to Aidan's.

Not long after their wedding, Maggie was deeply upset by the sad news of the early death of her favorite author, Miss Jane Austen of England. There would be no more of Austen's fine novels for her to read. She made a point to reread them all out loud to her kitchen and household slaves, who seemed to enjoy hearing the romantic stories of the English gentry.

Thirteen months after their first child was born, Gareth Martin arrived, with his mother's auburn hair and his father's bright blue eyes. Their new son was named after Darcy's father and paternal grandfather, the man who had left Prudence her many fine books. Uncle Shane's library was even more impressive, with volume upon volume of book on various subjects in all shapes and sizes, providing ample knowledge and reading adventures for Maggie and her family.

At the insistence of Cornelius Finnegan, Maggie's small volume on various herbs, their use and application in healing body, mind and spirit, was added to the books on a shelf. Many copies of *The Nature of Herbs and Their Medicinal Remedies* were sold across the nation. A few copies were posted to her Aunt Brigid, to whom the book was dedicated, with others for her father, Prudence and Megan, as well as to Darcy's relatives in Ireland, Scotland and England. A proud Uncle Shane gave away many autographed copies of Maggie's book published in November of 1818 near the time of her twentieth birthday.

Not long after the birth of Gareth in 1819, the newspapers reported the first transatlantic steamship, the *Savannah*, crossing from Georgia to Liverpool in less than a month. That same month a letter arrived from Megan to announce the birth of her fraternal twins, Rebecca and Robert, the girl the eldest by thirteen minutes. Darcy had happily assumed his role as Aidan's father, since the toddler had immediately bonded with him. In Charleston, the Gallaghers had two healthy daughters and one son: Constance born in 1817, with her grandmother's red hair and her mother's green eyes.

By late 1819, three more states were born into the Union: Mississippi in 1817, Illinois in 1818, and Alabama in 1819. The American family of states was growing by leaps in numbers and vastly in boundaries. Immigrants continued to pour into the country, ships often arriving in Baltimore with many of those onboard Irish.

That October, Megan wrote to Maggie with astonishing news:

My Dearest Maggie,

I do hope that you are sitting down, my sister, for the news I have for you is both shocking and grand. Last week riding to the harbor in our new maroon cabriolet, I noticed a finely dressed, handsome gentleman who looked strangely familiar. On his arm was a beautiful mulatto woman dressed in the most elegant fashions. She wore a fantastic purple hat with gorgeous feathers and matching boa, stunning. Perhaps the initial reason I stared.

There are few free colored in Charleston, though the numbers do seem to increase. Kevin goes to a colored barber who bought his freedom. He swears by Samson's shaves and haircuts. But it is unusual to see a finely dressed mulatto woman near the wharf on the arm of a white man. Scandalous, even though we all know that many white plantation owners cavort with their female slaves, siring one little pickaninny after another, usually lighter in complexion than the mother but few truly white. That is what my mammy says. Sally Ann is kind and truthful in addition to being wonderful in her care of our children.

You can perhaps imagine my surprise in discovering that the handsome gentleman was our very own brother, Liam Niall, who ran away in 1814 and broke our father's heart. The dashing rouge looks so much like our father. Shame on Liam, I said! And I told him so!

Liam was quite astonished to find me in Charleston married to Kevin, with 3 children and the owners of a fine hotel. He now lives near a large sugar plantation in Jamaica where he supervises the export of sugar, the reason he and his wife, Antoinette, were in Charleston on holiday. Kevin immediately moved them into one of our finest hotel rooms. But that is not the whole of it, so take a deep breath, my dear sister. Our Liam has been on a dangerous and amazing adventure.

Originally, he signed on with a merchant ship out of Cork for the West Indies the day after he left home. The ship sailed to the Caribbean, with him homesick <u>and seasick</u> most of the way. Then, they were attacked by pirates who seized the ship and its cargo. Many pirates are Irish, it seems, and the passengers on his ship were given several choices: (1) to become a <u>pirate,</u> (2) be marooned on some uninhabited island, or (3) be set adrift in a dingy with others so inclined. No fair choices all around. One Irishman convinced Liam to join their band of renegades, so our brother was a pirate for the next year, during which time he conquered his seasickness. Needless to say, being a pirate was not something he wanted to write home about. I am sure that you must understand.

When Liam came down with a high fever, the heartless thieves left him to die in Jamaica where one of the more kindly in his marauding band took him to a local doctor. The doctor was a mulatto, part African and part Irish on both sides. His great grandfather, Seamus McGuire, was transported during the terrible Cromwell years in Ireland, and his grandmother was born to an Irish exile.

The doctor, Henry McGuire, grew fond of Liam. Why would he not with our brother such a charming devil? I cannot get over the fact that Liam was a pirate, brandishing a cutlass against innocent souls on the high seas. I was afraid to even ask him if he had killed anyone. Perhaps he took those stories you read to us too much to heart? Like 'Robinson Crusoe'? As fate would have it, Antoinette is Dr. McGuire's youngest daughter, presently 22, lovely and charming. Our brother is now 25. Just think! They have two children in Kingston: Arthur, 2, and Muriel, soon to be one. Three years ago, Liam was hired on at a plantation to direct the export of sugar to Europe and America.

It is rare that he sails with the sugar, but they were eager to see Charleston, as this ship returns directly to Kingston filled with cotton. Our meeting was a true Act of Providence. Perchance our blessed mother was whispering in his ear from the Otherworld so Liam might find me here ... a blessing beyond my wildest dreams.

Liam has promised to write to father and to you. I have told him of your life up until now and of our family in Ireland, including the recent death of our stepmother, Eileen, (whom he knew not) from the consumption that has been her fate these many years. Also, of the drowning death of young Mark, 11, and the fact that Brian ran off to join the army in his rebellion against our father who so generously married his mother and cared for those children all these years.

Liam wants to visit Maryland, perhaps through a shipment of sugar. And yet, he agrees with the new law that equates trading in slaves with piracy punishable by death. Praise God, he is no longer a pirate nor a slave-holder like us, yet, he works for a man who owns 100 slaves. Who knows what shall happen to those with slaves, something that deeply troubles our brother. His children are part African from ancestors sold into slavery, as well as part Irish, who might as well have been slaves. Their lives no bet-ter as indentured servants under the cruelest of conditions in Barbados and Jamaica.

What a modern world we now live in, my sister. Perhaps the steamboats that shall soon sail up and down the coast will enable us to visit one another. It is my prayer that our children may love one another as cousins. In spite of the fact that our childhood was not easy with mother leaving us so young and father having to work so hard, I am grateful for your love and kindness and for the love of my brothers. I miss Matthew and Sean and am happy to find Liam safe, happy and alive!

As you may already know, Matthew is marrying a Protestant cousin of Kevin's at Christmas. He met Heather at our wedding when she was 14. Now she is 17 and Matthew 23. I hear their love runs deep and Matthew is converting. I still attend St. Michael's Episcopal Church with Kevin. Upon examining my soul, I am not sure that it matters to God if I am Protestant or Catholic, though I believe in the birth, sacrifice, and salvation of my Lord and Savior Jesus Christ, so I guess that is all that matters.

The twins are fussing, so I must go. Two babies at once are a great deal of work that drives me near to distraction. My mammy is not a wet nurse. I know I could not survive without my slaves. Even after meeting Liam and Antoinette, Kevin talks of buying more slaves, even though Moses freed the children of Israel from the land of Egypt where they were all slaves once upon a time.

My love to Darcy and all the young Brosnans. I am pleased that Aidan was adopted by your fine husband. It is a very good thing indeed. Please write to me soon. I miss you and I always remember you in my prayers.

All my love always,

Megan Caitlin

Maggie was thrilled to learn that her eldest brother was still alive and prospering, though she found it difficult to stop crying as a pen was applied to paper to immediately write to her father. Because of her own secret covert position against slavery, it pleased her that her new sister-in-law had descended from both Irish exiles and African slaves. It only seemed right that Antoinette had married Liam, scandalous news that it was indeed at Marcus Manor.

Not long after she officially moved to the plantation, Maggie started to teach her household slaves how to read and write.

"But it is against the law to educate our slaves in the English language!" Uncle Shane protested in front of two of the kitchen slaves. "Surely you know that! Do you want us all to get thrown into jail and fined a great sum?"

"Oh, fiddle de de, Uncle Shane! No one is going to jail," Maggie said, kissing his cheek, "least of all you," she added, fully understanding that any full-blooded Irishman was highly susceptible to the charms of nearly any attractive woman.

Nonetheless, a number of slaves still secretly gathered in the kitchen to learn the alphabet and numbers, mostly the women and the children, after Shane and Darcy had left for the fields or were down at the river to supervise the loading of tobacco into cutters for the merchant ship anchored off shore. She took Moses into her confidence, agreeing to teach him to read and write, if he promised not to tell his master.

One day, Darcy walked in and caught her teaching the alphabet to a group of women. He heartily complained, but she explained that their children needed someone to read to them besides her, since she had a great deal to do in running the manor house. Within a few weeks, not just the slaves, but a number of the Piscataway gathered around the kitchen table to draw letters and numbers on the margins of discarded newspapers. Missionaries had taught Yuma to read and write, mostly from the Holy Bible. Now, the shaman relished reading books from the library, such as *The Decline and Fall of the Roman Empire*. The old medicine man was amazed to learn that such places, such fierce warriors and emperors had existed long ago on the other side of the world.

The Piscataway always treated her with respect. Frequently, Maggie inquired after their customs and spiritual practices, sharing her knowledge of herbs and helping to heal them, especially with Yuma. In turn, the medicine man had taught her about the local herbs, roots, barks, and of the nuts and fruits of certain trees in the woodlands. The spiritual beliefs of the Piscataway and the Africans seemed similar to her, reminding her of what she had learned of the Old Religion from her Aunt Brigid in Ireland. It was easy for her to equate the one with the others. Had the Druids also perhaps taught their ancestors, she wondered? Their afterlife sounded much the same and was only culturally different. After being forced into baptism as Christians, many of them still held fast to the teachings of their forefathers, the same as she embraced the teachings of the Druids rather than blindly accepting the words of the catechism.

At times, Maggie tended to be forceful in expressing herself to her household slaves, especially Ruth and Rebecca. She told the women to pass on the information to the men and the children, with the sharing of books to remain their secret. The two slaves appeared to enjoy their unusual relationship with their mistress, with her constantly trying to stop them from thinking of themselves as slaves. The two women would go out of their way to please her, while she secretly considered Ruth and Rebecca as her only true women friends on the plantation.

In spite of all that, Darcy constantly reminded her of her need to "know her place" as the mistress of Marcus Manor. And yet, the other local white women avoided her, most having been taught to hate the Irish from the cradle.

Books were read to her slaves the same as she had read to her family and friends in Ireland. She taught the African midwives about her use of herbs and often assisted in the delivery of a baby in the slave quarters. The respect she received from all the slaves had not escaped her husband's notice.

"With you at Marcus Manor, peace seems to reign supreme," Darcy said in the privacy of their bedchamber one evening.

After another eighteen months, their first daughter, Brigid Kelly, was born with her father's blonde hair and his brilliant blue eyes. Daddy's girl also inherited her mother's spunk. It was fun for Maggie to finally dress a girl as their three rambunctious boys ran up and down the stairs and all around the yards.

Most of the Brosnan children's playmates were the slave children. Down the road at the Plunkett Plantation, the master's children were never allowed to play with the slave children. Skin other than white, Jeremiah claimed, was vastly inferior, especially black or brown skin. According to Jeremiah Plunkett, the white race was the chosen race, and he claimed that was written in the Holy Bible by God, though he was unable to locate the exact scripture.

The children at Marcus Manor avoided the Plunkett children at all times.

"Why are you called a *red man*, Yuma?" Maggie inquired one day. "You don't look red to me."

The old shaman laughed. "It is the way of the white man. I hear that the English do not care much for the Irish, and the Irish not in the least for the English, both of them white. Is this true?"

"Sometimes," she thoughtfully said. "There are shops in Baltimore with signs in the windows that read: 'No Irish Need Apply.'" Maggie said. "Darcy is part English, part Scot and part Irish, but it seems to me that too many Irish have already sailed to America. And lately, the government is taking the land away from the Indians, from tribes here long before the white man. It is unfortunate that we cannot all live together in peace and harmony."

The eldest son of young Master Brosnan, Aidan Padraic, was the strongest and tallest until some of the African boys grew bigger and taller than him. At times, Aidan seemed older and wiser than his years. He was especially fond of reading, although his sister Brigid could annoy him on occasion with her constant chattering when he was trying to concentrate on a book. Alone in the library, Aidan would read for hours. He was always asking for more books. He even staked a claim for a shelf of his own in one corner near the bottom.

More books were often required in order for Maggie to teach the children more about history and geography, also additional maps for some of the walls. There were no schools nearby where their children might be properly educated. Darcy spoke of sending Aidan to Boston or London for his education, but Maggie would not hear of it. She decided to teach her children herself as she was once taught in the hedge school before she began to read the many fine books in the vast library of Prudence Pratt. All the many books in Uncle Shane's library would provide an excellent education for their children.

In 1821, the newspapers reported the re-election of President James Monroe. The state of Missouri joined the Union on the Compromise Bill as a slave state, while Maine became a free state. Mexico gained its independence from Spain, and soon afterwards, Moses Austin settled with 300 American families in the Territory of Texas.

In spite of her reservation concerning Church doctrine, Maggie was pleased when the first Roman Catholic cathedral in America, the *Assumption of the Blessed Virgin Mary*, was dedicated in Baltimore. Under duress from his Uncle Shane, Darcy agreed to take the entire family to the dedication. That same month, Napoleon died on the island of St. Helena, which made Darcy pensive and reflective. That was also the month that Padraic O'Reilly and Prudence Pratt began to court in Dingle, Ireland, which was no big surprise to Maggie. She thought it was about time!

In July of 1823, right before the birth of Brian, the first steamboat navigated the Mississippi River to Fort Snelling. Their new son was named after Brian Boru, an Irish High King who ended the Norse conquest of Ireland, with Kevin as his middle name after his uncle in Charleston. His hair was a tawny brown and his eyes the same amber as his mother's.

In September, Padraic Desmond O'Reilly married Prudence Elizabeth Pratt in a simple ceremony at St. Mary's Catholic Church in Dingle. After a two week honeymoon in Dublin and Glendalough, Padraic fully moved into the fine house on Goat Street. Matthew and Heather moved into the farm to take over the family business with the assistance of young Sean Joseph.

Among Maggie's special treasures were the letters she received from her Aunt Brigid filled with information about the various members of the family and about her old friends and former patients in Ireland. That was how she learned that Prudence was starting to rely on her father's management of her properties around the peninsula. At last, Maggie had the stepmother she had always wanted, even though she now resided far away with her own young family in America.

On Brian's first birthday, a necklace and matching earrings of amber were the gifts from her beloved husband, which reminded her of how her father had always said that her eyes were the color of fine amber stones. By then, Darcy had made many of her dreams come true, for she now resided in the grand manor house of her dreams not far from a river that flowed into the wide expanse of the Chesapeake Bay. The bay was not far from the fertile fields of their plantation from which fine tobacco was being exported to Europe purchased mostly by the British, which still never set quite right with Maggie.

"Our tobacco imported to England should be mixed with a proper amount of gunpowder grown near the river," Maggie teased, "to explode in their faces upon lighting a pipe," she had said more than once. "Or send along enough to blow up the British House of Parliament and hold them hostage until Ireland is granted freedom from the Crown."

"Now, now, Mary Margaret," Uncle Shane said. "That would not be good for business."

"But it might be good for Ireland."

From the start, Shane was very good to her. He never complained about the boys fighting, the babies crying, the children screaming or the dogs barking. The man was an obvious saint.

"Since my grandchildren seldom visit, it is yours that bring me joy and it is your children who shall share in the bounty from this place."

They had managed to provide Uncle Shane with a sense of family, something missing in his life for a while. One day, a lawyer was summoned and all were asked to gather in the library.

"I am leaving Marcus Manor and all of its land to you and your bonny wife," Shane said to Darcy and Maggie. "My children have done right well. My daughters reside in the lap of luxury with doting husbands and everything they might ever want. The plantation shall one day be yours."

In March of 1825, President John Quincy Adams was inaugurated as president, the first son of a president to become president. A week later, Uncle Shane suffered a fatal heart attack at the age of sixty-four. His heart was weak for years, but he was never a man to be kept down. Maggie had sensed the Otherworld calling to him, perhaps to reunite him with his wife. And yet, for several years she was aware of his intimate alliance with Chenoa, the younger sister of Yuma. She was an attractive woman with a merry laugh widowed years earlier during an outbreak of yellow fever. Only the prior summer, Chenoa had fallen off a horse which resulted in her death. Since her loss, Shane appeared to have taken a turn for the worse.

On the day of Uncle Shane's burial, two white doves perched on the branch of the oak tree not far from the porch. In way of the Piscataway, the spirits of Shane and Chenoa were in those two white birds. As the doves flew off toward the setting sun, Yuma confirmed her suspicions.

After another week, young Brianna Louise was born. It seemed to Maggie that deaths and births often occurred in a family in the same year. In less than a year, her new daughter's hair was long and dark and her green eyes sparkled. The independent and willful child already showed promise with her creativity.

That October, the newspapers reported that the Erie Canal now linked the Great Lakes with the Atlantic Ocean through the Hudson River. Prudence wrote about the first public railroad with a steam locomotive in England, in addition to her great happiness in being Padraic's wife. Her father was happy to once again be married to a woman he truly loved and could cherish.

In January of 1827, the Duke of Wellington became the British Supreme Commander, a post Darcy deemed rightfully his with his special wisdom and panache. Her husband missed the reunions with his fellow officers from Waterloo, which the Iron Duke hosted yearly to honor the bravery of his men on the field of battle on that fateful day of great victory and great loss.

That was also the year that the Baltimore and Ohio Railroad was chartered, the first commercial railroad in America. That March, the first Negro newspaper, *Freedom's Journal,* was published in New York, with Maggie's copy safely hidden away in a trunk. In July, slavery was abolished in the state of New York, but in August, race riots broke out in Cincinnati, which forced 1,000 Negroes to leave for Canada where slavery was no longer sanctioned. By November, the Creek Indians lost their land, which was not good at all, in Maggie's opinion. The government was making Yuma more uneasy every month of every year.

On November 10, 1827, Maggie made up her mind that their last child was born. Timothy Thomas was bald at birth, but in a year's time his hair was a light brown and his eyes the amber of his mother's. He was the spitting image of his mother in a boy's body. Seven children seemed enough to Maggie. Herbs were brewed with Darcy's full consent, for her husband now had six children of his own: four boys, two girls, in addition to young Aidan.

By the age of ten, Aidan Padraic decided to become blood brothers with Pilan, translated as *supreme essence,* a young Piscataway brave. The two boys explored the woods and streams together, climbed the hills and fished the river. The two young braves were the same age. Pilan had also learned to read and write at the kitchen table and often joined Aidan in the library to read a book. Going through life side by side was a great adventure for the two young boys.

By late 1828, the Gallaghers in Charleston had six children. Liam and Antoinette had five youngsters in Kingston, Jamaica. In Ireland, Matthew and Heather already had three children. Sean supposedly had a sweetheart he planned to marry. Darcy had nieces and nephews that numbered twenty. An entire new generation had been born in various parts of the world to carry on the standards and bloodlines of the O'Reilly's, the Brosnan's, and the Gallagher's, for many generations to come—and that seemed like a very good thing, indeed, to Maggie.

40

The Slave Market

During the past year, the first man born in the backwoods of the Carolinas to Scot-Irish immigrant parents from Antrim, Ireland, was elected as the seventh president of the United States. Andrew Jackson was nicknamed Old Hickory and one of the foremost heroes in the Second War for Independence. He led the Battle of New Orleans to the overwhelming defeat of the British. Prior to his election, Jackson had also prospered as a slaveholding lawyer in Tennessee. Members of the National Republican, or Whig Party, called him *King Andrew I,* or a *hooligan,* for voting against the Second Bank of the United States, a private corporation but government sponsored monopoly.

The present pontiff of the Roman Catholic Church, Pope Pius VIII, governed during a propitious time for Roman Catholics. The new Prime Minister of Great Britain, the Duke of Wellington, had approved the efforts of Daniel O'Connell in passing the Catholic Emancipation Bill drafted by Sir Robert Peel.

In Dingle, Ireland, Padraic O'Reilly immediately sat at his desk to write a letter:

My Dear Mary Margaret,

It is a grand day for Irish Catholics, and for the moment, God save King George IV, though he happens to be a bloody Anglican Protestant. The next task for Darcy's former illustrious commander is to free Ireland from the Crown. As long as there is life in this body, I shall cling to that hope for my beloved Ireland.

An antislavery pamphlet published in Boston, *Walker's Appeal,* was purchased by Maggie, but refused even slight perusal by her husband. In fact, Darcy was adamant about wanting "the damn pamphlet out of the house!"

"Our slaves are well cared for!" he ranted.

"Would you like to be a slave, Darcy?" Maggie inquired, fixing him with her amber gaze.

Her husband remained silent and turned away from her.

Near Christmas, the first stone arch railroad bridge in the United States was dedicated near Baltimore. It was the holiday on which her husband presented her with a copy of Noah Webster's first *American Dictionary of the English Language.* The children could now look up the meaning and spelling of words in the library at Marcus Manor.

In January, the first U.S. railroad station opened in Baltimore, but it was months before the passenger service published its timetable in the *Baltimore American* newspaper. The train ran from Baltimore to Ellicott Mills, with some tickets purchased by some for the pure joy of taking a ride on a train. That September, a horse beat a locomotive named *Tom Thumb* near Baltimore. Many still claimed that the train would never replace the horse.

Free men boycotted slave-produced goods a month after the 1st Negro Convention in Philadelphia.

In the autumn of 1830, her father wrote from Ireland:

The man has liberated us all. Irish Catholics are now free to own property and hold positions of respect in the government and in commerce. O'Connell has a brand new crusade now, the abolishment of slavery in the civilized world, commencing with Great Britain. Since you own 40 slaves, and Megan and Kevin now own 12, I shall write a letter to them next. Kindly give us your thoughts on this important moral issue.

"What do you want me to say to my father concerning the abolishment of slavery in America?" Maggie inquired, boldly staring into Darcy's blue Irish eyes.

"In spite of O'Connell, I wonder if you understand how fortunate you are to have a husband who is tolerant of your position against laws considered just in a country free of monarchy?"

Taking down her long hair, his warm hands were soon on her warm flesh, reaching for her breasts and pulling her close to him. Darcy nuzzled her neck, toying with her nipples between his persuasive fingers. "Do you love me?" he whispered, kissing her neck.

Turning to face him, Maggie inquired, "Do my eyes not tell you of my love, my husband?" She kissed him. "Does my kiss not tell you how very much I love you?"

Soon, they were together in the bed, bodies intertwined, limbs wrapped around limbs, savoring wet kisses. When suddenly she pushed Darcy away from her and sat up.

"How much might you earn by selling me, Darcy, making me some man's sex slave?"

He scowled. "I do not find your question the least bit amusing."

"Perhaps to Jeremiah?"

Indignation filled his countenance as he stared at her and narrowed his eyes.

"How can his stupid wife look the other way as if she has no brain and no eyes with which to see? What sort of woman must she be?"

"That is no business of ours," Darcy said. "I am hardly Jeremiah."

"No, but who in this free country was free to decide that one man might sell another because his skin is a different, darker color?" she flared, standing in her nakedness, deep anger kindled inside her. "What fine, upstanding Christian made that choice, one of our noble Pilgrim Fathers, no doubt?"

Darcy stood and sighed. "I do not want to talk politics with you, Mary Margaret. Please let us not quarrel over such matters." He stepped closer and reached for her. "I love you, Maggie. I love you madly."

301

"And I love you," she said, instantly melting into him, for Darcy was the man she loved. Even good men appeared to own slaves, she silently told herself, but how did that make it right?

The next January, the first issue of the *Liberator* was published in Boston by abolitionist William Lloyd Garrison. After reading every single word, the paper was safely hidden away in her secret trunk in the far corner of the attic. It was in June that the matter of buying more slaves had come up, one slave for the house, others to care for the horses and work the fields.

This time, Maggie insisted on going with her husband to the slave market, and that was in spite of Darcy's very strong objections. On the previous night she had laid awake for hours questioning their need to purchase even one more slave. Many states had already abolished slavery. Why did more human beings need to live in bondage at Marcus Manor? All the others were there for many years. For twelve long years she had devoted herself to educating and refining her slaves. Fifty slaves were to be sold from a plantation on the eastern shore forced into bankruptcy. New slaves were no longer legal to buy from Africa, but the rumors persisted just the same. Megan had written of exactly that matter in one of her recent letters.

She thought perhaps it was because of the summer heat that all the slaves were stripped down, men bared to the waist, women only partly clad, small children stark naked. The men on the platform glowed with an oil, perhaps to emphasize the muscles in their arms, legs, chests and backs, and not just on the young bucks, either. The oil made the men look stronger. The male slaves at Marcus Manor usually wore shirts, except during the hottest weather. Maggie seldom ventured into the fields during the dog days of summer, since she was usually too busy with weaving, sewing, preserving foods, and other domestic chores. No naked male bodies were seen by her except for those of her sons and her husband, and Aidan, of course, once upon a time. There had certainly never been men on public display to be auctioned the same as animals.

The vision before her of the brawny, young blacks on the platform stirred strange yearnings down deep inside her, primal feelings that actually made her blush. African slaves were referred to as "savages" by the Preacher McKay and all the other white men. Such yearnings were only aroused before by the men she loved, not by strangers, and certainly never before by slaves. Still, what was it like for these men in their native Africa, she wondered, nearly naked, hunting lions or tigers with a spear? Africa was like another world that she had only read about and explored within her mind. She had taught her children and the slave children what little she could glean of Africa, and she loved to hear the stories of Africa sometimes told by the elders in the slave quarters, stories passed down from one generation to the next.

The two young manacled males on the platform appeared to be in their teens. Each of them kept glancing at a pretty woman and younger boy standing on the sidelines. The pathetic expressions on their faces tugged at her heart. Most of these slaves had been together for their whole lives. The former owner's unexpected death had left his widow deeply in debt. The two boys about to be sold again glanced at the attractive quadroon and the boy of about ten years, perhaps her son. Tears streamed down the woman's face as she watched another black man being taken to the back by his new master, Jeremiah Plunkett, who was standing with his overseer, Jethro Covey. Maggie could hardly stand to even look at the red-eyed, potbellied Plunkett, who had just purchased four more male slaves to work near to death. Plunkett was suspected of killing two of his slaves during the past year, but the local sheriff did absolutely nothing at all.

Suddenly, Maggie detected a connection in the Otherworld between the dark male slave and the pretty quadroon. That was when she made up her mind to buy the woman. If the woman worked at Marcus Manor, at least she would be near her man and could perhaps see him and be with him on occasion.

"Buy those two," Maggie urgently whispered to Darcy.

"I only need one man," he said, "An older one. I will buy another woman for you to help out with the children in the house."

"I know which woman," she said, noticing the quadroon was now openly weeping, with her eyes still on her manacled man standing next to Plunkett. Suddenly, Jeremiah spit tobacco on the ground and leered at Maggie. "Buy those boys," she demanded, noticing gossamer threads connecting them to each other. "They are young and strong, Darcy. I know what I'm talking about. Buy them."

Briefly hesitant, Darcy held up his hand and said, "Three hundred for the two of them."

The auctioneer glared at him and said, "You can't have both of them for three hundred."

"Four hundred for the two," another man called out from the back.

"Three hundred each," Maggie called out, carefully adjusting her bonnet, for she was the only white woman attending the slave auction that day.

The two boys nudged each other and grinned.

"They'll be hard workers. I could use a strong boy in the house, Darcy." Maggie's stomach was giving her fits, but she simply had to have those boys. They should not be separated, she was convinced of that.

The auctioneer was amused. "Is that an honest to goodness bid, Mr. Brosnan?"

His jaw set, Darcy refused to even look at Maggie as he nodded his head and said, "Yes."

The two black boys looked pleased.

"Three-fifty a piece," hollered a man in the back.

"Four hundred each!" Maggie shouted out, thinking, *this is fun*, as her husband suddenly turned pale.

"Well?" said the auctioneer, narrowing his eyes.

"Four hundred each," Darcy half-heartedly said.

"Four-twenty-five," the man in back quickly countered.

"Four-fifty," Darcy said before his wife could open her mouth.

The boys were bought for $900, surprisingly, not more. They looked somber as the woman in shackles and the three other women near her age climbed up onto the platform. It was a pitiful sight, Maggie thought, fighting the tears starting to fill her eyes from seeing women in chains, half dressed, to be sold as slaves. The young boy was crying. The quadroon, the prettiest of the lot, would not come cheap.

Jeremiah Plunkett started out the bidding by shouting, "Five hundred!" .

Cringing inside, and knowing exactly what the fornicator had in mind, Maggie was suddenly torn. The quadroon's man would be on his plantation. What was she to do?

"Five-fifty," Maggie said, raising her hand as she gently nudged her husband. "She's the one."

Darcy nodded to the auctioneer.

From the looks on the faces of all the men present, each man wanted to bed that slave. But that was not going to happen, if Maggie Brosnan had anything to do with it.

"Six hundred," was the bid from the back.

"Six-fifty," Jeremiah hollered out.

"Seven hundred," Darcy countered, for he truly despised Jeremiah.

"Seven-fifty," Jeremiah yelled, his eyes becoming slits as he leered.

"Eight hundred," said the man in back.

"Nine hundred!" Darcy countered, his arms now folded defiantly across his chest as he glared.

Sarah ended up costing them $1,000, but Maggie thought she was worth every penny. Eleven-year-old Harry cost another $500, but he was her son. Gerard, her brother, looked younger than his fourteen years standing next to his half-brother, Henry, thirteen. Darcy had all the chains removed.

Upon their arrival back at the plantation, Darcy immediately put Moses in charge of the four new slaves. Their reactions showed that their treatment was not what they had expected. Maggie spoke to them as though they were four new house guests arriving for an extended stay at Marcus Manor, as her husband listened to her in utter and complete astonishment.

A short time later, Darcy inquired, "Would you like to take a walk by the river?"

"It seems like a beautiful evening for a stroll, my darling."

Walking along their usual route, Maggie slipped her arm through her husband's, with both of them silent as they strolled beneath the shade of the tall woodland trees.

"You cost me some serious money today, Mary Margaret," Darcy finally said.

"Twenty-four hundred dollars does seem like a lot. But I hear tell that slaves are getting more expensive every day. Young men in the South can cost as much as $2,000 for just one." She could tell from his tone that her husband had something serious on his mind. "You will not be sorry, Darcy. You should be happy that you kept a family together. Uncle Shane never separated families. I hear it is rare for slave masters, but what can you do besides be like your dear, wonderful uncle who left us this fine plantation? It was the Christian thing for you to do."

His audible sigh amused her, as he suddenly turned to face her. "I did not need four new slaves. I would have preferred a man in his thirties with some experience, not those in need of training."

"Those boys are strong. And Sarah's husband can always pay her a visit." Maggie paused. "I will never let her go to that plantation, Darcy. She would be raped for a certainty. Those are horrible, evil men."

Again, they walked on toward the river in silence. Darcy extended his hand to her to help her over the creek.

"Kerry Creek," Maggie softly said.

Darcy smiled. "The river already had a name when we arrived. I know you would have liked to name it yourself." He chuckled, wrapping her arm through his, his dark mood having lifted.

"I find it charming that our river is called the Gunpowder River. And it is quite amusing that the Indians once thought that they could plant gunpowder the same as they did corn."

"Have you named any of these trees or shrubs that I should know about?"

"Of course not, Darcy."

He turned to her, wrapping his arms around her and gazing deeply into her eyes. "I am still glad that I married you, even though you forced me to buy too many slaves today." He softly kissed her.

"It is a good thing that you married me with all of these children we have. For soon there shall be eight young Brosnans," she said and she softly kissed him.

"You said there would be no more children. That seven were enough."

"My herbs seemed to have failed me. We shall have another daughter. And now, I have a new slave to help me care for her, and our boys have new playmates. That is a good thing, Darcy."

"You are a very clever woman, Mary Margaret. The two daughters we already have are bonny indeed, and now there shall be no more need to worry. If you would like to know the truth," he said and he kissed her,

"I would like to make love to you right here on this spot," and his hands moved over her as he kissed her neck and her lips again.

Pulling away from him, Maggie said, "I do not want our slaves or our children finding us buck naked in the woods, Darcy," and she slapped at his roving hands. "You must use your head to maintain your reputation as a respectable plantation master and fine gentleman."

And she turned from him and ran, knowing that Darcy would run after her and soon catch her. Then they would make love in the cabin down by the river, the fire of passion easily rekindled between this husband and this wife, who joyfully resided in the Land of Mary, the Divine Mother, not far from the Chesapeake Bay.

41

The Call of Destiny

The white gentleman dressed in the navy blue, pin-striped suit standing at the podium had large, dark, startling eyes filled with light behind his round spectacles. He was speaking in a strong cadence about "the abject shame and miserable crime of slavery condoned in these United States," calling out for the emancipation of all colored Americans so that they might also enjoy "life, liberty, and the pursuit of happiness" as promised by the Bill of Rights drafted by our founding fathers.

He riled on against the tobacco and cotton states, some still trading in new slaves from Africa, he claimed, men, women and children kidnapped and sold into bondage. He condemned the practice of slavery in America, outlawed by Great Britain in 1808. The United States had passed a law in 1819 that equated slave trading with piracy, and this was 1832, a full thirteen years later!

The eloquent man seemed thoroughly disgusted with those who still used slaves to harvest the cotton to export the world over, slaves numbering in the hundreds on some plantations, forced to work without rest and without mercy, having been born into bondage for many generations. The states below the Mason-Dixon Line were the worst offenders, and that included Maryland and Virginia.

Apparently, Garrison was often confronted by angry mobs of slave-holders by speaking out like an inspired preacher, being a devout Baptist and friend to many Quakers. The Society of Friends was anti-slavery and pacifists who also supported his crusade of non-violence. The Constitution was labeled by him as a "document of slavery." The audience was encouraged not to vote in order to defy its evil government, to resign from political parties, and to denounce the Union. Garrison was frequently referred to as a "radical anarchist," especially in the states in the South.

The man spoke without fear of how "inhuman and unchristian it was to own even one slave." He was plainly appalled by the masters that inflicted harm or forced slaves to perform the most menial of tasks without rest, nourishment or adequate clothing. Some masters did not even provide shelter free of vermin to protect the slaves from the summer heat or the winter cold. Slaves were treated the same as chattel, the women forced into prostitution, unwilling, licentious concubinage with a master, to be beaten, raped or murdered by men breaking marriage vows with the gall to call themselves Christians on Sunday mornings. Children born to such unions became slaves in turn and were "forced to serve the same racist, rapist master."

"What righteous man turns his child into his slave? Tell me that!" Garrison shouted in indignation, and that time he looked right at Maggie.

Suddenly shivering from head to toe, the repugnant image of Jeremiah Plunkett filled her mind. She had actually prayed that Plunkett might end up burning up in the hell that Preacher McKay so graphically described in his fiery Sunday sermons. Plunkett was known to constantly take advantage of the young girl slaves and had already sired many children with them. Perhaps it was only right for him to burn in hell, Maggie thought, although she never put much stock in the place described by the preachers. She only humored the pastor to keep the peace.

The man standing on the platform now stalwartly declared that it was ungodly to sell or buy even one human being. Parents were separated from their children, brothers from their sisters, husbands from wives, with babies and toddlers sold by the pound. It was an outrage the public needed to know about. With slave traders selling families "down the river" to Virginia, Tennessee, Kentucky, North and South Carolina, Georgia, Alabama, Mississippi and Louisiana, with Texas, Arkansas and Oklahoma also involved in the slave trade, though still outside of the

Union. Trafficking in human flesh was indeed a grievous crime in the eyes of William Lloyd Garrison in his relentless pursuit to make slavery illegal in the United States of America.

Garrison was younger than Maggie had expected, younger than her, perhaps not yet thirty. His scalp was shiny where his dark hair receded and reflected the light of the candles. Darcy still had a full head of hair at the age of forty-two. Uncle Shane had all his hair when he passed. And yet, Garrison was filled with the Spirit, and it was plain to her that the man meant business.

From the time that she read the first issue of the *Liberator*, Maggie still remembered his statement: "I do not wish to think, or speak, or write, with moderation ... I am in earnest. I will not equivocate. I will not excuse. I will not retreat a single inch. AND I WILL BE HEARD."

Garrison was being heard, especially by her, as he eloquently and passionately spoke out for the rights of America's colored inhabitants. Mary Margaret O'Reilly Brosnan had heard the *call of destiny* from the Otherworld, and she had also begun to tremble slightly from head to toe. At that very moment, she knew in her heart that she had to somehow join his crusade to abolish slavery. Prudence had written to her about his lecture, and of how Garrison's crusade was defended by Daniel O'Connell. At the time, their Kerryman was working tirelessly to liberate slaves all around the world, particularly in America.

During the past year, the rebellion of the preacher Nat Turner in Virginia had preyed on her mind. The slave incited an uprising, his band growing to seventy slaves that in thirty-six hours murdered sixty white men, women, and children before the militia finally ended the carnage. In reprisal, white vigilantes murdered over 100 slaves, most of them not even involved in the rebellion. Turner had escaped, but was later captured and hanged for inciting insurrection, for killing citizens and burning private property.

That was when Maggie remembered Liam's letter:

I am not sure how to tell you about our situation here in Kingston. Over the Christmas holidays, a slave rebellion broke out in St. James Parish and rapidly spread, with the fury still ongoing. Who knows how long the slaves shall persist in their madness? The insurrection was led by Paddy Sharpe, a Baptist Deacon with whom I am well acquainted. I never dreamed he might incite such a fury among us.

311

Over 20,000 slaves soon joined in, looting and razing plantations, killing owners and their entire families. The problem was that the slaves thought they were freed by the British Parliament. Not yet true, although O'Connell is doing his best to free all slaves under British rule. I pray he succeeds. Slavery must be eradicated, if such an ideal can ever hold sway in a world such as ours where avarice and greed rob the human soul of all decency. The plantation where I worked was burned to the ground. Mr. Wilton and his family slaughtered with machetes used to harvest the sugar. It was revenge on their heartless, mindless, soulless masters, all of them.

There is nothing left for me here now. The sugar was destroyed by the oppressed who can no longer tolerate abuse at the hands of evil men. Men who seemed to have lost all sense of decency, perhaps from the moment they became slaveholders.

It is hard to describe these men. Over the years, I have seen terrible things done to men and women, some beaten to death or far worse. Some masters were sadistic indeed. I shall spare you the details of their numerous sins and means of torture. Surely they shall all burn in hell and be made to pay for their grievous crimes.

I know you own slaves, my sister, so this may be difficult for you to hear from your brother who loves you, but you must know in your heart the true wickedness of such commerce. One day slavery will be abolished in America. It must be, if there is a God in heaven.

I am married to Antoinette, a mulatto, who I dearly love. For now, we are safe. We have four wonderful children, part African, with some nearly as white as I am. Arthur, 15, is a fine boy who now seeks adventure. Muriel, 13, is a true beauty like her mother. Padraic, 11, looks much like me and our father, his namesake. Deidre is a charmer at the age of 8 as well as being something of a spitfire.

We will start a new life together where slavery does not exist. I shall write to you again when we are settled God only knows where, with our immediate fate uncertain. I know sugar, but there are rebellions on other islands as well. In the Caribbean, violence is now possible from black men or white men. It is unfortunate, since I am very fond of life in the tropics.

Please free your slaves, my dear sister. It is the right thing for you to do. It is not fair that any human being should live in bondage even to a kindly master like Darcy. The end of slavery is at hand. Please do what you can to be a part of that process, for the sake of your own soul. One day I hope to see you again. Until such a day should prove to be our mutual good fortune, I remain,

Lovingly your brother,
Liam Niall

The modestly dressed middle-aged woman introduced herself as, "Mrs. Jacqueline Carrington."

A mob of ruffians had rushed into the building where the lecture was taking place, shouting and forcing everyone outside, hollering, "Nigger lovers!" and other equally offensive obscenities. The rowdy men seemed educated and were well dressed. In Baltimore, freemen had businesses. Two in the group of rabble rousers were also freemen, for several free blacks owned African slaves in Baltimore.

While briskly walking down the street a safe distance from the building, Maggie learned that Mrs. Carrington was a widow with six children and fourteen grandchildren. She was also a Quaker and an avowed abolitionist.

"What do you think of our cause?" she inquired. "Are you interested in helping to free the slaves?"

"Yes," Maggie said without thinking, knowing something had to be done. Trepidation was all over Shannon's face as she listened to the conversation.

She had talked Shannon into attending the lecture, which was Maggie's main reason for being in Baltimore, besides a much needed break from her children. The birth of Triona was difficult and her milk never came in. The baby was turned over to a wet nurse, one slave still nursing her own child. It was the first time Maggie had any free time so soon after delivering a child. That, of course, was because of her slaves.

"Mrs. Brosnan has a tobacco plantation," Shannon nervously said.

"I see," Mrs. Carrington coolly replied. "How many slaves do you have?"

"Forty-two, counting the newborns," Maggie said, instantly feeling guilty. "We lost two this year," she went on, appalled right after she said that.

"They died in slavery," Mrs. Carrington said, with blame plain on her face.

In silence, Maggie and Shannon simply stared at the formidable woman.

"My husband and I owned slaves," she said. "My George died a slaveholder."

"Then you ... understand," Maggie said in a bid for sympathy.

"Four years ago I became a Quaker. I heard Mr. Garrison speak in 1829, and after that, I freed my slaves, arranging indentured positions for a few of them. Four of the faithful remained, but they are free now." She paused. "The *spirit* told me to speak with you, Mrs. Brosnan."

"*Spirit?*" Shannon said, quickly sucking in her breath.

"I knew we needed to talk, you and I. I was divinely directed to you," she said.

"I understand," Maggie said, as a strange sense of peace suddenly enveloped her.

"I live in Delaware and came all this way to hear William speak. He is such a fine man with such a good heart. I am staying at the Bentley Hotel. Would you care to join me for breakfast or lunch sometime tomorrow, so we can speak privately? It will be my treat!"

After quickly glancing at Shannon, Maggie said, "We were planning to shop at the new emporium tomorrow. I need some fabrics and some trinkets for my children." She paused. "Breakfast might be all right. I will be returning to Marcus Manor the day after tomorrow."

"I will meet you in the lobby at eight o'clock sharp tomorrow morning," Mrs. Carrington said. "I need to speak to you about the railroad."

"The railroad?" Maggie repeated.

"Good evening, ladies," she said, "Until tomorrow morning," and she briskly walked away.

42

The Underground Railroad

The hotel lobby was not necessarily spacious, but the dining room was pleasant enough. Mrs. Carrington was there as Maggie came through the door. After an exchange of small pleasantries on that sunny May morning, they were both soon seated at a corner table in the dining room enjoying a steaming cup of tea.

"It is more private in here," Mrs. Carrington whispered, picking up her napkin to spread over her lap.

Having never eaten in a hotel before, Maggie felt as though she was on a brand new adventure. For some time, she had not acquired any new white women friends. Most of her time was spent with Ruth, Rebecca and Sarah, her house slaves, either working or teaching them, and often laughing together. Sensing herself on the threshold of great change that was both frightening and exciting at the same time, she closely watched as the waiter filled their glasses with water.

"I have not yet ridden on a train," Maggie confessed, "My husband has promised to take us on a train sometime soon. Our plantation is not far from Baltimore on the Gunpowder River. We have a sloop and often go sailing. Darcy has already taught the children how to sail, so we do not feel a tremendous need to take a ride on a train." Her laugh was nervous as she continued, "We have spoken of taking a steamboat to visit my sister, Megan, and her family in Charleston, South Carolina. They own an inn." Maggie knew she was rambling. She was anxious about being with a strange woman, an *avowed abolitionist,* who wanted to talk to her about "the railroad." Her present set of circumstances seemed beyond astonishing to her.

"I have only ridden on a train twice," Mrs. Carrington said, picking up her cup as a curious expression spread across her face.

"I see. And did you find it ... pleasant?"

"Far less jarring than a stagecoach."

"Stagecoaches, wagons and carriages can be rather jarring over a long distance."

The waiter informed them of the breakfast buffet. The long table had a stack of white plates and an assortment of fruit, scrambled eggs, potatoes, sausages, bacon, bread, biscuits, gravy, sweet rolls and various kinds of jam.

"This looks delicious," Maggie said. "Sarah and Rebecca make a wonderful breakfast for my family every morning. I have eight children, Mrs. Carrington. My youngest, Triona, was only born in January just days before my eldest son, Aidan, turned fifteen. He is tall and handsome like his father." She hesitated, reflecting on how much Aidan really did look like Aidan: the same dark eyes and dark, wavy hair. Sometimes he could take her breath away when he walked into a room. Young Aidan was nothing whatsoever like his sister, blue-eyed, blonde Brigid, who resembled her father and showed signs of becoming a true beauty.

"Your husband is not interested in freeing his slaves?" Mrs. Carrington inquired.

"No," Maggie said, jarred back into the moment. "Darcy says we could not survive financially without our slaves."

"It is quite an adjustment, I can assure you."

"I imagine that it would be."

"What about joining me as a conductor on the railroad, regardless?"

"A conductor on the railroad?" Maggie blurted out, immediately receiving disparaging glances from the people at the very next table.

Mrs. Carrington tried to politely shush her. "We must be very discreet, Mrs. Brosnan," she whispered, "If we are to free slaves and help them reach safety in the North," she now whispered even softer, "You would like to help free the slaves, would you not, Mrs. Brosnan? Perhaps if, in the beginning, the slaves were not necessarily your slaves?"

Taking a bite of sausage, Maggie thoughtfully chewed, considering her companion's dangerous and outrageous proposal. "I thought it was just rumors about the Underground Railroad," she whispered, "mostly around the Ohio River in Illinois and Indiana. Free states, you know, with slaves escaping from Kentucky and Tennessee, the cotton states," she quickly scanned the room to see who else might be listening before again filling her mouth with egg and chewing. All of sudden, she was really hungry.

Slowly nodding her head, Mrs. Carrington took a bite of bread with jam but said nothing.

"Is it really a *railroad?*" Maggie felt silly asking her, but she really wanted to know.

Chuckling softly, Mrs. Carrington said, "In a sense. You see ... we create a pathway, or trail, you might say, through our hiding places, where slaves can stay and eat and sleep before moving on," she whispered softer, "to the next conductor on the railroad," she said, smiling as she took another bite and chewed for the longest time before she swallowed. "Where is your plantation?"

"Marcus Manor is north about twenty-five miles from here, not far from Joppa on the Gunpowder River and the Chesapeake near the trail," she nervously added, wiping her mouth with her napkin.

"I am north of you near the Chesapeake and Delaware Canal close to Bohemia Village in Maryland, not far from Kirkwood and near Pennsylvania. Many abolitionists live near the border to help runaways reach Philadelphia and sometimes go on to Canada," she had whispered every word, looking up to smile as the waiter poured more water into her glass. "Thank you," she said to the waiter, and after he left, she turned to Maggie and inquired, "More eggs?"

The two plates were refilled to accommodate two hearty appetites.

"Is it not dangerous ... being an abolitionist? All those angry men the other night, vulgar in front of the ladies," Maggie said, thinking of how she was always fascinated with the forbidden, perhaps the same as the disciples and Jesus with the Sanhedrin. What about Darcy, she wondered? How was she going to avoid getting caught being a conductor on the Underground Railroad?

"We could end up in prison," Mrs. Carrington said in a matter-of-fact tone as she cut into a sausage and grinned. "William, Mr. Garrison, was in jail. And I nearly was right here in Baltimore."

"Jail?" Maggie had forgotten to whisper.

The couple at the next table turned and stared at her.

"There are risks," Mrs. Carrington now whispered, "I would advise you to take some slaves into your confidence, those you trust the most, who might be willing to help others in terrible bondage escape from the shackles of a cruel and heartless master. The slaves that love you will help you for that reason, if not for reasons of their own."

"I can think of some who might want to escape from a cruel master, but not my slaves. We do not beat them. We feed and clothe them properly. They have shoes, even the children. They are like family to us."

Appearing to study her, Mrs. Carrington said, "One day this country will abolish slavery, but it might take some time. Right now, the problem is the value of cotton on the open market, the money made exporting. Free labor, of course, is better than paying for workers. There is much greater profit."

"I am not sure that I can accept Mr. Garrison's view on the men not voting. My husband would fight to vote. Next week, Darcy is attending the Democratic National Convention in Baltimore. My Darcy was one of Wellington's invincibles," she said proudly, "He helped to defeat Napoleon and was severely wounded at Waterloo. His leg still gives him trouble on rainy days."

"You have a good marriage, then?"

"A wonderful marriage." Maggie hesitated. "Which is why it is going to be hard for me to betray my husband by helping the slaves, perhaps even our slaves?" She took a deep breath and ate more sausage, chewing vigorously in an attempt to dispel her growing anxiety. "You will tell me all about how to do this, right? It is sort of like belonging to a secret society, is it not? I know about that, Mrs. Carrington." She thought of her Aunt Brigid and their secret rituals in Ireland, but she doubted this would be anything like that. She and her kitchen slaves had secretly performed rituals in the sacred oak grove near the river on many occasions.

Smiling brightly, Mrs. Carrington picked up her cup of tea. "Please call me Jackie. All my friends call me Jackie. Mrs. Carrington is much too formal."

"And all my friends call me Maggie," she said, knowing how Ruth and Rebecca still insisted on calling her 'Missy Maggie' even though she considered them as her friends.

"Okay, Maggie," Jackie said, holding out her hand across the table.

At first hesitant, Maggie shook her hand. "Do you have secret signs and words or phrases I shall have to learn?"

"Of course. It might be best for me to visit your plantation and survey the lay of the land, so to speak. Tell your husband that I am your new friend from Delaware. That should please him. I am a property holder and my husband was highly respected in the community."

"I see," Maggie said, drinking tea from her cup. "Does that mean I need to come and visit you sometime?"

"Good idea! Then you could meet the other abolitionists, women like yourself, and stalwart, honorable men who favor freedom for all, regardless of race."

"You promise to teach me exactly what to do and tell me how I will know I have someone to feed and hide." Reflective for a moment, Maggie said, "I have an old cabin down by the river where I might hide some slaves and feed them." Chewing on the last of her sausage, her whole body suddenly began to tingle.

"We have already shaken on it," Jackie said.

"We have?"

"Yes, ma'am. Congratulations! You are now officially a conductor on the Underground Railroad, an avowed abolitionist. You have heard the call and accepted the challenge."

"I have?" Maggie said, now thrilled through and through. "Well, I'll be!"

43

The Slave Driver

After spending five days in the city, the return trip to Marcus Manor included many new treasures for the house, especially for the kitchen, along with a new bathtub. Readymade fabrics were purchased made in England, colorful bunting for the slaves. Darcy already had a new pair of deerskin trousers, which pleased him immensely. The Piscataway women helped her to make them. There was more gingham and calico and lots of new buttons. Cloth no longer needed to be hand woven, which had been tedious and time-consuming. There were two new harmonicas for Dermot and Gareth. The boys had shown signs of musical talent. Aidan and Dermot played the fiddle, the same as Liam and her father back in Ireland.

The moment Maggie entered the house, Rebecca came running, screaming, "Missy Maggie, Missy Maggie ... that man is beating Isaac near to death. Come now, missus, please come now!" Tears streamed down her face. "You got to stop him, Missy, or that man is gonna kill Isaac in about another minute!"

Instantly dropping everything, Maggie ran. On her way to the back door, she grabbed the shotgun in the kitchen that was always loaded in case some mad dog showed up in the yard. There was not the usual sound of children's voices. Apparently, some mad dog was hurting Isaac, and exactly who could that mad dog be?

Out in the yard, Rebecca shouted, "Come stop this man from beating him, Missy Maggie. PLEASE STOP HIM! I kept praying that you would come home."

Isaac, a strong man in his thirties, was tied to the hitching post near the barn. His knees had buckled under the severe punishment he had received. A large, towering man with sunburned arms extending from his rolled up shirt had his back to her. He wore a wide-brimmed brown hat with a feather in the band as he raised the bullwhip high up into the air, and the whip cracked on Isaac's bloody back.

The slave cried out in pain. Large, bleeding welts appeared on the dark skin of his back as Isaac's body sagged in his ropes.

"STOP IT! STOP IT, I SAY!" Maggie screamed, with her heart starting to race. She could hardly believe her eyes. Shaking with fury, she boldly stepped between Isaac and the burly man about to raise the whip again. Standing in front of Isaac, she shouted, "Unless you want a load of buckshot in your face and your belly, you had best stop what you are doing. Do you hear me? Stop whipping my slave, mister, or you are going to force me to kill you this very minute! If you don't believe me, try me! That slave you are whipping, Isaac, is the one who taught me how to shoot straight as an arrow. The Piscataway taught him! Drop that whip, drop it, I say!" she angrily shouted.

Evidently, several slaves were forced to watch the whipping. All eyes were now fixed on the large man with the ruddy, pockmarked face, who disdainfully glared at their mistress who was holding a loaded gun.

"You have no say in this, you're just a woman," he said in a pronounced Southern accent.

This man was plainly one of those ugly, mean sorts from the Deep South, Maggie quickly decided, a slave abuser. But what the devil was he doing on her plantation was what she wanted to know?

"How dare you!" she screamed, taking a step toward the man, "Who the blazes are you? I am the mistress of this plantation and we do not whip slaves! Do you understand me, mister? Slaves are NEVER WHIPPED at Marcus Manor!" she shrieked, aiming the gun at his extended belly.

That was when she first caught sight of Darcy out of the corner of her eye. He was running toward them with an alarmed look on his fine, handsome face.

Advancing on the madman with the whip, with her shotgun still pointed right at him, Maggie shouted, "We do not abuse slaves! Slaves are human beings. Drop that whip, whoever you are! Whoever the devil are you, anyway, mister?" she demanded, now fully enraged and knowing that she was the one in control, she was fully prepared to kill the bastard should he force her hand.

"Mary Margaret," Darcy said in a mildly apprehensive tone.

Slowly and deliberately, she turned to her husband. "Who is this man?" she demanded, with the shotgun still pointed at the offender. "If you hired this monster, you had better tell him he is dead wrong! Kindly inform this man that we do not whip slaves at Marcus Manor," she said, gritting her teeth. Then, she handed the shotgun to Darcy. "Here! You can shoot better than I can. You could take him out with one blast."

Then, she rushed over to Isaac and called out to Rebecca, "Bring him some water, quick!" Maggie suddenly turned to another slave and said, "Jacob, untie him and take him to his cabin. I will be there to tend to him as soon as I can change my clothes."

Rebecca got some water from the pump.

Jacob hesitated, turning to his master, who was plainly stunned by his wife's words and unfamiliar actions.

"Do as she says," Darcy told him.

The slave untied Isaac as Rebecca gave him water.

Turning to the slave abuser, Maggie demanded, "Who are you?"

He simply stared at her, plainly dumbfounded that a woman had such power.

"His name is Jake McClintock. He's our new overseer," Darcy said. "He's from Kentucky. His grandfather came over on the boat from Belfast." He appeared to be trying his best to make light of the odd and unanticipated situation.

"Good for him," she snapped. "Not all Irishmen are good men, Darcy. Surely you know that much from serving under Wellington. I will not have this man on our plantation. He nearly killed Isaac and I simply will not have it," she said, stomping her foot, "Do you hear me?"

"The nigger wouldn't obey me," Jake shouted in surly tones. "I caught him in a cabin reading a book. You know niggers ain't supposed to read. How come he's done learnt how to read?"

Slowly turning, Darcy now faced his wife with his questioning blue eyes.

"Perhaps you forgot to tell Mr. McClintock that if one of our slaves misbehaves we might lock him in a woodshed, no food for a day, but our slaves are never lazy, mean or impolite. They never run away, because we are very good to them. We treat them like human beings, which they are. Uncle Shane taught us how to treat our slaves. You remember that, don't you, Darcy?" Her eyes were fixed on her husband and her jaw was set. "It seems that you neglected to tell Mr. McClintock that we do not whip slaves at Marcus Manor," she said, sighing in her exasperation.

Darcy and the overseer exchanged mystifying glances.

Turning to Ruth, Maggie said, "I'll go change and see to Isaac. Make some soup with lots of fresh vegetables, garlic and onions and the right herbs for healing."

Ruth nodded and hurried into the house.

Striding toward the house, Maggie turned around on the porch and quietly said to her husband, "I will see you at suppertime. I bought you a new bathtub, Darcy. I hope we will have the chance to use it sometime soon. I have some other nice things for you, too."

His expression softened. "Did you have a nice visit with Shannon and Cornelius?"

"Very nice," she said, smiling, and she turned and entered the house.

During the past month, Darcy had brought up the matter of hiring an overseer to help him with the slaves. He said he thought things were getting far too friendly with them. Since his Uncle Shane's death, he had thought about having another white man on the plantation, but Maggie never agreed. She pointed out that their slaves were not in any way unruly. After meeting Jackie Carrington, she seriously doubted that any slave could be happy after hearing her tragic stories of abuse and horror, and not only in the Deep South, but not far away on the Eastern Shore of Maryland. Some of her tales made the hair prickle on the back of her neck. No human being should ever be treated that badly.

Liam and Antoinette would be happy to learn of her covert decision, even with her own slaves not immediately freed. After all, her father had hidden guns and ammunition for the United Irishmen. But what about keeping secrets from Darcy, she wondered? Never before had she ever tried to deceive her husband in any manner. The thought of the two of them being on opposite sides troubled her. After all, she planned to defy the law. What would happen to her children if she were sent to prison?

Hurrying toward Isaac's cabin, Maggie could see Rebecca had already applied a balm to his wounds, something designed with herbs for far less serious and repugnant injuries.

"I am mighty beholden to you," Rebecca said to her. "That was a brave thing you did, Missy. You done saved Isaac's life."

Isaac winced. He tried to raised up and turn over.

"Never you mind, Isaac. I would imagine that you are going to have to sleep on your stomach tonight and perhaps for a few days."

"Yes 'um."

Isaac had always enjoyed playing the butler in an old white wig that Master Shane had given to him when he was a boy. He often wore the wig during parties in the manor house, being naturally playful and theatrical was his nature. Isaac had always done an excellent job reading books to the children. Reading to them helped him to learn more himself. A slave driver such as Mr. McClintock was unlikely to ever cotton to slaves that could read. That might have been too much for the man, since he was probably unable to read himself.

"You are strong, Isaac," Maggie said. "I know you will heal from these wounds. I promise you that nothing like this will ever happen again, but you have to forgive me for not being here sooner. I am so terribly sorry that this happened to you." Tears filled her eyes as she picked up the bowl of soup and held a spoonful to his mouth. "He is not staying at Marcus Manor. I can promise you that, Isaac. I have no doubts about that in my mind at all."

Isaac tried to rise up. "You ain't got no need to feed me, missus," he said, plainly embarrassed. "You done enough for me already. I'm mighty grateful to you for your kindness. You are an angel, Missy Maggie." He forced a smile. "A gun totin' angel is what you are, for a certainty!"

Smiling, Rebecca said, "I'm just glad you're alive. I was a feared the man was going to kil you, Isaac."

"I am so glad you are alive," Maggie gently corrected. "Don't forget to use proper grammar, Rebecca," she said, lightly touching her arm. "I have some new calico for you," and she again turned to Isaac. "I'm going to prepare some tea that will help you sleep and ease your pain. When you are feeling stronger, I have something private I want to share with you and Rebecca. I have received a divine calling that may be your calling, too. But you rest now, Isaac. Mr. McClintock is leaving this plantation tonight."

"The master, he say we need an overseer, but I never heard him tell him to beat us. I guess that is just the way those men treat niggers. They don't know no other way. I hear tell that's how it is down in Kentucky and down the river. Those slave drivers are mighty mean men, Missy Maggie, mighty mean."

"Well, he is not going to beat my slaves anymore, or I shall take that cat of nine tails to him! What do you think about that, Isaac?"

Isaac and Rebecca grinned.

So did Maggie.

"I believe you," Isaac said. "I surely do believe you!"

"Meanwhile, I'm going back to the house to take a bath in my new bathtub."

"I'll come fill it with warm water for you, Missy Maggie," Rebecca said.

"No. You see to Isaac. There are plenty of others to help me with that." She turned to Isaac again. "I will come down and check on you tomorrow, Isaac. Meanwhile, please eat your soup. I will soon be sending you that tea and you must drink all of it."

"Yes 'um."

Maggie was halfway back to the house when Darcy caught up with her. "Would you really have shot the man, Mary Margaret? Really?" he inquired.

"If he kept on beating Isaac, I would have been forced to kill him … sure as shooting." She defiantly faced her somewhat flustered husband and folded her arms in front of her as she stared him right in the eyes.

"You are surely acting like a nigger lover, Maggie. You surely are!"

"I am a nigger lover, Darcy. I see no reason not to care for someone because their skin is a different color. I happen to be an Indian lover, too, in case you haven't noticed. I love all the savages, Yuma and the rest of them are my dear friends. The truth is that I am mighty surprised to hear such talk coming out of your mouth, Mr. Suddenly Uppity-Uppity!"

"Sometimes you do amaze me! You truly do!"

"Well, when I cease to amaze you then you will probably no longer find me the least bit attractive!" She thoughtfully paused. "We women really do need to amaze you men or you might leave us for another woman who is much more amazing."

They walked a few steps before she stopped and turned to him. "You have sent him away, right, Master Brosnan? You have told Mr. Jake McClintock, whose grandfather hails from Belfast, to hightail it out of Marcus Manor and go back to the Deep South where scoundrels like him get away with being despicable oppressor of the downtrodden and enslaved. You have told him that, right, Master Brosnan?"

"And if I have not?" he said, with his eyes a steely blue.

"Then you can sleep in the conservatory and play the piano all night long to bang out your frustrations, for all I care!"

"You are not serious?"

"I certainly am! He goes or I go … and I am not jesting, Darcy Donal Brosnan!"

"Where will you go?"

"Back to Ireland … and I will take my children with me. We will live with my father and Prudence in Dingle. They would be delighted to have all their grandchildren and me there with them. Then we could visit your parents in Dublin, and the children would have the chance to meet all their Irish relations. It's my guess that we would be quite welcome and find a home large enough to accommodate all of us rather nicely, don't you think?"

For a long moment, Darcy just stood there studying her. "You are not going to Ireland," he finally said. "And you are not taking our children away from their home."

"Fine! Then Mr. McClintock is going back to Kentucky, or anywhere else he can find sadistic employment. Vermin like him live on the eastern shore, hear tell." She pointedly turned to him. "Well, Darcy, is it Jake McClintock or your wife and children?"

He audibly sighed. "All right," he said, and he started to leave when he suddenly stopped and turned to her with a scowl. "Is that a bustle you're wearing?"

"It is the latest fashion. You do want me to be fashionable!"

"Turn around," he said, striding fully around her to stare at the protruding bustle in back. "Why ever would a woman want to make her derrière appear so out of proportion and extended? I find nothing attractive in a bustle."

"It is the fashion, Darcy!"

He laughed. "And I would rather see your fine backsides!" He tried to swat the bustle as Maggie quickly stepped aside, "and I would rather touch your fine backside, as well." Darcy grinned. "There is nothing appealing to a man in a bustle. But you most certainly are one amazing woman, Mary Margaret!"

"My dear husband, you have not even begun to see how truly amazing I can be! Just you wait and see!"

"Oh, I can wait, Mary Margaret. I can wait!"

44

The Gunpowder River Line

After another month, Jacqueline Carrington arrived for an extended visit. During the time set aside for their secret purpose, Jackie diligently taught Maggie the signs, signals, methods and words used by 'conductors,' also sometimes called 'station masters,' on the Underground Railroad. There were folks that Maggie needed to meet, mostly in secret, some living slightly to the south or north of her plantation. Eventually, Maggie would meet still others. Letters needed to be written in a special manner to inform her of important meetings. In the future, more private meetings might better serve the cause in the business of assisting, hiding and caring for runaway slaves.

The old cabin down by the river seemed ideal to her for her purpose, the cabin Maggie and Darcy often used for trysts away from the prying eyes of their slaves and their children. The cabin would provide shelter for those heading north to escape from their abusive masters, some desperate to reunite with friends or family in Philadelphia, New York, Boston, smaller towns, or even in Canada. Most still had a long way to go on foot to escape the slave traders and catchers, with the distinct danger of being returned to their masters, or murdered, especially below the Mason-Dixon Line at the northern border of Maryland just fifteen miles from Philadelphia.

Darcy appeared pleased with his wife's new friendship with an educated, respectable woman who owned 200 acres of prime land in Delaware.
He had heard fine reports regarding her late husband, Elmer Carrington,
in both commerce and politics. Elmer was present at the signing of the
Declaration of Independence. That pleased Darcy immensely as he talked
of the first Democratic National Convention to be held in Baltimore.

"Of course," Darcy said, "President Jackson is running for re-election
with Marten Van Buren as his vice president. Frankly, I fail to see how
the men can possibly lose."

During supper on those June evenings, there was no mention of the
real reason for Jackie's visit to Marcus Manor. The topics of conversation
usually involved current events, including the rapid growth of the population in the city of Baltimore.

"There are well over 130,000 people in the city now," Darcy said. "I
find that amazing."

"Yes, Mr. Brosnan. But I have heard that the working class tends to
behave rather badly. There have been petitions complaining of black women
washing clothes in the streams far too boisterously, as well as complaints of
the Irish laborers singing loud late at night and disturbing the peace. There
is apparently too much cursing and gambling going on in the marketplace."

"I have heard complaints against the free colored and the Irish from
Shannon," Maggie said. "But you cannot blame them for singing and
carrying on, considering their meager wages. I am surprised there aren't
more brawls outside the pubs the way it often was in Ireland. Shannon
calls Baltimore—Mobtown."

"It is best to raise a family in the country," Darcy said.

Everyone agreed that the city officials had their fair share of problems. But there was no mention that evening of the 3rd National Black
Convention in Philadelphia, or of the organization of the *New England
Anti-Slavery Society* that year with Garrison as one of the founders. Women
were not welcome, unfortunately. Maggie sympathized with the threats
on Garrison's life: $5,000 offered by the State of Georgia for his arrest
and imprisonment. The dangers involved with being an abolitionist were
plain to her, and being a conductor on the Underground Railroad was
surely going to complicate her life. Deceiving Darcy was the bitterest pill
for her to swallow. And yet, she had responded to the *call* and accepted
the challenge.

Back in Ireland, care always had to be taken in performing the seasonal rituals and making amulets to dispel evil and attract the good, as well as talk of the stars and the planets. Maggie always used discretion in conversing with the fairies, keeping the truth from her father and the priest. Her father never learned of her veil, and yet, he was aware that her Kelly blood linked her to the old ways. A time or two, her father had called her "the latest Kerry witch." Nevertheless, it seemed that her promise to Jackie made her a high priestess of a different order, the rituals different but also life preserving and life saving. It was Maggie's hope to save many slaves from evil masters who seemed ignorant of laws far higher than those fashioned by men. Her sincere prayer was to honorably fulfill her sacred obligation.

Not long after Jackie's departure, Maggie met in secret with Peter Gulliver of Joppatown and Wilmer Dayton of Edgewood, two other conductors on the railroad. Within a fortnight, her first runaways occupied the cabin. The lit lantern signaled this as a place of safety. To her surprise, Maggie was not nervous, although conductors seldom knew when a runaway might appear. Even so, dried beef, nuts and fruit were left in a tin. Rebecca and Isaac helped out, even though Isaac appeared scared stiff.

"Missy Maggie, please don't go getting youself into a whole lot of trouble helping these runaways. I knows a man down south got hisself hanged on his own oak tree for helping slaves escape. Yous gotta be awfully careful, Missy Maggie. They just might lynch you!"

With a tin of hot potato and leek soup and a fresh loaf of bread, Rebecca approached the cabin by making certain noises before she entered. Apparently, some slaves had never slept on a bed before reaching the cabin by the river.

"They was mighty glad for the potato soup," Rebecca said, "And for the apples and nuts, mighty happy, those two. The men blessed me twice and says to tell you they was remembering you in their prayers probably forever from this day forward."

"They were," Maggie gently corrected, determined to remember those men in her prayers on that night with no need of names.

"They be moving on at first light. I said to lock the door and turn off the lantern so as not to attract any attention." Rebecca paused. "I don't think anyone saw or even suspected, 'ceptin' Isaac ... and maybe Moses. Did you say anything to Moses?"

"I did. He seemed even more scared than Isaac. I told him I want you all to be free. That is how it would be now if I had my way, but you already know that, don't you, Becky."

"Yous," she said, instantly stopping, "You are a mighty brave soul, Missy Maggie. Probably the bravest woman I ever did meet in my whole life. I am mighty glad you are my mistress. I would never be anyone else's slave in this whole wide world, exceptin' yours, and that is the honest gospel truth."

It was official.

That night Maggie became a conductor on the Underground Railroad. Her first two passengers had arrived safely at her station, and gratefully, both were gone by morning. There were wild flowers in the old tin cup beside the bed. Seeing the flowers brought tears to her eyes and convinced her that she was doing the right thing.

All that year, slave rebellions had broken out, along with several Indian wars. More native tribes were dispossessed of their lands. Megan wrote of the first Negro hospital chartered in Savannah, which made Maggie wonder what her sister might think of her recent calling.

More passengers arrived, some not even staying the night. All were grateful for the food, clean water and a safe place to rest and hide. An important new phase in Maggie's life had begun.

There was now a new station established on the Underground Railroad known as the Gunpowder River Line.

45

Moses and the Children of Israel

It was common knowledge on the various nearby plantations that Israel often visited with Ruth and Rebecca at Marcus Manor. The Plunkett slave also had other friends on the Brosnan Plantation during her twenty-eight years in bondage. Upon her arrival at the Plunkett Plantation, Israel was not yet two-years-old. She was purchased for twenty dollars, her weight at auction. It was Plunkett who gave her the name.

The slaves at Marcus Manor seemed happier to Israel than those on her plantation. She thought maybe it was because of the way the master and his fiery Irish missus with her long red hair and golden cat eyes treated them. Israel had always considered the mistress comely, in spite of having borne her husband eight children. Missy Maggie always had a nice word to say. That was why Israel tried to stay away from Jeremiah, although he was the one who had fathered her three children. All three children looked more like her, except for her youngest child, Rachel, with her light eyes and light silky hair.

Israel had nothing but contempt for the pot bellied, ruddy faced, drunken old white man who continued to repeatedly force himself on her. His mere touch could make her skin crawl. The sight of him could make her sick to her stomach. That year he had severely beaten her and broken

333

her wrist after finding her in the arms of the man she loved. Lazarus. He was a slave acquired at auction two years earlier, a Carolina slave who worked with rice, and in the beginning, knew nothing of tobacco. But Lazarus was well acquainted with brutal masters and cold-blooded overseers with a whip.

On her frequent visits to Marcus Manor, Israel often brought along one or more of her children, especially on Sunday afternoons. The oldest, Salome, was nearly fifteen, Daniel was fourteen, and Rachel was twelve. Rachel was the prettiest with brown ringlets that framed her face.

One Sunday after church, Rachel was acting truly strange.

"Good day, Rachel," Maggie said. "Would you like some lemonade?" A strange sensation tugged at her center as she looked into the girl's sad, light brown eyes.

"Yes, ma'am," Rachel replied, glancing at her mother who was tightly holding her hand.

Instantly shaking her head, Israel's expression looked strained as she stared right past Maggie. "Thank you'all jest the same, ma'am, but we be going to the slave quarters. Theys expecting us." The slave seemed really distant, not at all her usual self. "Your kindness is much appreciated, Missy Maggie. I needs to speak with Rebecca about some herbs, and I'll be needing some arsenic to poison the rats in the barn," she said, straightening up. "We be going now," she said, starting to take long strides toward the slave quarters, dragging Rachel along, with Salome and Daniel trying to catch up.

Puzzled, Maggie watched the four of them as a sudden, powerful sensation gripped her midsection and almost made her dizzy.

Ruth walked up to her. "I need to take some herbs to the other kitchen, some for cooking and some for healing. Will that be all right?" and then she whispered, "We got visitors."

The word *visitor* meant one or more runaways at the cabin. That year, Ruth had become an abolitionist. Being a slave abolitionist amused her. But she was emboldened by her mistress's desire to set her free. Her mistress had never given Ruth any reason to doubt the sincerity of her words or any of her promises.

Collecting herself, Maggie said, "Here on a Sunday, huh? The Lord's day?"

"Yes, ma'am, a young woman with two young children about seven and ten. I'd say they're mighty hungry. Should I take them some food?"

"Right away," Maggie said, and yet, she had hoped to soon join Darcy and the children in the parlor to play the piano. "Did they come on foot or by boat?"

"Across the river in a rowboat. They made it all the way from Georgia."

"Merciful heavens! You had best use the basket. Take a loaf of that bread you just baked and some ham and greens and apples and pears."

"Yes, ma'am," Ruth said, starting for the house.

"Ruth," Maggie said, following after her, "Whatever is the matter with Rachel? Something seems terribly wrong. I can sense it."

As Ruth turned, she hesitated briefly before she said, "It's Plunkett, that mean old cuss ... he says he's going to sell Salome and Daniel down the river."

"What?" Maggie gasped. "They are his children! Heaven only knows what might happen to them if he did! Why ever would he do such a horrible, despicable thing?"

"That is not the whole of it," she said, appearing to struggle.

"Tell me, Ruth. What has happened?"

"The master ... that crazy man ... he done raped Rachel," she said, sinking into a chair.

"What?" Maggie screeched.

"Rachel is his own daughter, Missy. He's done gone and raped her like he did her mother." Ruth started to sob. "What sort of man does a thing like that to his own daughter? Daniel wants to kill him, and Salome, he tried to *do it* to her, too, except she done run away into the woods where our Piscataway stopped him from committing evil against that child. He wants to sell his beautiful children down the river. Why, Missy? Salome is most as white as him. He done fathered twenty-two children, and only six with his wife, and she don't do nothing to stop him! Nothing at all!"

Her eyes filled with tears and Maggie started to pace back and forth as an intense anger welled up inside her. Her blood was soon throbbing in her temples. She had half a mind to get the shotgun and finish off Plunkett herself. Her heart was pounding so hard it made it nearly impossible for her to think.

"We have to get them out of here," she said, "I don't think it can be tonight, but we have to. Maybe they can go with the woman and her children. I need to think about this, Ruth. Merciful God in heaven, whatever am I to do?"

Ruth stood and faced her. "Something else ... Mr. Plunkett says he's selling Israel down the river, too! That way I guess he can have the young'un to do with as he pleases, so his baby can have his babies. That's what!" she said, fighting back her tears.

"Ruth! No!"

"Israel says he near beat Lazarus to death yesterday. He doesn't want them together. He also says he's no 'bloody nigger lover like those white Irish trash Brosnans'! He called you white trash! With you a lady and your husband a fine gentleman, like as he's not the biggest white trash I ever did see in all my born days!"

"Good law, Ruth! He is a sorry excuse for a man ... for a human being."

Brianna ran into the kitchen in a bright yellow dress, her long dark hair flowing down her back, her green eyes bright as she hugged her mother. "Mommy, when are you coming? Daddy is playing the piano. We want to make family music like you did back in Ireland. Will you be there soon?"

"How many times have you been told to ask permission to enter a room without blurting out what is on your mind when grownups are talking?" Maggie scolded. "Have you not been told?"

"Yes, ma'am," Brianna said. "But are you coming ... soon?"

"In a few minutes. I will bring in some strawberries from our strawberry patch."

"Yum!" Brianna said and she ran back to the parlor.

The piano music filtering down the hall made Maggie smile before she turned back to Ruth. "Take those folk some food. I know this is your day off, Ruth, but ..." she started.

"Sakes alive, Missy, I don't give a Sam Hill about a day off when the whole world is falling to pieces. You just skedaddle in there with your family and have some fun, you hear? Any time you want me, you just send for me and I'll be here. Somebody needs to look after those ... *visitors*," Ruth said. "I know you'll think of something to help out Israel and her children. We can't have them sold down the river!"

It was around eight o'clock the next evening after supper when Israel ran screaming into the kitchen through the back door of Marcus Manor. Her three children ran in right behind her and every one of them looked scared to death.

"I kilt him," Israel cried out. "Kilt him dead! I done it! I done kilt my mean massa. I'd rather die than go down the river," she shrieked, throwing herself onto the floor. "Died right dead right this minute. I'm thinking bout throwing myself into the river ... and I dun know how to swim. I dun know how," she howled, getting up, about to run out the back door.

Entering the kitchen to check on the commotion, Maggie found Rebecca and Ruth trying to restrain Israel and her frightened children desperately clinging to their mother. Maggie closed the kitchen door behind her just as Aidan tried to push his way in, but she blocked him.

"You just go about your business back in the parlor with the other children. This is none of your business."

"It could be my business, if you'd allow it," Aidan said, trying to see past her, with Israel sobbing near the back door. "It's not like I happen to be dumb about what goes on around here, Mama, if you must know the truth. There are things I know from Yuma, from the other braves and Mia."

"Please go, Aidan. I'll call for you if I really need you. I promise."

Reluctant, Aidan backed off. "I expect you to keep your promise, Mama," he said and he left.

After entering the kitchen, Maggie noted the pure torment on Israel's face.

"I kilt him," Israel cried out. "I kilt Master Plunkett ... I put arsenic in the stew."

"My Law!" Maggie said, and instantly she sat down. "For the rats in the barn," she softly said, remembering the slave's words on the prior Sunday.

"He done raped Rachel in the barn! Our baby! He done raped our very own baby girl in the barn, Missy Maggie," Israel shrieked, her slender body violently shaking as she convulsed in sobs.

Rebecca and Ruth looked at Israel in an apparent state of shock and at her three children now hysterically weeping too.

"What kind of man is he?" Daniel cried out, seeing the loaded shotgun. "I'll kil him maself, even if he is my Pa. He's no kind of father to me."

337

Rushing over to block the gun, Ruth cried out, "You'll not be killing anyone, Daniel. Enough harm has already been done on this day!"

"I ain't going down the river!" he cried. "I'll kil myself ... an' I'll kil him."

"Master Plunkett raped you?" Maggie asked Rachel, instantly noting the shame and torment in the child's reddened eyes and face from her crying.

Nodding, Rachel hid her face. "He done tried to rape Salome, too. We be his children. Why's he done this? Why is he selling us down the river?"

Those questions nearly broke Maggie's heart. Plunkett's acts were always mean, vile, even unthinkable, but what had Israel actually done? "You poisoned his supper?" she said, knowing how a woman could be driven to such acts, knowing how Israel had suffered at his cruel hands.

"I kilt him ... and Matthew and Mark. I kilt them, too, the ones named after those chapters in the Bible. But Luke and John, theys away with that crazy woman, Edna. I can't stand her. All four of 'em jest keeled over at the supper table. The man with his face in his stew ... and he only et half of it." She looked up with a strangely pleased expression on her face as Rebecca and Ruth simply stared at her in amazement.

"Lord Almighty!" Rebecca cried out. "Looks like she done killed four people. She thinks she killed the missus, too!"

"Four?" Maggie managed. "Israel has killed four of the Plunketts?"

All three children nodded together, looking oddly pleased with their mother, proud of her evil vengeance on the unrepentant Plunketts.

"I done fed some stew to that mean old hound, Leviticus, too," Daniel said. "I sure do hope it kils him. That thar dog bit me something awful and nearly took a hunk out of my backsides. I could hardly sit down for a month."

Staring at the boy in disbelief, Maggie said, "Well, it seems to me that you will have dead people all over the place if someone doesn't get rid of that stew. Get Aidan!" she said to Rebecca, "And someone with some common sense has to go over and see how many dead people there really are at the Plunkett Plantation. I'm so glad that Darcy went to that political meeting," she said, turning to Daniel. "You may have poisoned every creature in the barnyard, boy. Did you think about that?"

He shook his head. "No, ma'am. But I sure did want to do in that Leviticus. I dun hate that dog! Should 'a et him for supper a long time ago. That's what!"

It was all Maggie could do not to laugh, but with the present set of circumstances, matters appeared far too grave for laughter.

"Get Moses," she said to Ruth, "Right away, Ruth!"

"Yes, ma'am," she said and Ruth ran out the back door.

In another hour, Moses and the three children of Israel were in a wagon ready to leave for Philadelphia. Moses had written permission from Mrs. Darcy Brosnan for the open road just in case he was stopped by someone looking for runaways. He was to claim the children as their slaves.

"I am giving you your freedom, Moses," she said, handing him an envelope with a letter stating that fact, along with some money. "I will tell Darcy. After all, there are five dead people down the road, along with three dogs dumb enough to fight over poisoned food. Aidan has gone for the doctor, though I guess it should have been the coroner. I don't know what is going to happen to Israel, but I can't let you take her, because sure enough, they will come after a murderer and hang her from the nearest tree. I'm smart enough to know that there will be no fair trial or justice for an abused slave who poisoned her master and mistress, his sons, a house slave crazy enough to eat out of the same pot, and the Lord only knows how many animals!"

"I'll be back, Missus," Moses said. "You and Maser Darcy have been very good to me. I feel bad enough now leaving without telling the master."

"You take those children to safety. I'm counting on you, Moses. You're the same as your namesake in the Bible taking those children to the Promised Land."

Tears filled his eyes as he looked down at his mistress and nodded.

"There are names and addresses in the envelope. Get in touch with Mrs. Matthews in Philadelphia or Arthur Tappan. They know me and will help you out. You will find someone. I will deal with the backwash here. Don't you worry, Moses. I will think of something."

By the time the wagon disappeared into the deepening darkness of night, Israel was nowhere to be found. Had Yuma hidden away the pathetic slave, she wondered? Aidan had advised his mother to have nothing to do with the protection of Israel or she might be implicated in the dastardly multiple murders.

After all, it was Brosnan arsenic used to poison the stew in the slave's ultimate act of revenge on the cruel and heartless Plunketts!

46

Steamboat to Charleston

The weather was perfect for an ocean voyage. It was a balmy July in 1836, with all the children excited about being cabin passengers on the *Lady Bug* with its bright red shutters dotted with black dots and its deck stacked high with wood for the furnace. Even Aidan enjoyed watching the great paddlewheel turn as the boat glided down the eastern seaboard toward Charleston, South Carolina.

After an absence of so many years, Darcy was eager to see Kevin again. Maggie was constantly talking about Megan, wondering how they might appear to one another after twenty years. All the children were going on the journey in spite of the ten dollar fare. Her husband was still unaware of her covert activities to help runaway slaves, even after the Plunkett affair with its five ghastly murders. Moses had willingly returned from Philadelphia after delivering Israel's children to the right people. His wife and children were still on the plantation. Darcy was angry with Maggie for giving Moses his freedom. The fact that Jeremiah had raped his own daughter seemed reason enough for her to help Israel's children escape, but he was concerned that they still might end up implicated in the gruesome mess.

When Moses returned to Marcus Manor, glasses of whiskey were shared in the library, with Darcy extremely relieved to have him back.

Maggie realized that Moses was Darcy's closest friend on the plantation other than Yuma, who was always more of a father figure. That was the truth whether Darcy could accept it or not, in her honest opinion. She was unyielding in maintaining that Moses was no longer a slave but a free man.

Besides her sincere desire to see her sister again and meet her nephews and nieces, Maggie's covert reason for traveling all the way to Charleston was to meet an indomitable Southern abolitionist, Penelope Worthington, the widow of the late Jonathan Worthington. The Worthington's were supposedly highly respected in Charleston society. Maggie had already corresponded with Penelope for two years, for she was another secret member of the *American Anti-Slavery Society of Philadelphia*.

Before heading farther north, several runaway slaves that safely reached the cabin at Marcus Manor were previously hidden on the Worthington Plantation. Penelope was also a member of the Congregational Church which was fervently opposed to slavery. The slaves on her rice plantation were freed after the death of her husband, the master. Those who remained were paid a fair wage, which was a hardship in the beginning. But all seemed to enjoy a sense of family with the Worthington's. Communality with slaves was something the two women shared, which made them soul sisters in a righteous cause. According to Penelope, slaves born in America, as descendants of Africans, should not think of themselves as purely Africans as she had written in a letter:

> *We are all Americans, regardless of our country of origin or the color of our skin. Our colored brothers and sisters should be treated equally with the same rights and privileges as Americans of African descent, the same as I am an American of English descent and you are an American of Irish descent.*

The family gathered on deck with the other passengers as the *Lady Bug* docked at the Port of Charleston. The Brosnans felt fully rested after just one night of sleep, surprised that only two days and one night were required for the journey from Baltimore to Charleston. Out in the harbor was Fort Sumter, named after Thomas Sumter, a South Carolina Revolutionary War Patriot. The harbor was filled with many different kinds of boats, as well as ships being loaded with bales of cotton and barrels of rice for export. Out on the deck, the captain had extolled the many fine virtues of the charming southern city.

A large carryall transported the family to the *Dublin Hotel*, which was not far from the harbor, with its bright green shutters decorated with shamrocks, the hotel having been renamed after the Gallaghers assumed ownership three years before. Kevin and **Megan** had managed to bring a touch of Ireland to the Carolinas. The color green was also used in the lobby and in nearly every room. Emerald green draperies added a touch of elegance in the hotel's restaurant.

On the next day, the Brosnan family was treated to a carriage and walking tour of the city of Charleston. Megan was their able guide in pointing out the iron battery benches and houses with bric-a-brac on all sides. The Edmondston-Alston home looked impressive. The Nathaniel Russell house was built by a man once called the King of the Yankees, a Rhode Islander who had found his fortune in Charleston. And then, there was the Heyward house.

"Thomas Heyward, Jr. was an original signer of the Declaration of Independence," Megan proudly said. "George Washington slept here, and he kept his inaugural promise to tour the South. He rented the house for an entire week."

"I understand that the Courthouse was designed by James Hoban, the Irishman who designed the White House," Darcy remarked.

"Why, yes," Megan replied in tone of pride.

Next, they visited City Hall and the Council Chambers where Kevin was an active member.

The steeples of many churches were highly visible in the city, commencing with St. Michael's Episcopal Church, which the Gallaghers still regularly attended.

"The bells of the church have made several trips back and forth across the Atlantic. They were crafted in London, and then claimed as a war prize by the Crown in the Revolution. And then, later the bells were returned to us. Fortunately, the bells escaped capture during the Second War for Independence," Megan explained. "Let us hope that there are no more wars to threaten our fine church bells."

The new wood frame Gallaher house was not that far from the hotel. It was three stories with lots of rooms and painted white with bright green shutters that featured Irish shamrocks. A rope design framed all the windows, an ancient Chinese symbol that signified that a merchant lived there. The piazzas faced west and south to catch the breeze and cool the house during the extended days of summer. On one piazza was a jogging bench on which the children often bounced up and down.

Both Maggie and Megan preferred to take their meals with the family at home, and yet, the hotel required Kevin's constant supervision. The summer weather was pleasant enough to often lunch on the verandah, with the youngsters racing off to the gazebo to watch the ships sailing in and out of the harbor.

On some afternoons, the new game of baseball was played on the lawn, with chess and checkers in the sitting room and card games of poker played with seashells. In the evenings after supper, there was often music and singing in the parlor. On occasion, Maggie and Darcy played duets upon the piano.

"I am truly delighted to finally hear my sister play the piano," Megan said.

One evening during supper, there was discussion concerning the recent tragedy in the Territory of Texas. After the Mexican General Santa Ana captured the Alamo, all the men not killed in the siege were immediately executed, with the women and children sent away with a Mexican escort.

"Three thousand highly trained Mexican soldiers fought 250 Americans, mostly untrained," Aidan said in a tone of some disgust. "Why didn't Sam Houston send in some reinforcements?"

"It was a massacre," Dermot said.

"Houston is Scot-Irish, the same as President Jackson," Megan said, "As are you, Darcy, except that you have English blood as well, correct?"

Darcy smiled and nodded.

"Houston served under Jackson in the Creek Wars," Kevin said, "He was Governor of Tennessee before he secured freedom for Texas. And now, he is Governor of the Republic of Texas. Yes, sir, not bad if you ask me?"

"Texas will probably be a state one day," Darcy said.

"We now have twenty-five states," Peter Gallagher said, smiling.

"Arkansas became a state last year," Timmy added.

"Yes, Timmy," Maggie said, "That is correct."

"What is Arkansas?" four-year old Triona inquired.

"It is a state in the United States of America," Timmy impatiently told his little sister. "You are too young to understand all that, but you will learn soon enough. Mother is an excellent teacher."

"Great Britain abolished slavery two years ago," Brigid said, coyly glancing at her mother before she turned directly to her Aunt Megan. "How soon do you think it will be before the rest of us are forced to free our slaves?"

At the age of fifteen, Brigid freely voiced her opinion. She now glanced from her mother to Betsy, the household slave near her own age, who was serving supper. Brigid had not failed to notice that the Gallagher slaves were not treated as well as the slaves at Marcus Manor. It was something she had already discussed privately with her mother.

"In 1833, over 700,000 slaves were freed in the British colonies," Aidan commented, "It caused economic hardship throughout the Caribbean, but they will surely recover in time."

"How do you happen to know that?" Darcy inquired.

"I read the newspapers, Pa. What are folks supposed to do with 700,000 colored suddenly free, most still illiterate and only knowing how to follow orders to cut sugar cane they have already apparently destroyed? Mother was right to teach our slaves how to read and write."

Darcy looked askance, first at Aidan, then at Maggie. "Mainly the household slaves," he hurriedly explained to Kevin, "to help them read to our children." He sipped wine from his glass while tentatively glancing around the table to perhaps more closely examine the expressions on the faces of all his eight children.

The Brosnan youngsters glanced at one another with faint smirks before most of them received a stern glance from their mother. The knowledge the Brosnan children had of certain activities of their mother was far greater than that of their father. Only the past spring, Aidan and Mia were compromised in the cabin when two runaways found them naked together in bed. That was the night that Aidan officially became a conductor on the Underground Railroad.

"Rebecca reads to me," Triona volunteered, "Mostly fairy tales and nursery rhymes." Her young face glowed in apparently being able to disclose that information.

"I suppose the Crown had to free the slaves after all those killings in Jamaica and Trinidad. Hundreds were murdered," Kevin said, "After that horror, no one was willing to go there for fear of being murdered in their beds in the middle of the night." He cringed and shuddered. "Innocent children murdered in their beds! Imagine?"

"That was why our Liam and Antoinette left for Hawaii," Megan said, "His employer and his entire family were murdered in their beds! Nothing I would ever like to consider!"

"I received a lovely letter from Liam right before we boarded the boat for Charleston," Maggie said. "He says that living on the island of Kauai is like living in Paradise. The sugar is doing well, the climate being quite similar, I should think?"

"Most certainly," Darcy said, "It sounds like a wonderful place with all the islanders so outgoing and friendly."

"Captain Cook discovered the Hawaiian Islands in 1778," Gareth announced. "Twenty years before our mother was born in Ireland."

"And twelve years before our father was born," Brian added. "Father is forty-six. He's thirty-four-years older than I happen to be now."

"Must you remind me?" Darcy said in good humor.

"King Kamehameha III is only twenty-two-years old. He's three years older than Aidan and is already king of the Hawaiian Islands!" Dermot said. "Too bad I wasn't born to be the king of paradise."

"Not with the Crown constantly trying to take away your land. No kings in this family, I fear, Dermot," Maggie said. "Or queens, for that matter. Though I do hope you girls end up marrying well. Find yourselves a fine man like your father!"

Darcy affectionately smiled at her.

"Mine, too," Megan said, smiling at Kevin, seated at the other end of the long table. "Constance has a handsome beau who seems to be seeking her hand. Raymond has family in Atlanta and New York City. He's a bit of Yankee, that charmer. You will meet him on the weekend. He went to Atlanta by train, which is the latest way to travel that seems to be catching on."

"Our Irish immigrants are building railroads everywhere, it seems, the same as the canals," Darcy said. "Only the railroads are taking the business intended for the canals. It's very hard to keep up with all the progress going on these days."

"I should like to take a wagon train to the new Indian Territory in Oklahoma," Aidan said, cautiously glancing sideways at his father, "Or go out to California. Yuma and the Piscataway would like to go with me, of course."

"Wow!" Robert said. "I'd love to go out west. That would be some adventure. How about taking the Oregon Trail together, cousin?"

"You are needed right here," Kevin said in a strong voice. "We are thinking of building a second, bigger hotel. Your place is right here in Charleston, Robert."

Robert rolled his eyes and audibly sighed.

"You seem to be doing rather well for yourself, Kevin," Maggie said. "I'm pleased for all of you. Or ... should I say *you all?*" she teased. "You all sounds more Southern than Irish to me these days. Good Law!"

Everyone laughed.

"I suppose you cannot reside in Charleston without sounding Southern, eventually," Megan said. "It rubs off on you."

"What do you think of that Irishman McCormick inventing that gol dang reaper?" Darcy said. "They say that eventually the reaper is going to revolutionize agriculture. He is selling the machine on credit with a money back guarantee. Imagine that?"

"That is something!" Kevin said. "Lately, we've been watching our prices at the restaurant. I hear tell that in New York City at Delmonico's a man can get soup, steak, half a pie and several cups of coffee for twelve and a half cents! And I'm doing that for eleven cents right here in Charleston!"

"Good Law!" Maggie said. "That is a bargain, Kevin."

"You have excellent food at the Shamrock," Darcy said. "It reminds me of being back in Ireland."

"How about that colored man, Henry Blair, getting a patent for his corn planter," Maggie said, quickly glancing at each of her children around the table. "I've heard he has also invented a cotton planter. Maybe that will help the slaves in the South. Or perhaps you can do away with the slaves entirely," Maggie said, now purposely making eye contact with each of her children in turn.

Aidan winked at his mother.

"I'm so relieved that we own no rice or cotton plantation. There are no crops to worry us," Megan said. "Maggie says that your tobacco is not doing so well of late. Is that right, Darcy?"

Darcy scowled. "Yuma thinks we should grow corn instead. I've been thinking about it. But I am not yet convinced that we can make a profit from growing corn."

"If we start planting corn, we shall need Mr. Blair's corn planter," Maggie said with a thrill in her voice.

"That is possible," Darcy cautiously said.

All at once, Maggie realized that she had made an important point in the Deep South of Charleston and that pleased her immensely.

47

The Devil's Daughter

The day before Martin Van Buren was sworn in as the eighth president of the United States, President Andrew Jackson and the Congress recognized the Republic of Texas. That same month the colored citizens of Canada were given the right to vote, the men, not the women. But it was a step forward in securing the rights of free colored outside the United States. Free colored in America were not allowed to vote in twenty-six states, with slavery still a fact for many, especially in the Southern States.

That June, after the death of her uncle, King William IV, Queen Victoria ascended to the British throne at the age of eighteen. She was the first monarch to reside in the lavishly remodeled Buckingham Palace. England soon issued its first stamp: 1P Queen Victoria.

In a letter from Prudence received in July of 1837, she wrote:

All hail to the Queen, only the fifth to so rule in over 1,000 years, the first to rule Great Britain in 117 years! Perhaps a woman is better suited to ruling such an empire during these truly modern times? May the Lord bless and keep our new queen. All hail Queen Victoria! Perchance she shall be the one to grant greater leniency to Ireland.

That was the same year that Jedidiah Plunkett, Jeremiah's younger brother, and Luke, his oldest surviving son, took over the management of the Plunkett Plantation. That was the case even though none of the local tobacco growers were prospering in any manner whatsoever, with the tobacco stunted and coarse. At Marcus Manor, corn was now being grown and it showed promise. The new corn planter was a definite asset to all the slaves.

Down in Kentucky, Jedidiah had grown tobacco. He brought along his wife and three youngest children to Maryland. Luke, now age twenty, was not present on the evening that the deadly stew was consumed. Neither was his younger brother, John. Both boys were in Baltimore with their maiden Aunt Edna, who suffered from severe arthritis. Having only one indentured servant, she had required their help. Luke enjoyed the city life, unlike John, sixteen, who despised crotchety Aunt Edna and Mobtown, where the gangs caroused at night, shouting and fighting, especially the poor Irish.

The eldest Plunkett girl, married with two children, and her younger sister, Mary, were also not present on that dreadful, fateful night. Four Plunkett children had survived, and yet, four cats and four dogs had perished, all of them buried on the plantation, including Mary's favorite tomcat, Boots, along with Numbers and Deuteronomy, their father's two hunting hounds. The crazy dogs had fought over the poisoned stew. That had made Luke wonder if anyone ever expected to have poison in their food. He lost twenty pounds that year, now fully understanding why kings had tasters. Luke was fearful of eating any type of food prepared by a slave.

Over the years and at various times, Luke had spoken with Aidan of his desire for a different kind of life. He had never thought that he was cut out to be a farmer. Before the "gol dang stew" there was always the hope that another brother might take over the plantation. Luke's aspiration to study law was often summarily dismissed by his father, along with any talk about going into politics. What Luke had never needed to disclose to Aidan was how sweet he was on Aidan's sister, Brigid. In Luke's mind, her beautiful blonde hair glowed in the sun like strands of the purest gold. Her blue eyes were as two precious stones of sapphire. And her mind was as quick and as sure as a mink's trap. Luke was plainly taken with Brigid, while Aidan preferred heated debates with his sister regarding various laws and practice. For, in Aidan's opinion, Brigid would make a truly fine lawyer herself.

Whenever there was a chance for them to get together and talk, Brigid and Luke often spoke of politics and about changing laws. Luke thought women should have the vote, and that point of view served to fan the flames of Brigid's aspirations with regard to women's rights. Besides the fact that she was extremely pretty, Brigid was also skilled in the use of her father's new Colt revolver, in addition to his Baker rifle, her father's keepsake from the war fighting Napoleon. Every Brosnan child was taught how to shoot a gun. Their mother had insisted that the girls needed to learn to shoot the same as the boys. Brigid's marksmanship was every bit as good as that of all her brothers. Luke was quick to point that out, especially to her eldest brother, Aidan.

Luke Plunkett was not a bad-looking man. In Maggie's opinion, he had taken more after his plain-looking, though obnoxious mother than his revolting and reprehensible father. Plain though rugged features seemed suitable on a man, especially with his well-trimmed moustache and clear blue eyes. Aidan always said that the same face on his sister Mary was likely to make her end up much the same as their spinster Aunt Edna. Mary also had her father's disagreeable disposition and vile temper. In Aidan's opinion, he could never imagine a man attracted to such an unsightly, bigoted sort of woman. Her father had always gone after the good-looking slaves, including his very own young daughter, which was certainly the worst decision the man ever made in his life.

All the Brosnans tried to avoid Mary, for Mary, along with her brother John, continued to ask countless questions about Israel, the poisoner. John and Mary Plunkett also frequently inquired into the whereabouts of Salome, Daniel and Rachel, their actual half-brother and half-sisters, who they usually referred to as "lying pickaninnies in cahoots with their evil mother" in plotting the murders of their family and beloved animals. A reward of $2,000 was posted in Maryland and Virginia for the capture or hanging of Israel, with all the slave catchers on the lookout for years. Neither Israel nor her children had ever learned how to read and write, so it seemed highly unlikely that anyone would ever hear from them again. However, Maggie had received a letter from Philadelphia disclosing that the children now safely resided somewhere in Canada.

During the past year, Brigid had done nothing to discourage Luke, who constantly brought her flowers and small gifts. She thought he was intelligent and kind and not at all like his father. In fact, she was the one who constantly encouraged him to attend *William and Mary's College* to study the law.

With the return of the Plunketts, Maggie was learning to exercise greater tolerance toward the youngsters than she ever had with their elders. She hoped they at least possessed some degree of moral fiber.

No one suspected that all hell might break loose on that September evening. Then again, young John Plunkett was convinced that old Yuma had helped Israel escape from justice. The slave he was confident had poisoned and killed his parents. The "savages" had helped a criminal escape from the law, which had caused John cruel and grievous suffering. For that reason, after finishing off the better part of a fifth of his daddy's favorite whiskey, John entered the Marcus Manor Plantation land and proceeded down to the Piscataway camp near the river. He was carrying his daddy's loaded revolver in order "to kill himself a lying, murdering, cussed savage."

Right after John staggered out the front door of the Plunkett Plantation, Luke ran across the road to let Aidan know of the evil intentions of his foolish, drunken brother. As fate would have it, neither Aidan nor Darcy happened to be at home. They were attending a meeting at the church with the other local farmers to discuss the prospects of getting their produce to market.

"The gun is loaded," Luke said in a state of panic, with his father's loaded rifle in his hand.

"Do you want the revolver or the shotgun?" Brigid asked her mother. "Someone has to stop that drunken fool."

Picking up the shotgun, Maggie said, "I wish the men were here. Your Pa insisted that Timmy go with him to the meeting and he isn't even ten yet. What does Timmy know about selling corn, for heaven's sake?"

Glancing down at the rifle in his hand, Luke said, "I hope I don't have to shoot my own brother. I hope the drunken fool doesn't force my hand." He was shaking his head with a woebegone look on his face. "The truth of the matter is ... John is a much better shot than me, even when he's drunk."

"Are you going to shoot somebody?" Brianna asked from the open doorway.

"What's wrong?" Triona asked, wrapped in a towel as Rebecca tried to dry her long red hair. "Are you going to shoot a mad dog or a bear, Mama?"

"A crazy bear," Brigid said. "Come on, Mama! Let's hurry!"

Rebecca frowned. "Is something wrong?"

"Yes, Becky. Take care of the girls," Maggie said. "We have to go down by the river."

Maggie, Brigid and Luke hurried out the back door just as Mia came running up to the house.

"He's going to kill somebody, Mrs. Brosnan. He's drunk and he's waving a revolver. John has gone crazy. You have to stop him, Luke. He's going to kill my people!"

All of them hurried down the path through the woods, hearing drunken shouting in the distance. The campfire was still burning in the clearing when Maggie stepped forward, her shotgun cocked and ready. Young John Plunkett was ranting and raving on her land.

Suddenly, John shot into the air. Plainly, the young man was not ready to listen to what she or any of the braves might have to say. He staggered around a clearing before he grabbed hold of a small tree to steady himself.

"Where is she?" John slurred, staggering to grab onto another small sapling for support. "You tell me where that fucking, murdering slave is, or you're a dead man, you hear me, you fucking savage! You have no right to be on a white man's land, none at all. You go on out to the Indian Territory with the rest of the goddamn savages!"

"Watch your language, John. There are ladies present," Maggie yelled with the shotgun pointed right at him. She stepped forward into the light of the fire.

Out of the corner of her eye, Maggie could see Red Bird with his rifle pointed at John from inside the cabin. His brother, Henry, had no weapon, but Long Bow's hand rested on the hatchet at his belt. An excellent hunter, the brave would never hesitate to use his weapon with great accuracy and skill. Long Bow always hit his mark.

"What do you think you're doing?" Brigid called out, now standing next to her mother and pointing her father's revolver at John. "It's loaded,

John. So don't tempt me. You're trespassing on private property. You know that I can shoot as good as you can or better. So can my mother! You had best put down that gun and save us the trouble of having to kill you!" she shouted in a tone that surprised her mother.

In the shadows until then, Luke cautiously stepped forward. "You had best stop whatever it is you think you're doing, John. You're as drunk as a skunk and you know it. Drank daddy's best whiskey to get up your courage to come over here and act the fool. Israel is not here, John. You are just going to get yourself killed if you don't watch it."

"That's right, John," Brigid said, defiance on her face as she took another step toward him. "Israel is not here. She never has been here. You're just being plain, stupid drunk."

"You're all jest a bunch of nigger lovers," John slurred, hanging onto the tree, "Nigger lovers and savage lovers that done stole our slaves. You're slave stealers that thar's what you are ... the lot of you!" he said, pointing his gun at Brigid. "You're turning my brother into a nigger lover too, Miss Brigid Kelly Brosnan. Why ... you're the devil's daughter that's what you are. You're the fucking devil's Irish daughter that stole Luke's heart away. That's what you've gone and done. Stole his heart, making him half crazy, you nigger lovin', savage lovin' crazy woman, Irish devil's daughter!"

At once, Red Bird stepped out of the cabin with his rifle aimed at John.

Women and children peered from the windows at the crazy white man and the two white women holding guns. Mia watched from the shadows.

"Put down your gun," Yuma ordered from where he stood near the fire. "Your slave is not here. Neither are her children. They are far away I know not where."

Twirling around, John took aim at Yuma.

Red Bird cocked his rifle.

Staggering forward, John yelled, "It was you, you goddamn savage. You hid her away," and he fired, grazing Yuma's arm.

At that exact moment, Brigid and Red Bird both fired.

Instantly, John crumpled to the ground.

"Brigid!" Maggie yelled. "Why did you shoot?"

With tears streaming down her face, Brigid cried out, "I love Yuma, Mama. He's like a grandfather to me. How can I let a drunken fool kill him on our land for no damn good reason?"

Rushing over to his brother, Luke knelt on the ground. "Is he going to die?" he asked Yuma, who was holding his bleeding arm.

"Brigid is a good shot," Yuma said, "Right through the heart. I think the one in the belly was from Red Bird. John never should have shot me. I did your family no harm," he said. "We taught all the Brosnan children how to shoot well, Darcy and me."

Staring down at John's lifeless body, Brigid dropped the revolver on the ground.

"Through the heart?" Brigid faintly said, "Well, I guess John Plunkett never should have messed with the devil's daughter!" and she dissolved into tears in her mother's arms.

48

An Act of Providence

On April 27, 1838, a great fire devastated half of Charleston: 1,158 buildings on over 145 acres burned beyond recognition, including St. Mary's Church, the synagogue, and the homes of friends of the Gallaghers in Ansonborough. Marketplace buildings were also destroyed, and yet the loss of life was insignificant, according to Megan. An act of providence had spared their hotel and home from the fiery fury, but the framing for the new hotel was lost. The next month, Kevin started over building with brick. Many buildings and homes were rebuilt with bricks as an added precaution.

In spite of the terrible fire, the June wedding of Constance Mary Gallagher, twenty-one, to Ronald Raymond Rathmore, twenty-eight, took place as planned at St. Michael's Episcopal Church. The reception was held in the Shamrock at the *Dublin Hotel*. Soon, the couple honeymooned in Savannah, and later, boarded another train to Atlanta where Ronald would practice law with his uncle.

Commerce in Charleston suffered immensely. Many folks moved away rather than start over. Penelope Worthington moved to the abolitionist community in Philadelphia. It was suggested that one of her former slaves had started the fire, which was a lie to discredit her free colored friends.

Bond was posted for the release of Chester from jail, with Penelope paying for the lawyers. He was finally acquitted. That year Penelope helped many slaves, including one interested in buying his freedom. This was disclosed to his master. After that, Penelope Worthington was excluded from most social events in the city.

With her entourage heading north, Penelope Worthington stopped by Marcus Manor on the day before the wedding of Aidan and Mia.

"The beautiful young squaw is with child," Penelope said to Maggie in the guest room. "And your Aidan is a very handsome young man."

"They have been sweethearts for many years. Aidan begged Mia to marry him when he was sixteen. Sometimes passion cannot be contained, Penelope. When we learned of the child, we agreed to the wedding. Aidan is now twenty-one."

"I completely understand. I was not a virgin when I married my Jonathan, though not yet with child. The fire of passion between us all consuming. I have never told anyone that before," Penelope said, blushing. "My daughters have fine marriages. My Bess is upset with losing her home. Her husband has lost everything. They have my plantation now to start over again. My Karen lives in Atlanta where Constance resides. My grandchildren are the same age as yours. I hope they can all be friends."

"I have written to Constance about your family."

"Maggie, please speak with your husband about freeing your slaves. It is not right for any man, woman or child to be held in bondage. Britain has freed all the slaves in the Bahamas."

Hesitating, she said, "Many of our slaves already consider themselves free. Darcy doesn't know that I recently helped four escape, those I had forced him to buy. But after Israel poisoned the Plunketts, I sent them on to Jackie. I could not bear to separate the family."

"I remember the slave who poisoned the master who had raped his own daughter. I understand she also killed his wife and two sons in the process, an unfortunate set of circumstances." Narrowing her eyes, she said, "That slave was acting as an avenging angel. After all, consider her name, Israel! She and her children could no longer remain in bondage to the evil Philistine. God shall forgive her, Maggie, though she should have perhaps been more discreet in her wicked business. Your praises shall also be sung by a heavenly choir for seeing that Israel's children reached freedom from their evil, fornicating father-master."

"I am not sure that my Darcy will sing my praises! After those killings, he refused to buy Joshua, Sarah's husband, who I could not allow to be sold down the river. That was what happened to some Plunkett slaves before Jedidiah arrived and before John was killed."

"Does your Brigid still think she fired the fatal shot?" she asked in hushed tones.

"That is highly debatable. I was there, of course, but it was very dark. No moon at all, just a dying campfire. It was not easy to tell exactly who killed John."

"Your daughter must be an excellent shot."

"All my children shoot well. For the longest time, Brigid was sure that she had killed him. But Luke, his brother, could not bear to think she had. Brigid was trying to stop John from killing Yuma, the medicine man who died last year at the age of eighty. Luke has begged Brigid to marry him. He seems out of his mind in love with my daughter. He writes her countless love letters."

There was a knock at the door.

"Mother," it was Brianna. "You need to come now. Aidan wants to talk to you," she said, opening the door and sticking her head in.

"I will be right there," Maggie said, turning back to Penelope, "Come see my Aidan marry his Mia. I shall be a grandmother soon. I cannot believe that I am nearly forty-years old. The years just seem to fly by, do they not, Penelope?"

The trees were cloaked in the brilliant shades of autumn when Dermot announced his plan to marry Priscilla Patterson of Baltimore and bring her to the plantation.

All the young Brosnans, particularly Brigid and the older boys, had discussed a bold plan to turn the plantation into a farming community, with the Piscataway and the free colored sharing in the profits, especially with the newly acquired Plunkett land that added another 200 acres and thirty more slaves. The corn was doing just fine.

All the children were in agreement on freeing the slaves. But first, the Plunkett slaves needed to be treated with kindness to gain their trust, rather than have them stealing, cheating, lying and being afraid of being sold down the river. Apparently, it was not easy for slaves physically disfigured and emotionally damaged by rape, starvation, and torture by Jeremiah and his evil slave driver to learn trust. Over a dozen slaves were murdered on that plantation over an equal number of years, with their remains sometimes thrown into the Gunpowder River.

It was Darcy's father, Gareth, along with Prudence and her father, who had so generously sent them the money to acquire the Plunkett land as an extension of Marcus Manor. Everyone said there would always be a home for them in Ireland, in Dingle and in Dublin. Evidently, Padraic O'Reilly had proven himself as an astute property manager in acquiring land all around the peninsula, even as far away as County Cork.

By that time, all the Brosnan children had joined their mother in her secret activities and considered themselves conductors on the Gunpowder River Line. That was true in spite of the hideous threats made by other slaveholding farmers in the area. The boys especially relished the intrigue and adventure, all of them feeling that their father should free the slaves. Their views already shared with their many friends still in bondage. The younger colored responded favorably to the idea of community farming. But there was considerable suspicion among the Plunkett slaves. Their past abuse had indeed produced a sense of deep distrust and suspicion.

A few of the other farmers in northern Maryland had already freed their slaves. Some former slaves stayed on to work for a wage, having spent all their lives in the area. The main problem was the plantation owners on the eastern shore with large tracts of flatland bordering the Chesapeake Bay. Their reputations for abuse were just as grave as the reputations of slaveholders in the cotton states of the Deep South.

Recently, a young runaway slave named Frederick Bailey had escaped by train and steamboat to New York where he married and traveled on to New Bedford, Massachusetts under the name of Frederick Douglass. His mother had died when he was seven, the same as Maggie's, and he suspected that his first white owner was his father. The same as Jeremiah, the master never admitted his paternity like so many other morally flawed male slaveholders.

By the end of the year, the colored citizens in Pennsylvania and Michigan had lost their right to vote, with petitions to vote filed in New York. White and colored abolitionists were murdered by angry mobs. In Philadelphia, a mob destroyed the meeting hall, burning and terrorizing in the colored neighborhoods. The authorities did nothing. And yet, the first abolitionist Congressman was elected to the House of Representatives in Ohio: Joshua R. Giddings. It was definitely a moment of triumph for the movement.

Gareth fell in love with a Piscataway girl, the same as Aidan, Her name was Shining Star. For that reason, it was not long after Aidan and Mia married that they wished to marry too. Maggie mixed herbs for Star and asked her to come to her whenever she needed more. It was more often than she had ever used her herbs, which caused her to reflect on her passion for Darcy and the many beautiful and intelligent children produced from their union.

By 1839, a country schoolhouse was built down the road. The young teacher from Baltimore by the name of Ralph Upton taught the young Brosnans, along with other children in the area. The older children thought their mother was a far better teacher, for she also taught the songs and dances of other countries. Their father often told tales of his service involving the war between Wellington and Napoleon. After such stories, their mother would often test them and make them grade their own papers.

Young Ralph Upton often sought Maggie out for advice. He was surprised to learn that their slaves could read and write, use numbers and read maps, with some possessing knowledge of the Romans and the Greeks. The teacher began to borrow books from the library. He was flabbergasted when he discovered that the Piscataway could also read and write and that everyone sang the praises of Maggie Brosnan.

An attractive age twenty-two, Ralph Upton was also charmed by young Brigid, seventeen. Her brothers accused her of leading men on after their trip to Charleston where the Southern belles could drive a man crazy with all their flirting and giggling. Dermot and Gareth found their female cousins in Charleston altogether exasperating.

"You caught it from them," Gareth said to Brigid. "It's a Southern disease!"

"Well, I am a Southerner," Brigid said, batting her big blue eyes at her brothers. "We do live south of the Mason-Dixon Line."

On a regular basis, young Ralph Upton would stop by for a lemonade or to inquire about another book, which made Maggie wonder what young Luke Plunkett might think about the situation. After all, it was Brigid who had talked him into studying law at the college of *William and Mary*. Luke had already proposed to Brigid several times, with her daughter still apparently unable to make up her mind.

That June, two American slave ships were escorted into New York Harbor by the HMS *Buzzard,* the brig *Eagle,* and the schooner *Clara.* The captains and the crews were to be tried in the American courts. Two weeks later, more slavers arrived manned by British naval officers as prizes of another ship on the African squadron. A commission in Sierre Leone refused to try any ship flying American flags. The British were plainly trying to force the Americans to enforce their laws against slavery.

That August, there was a major issue with another slave ship, the *Amistad.* A strong African had overpowered and murdered the captain and three members of the crew. He then ordered the Spaniard who owned some of the Negroes to sail the ship back to Africa. The intended slaves were told by a sadistic seaman that the men were cannibals and planned to eat them. The Spaniards sailed west instead of east. With the *Amistad,* the illegal trading of slaves was finally challenged in the American courts, with the aid of several stalwart abolitionists.

On January 13, 1840, a new generation arrived with the birth of their first grandchild on his father's birthday, the day that Aidan turned twenty-four. The new boy had a shock of dark hair and was named Darcy

Yuma. It concerned Maggie to hear Aidan and Mia talk of moving to the frontier. A plantation with 500 acres seemed enough to keep her entire family together, indefinitely.

That summer, young Darcy was crawling around on the floor in the parlor when Maggie said to Aidan, "Your father needs to free the slaves. Please talk to him, Aidan. I need your help with this."

"I suppose you also need my help with the Piscataway," Aidan said. "Sheriff Packer was here again. They've been keeping a close watch on our native friends since crazy John got shot four years ago. Not to mention the nasty business with Israel that we would all like to forget about completely. I guess they need to make sure there are no Indian uprisings at the Marcus Manor Plantation."

They all laughed.

"The sheriff told me to go to the Indian Territory," Mia said. "But it seems to me that we will not be going anywhere until after our next child is born," she said, brightly smiling at her husband.

"Oh, my!" Maggie exclaimed. "That's wonderful news. I hope this one is a girl."

"Mia informed me of her condition only this morning, Mama," Aidan said as he walked over to kiss his wife. "Mia is like you, Mama, she had a dream about a little girl. I told her how you always knew who was coming next from your dreams. That's my Mia."

"Is that right?" she said, momentarily studying her son. "I think we need to have that meeting with the slaves and discuss everything out in the open, son. Then maybe your father will be forced to free them. What do you think, Aidan?"

"You pick the auspicious time of the sun and the moon and speak with Red Bird, our new medicine man, and we will do it. I cannot promise you what Pa will do. The Piscataways are already in on the matter," he said, heading toward the front door. "Right now, I need to find Pilan and check on that corn."

Rushing after him, Maggie called out from the porch, "Aidan, Pilan seems sweet on Brianna and she's only fifteen. I saw them out walking together. Pilan is twenty-four, the same as you." She sighed in exasperation as she waited for his response.

"You were seventeen when you had me, Mama. I guess you just can't stop love!" he said, laughing as he walked on down the lane.

Early evening, Darcy entered the kitchen with a grim look on his face and removed the rifle from its rack behind the door. "I caught some runaways in that cabin down by the river," he said to Ruth and Rebecca. "Why the hell was that lantern doing burning out front? Is that some sort of signal or something? Exactly who around here is up to no damn good?" he demanded.

The lantern now flickered on the back porch as the women glanced at one another in a guarded manner, all the more rapidly peeling potatoes and shelling peas, with their eyes glued to the bowls. Only the night before there was the big meeting in the barn with all the slaves. Their mouths were closed tight.

Briskly entering the kitchen, Maggie inquired, "What are you planning to do with that gun, Darcy? Are you going to shoot somebody? Is there a black bear in the woods?" Then she noticed the lantern and rolled her eyes. "Why did you bring that lantern all the way to the house..." she started out, immediately sensing that the jig was up. Even so, she studied her husband for a very long moment.

"I caught two runaways in that cabin down by the river. I have Moses standing guard. I gave him the revolver I've carried with me since that Plunkett affair."

That was about the shooting of young John, with their daughter never discussed. Red Bird had accepted the blame. He was never legally tried after all present said that John was drunk and trying to kill everyone. Since then, it was the 'Plunkett affair,' with Brigid convinced that she had done what she had to do. After all, she was grateful to never be hanged or imprisoned.

"You are not going to use that gun on those runaways, Darcy," Maggie said. "You are not going to shoot anyone."

"I need to turn those darkies over to the sheriff," he said, looking stern, and he started for the back door. "I told Isaac to hitch up the wagon and saddle up some horses."

"You are not going anywhere, Darcy!" she said, grabbing his arm and nodding to the women to go out and check on things. "They are my runaways, Darcy. Don't you understand? I cannot believe that after all these years you have never caught on to my clandestine activities!"

The expression on his face was now one of bewilderment.

Entering the kitchen with the lantern, Aidan said, "Well, Mama, it seems to me the time has finally come for that talk you've wanted all of us to have."

"I am a station master," Maggie said to Darcy.

Stunned, at first he scowled, and then Darcy said, "A station master? What the devil is that?"

"Tonight, it looks like we are about to free about seventy slaves. That way, none of them will ever be forced to escape on the Underground Railroad."

"You won't be needing that, Pa," Aidan said, taking the rifle from his father.

In utter dismay, Darcy watched Aidan put the rifle back on its rack as he stood in silence and tried to make heads or tails out of what was going on right before his eyes.

Maggie nodded to Rebecca and Ruth and they hurried out the back door.

"You are in cahoots in this with your mother?" Darcy said to Aidan, slumping into a chair and whacking the table hard with his fist. "Freeing slaves? Helping runaways? Working on the Underground Railroad?" he said in a tone of some astonishment. "Well, I'll be damned!"

Aidan turned to his mother and the two of them exchanged meaningful glances.

"Risking our lands and our properties? Getting us all thrown in jail? Are you both crazy as loons—or what?" he shouted out in desperation.

Dermot and Gareth entered the kitchen, followed by Brigid, Brian and Brianna. All eyes were on their father who wearily shook his head with a woebegone expression and sighed in a fully disturbed manner.

"I am fifty-years old, Maggie. What the devil are you doing in this here runaway business?" He paused and took in a very deep breath. "It's not that I've failed to notice you running off to all those crazy meetings with your abolitionist friends." Again, he wearily shook his head. "I know all about your friends Jackie Carrington and Penelope Worthington and their anti-slavery antics up there in Philadelphia where that mob burned down their meeting hall. That was probably because of that crazy, radical, anarchist Garrison preaching treason against the United States government."

All the children now turned to their mother in plain sympathy, knowing of her fondness for Garrison.

"Do you know about the *Amistad,* Pa? About the Africans in jail in Connecticut and the abolitionists trying to help them?" Aidan inquired.

"Do you know about ships flying American flags still dealing in African slaves when it is against the laws of the United States?"

"Trading in slaves is punishable by death," Dermot said.

"I know that," Darcy said, "I read the newspapers. I do not trade in slaves. I do not bring them here from Africa. And I have never sold one. Just had the four new ones run off." Suddenly, Darcy stopped cold, as the truth dawned on him. Slowly, he looked from one child to the next before he turned to his wife. "Am I to understand that you are the one responsible for those slaves running off ... slaves for which I had to pay a whole lot of money at your stubborn insistence?"

Sinking into the chair opposite her husband, Maggie coyly smiled and noted the sheepish expressions on the faces of each of her older children.

Timmy and Triona entered the kitchen.

"Is supper late?" Timmy asked.

"Supper is going to be late for everyone," Brigid said.

"I have been biding my time, Darcy," Maggie said, "After working on the railroad for nearly eight years, along with our children now being conductors on the Underground Railroad. I am quite proud of our children, every single one of them, Darcy, I am proud as punch."

"You mean to tell me that this here is some kind of mutiny ... right here on my plantation?"

"Seems so, Pa," Gareth said. "We need to free our slaves. We had a big meeting last night. They are ready to work with us as sort of indentured farm workers, who work for seven years to acquire two acres of our land."

"What?" Darcy shouted as he leapt to his feet. "What are you talking about? What sort of plan do you have to give away our land ... to give away your inheritance? Are you daft ... the whole lot of you?"

"It's time, Pa," Aidan said. "Lots of slaves are being freed. It is time to free ours. Tonight!"

"It is time, Darcy," Maggie said, standing to face her flustered husband.

"It is time, Father," Brigid said. "The boys have a wonderful plan for all of us to work together and share. We love you, and we know that it is going to be just fine. It is the Christian thing to do, Pa, the humane thing. You wouldn't want to be a slave, would you, Father?"

"They don't want to leave," Brianna said. "They like you, Pa. You have always been good to them. They have always worked hard for you. It is a fair plan that the boys cooked up, a fair plan for all of us."

Rebecca and Ruth walked into the kitchen.

"I need to finish fixing supper," Rebecca said. "We both do," she said. "Your younguns must be mighty hungry." Rebecca smiled at Timmy and Triona, who vigorously nodded.

"Are the visitors okay?" Maggie inquired.

"Yes, Missy Maggie. Those two are on their way to Philadelphia. I did what you said."

Darcy shook his head and forlornly sank back into the chair.

"It was an act of providence that you caught those runaways tonight, Darcy. It was Spirit providing us with an opportunity to tell you about our plan to free our slaves and live in harmony on this land in a state named after the blessed Mother Mary."

Turning to face her children, Maggie said, "Now, let us have some supper and discuss this like one big happy family." She smiled at Darcy. "Then, tomorrow we will have that meeting with our slaves and tell them they are free. They may go or they may stay, according to their desire and the plan regarding the land here at Marcus Manor."

49

Cholera

The high fevers started out with the Piscataway working out in the fields. In the beginning, no one was able to determine the cause. After three braves and two squaws started vomiting and burning up, Red Bird thought it was yellow fever. Herbs were mixed and healings performed in the long house. Next, several colored workers started running fevers, followed by vomiting and dysentery, which was far worse among the children.

"You don't look so good," Maggie said to Gareth shortly before supper, as she reached for his forehead that was warm to her touch.

Immediately, Gareth ran out the back door for the outhouse.

Shaking her head, Rebecca said, "He's got it, Missy Maggie. Old Tom says it's the cholera. He has seen it do its evil down in Kentucky at Jedidiah's plantation where it killed twelve slaves in two weeks, young and old alike."

"Good Law!" Maggie exclaimed.

"I don't feel so well," Aidan said, slumping into a kitchen chair.

Instantly, his mother's hand was on his forehead and she turned to Mia and said, "You stay away from him in case he's contagious. You are with child. Sleep with the children or in my bed."

"Yes, Mother," Mia said. "Red Bird says it's because of the well, except he thinks there was yellow fever down by the river. Henry and Swallow both have high fevers."

"Boil water and get my herbs. Make soup with a chicken and onions and other vegetables. They will receive nourishment from the broth. Make some healing tea. I shall do everything I possibly can," Maggie said.

Aidan's fever was not as high as Gareth's. Star was pregnant with their first child and now she was running a fever. The vomiting and diarrhea started with both of them at the same time. Then, Timmy and Triona started throwing up. Beside herself with fear, Maggie had trouble deciding who to attend to next or more often than the rest with so many of her children sick at the same time.

"I am not feeling so well," Darcy said after supper, and he headed for the stairs.

"Don't you go getting sick on me, too, Darcy," Maggie said in a tone bordering hysteria as tears spilled from her eyes. "I need your strength with four of our children running high fevers. Good gracious, Darcy! There is cholera down the road. Five have already died. We need to dig us another well. I don't want you dying on me," she said, throwing herself into his arms. "I need you, Darcy. Don't you dare die on me, do you hear me? Don't you dare die!"

"I don't plan to die, Maggie," he said, burying his face in her long hair. "But right now, I need to lie down for a spell. I've had a very difficult day."

"All right, lie down and get some rest. I'm just glad that Dermot and Priscilla are still in Baltimore. I don't need one more sick person in this house to worry me near to death."

"You must be happy that Brian is in Baltimore studying to be a dentist. First school for dentists in the whole world," Darcy said in a tone of pride.

"Praise the Lord that Brigid and Luke are in Philadelphia. I'm still surprised that Luke is an abolitionist lawyer for our Anti-Slavery Society. His daddy must be rolling over in his grave every single day. You lie down and rest, Darcy, and I'll take care of my sick children."

"Our sick children," he corrected. "I won't kiss you just in case."

Grabbing his face, she kissed his mouth. "If you die, I'm dying with you. You stay well, Darcy Brosnan, you hear me? Because I am not ready to die and neither are you!"

"I hear you," he said, and slowly, he ascended the stairs. "I trust the chamber pot is in there?"

"It is," she said, hurrying into the kitchen to open a cupboard where she removed several jars of herbs.

Aidan was propped up in his bed reading *Two Years Before the Masts* by Richard Henry Dana. Dana's life as a sailor fascinated him. The man had sailed around Cape Horn to California and all the way back to Boston in 1836, with the ship's cargo cowhides. Dana entered Harvard Law School and had greatly improved upon the lives of seamen before he made the choice to openly opposed slavery as a lawyer.

The Last of the Mohicans by James Fenimore Cooper was on top of Aidan's dresser. That book had already made the rounds in the family several times. He was reading the story to Triona. At ten, she could read fairly well herself, but she still liked to hear her big brother dramatize the tragic tale.

Holding out a cup of her special tea, Maggie said, "Drink this, please, Aidan."

"I told him that you were bringing him a cure," Mia said from the doorway.

"Yes, ma'am," Aidan said and he sipped. "Not bad, Mama. Your cures always make me feel better. This one doesn't taste nearly as bad as the last one."

Reaching for his forehead, Aidan felt hot to her touch. Twenty-six and the father of two, with another child on the way, he still talked about going to California. "You shouldn't read that book again," Maggie said, "His adventures just make you want to leave us. You have a fever, Aidan. Do you have the runs, too? You keep away from him, Mia."

Mia disappeared down the hall.

Maggie stared at the book in his hands. "Mr. Dana didn't like California very much. He could hardly wait to get back to Boston. He thought the Spaniards were lazy and that California was highly uncivilized."

"The clipper ships are faster these days, Mama," Aidan said.

"Gareth and Star have the runs something awful. They're throwing up and burning up," Mia called from the doorway, hanging onto the frame and looking anxious. "I'm keeping my distance from them, Mama."

Fear gripped Maggie as she said, "I will see to them in a minute. You stay out of this room, too, you hear me?"

"Yes, ma'am," Mia said, nodding to Aidan. "I'll put the children to bed. They nearly wore me out today, but they have no fevers, praise the Lord."

"Moses has gone for the doctor," Maggie said. "He says it's the cholera. Three men and four women in the cabins are having an awful time of it, along with five of the children."

"Oh, my!" Mia gasped. "I would help out if I wasn't with child."

Upon reaching the hall, Maggie stopped short. Pilan was coming down the hall carrying Brianna in his arms. "She wants her mother," he said, "so I brought her up here. I'm not sure what to do. Red Bird used his herbs, and so far I seem to be all right. But Brianna is burning up with fever."

"Put her in Brigid's room," Maggie said, turning to Aidan. "You swallow those herbs and pray. The Lord must spare my family. I am not ready to lose one of you, not one!" and she ran down the hall trying her best not to cry.

The first in the family to die from the dreaded cholera was young Triona. Until the very end, Aidan was reading to her from *The Last of the Mohicans,* with his copy placed in her casket with three chapters still unread. Young Timmy fought hard, holding on fast, saying that he planned to live to be a hundred. Gareth and Star were buried side by side, having suffered the worst of it, taking their unborn child with them to the Otherworld.

For several days and nights, Maggie and Darcy had taken turns sitting up with one child or another. Their mother and father told each of them how very much they were loved and how important each child was to the parents, to their brothers and sisters, and everyone else on the plantation. Day and night, Maggie wandered from one room to another to administer more herbs or try to feed a child when the child was no longer able to keep any food down. Constantly, she was crying and continually praying to Mother Mary and all the saints and to every Celtic god in Ireland to please spare her dear, dear children. But all the while she understood that the fate of each child was up to the Lord of the Otherworld by whatever name might be petitioned.

Her ancient ancestors, her mother, her grandparents and great grand-parents were called upon to look after and care for her sweet, darling, dearly departed children, especially had she called upon great grand-mother Kelly. And yet, every one of them was needed to care for Triona, Gareth, Star, and their unborn child. Ultimately, destiny had its way, in spite of everything that Maggie and Darcy had earnestly hoped and prayed for and desperately tried to do.

Crying herself to sleep during the few stolen hours she could find, Maggie was keenly reminded of how both Aidan and Niall were buried in the sea. It was Darcy who was her knight in shining armor, the man who had rescued her from all her losses and her despair. Lying awake in her bed nearly sick herself with worry, Maggie was forced to review the tragedies and the triumphs of her life. She was greatly relieved that the Lord of the Otherworld had spared Darcy once more, besides those of her remaining children, for she dearly loved and treasured each and every child.

Five Piscataway had died, along with nine former slaves who died free. The Preacher McKay refused to bury "niggers and savages" in his churchyard cemetery. For that reason, another cemetery was set aside and consecrated at Marcus Manor where all might rest together in eternal peace as members of one extended and beloved family. Their two chil-dren and daughter-in-law were buried in the same ground hallowed by many different kinds of sacred rituals: Druid, Christian, Piscataway and African. The land was not far from a grove of sacred oaks on the banks of the Gunpowder River.

The elders were gathering beyond the veil to see to the needs of all placed within their sacred care, regardless of race, religion, age or circum-stance. That was something that Maggie knew in heart was absolutely true.

Burials were performed on three separate days near the time of the full moon. First, the Piscataway held a sacred ceremony, which was fol-lowed by Christian and Druid prayers. Later, sacred African rituals were performed with drumming. All the rituals helped to soothe the hearts and the souls of those left behind to go on in a world where shadows could still obscure the light more often than she might like. The cholera had claimed many in the epidemic, and not only those residing at Marcus Manor.

"They will be having a party," Maggie said, weeping, as Darcy wrapped his arms around her on the last night of mourning, with tears coursing down both their faces.

"They shall welcome us when our time comes," Red Bird solemnly said.

"They will do that, along with all our ancestors," Maggie said, walking through the woods under the light of the moon with her Darcy. She was deeply grateful that her husband and her six other children were still alive upon the earth.

50

Great Famine in Ireland

The first year of the potato blight, 1845, was not the worst year of the Great Hunger in Ireland. The year 1847 became known as Black '47. It was the worst year in County Kerry and throughout Ireland. Many tenant farmers lost everything, mainly those with less than an acre on which to grow potatoes. During the past two years, over 10,000 farmers had lost their homes and land, emigrating to England, Canada, Australia, Latin America, and mainly, the United States, which was an irresistible option for the sons and daughters of Erin. Those who survived the passage in the *coffin ships*, as they became known, arrived in Boston, New York City, Philadelphia and Baltimore. The same as with the slavers, throughout the years, sharks followed the ships to feed upon the bodies tossed overboard.

In the autumn of 1847, her father wrote:

My Dearly Beloved Children,

An enormous number has already perished in the land of your ancestors, because of this famine that has descended upon us without knowing the exact number gone in just this year alone. Many blame the fairies. Death is not usually the result of starvation but from some illness: fever, dysentery, smallpox, influenza, TB, measles and bronchitis. The farmers are forced by Great

375

Britain to work twelve hours six days a week to build roads that lead nowhere and walls that enclose nothing, the length and breadth of Ireland.

It is a sad business indeed to bear witness to the devastation with no power to alleviate the suffering, considering the miserable state of countless souls. Our means insufficient to stay the tide of human degradation when food grown here fills bellies elsewhere, unbridled gluttony and greed a plague created by the Crown's unwillingness to show charity to the Irish people, forcing a sick man to work at useless tasks to feed a family. They pay a man to dig his own grave and those of his family, with many too weary for the pitiful task, falling by the road to die alone and Godforsaken.

I am grateful that you are away from all this suffering. Prudence serves soup in front of our house five days a week. We tend the sick whenever possible. If you can, please send money and clothing. At the Dingle Poorhouse hundreds die monthly and are buried in the pauper's cemetery at Cnoc a'Chairn, all poor Catholics. I beg Matthew and Sean to see it through, having already lost three children to immigration, never to see my grandchildren, to only briefly hold young Aidan now thirty-one-years old. I am sure that he has grown to be a fine man by now. My life is fully blessed by Prudence's love and endearing companionship.

I pray that America wins this war with Mexico. You now have Texas and Iowa, 29 states. I read about the annexation of California and New Mexico. America seems to grow larger by far each and every new year. I am sure that you will miss the children should they go to California. I hear the city is now called San Francisco. The west must be very exciting. It seems to me that O'Reillys live everywhere in the world these days.

We trust that you enjoyed your birthday gifts: "Jane Eyre" by Charlotte Bronte and "Wuthering Heights" written by her sister Emily, both women fine writers. Prudence has already read "Jane Eyre" and shall send you her thoughts on the story very soon. I have learned much from the books in this library and read nearly every evening. I remember when you read to us in our farmhouse that Matthew and Heather now fill with love, hard work, and my four delightful grandchildren.

Fortunately, in catering to the gentry we do not suffer from the famine. However, our hearts bleed to witness the horrors inflicted on poor Catholics. The abominable Protestants use food to "convert to the true faith of Christ." A pox on them, I say, begging your pardon, Darcy. You can see that I have changed little in my 74 years.

I am amazed to think you are now 49 years, Maggie, with Liam 53 and already a grandfather to eight. We Irish do multiply, and yet, the famine has subtracted greatly from our race. May God bless you and keep you and your family and my descendants everywhere in this world.

You ever loving father,

Padraic Desmond O'Reilly

Maggie was grateful to receive the two novels, and grateful that her family had not starved like so many others. Her heart ached for those in her native Ireland. Clothing and money were sent during each of the famine years. Some money provided passage to America for a few to escape from the terrible times of the Great Hunger.

In the spring of 1847, Maggie and Darcy listened to Aidan and Pilan discuss the possibility of fewer hardships being endured by sailing to California on a merchant clipper ship rather than taking a covered wagon all the way to the West. The *Golden Gander* would take three to four months for the voyage with room for only twelve passengers. The young men's heads were filled with romantic notions of sailing the high seas at the age of thirty-one, accompanied by their wives and many children. Perchance it was better than trying to take a wagon 3,000 miles across high mountains with unfriendly Indian tribes all along the way. But it was still very hard for Maggie to accept.

Passage for each adult: Seventy-five dollars, with each child fifty dollars to include the food. The price of two wagons and all the supplies would have been more and it would have taken much longer to reach California.

Brigid and Luke arrived with their two youngsters to say their fond farewells to their family members. Having her family together with her for a few days caused Maggie to wonder if she would ever see them all together again.

"Good gracious," Maggie cried, reaching for William, Aidan's youngest child, with one arm, and for Brianna's three-year old Charles with the other, tears streaming down her face. "Shall I ever see you again? Shall I live long enough for that, my darling grandchildren?" Quickly glancing at Aidan and Mia's three children, with Elizabeth in Brianna's arms, her long dark hair and green eyes so like her mother's, Maggie was unable to stop crying.

"We shall surely see you again one day, Mother," Aidan said. "Trains might well reach from one coast to the other before too long."

"I reckon California will be a state one day," Darcy said.

"You can always take a clipper ship," Brianna said. "I'm looking forward to the voyage. It will be summer as we sail around South America, the best time of the year for sailing, I hear. And it will still be summer in California when we arrive. Isn't that something, Mother?"

"I hope you don't get seasick," Brigid said. "On the way to Charleston, you threw up and your puke landed on the side of the steamship. It was quite disgusting!" she said, laughing.

"I'm sure I've outgrown that," Brianna haughtily replied, "though I will probably have my hands full with these two." Charles was clinging to her, as Elizabeth toddled over to Pilan and her father picked her up.

"We shall have more children," Pilan said. "Brianna is taking along her herbs should the opportunity arise for such activity onboard ship. Morning sickness might not be much fun at sea."

"Is it ever any fun?" Maggie said, "I understand Red Bird supplied you girls with some remedies as well."

"Yes," Mia said. "I will wait until we reach California, but we would like more children."

"You just keep having them," Darcy said, "They're beautiful children and very smart. Young Darcy reads quite well. Even Brown Bear can read."

"You should call me Patrick, Grandpa," he said. "I don't want the sailors to know I'm an Indian or it might scare 'em," the four-year-old said.

"You are not going to scare them," Aidan chided. "You should be proud to be half Piscataway and don't you forget it."

"I am proud," Brown Bear said. "Thanks for the books, Grandpa. I'm going to read them on the ship. The *Golden Gander* is a pretty ship, isn't she?"

"She surely is. Prettier than any ship I ever sailed on. It is going to take longer to sail to California, however, than it takes to sail to Ireland."

"Much longer," Maggie said. "I hope storms don't spring up on you all of a sudden."

"I'm excited," young Darcy said. "But I guess it won't be much like sailing on the *Maggie,* will it, Grandpa?"

"Our sloop is only twenty-foot. This ship is 225 feet long and forty-one feet wide with its three square-rigged masts. It's a fine-looking Yankee Clipper ship." He reached over and pulled young Darcy into his arms. "And I surely will miss you, young Darcy. I shall miss you very much."

"I will miss you, too, Grandpa."

"It is most unfortunate that this ship is not sailing to Ireland with our corn," Aidan said. "After we reach California I shall contact my cousin, Seamus McKenna, and see what can be done to help out with the famine. In his letter he said that he has done right well in San Francisco."

"Good lad," Maggie said, giving her son a hug and a kiss.

Soon, Maggie was kissing each and every one goodbye.

Before long, the stately *Golden Gander* sailed toward the *Patapsco River* and the *Chesapeake Bay* in order to reach the open Atlantic Ocean on its long voyage to the West.

"I'm glad you allowed me to tell Aidan about his natural father," Darcy said on the way home in the carriage. "It was time he was told of the first Aidan back in Ireland. Perhaps he should have been told long ago. But I do love him as much as any of our other children. You do know that, Maggie. I consider Aidan as my own son."

"I know," she said, resting her head on his shoulder. "You are a good and loving man and a fine father, Darcy. It was very wise of me to marry you."

"I am the lucky one," he said, kissing the side of her head, "Even though you made me give all my slaves their freedom." He pensively paused. "Uncle Shane may very well have done the same by that time, come to think of it."

"He would have. I know it. He told me in a dream more than once."

"Is that right? You and your dreams."

There was a long silence.

"What do your dreams tell you of this famine in Ireland?" Darcy inquired, sadly shaking his head, "And about the safety of our children on their long voyage around Cape Horn?"

"The famine will not be over soon enough, I fear. There is yet more suffering for the Irish is what my mother tells me." Maggie paused. "Our children will arrive safely in San Francisco. Great grandmother Kelly has promised to watch over them until the ship sails into the San Francisco Bay."

"I am counting on your great grandmother to keep our children and grandchildren safe, but I pray your mother is wrong about this famine. I pray the end comes soon with the help of the good Lord and all His many angels, if not with the help of the parliament of Great Britain."

51

Gold in California

The children were safely in San Francisco for less than a year when an employee constructing a sawmill for a man named John Sutter discovered gold. The two men were not really interested in starting a gold rush, the stories filtering into the countryside at first seemed too fantastic to believe.

A San Francisco merchant named Sam Brannan, thinking a gold rush might make him rich, dreamed up a scheme. He ran through the streets of San Francisco shouting, "Gold! Gold from the American River!" holding up a bottle of gold dust, and thus he ignited the Rush for Gold. His run was followed by the purchase of every pick axe, pan and shovel in town. A pan that had sold for twenty cents became fifteen dollars. In nine weeks, Brannan made $36,000 and was a very rich man indeed.

The rumors of gold were discounted until 1848 when President Polk said: "The accounts of the abundance of gold in that territory are of such extraordinary character as would scarcely command belief were they not corroborated by authentic reports of officers in public service."

In the *New York Tribune,* Horace Greeley wrote: "Fortune lies upon the surface of the earth as plentiful as the mud in our streets. We look for an addition within the next four years equal to at least $1,000,000 to the gold in circulation."

GOLD FEVER was epidemic by 1849, with young men streaming West by horse, by wagon, and on ships. The *Forty-Niners* left home in '49. Numbered among them was Brian Brosnan on a clipper ship, the *Golden Swan,* in search of his brothers Aidan and Pilan, panning for gold on the *American River.*

"You will help Aidan," Maggie said. "It was tragic losing our Mia in childbirth, but at least their son survived. It took me back to the time when my mother died when your Uncle Sean was born. Kiss young William Gareth and each of the children for me, Brian. Kiss them all for Grandma and Grandpa Brosnan."

"Of course, I will kiss them all. And I will help out wherever I can. But the main reason I'm going to California, Mama, is to make my fortune. After I have enough gold, I plan to find myself a beautiful and proper wife."

"I thought you loved Sylvia. Perhaps you should take her with you. Brianna says that prostitutes work the mines and take away the men's gold. I don't want you getting a terrible disease from some harlot. So you be careful, do you hear me, Brian Boru? Damn careful!"

"Mama, you know Pa doesn't like you to swear."

"Do not correct me, young man! You marry some decent girl, not some saloon harlot, do you hear me?"

Brian grinned. "Yes, Mama, I hear you, I hear you loud and clear."

"I thought you were going to be a dentist. You have your diploma."

"I may be a dentist in San Francisco. I will have to see after I get there."

"Well, I don't know exactly what we are going to do without you. Timmy wants to leave, too. I can't have four children all the way to California. You understand that, don't you, Brian?"

"You can't hold onto us forever, Mama. You have to let us find our ways the same as you did coming to America at the age of seventeen. Shucks, I'm already twenty-six, and I want to see the West, the wild frontier."

Besides the free colored and a few Piscataway, Maggie still had Timmy, twenty-one, on the plantation. Dermot, thirty, Priscilla, twenty-six, and their five children were also there. Maggie often read books to the children and told them the tales of the Tuatha De Danaan and of Ireland's once proud high kings. Dermot was a respectable farmer. Some of the locals still made a fuss about the "niggers" who were no longer slaves, farming. They claimed some had stolen their chickens, calling the colored "niggers," and all the Brosnans "white trash" and the Piscataway "gol dang savages."

That summer, Maggie learned her Aunt Brigid had died in her sleep at the age of eighty-four. The doctor said it was probably her heart. But Maggie knew from her dreams that her aunt was ready to go weeks long before the letter arrived. On the night of her passing, she had a dream where all of them were together in the sacred grove near the deep blue pond with the patches of lavender and purple heather. Aidan was also there. He let her know that young Aidan was doing fine in California. Their son was richer by far than any smuggler he had ever known.

Thank you, Aidan said without appearing to speak, *Our lad is a fine man. Bring him home to Ireland one day, back to his roots so he might better understand the blood that flows in his veins is the sacred blood of our thrice blessed Erin.*

By 1850, the Famine in Ireland had taken an enormous toll. More than a million people had died and another million had emigrated, with no knowledge of how many actually died on the crossings, or soon after reaching the far distant shores. The largest number immigrated to America. The new influx of Irish was partly responsible for the Piscataway following the Trail of Tears to the Indian Territory in Oklahoma. Over 90,000, from numerous Indian tribes, were relocated by the United States government.

That same year, Sean Joseph was apparently struck with GOLD FEVER. He booked passage for his entire family, including his seven children, from Cobh to San Francisco. By that time, Aidan owned a hotel, *The Brosnan Arms,* along with the nearby *Indian Gold Saloon.* Brianna and Pilan owned a mercantile store where the latest fashions from Europe were sold. However, Brianna also designed dresses and hats. Maggie and

Darcy were proud of the accomplishments of their children in California, including the fact that Pilan and Brianna owned a fine three-story house with two indentured Irish servants to help them care for their four growing children.

That September, California became the thirty-first state. Everyone in the family in San Francisco celebrated together that night, including young Padraic, Liam's son, and two of Matthew's sons newly arrived from Dingle. Aidan wrote to his parents about the fireworks lighting up the night skies and everyone dancing in the streets.

That December, Maggie and Darcy visited Brigid and Luke in Philadelphia to attend the lecture of a former slave named Frederick Douglass. He was an imposing, dynamic man and an eloquent speaker who called out for racial equality. His autobiography was published in 1845, *Narrative of the Life of Frederick Douglass, an American Slave, Written by Himself.* Soon after his book was released, his former owner tried to take him to court to return him to slavery. Douglass escaped to England. Those in the anti-slavery groups raised enough money to secure his freedom. Famous for his assistance in freeing blacks, in his lecture, Mr. Douglass called for the abolishment of slavery in the United States of America.

"Mr. Douglass visited our *Liberator*, Daniel O'Connell, before his death in Rome back in 1847. Imagine, Mr. Douglass and Mr. O'Connell having tea in London," Maggie gushed.

"They probably drank something stronger than tea, Mother," Luke said. "It is most unfortunate about the Free Church of Scotland demonstrating with their uncouth signs, 'Send Back the Nigger,' so tasteless and unnecessary."

"He criticized them for taking money from our slaveholders," Darcy said, "And the Scots are a stubborn, opinionated lot for sure."

"Aren't they though?" Maggie teased, "Quite stubborn and quite opinionated."

In the group dining together on that evening was Jackie Carrington and Penelope Worthington, with all present voicing their concern over the passing of the recent Compromise Bill.

"Abolishing the slave trade in the District, while still allowing slavery to exist in our nation, is an enormous contradiction!" Penelope said in her distinctive southern accent.

"Pacifying the Southern politicians, who claim an imbalance, with California a free state, is hardly a fair reason to pass the Fugitive Slave Act," Luke said in a tone of exasperation.

"Everyone is upset about this," Darcy said. "Douglass said as much in his speech."

"What about the slaves?" Brigid said, "Those trying to start a new life? This is a disaster, Luke. You have to know that."

"You and the other lawyers need to repeal the law," Penelope said. "What about life, liberty, and the pursuit of happiness for all Americans? Hypocrisy right there in our Constitution, my Law, maybe Garrison is right about the men not voting!"

"I'm sympathetic with Mr. Douglass's recent falling out with Garrison," Jackie said.

"I thought you called him William?" Penelope chided.

"But, if he had his way, there wouldn't be a United States of America," Jackie defensively replied. "He tells men not to vote. He wants to destroy the Union. I simply cannot go along with that idea! I just can't!"

"Now, ladies," Maggie said. "Let us not quarrel. We are all entitled to our differences."

"In my opinion, Garrison is a radical anarchist!" Darcy announced. "I will not be surprised if they put him in jail again for a longer period of time. He speaks treason and raises havoc for the abolitionist as much as he helps them. I'm sorry, but that happens to be my position on the matter. I do not care in the least for Garrison."

"Mr. Douglass is right," Luke said. "The Constitution should be used to win the rights of our colored citizens. There is no need to disband the Union ... just the need to free slaves from their masters everywhere across the land."

"I love his motto for the *North Star*: 'Right is of no sex ... Truth is of no color ... God is the Father of us all, and we are all Brethren,'" Brigid dramatically quoted. "He is a wonderful man, Mr. Douglass, so striking and so very eloquent."

"She memorized it," Luke said. "He is certainly one of our best advocates with a voice to be heard."

"Mr. Douglass calls his paper the *North Star* because slaves escaping at night on the railroad are told to follow the North Star," Jackie said, smiling.

"Mr. Douglass is an advocate of women's rights, too, Mother. He spoke at the first Women's Rights Convention in Seneca Falls back in '48," Brigid said. "I was there and he was brilliant!"

"He thinks we should have the vote," Penelope added. "Now, wouldn't that be something? Women voting?" Straightening up, she austerely added, "I certainly wouldn't have voted for that slaveholder, Zachary Taylor."

"A bundle of contradictions," Penelope declared. "I never did like him. Praise the Lord he got sick and died."

Darcy and Luke exchanged glances of feigned horror, with the women giddily pleased.

"One crusade at a time is sufficient, ladies," Luke said in good humor.

"That Sojourner Truth is doing an amazing job in this country. She is also one fine lecturer," Maggie said. "I am mighty proud of her work."

"So am I!" Penelope added.

"I am quite unhappy with Daniel Webster as Secretary of State under Fillmore. He is undoubtedly the reason that this Fugitive Slave Law was passed," Darcy said in a tone of disgust.

"Federal officers to be at the disposal of slaveholders seeking fugitives," Luke said, "Unconscionable! We shall endeavor to do our best to keep him out of the presidency in '52. I know powerful men whose ire he has raised to a high fury by signing this act into law."

"Both men are sincerely hated in the North," Brigid said. "I would never have voted for him, either," she said to Jackie, giving her husband a firm nod.

"My Brigid is always generous in rendering her unbiased opinion," Luke said, prideful amusement in his tone. "She would make a fine lawyer herself, my lovely wife. Her brother Aidan is certainly right on that score."

"Well, with women now doctors, I suspect the law will be next," Maggie said.

"That is a formidable thought," Darcy said, turning to Luke. "Good luck, old chap!"

"What do you think of that Dana getting the Navy to abolish flogging?" Luke said. "He is a tremendous asset to our movement, as well."

"Excuse me for changing the subject, but our family members have once again been forced to rebuild their businesses after all those horrible fires in San Francisco," Brigid said. "Our Brian and his Uncle Sean faired the best, it seems. My Irish cousins are determined to rebuild, repeatedly, if necessary. They absolutely adore California."

"Aidan has joined the Vigilante Committee in fighting the gamblers and cutthroats who started those fires ... horrid bunch of rabble rousers," Darcy added.

"Hasn't there already been three fires in San Francisco just this year?" Penelope inquired.

"May, June and September," Maggie said, "All of them arson. And yet, the city is resurrected time and again. The men just go back to the gold fields. That metal seems to be just lying around out there in California, Oregon, and Nevada. Aidan sent me a nice nugget for my birthday."

"That is how our Brian gets the gold for his patient's teeth," Darcy said, "All those forty-niners running around with gold in their pockets. Just last year, our Brian married Molly from Tralee. Just like his Pa, he fell in love with an Irish girl with long red hair and light brown eyes," he said, and he winked at Maggie. "It worked mighty fine for me."

"Brian wrote that all this rebuilding going on out there reminds him of an old Egyptian myth about the Phoenix," Maggie explained. "Just like that bird, San Francisco keeps rising out of its ashes again and again and again."

52

The Fugitive Slave Act

In early April of 1851, both Moses and Johnny went missing, both of them free men. Moses, now fifty-eight, had a young wife and three small children on his two acres of land with its newly erected cabin not far from the river. Moses was in charge of the Plunkett land, so he had no reason to leave. Johnny, twenty, had once before run off because of a girl on another plantation. Lately, he appeared happy and had shown an interest in a young Piscataway girl. The situation truly puzzled Maggie.

"Did you have a fight?" she asked Katie, the young wife of Moses.

"Lordy no, Missy Maggie! I love Moses to pieces." Tears filled her eyes. "Do you suppose he's done found himself another woman?"

"He always says what a fine woman you are, Katie. About how much he loves you and the children, even though his older youngsters left and went north. You are so much younger than he is that he worries about you finding another man. You're only thirty-five."

"Good Law! I don't have eyes for no man but him. While I was still working for the Plunketts, I had my eye on Moses. It was sad when his Esther died. I guess she was too old to have more babies. But I was thrilled when Moses took to me. I could hardly sleep after he asked me to marry him. I couldn't wait to be with that man."

"If he's not back by tomorrow, the men are going out looking. The woods and the river have already been searched, haven't they?"

"Oh, yes. We done searched everywhere. I done been scared to search the river. And Moses, he was a good swimmer. He could swim across the Gunpowder at its widest part and all the way back again. That is a mighty long way, Missy."

"A mighty long way," Maggie said. "I've seen him help runaways swim. I guess it wouldn't be good for the colored to go looking for him outside the plantation. I don't want anyone else kidnapped. These slave catchers have Federal marshals helping them take folk they have no business taking. They get ten dollars for bringing a slave back alive."

"They gets five dollars for a dead nigger," Katie said. "Like some buck shot in the woods. There are terrible things happening to our kind, Missy Maggie."

"You know we help runaways. It'll be best if Darcy and Timmy do the searching."

"Yous probably right. The way folks been carrying on calling you white trash, yelling, 'nigger, nigger,' whenever they see one of us. I hate to say it, but those Junipers from Georgia, theys almost worst than Jeremiah, and that's saying something."

"I think you might be right."

"Theys the white trash beating one slave near to death."

"One day, things will change, Katie. But it's probably going to take some time."

Guns were cleaned and loaded, two Colts and two new Hawkins rifles. Darcy and Timmy saddled up, with plans set into motion as soon as Reynard Juniper started talking about "lynching niggers down in Georgia, hanging 'em on a tree to feed the buzzards." Then he would laugh and spit tobacco, his ugly face contorted pathetic-like. "That's jest to keep the other niggers in line," he said, spitting on the ground again not far from the hem of Maggie's new dress.

That was the last straw. It was all Darcy could do not to knock the fool on his posterior that very minute. Darcy's face flushed. Maggie knew all about riling Darcy. He was not safe to be around when he was truly angry. That was something his sons had learned early on.

"I may have to accidentally shoot that redneck son-of-a-bitch," Darcy said, narrowing his eyes as he climbed up onto Wellington III. The sire was old and lame. His grandsire had passed away back in 1834. Wellington I and II had run a race or two, which was as good as any thoroughbred in a race of kings, Darcy had often boasted.

"Isn't he a bit frisky for you to ride to hunt those men?" Maggie inquired. "Welly is high spirited and bucks like crazy when Dermot even tries to ride him."

"Don't you mean ... aren't I a bit old for his saddle?" Darcy said with a wink, pulling out his Colt and reinserting the gun into its holster. "Timmy is riding Penny. We're taking along Horace for Moses to ride."

"You know how much Reynard hates free colored. How many times has he threatened Moses?" Maggie inquired. "He could just as well be behind all of this."

Darcy frowned. "The men may show up while we're out looking for them. Who the devil knows?"

"Neither of them said one word to me about leaving," Maggie said. "After all these years, I still find Horace a strange name for a mare, don't you, Darcy?"

"It is too late to rename her. Timmy always called her Horace the horse, even though we said the name didn't seem right for a filly."

Maggie laughed. "It always made us laugh, and the horse didn't seem to mind. She's a fine mare." She paused. "Do you have enough bullets with you to deal with their kind?"

Darcy nodded. "Dermot and Priscilla will be at the house. I won't leave you here without another white man on the property, even though I know what a good shot you are. But don't you go shooting Reynard like you said you might, okay? Leave him for me!"

Maggie smiled. "Well, don't you go getting yourself killed by some mean, ornery slave catcher, or I may have to find the renegade and kill him myself!"

"I don't plan to, my darling."

"Becky says we've got visitors down by the river, couple of runners headed for Philly."

"You'd best be careful with Juniper nosing around. He's a mean man, and we don't need any more trouble with the law."

"Those slaveholders on the eastern shore can be mean sons-of-bitches just like the Junipers. I wish to heaven that they'd have stayed in Georgia. Do you suppose our family in the south is sadistic with their slaves? I have met more than a few loathsome bastards I would never ever care to sup with!"

Looking at her askance, Darcy said, "That's no kind of talk to come out of the mouth of a beautiful, refined woman like you. You surprise me, Mary Margaret."

"It's nice to know you still find me beautiful. Maybe I should swear more often."

"One more for the road," he said, leaning down toward her.

From tiptoes, Maggie kissed his lips. "I'm quite serious about you staying alive!" Grabbing his leg, she pressed against him. "Timmy, too. Don't you let anyone hurt our boy."

Riding around the corner on his horse, Timmy pulled up to a stop, with another horse tied to his saddle. "Come on, Pa. Isaac says some mean slave catcher has been hanging around who has a reputation for kidnapping free men. Those sort are barely human, seems to me. Luke needs to get that law changed." Tim smiled and nodded at his mother. "I'll take good care of him, Mama, the best I can, anyway. The truth is … Pa's a much better shot than I am."

"He will take care of you, too, Timmy. You just go on and hurry back, please!"

The men turned their horses around and cantered off toward the arch.

Within another fortnight, everyone on the plantation was worried. Katie kept coming to the house and bringing along all her children. Two free families moved away because of the vulgar and frequent taunts of the Juniper family. There was still plenty of prejudice against Quakers and abolitionists, some of them murdered, their homes burned. Colored children were not allowed to attend school in states in the Midwest or the South. Even the latest local teacher had refused to teach the colored children. Maggie still taught everyone interested in learning at the kitchen table of Marcus Manor.

After a month had passed, three men on horseback rode through the archway of the Marcus Manor Plantation. Catching sight of them from an upstairs window, Maggie ran down the stairs and on down the road, holding up her skirt and calling out, "Darcy! Timmy! Moses! Oh Law, praise the Lord and all the Irish saints that I can think of … all of you are alive!"

Soon, Katie and the children came running, with their eldest son, Mark, calling out, "Papa! Papa!"

Right away, Moses was off his horse, picking up his son and hugging Kate, as the smaller children clung to his legs.

"We tried to find Johnny," Darcy said, getting off his horse. "They said he was already in Mississippi picking cotton. They were probably lying, but who the devil knows?"

"Oh, Darcy! No!"

"The slavebreaker is called Remus," Moses said. "He nearly beat Johnny to death trying to break his spirit. They probably had him bound and gagged in the cellar. Missy, it's right terrible what these folk do to our kind. Those slaves don't have any spirit left in them. They've been worked near to death. I've never seen anything like it, even with the Plunketts."

"They were on St. Michael's Island," Timmy said. "We had to go to several plantations, and we had to pay $200 to get Moses back."

"What? Oh, Moses," Maggie cried. "I'm so glad that you're safe. Two hundred dollars?"

Moses flinched when his wife touched his back. "They beat you?" Katie said in a tone of alarm.

"Beat him bad," Timmy said. "He was sick and bleeding when we found him. His back is infected. I asked that Harmond what he wanted with an old nigger, not much good for anything." In noting the alarm on his mother's face, he quickly added, "You have to talk like that to their kind, Mama. They don't know any other kind of talk. He wouldn't let us have Moses if I hadn't called him a nigger. I'm sorry, Mama, but Moses understands."

Moses smiled, pulling Katie closer to him. "You're what kept me alive, Katie. You and our children. I may be old, but I had to live for you and our youngsters."

"But Johnny," Maggie said, ready to cry.

"We did what we could," Darcy said. "He's young and strong. He might live long enough to be free again. Plunkett was his father, and we gave him his freedom. We can only hope and pray, Maggie. That's all that we can do."

"You did your best. You brought Moses home. It's high time you get out the good whiskey, Darcy, and you're in serious need of a bath," Maggie said, holding her nose.

Darcy laughed, leading Wellington down the long driveway.

The best Irish whiskey came out of the cupboard. Everyone had a glass, even Maggie. Rebecca and Ruth giggled throughout supper, for Missy Maggie was drunk as a skunk on one glass, but Moses was home again at last.

53

Uncle Tom's Cabin

The spring of 1852, Darcy could hardly believe what he was reading in the newspaper when he discovered that another Napoleon had seized the throne of France and declared himself Emperor Napoleon Bonaparte III.

"He's supposedly a nephew," Darcy said in a tone of exasperation. "His paternity suspect due to his mother's numerous escapades. He removed the Second Republic from power and crushed a coup d'état a month later. Imagine that?"

"The man plainly has his uncle's high opinion of himself," Maggie said, "And his spirit and daring, it seems to me. But frankly, my dear, I'm much more interested in hearing about the new public toilets in London and the baths in New York City! It is high time that something was done for the poor and the homeless, the Irish being much fonder of bathing than others, perhaps. And New York City is teeming with poor Irish immigrants."

"I enjoy bathing with you in our new tub. It is sweet fun having you scrub my back."

"I wash more than your back, my darling, which is still great fun for me after thirty-five years of marriage, with me an aging woman."

"You are hardly a crone, my dear. In fact, it amazes me how young you look upon seeing my own reflection in the mirror. You haven't aged a day since 1814. You are still my bonny Mary Margaret O'Reilly from County Kerry."

"I fancy your beard now that it is softer and not so damaging as we cavort about."

"Cavort?" Darcy laughed. "But where shall we cavort with our trysting place used by runaways all these years? Especially with Mrs. Stowe's novel pointing out the many cruelties of slavery. Her book seems a sensation the world over. It is already published in several languages."

"And Ohio has made it illegal for children under eighteen, and women, to work for more than ten hours a day. Is that not progress?" Maggie stood. "There are so many Irish women here because of the famine, much more than men, I fear. I do hope that Harriet's book abolishes the Fugitive Slave Act. That law has created so much unnecessary misery and suffering for our colored friends."

"Amen," Darcy intoned.

Uncle Tom's Cabin had generated a new level of awareness with regard to slavery, especially in the North. And yet, many were still afraid of slave catchers who captured free men and women to sell back into slavery, especially in the Deep South.

On September 27, 1852, George L. Aiken's rendition of *Uncle Tom's Cabin or, Life Among the Lowly, A Domestic Drama in Six Acts,* premiered in Troy, New York with singing and dancing. It was only one of many unauthorized dramatizations with no compensation whatsoever to the author, who considered theatrical productions immoral. No stage production ever received Stowe's sanction, in spite of the message having secured the defeat of Fillmore by Pierce at the polls.

"Arthur Wellesley, the Bugger who beat the French, is dead at the age of eighty-three," Maggie lamented that November. "Was he known as *Old Hookey* because of his nose?" she somberly inquired of her husband.

A misty-eyed Darcy nodded and said, "Old Atty for Arthur. And less flattering names among the men, of course. I fear he hanged too many for looting, an aspect of war he thought of as ungentlemanly. His discipline was the lash and the gallows, but his brilliance in combat was highly respected for saving many men's lives."

"You've told me this before, Darcy. In remembering the Duke, I think of Prudence's letter after attending the Great Exhibition in London. My father's complaint, the ostentation by the Crown with the famine barely over, in view of the Queen's pittance to Ireland: 2,000 pounds to feed millions! And they had the gall to rename Cobh, Queenstown!" Maggie said in a tone of disdain, "Outrageous, in my humble opinion."

"Your opinions are seldom humble, my dear. Your father said the American Display was pitiful, only coffins and carriages. Poor losers in two wars, I daresay."

"Prudence said that ladies fainted from the heat under all that glass."

"And they saw the young prince and princess," he said, picking up his pipe.

"The Prince of Wales and Princess Royal. Luckily, they timed things just right to view the royal equipage: two outriders in scarlet livery, grandly prancing. Two lords in waiting on horseback, followed by the Queen's open landau as she smiled and waved," Maggie smiled and waved. "Prince Albert was right beside her. Prudence wrote that the young queen is lovely and Prince Albert quite handsome, all that a queen and her prince are expected to be by their subjects."

"Their subjects?" Darcy grumbled. "Praise God that we are Americans." He paused. "But our time is called the *Victorian Age* ... after the queen. Imagine that?"

"Father was pleased to see your former commander there. Prudence said the Iron Duke wore a gentle smile beneath his beak, standing erect and soldierly, and that his distinguished white hair granted him a dramatic profile." Maggie rose and placed her needlepoint on the table. "Father's hair is still black as coal at the age of seventy-nine, with distinguishing strands of gray, Prudence claims, to make him that much more handsome." Briefly reminiscing over her father, she smiled.

"My hair is nearly all gray. Do I appear older than your father, perhaps?" Darcy frowned and pursed his lips. "What a horrid thought."

Maggie walked over and kissed his forehead. "You are incredibly handsome and strong for a man of sixty-two, grandfather to nineteen grandchildren. I've no plans to exchange you for a younger specimen, in accordance with Mr. Darwin's theory. You seem fit enough to me to last forever."

"That is incredibly good news," Darcy said, standing to slip his arms around her. "How many grandchildren and great grandchildren does your father have now?"

"Twenty-eight grandchildren, with the unfortunate loss of Patrick last year in that stupid duel over gold. Poor Liam and Antoinette! He should have stayed in Hawaii and raised sugar instead of running to the gold fields to end up dying in a duel over gold."

"Shannon seems to want children. Aidan said, should he have another son he will name him Aidan McKenna Brosnan. To think he has a red-haired Irish wife of twenty-two-years at the ripe age of thirty-seven. Brian says she's quite the beauty, and our Brian can be highly critical."

"Indeed. My father now has forty great grandchildren: Irish, Scot, English, German, African, Hawaiian and Piscataway. How say you on that score, Darcy?"

"Good gracious!"

"Would you care to go for a winter stroll, my dear?" Maggie inquired. "We might catch sight of that regal stag with his grand setoff antlers. I don't want anyone shooting him! Perhaps he will populate our woodlands with frisky fawns and venison enough for all if left to his own devices."

"I have told the men your thoughts on … Reginald, is that his name?" he inquired, kissing her lightly, breathing in her sweet lavender scent. "Perhaps he should move deeper into the forest or vacate our land entirely."

"He is our deer, Darcy. You must not shoot our deer. He must be allowed to die of old age … the same as we plan to."

He sighed and smiled at her.

After donning their winter cloaks, they walked outside into the lightly falling snow and followed their usual path through the barren trees to their favorite spot on the Gunpowder River.

In 1853, Liam wrote of an outbreak of the smallpox in Hawaii that claimed 5,000 lives, including his eldest daughter, her husband, and two of their children. Liam had taken on his three orphaned grandchildren to bring up. The situation reminded Maggie of their tragic losses to cholera back in '41.

In July, they boarded a train to New York to attend the First World's Fair at the newly constructed Crystal Palace. Maggie and Darcy, Brigid, Luke and their children, Dermot, Priscilla and their four stayed in the refurbished *Swords Hotel* in New York City.

According to the newspaper reports, over a million and a quarter had arrived to view the world's first workable elevator and all the various other exhibits. The Crystal Palace resembled the one built in London, although Maggie doubted it was anywhere near as grand. The children rode the carousel. In the evening they attended concerts. The crowd turned rowdy, with all the gambling and swearing, with more refined entertainment to be found at the hotel. On one evening, they attended a performance of *Uncle Tom's Cabin, Topsy's Reform* at the theater.

Upon their return to Marcus Manor, the Brosnans discovered that a fire had burned down the old Plunkett barn. Luckily, four horses escaped, with livestock sickened by the smoke. Moses managed to keep the house from catching fire by organizing a bucket brigade from the well to the house in the middle of the night.

"I nearly shot me a nigger," Moses said in heated anger. "I saw two Juniper slaves running through the woods, one carrying a torch. I nearly killed the crazy coon. It was that Charlie, yelling, 'we's gonna git you … we's gonna git you black bastards,' liken he's not a black bastard himself."

Apologetic, Moses turned to Maggie and said, "Sorry, Missy, but he is a black bastard. That was our barn! I ought to skin his hide."

"You can swear up one side and down the other, Moses, and you will never offend me."

Suppressing a grin, Darcy said, "It seems to me that we need to post sentries with rifles and shoot to kill." He turned to Dermot. "Keep your rifle beside your bed in case someone tries to burn the house. You have my permission to shoot any arsonist."

"I don't exactly think that I need your permission, Pa, but thank you all the same," Dermot said. "How about making some of those 'No Trespassing' signs you've been talking about, Mama. We'll post them on the boundaries. That scum has no right coming here and burning barns and threatening livestock." Dermot turned to Moses. "I'm including you in this, you do understand, I hope?"

"Yes, sir," Moses said. "You think we should call us a meeting tonight?" he asked Darcy.

"How about first thing in the morning," Darcy said. "That son-of-a-bitch could have killed my family and my friends," he said surveying the damage. "If Juniper wants razing, he'd best watch out. I'm seeing the sheriff tomorrow. If he can't keep his slaves in line, we just may have to have us a lynching party ourselves."

"And feed 'em to the buzzards like down in Georgia?'" Dermot inquired with a stern frown. "Like Mama says, Pa, just because the man happens to be a fool doesn't mean that we need to be fools too."

"His niggers need to learn respect," Isaac said. "Isn't that right?"

"That's right," Darcy said.

"See you all first thing in the morning," Dermot said.

"I'm afraid that's not the end of it," Moses said.

Slowly, Dermot and Darcy turned to Moses, as everyone braced themselves. It had been a long day on the train from New York with the children excited and cranky. Two carriages were needed to get them all home.

"What is it?" Maggie inquired of Moses. "What else happened while we took our children and grandchildren to the World's Fair? We were only trying to have a little fun for a change!"

"I'm awfully sorry, Missy Maggie, but guards do need to be posted. Three days back, I saw that slave catcher, Remus Clapton from the eastern shore, and this time he was carrying a gun."

"And?" Darcy demanded.

"Bobby and Chester went missing. Uncle Billy, too. He's just like that old Uncle Tom in the book. I told those young men not to go acting big around that slave catcher. And I told Uncle Billy to stay at home. Those three would never run off. Sally is expecting Chester's first child."

"Oh, Law!" Maggie said. "I am going to bake that man a nice blueberry pie laced with arsenic."

"You and Israel," Moses said, grinning.

"We'll discuss this in the morning," Darcy said. "This sort of thing has to stop. But now we all need some sleep. Post guards that are somewhat rested at least."

"It looks to me like we'll be building us a new barn fairly soon," Dermot said. "Maybe I said I needed one a bit too often. You think so, Mama?"

"Sometimes you get what you wish for in the darnedest way. You'll have your new barn, Dermot. You'll be building it in the heat of a Maryland summer."

On the very next day, Uncle Billy, age seventy, was found by the side of the road shot through the heart. He was always loved by everyone for his simple wisdom. He was a Plunkett slave and treasured his freedom. Uncle Billy would be sorely missed.

The other two young men were never found, even after Darcy and Dermot searched for two weeks. The slave catcher never showed his face again. Darcy thought it was because he was suspected of murdering an old free man. On the other hand, Maggie surmised that her secret rituals performed in the woods with Ruth and Rebecca just might have done the trick. They had conjured up the ugliest image of the devil anyone could possibly imagine and sent it after Remus Clayton with a vengeance, in the hope of scaring the no account into an early grave.

54

Vigilantes

In May of 1854, Anthony Burns, a fugitive slave from Virginia, was arrested by U.S. Marshals in Boston. Immediately, black and white abolitionists rallied to his cause. They attacked the federal courthouse with a battering ram, but failed. Burns' defense lawyer, Richard Henry Dana, also proved unsuccessful in his defense of Burns.

On June 2, thousands of people lined the streets, including Penelope Worthington and Jackie Carrington, many shouting, "Shame! Shame!" as Burns was led to a ship in the harbor. Over 2,000 police and armed troops, plus $40,000 in government funds were required to return one Negro man back into bondage.

"Good Law! No one would pay $40,000 for a slave!" Darcy shouted. "Whatever is the matter with Massachusetts, let alone our government? Is our legal system run by a bunch of fools incapable of committing to true justice?" he said to Dermot, who simply nodded in agreement.

"We need someone to run this country that will do something about the Southerners and their gol dang cotton, Uncle Kevin and Aunt Megan included. He has twenty slaves! He needs to free those slaves and pay them a decent wage. At least now we have the colored Ashmum Institute in Pennsylvania where free men can be properly educated. It's time, I say!" Dermot said in a tone of some heat.

"Jackie and Penelope said it was truly shameful. Burns barely got away before he was caught. He should have gone to Canada. Nothing good is going to happen to him, believe you me!" Maggie said.

"What's done is done, Mama," Dermot said, "That's what you always say. I guess it was his destiny. You always say its destiny when things happen."

"Well," Maggie said, "I guess it was his destiny. But I sure do hope he ends up helping us with the cause. I hope our government isn't low enough to ever try this one again."

"We've been lucky not to get caught. No fines or imprisonment," Dermot said, chuckling in a manner that instantly reminded her of her father, his own grandfather.

"You look more like your Grandpa O'Reilly every year. It's most unfortunate that you cannot meet him, Dermot. You would love your Grandpa O'Reilly and you would love Prudence," Maggie said.

"That's what you always say too, Mama. I'd love to go to Ireland one day."

"Sometimes Dermot reminds me of my daddy," Darcy said, "Especially around the eyes." He sat in his favorite chair and picked up the newspaper to scan the front page.

"You always say that, Pa. I guess I don't look much like either one of you. You had light hair when you were young." Dermot said to his father. "Gareth had Mama's red hair."

"Yes, he did," Darcy soberly remarked. "Timmy says his hair is more like his Mama's now. I don't know if that boy is ever going to get married. He needs to find himself a wife."

"He's only twenty-seven, Darcy. You were twenty-seven when you married me. There's still plenty of time for Timmy to marry."

"I married late because of your ... shenanigans," he cautiously defended.

"Mama says that she married a moron before she married you, Pa," Dermot said. "Aidan's no moron. So some good came from her shenanigans. I'm mighty fond of Aidan, proud of him with that big hotel and his own saloon. He's done right well for himself."

"Shannon will keep him young for a while yet," Darcy said, chuckling.

"Aidan is thirty-six. Dermot turns thirty-four with his seven children. Aidan only has five children. But now he has Kelly Sue. Isn't that the cutest name you've ever heard? There are more than a few Kelly's in this family."

"Brigid Kelly for starters," Darcy said.

"Molly Kelly for Brian," Maggie added. "She reminds him of me. That's what Brian tells me."

"Our family is not lacking in the red hair of Queen Mauve," Darcy said.

"That's because the Vikings invaded Ireland," Dermot remarked.

"Nearly everyone invaded Ireland at one time or another," Maggie said with a sigh. "Spaniards, French, Fins, Norwegians, Swedes, English, Scots, all of them came to Ireland to spread their seed throughout the land."

"I will not be surprised if Aidan catches up with us having such a young wife," Dermot said. "At thirty-three, Priscilla finds seven children enough. She's taking her herbs. Five boys and two girls are fine with me, with Stephen not yet a year."

"No one in this family has any reproductive problems, I'm pleased to say," Maggie said.

"Brigid took the herbs after four children," Dermot said. "You'd best keep your secrets. I hardly think that Pope Blessed Pius IX would be pleased with your birth control practices, Mama."

"Pilan and Brianna have five children," Maggie said. "Carla not yet a year, and Brianna wants more. Her designs are now purchased by the society ladies in San Francisco. Now, isn't that grand!"

In February of 1855, abolitionists in every state celebrated when the Wisconsin Supreme Court declared the United States' Fugitive Slave Law unconstitutional, which split northern and southern states even farther apart. That June, the Know-Nothing Party held its first convention. It was not only anti-Negro, but anti-Irish and anti-Roman Catholic!

Holding the newspaper, Darcy read aloud an excerpt spoken by a man in Illinois who had just missed being elected a senator:

"I'm not a Know-Nothing. That is certain. How can anyone who abhors the oppression of Negroes be in favor of degrading classes of white people? Our progress in degeneracy appears to me to be pretty rapid. As a nation, we begin by declaring that 'all men are created equal.' When the Know-Nothings get control, it will read 'all men are created equal except Negroes, and foreigners, and Catholics.' When it comes to this I should prefer emigrating to a country where they make no pretense to loving liberty, to Russia, for instance, where despotism can be taken pure, without the base alloy of hypocrisy." Darcy paused.

"The man's name is Abraham Lincoln."

"Amen to him," Maggie said. "I like the way that man thinks."

That October, the 6th National Women's Rights Convention met in Cincinnati, Ohio. However, Darcy was not keen for Maggie to attend. Penelope and Jackie promised her a full report. With Brigid and Luke in attendance, all of them were now convinced that women should have the vote.

At the American Anti-slavery Society, Susan B. Anthony spoke out against slavery and in favor of women's suffrage. William Lloyd Garrison shared her views on prohibition, with Darcy heartily disagreeing. Maggie's father, Padraic, was already accusing the "blessed Temperance Society in County Kerry" of robbing a man of his few remaining pleasures.

"Do you think that Great Britain will ever put an end to all their wars?" Maggie enquired. "They have taken over Hong Kong, and now there is this Crimean War. Will they ever stop this, Darcy? They are even worse than Napoleon, in my opinion, and should leave things well enough alone!"

"I doubt the queen or prime minister will ever seek your counsel, my dear."

In 1856, Aidan wrote in a long letter:

Dear Mother and Father,

What I have to say is not pretty. I have mentioned the lawlessness in San Francisco since the discovery of gold. All have benefited from panning or working the mines, but lately things have gotten out of control and made us fear for our families. You know of the Hounds in '49, ruffians whose idea of a good time was terrorizing peaceable folk by killing and burning. We have rid ourselves of the gamblers and cutthroats. They are all by now in Mexico or Los Angeles.

Perhaps you have read of James King, a newspaper editor and honorable man, shot in cold blood by James Casey, an ex-con serving as city supervisor through his corrupt cronies. King made Casey's criminal record public and Casey didn't like that. Outraged by his murder, 3,000 have answered the call for vigilantes, including yours truly.

We are backed by the bankers. The Law and Order fellows are not very happy, but that is too dang bad. Last year, Charles Cora, a notorious gambler, shot U.S. Marshal Richardson, with Cora arrested by his friends in office, the <u>corruption unbelievable</u>. So King says, if Cora escapes, then Sheriff Scannell should hang. Brave talk. Soon King was taking on Casey, disclosing him as an inmate in Sing Sing. So Casey shot him and he died that same day at home.

Soon everyone was talking Vigilante Committee, with Casey guarded by hundreds of his friends and a militia. I am proud to do what I can to help restore order. Each of us is known by a number. Our life, liberty, property and honor pledged. By the time King died on May 20, we had gathered together 3,500 armed men.

First, we battered down the door with a canon, and in we marched, Cora and Casey delivered after small protests. Both taken from the jail in a dramatic show of force like some theatrical production, Mama. You would have loved it. A local banker and officer of the State Militia, William T. Sherman, watched from the hotel roof.

Both men were given advocates to defend them and tried before a jury from the Vigilante Committee, found guilty, and hanged from a platform from a second story window at Fort Gunnybags, as it was called. An immense crowd witnessed the double hangings on May 22. The entrance to our headquarters protected by bags filled with coarse sand 6 feet by 10 feet. You would have been proud of our fortifications, Pa. It was as though we were ready for Napoleon III. Ha, ha!

We were all well armed the same as Wellington's Invincibles, though perhaps not as great in number as the British and Prussian armies in dealing with the boys of the Law and Order Party. They had the good sense to leave us alone with the two lawless men buried. The governor and mayor made formal pleas to no avail with the good sense to stand aside.

Belle Cora, the gambler's widow, still enjoys notoriety in the gambling halls dressed in black. He married her an hour before his execution in the same room from which he was hanged, eleventh hour honor among thieves. She has dressed in mourning weeds since that day. Brianna has made up new gowns for her in black silk, with Belle milking this for all it is worth. Is that not a hoot or what?

Our committee posted notices: WARNING! Notice is given that any person found Pilfering, Stealing, Robbing, or committing any act of Lawless Violence will be summarily HANGED, with it signed: The Vigilante Committee. Uncle Sean and Brian are with me, also Timmy and young Darcy, 17. Patrick was too young at 13, but he is already good with a Colt and a rifle. Don't you worry, since we are all happy as pigs wallowing in the mud in this wild western town. Come see us before the gold is all gone from all the wild miners arriving from all over this world.

I want you both to meet Shannon. You will love her to pieces. She reminds me of you, Mama, when I was lad sitting on your knee, your soft cheek against mine, giving me all the love you could muster. Shannon is the same. I am not leaving you out, Pa, except I am far too big to ride on your shoulders these days. You have both given me many wonderful memories, so come to California. The grandchildren need you and you need them, too.

Aidan McKenna is crawling at six months, with Kelly Sue already running. Peggy, 15, is a fine babysitter. She plans on having ten children, saints preserve us. William, 8, builds fires in the fireplaces. We hope we are not raising a pyromaniac the way that he loves to watch those flames. All the boys love to play baseball.

What do you think of that Senator Brooks from South Carolina beating Senator Sumner from Massachusetts near to death with his cane over slavery on the Senate floor? The South has political abusers besides slave abusers. I do what I can to help the free men and women here. These days our town is filling up with the Chinese.

That Pottawatomie Massacre in Kansas by John Brown's sons was a big mess, in my opinion. I didn't know vigilantism is accepted by the abolitionists.

I know Garrison and Douglass disapproved the murder of those favoring slavery. But these men terrorized those opposed to slavery, killing and burning. Brown's picture in the newspaper reminded me of Moses in the Old Testament accepting the Ten Commandments from God and taking the Children of Israel to the Promised Land. Perhaps Brown is Moses back to free the slaves from the oppression of their white masters! Think about it, Mama! Perhaps the peaceable way will never make it happen. John Brown may have a point that we need to consider.

I may vote for James Buchanan. Sorry you are unable to vote yet, Mama. Perhaps one day, if Brigid has her way, you will vote. May she and Luke win all their many crusades!

God bless you both, and God bless our Vigilantes out here in California.
Your loving son,
Aidan Padraic

55

A Wake in Dingle

Her father had never planned to live forever. But Maggie had hoped that he might live for the rest of her days. She had wanted to see his handsome face again before he was buried in the rich soil of Ireland. The new doctor in Dingle, Timothy Guerin, who replaced Dr. O'Malley after he succumbed in Black '47, said that it was her father's heart. At least he had lived a good, long life and was happily married to Prudence for many years as she now wrote to them in her letter:

My Darlings in America,

It is unfortunate that the new transatlantic cable is not yet through Dingle to send a telegram to inform you of the sad passing of your father into the Otherworld on May 7, 1857, his 84th birthday. We had a lovely day together on his fateful day.

After he enjoyed his favorite breakfast, we strolled along the cliffs above the sea in the sun to revisit the Ceallaigh ogham. For some reason, Padraic was drawn to the ancient stone on that morning, ever respectful of your mother's ancient ancestors, telling me how she had brought him there as a lad to introduce him to the spirit of the Ceallaigh's.

At midday, we lunched at a new restaurant, the Unicorn, a whimsical name but with excellent food. The ale was also very fine. We reminisced about our lives, our wonderful trips to London and Paris, Edinburgh and Glasgow by train, sailing through the canals of Amsterdam and seeing the bright tulips bloom in Holland in the springtime.

Ona made Padraic his favorite supper that evening: succulent duckling with orange sauce, a tasty sage dressing, parsley potatoes, collard greens, a fine port, and his favorite chocolate cake. We prayed that his last supper did nothing to contribute to his passing in his favorite chair near the fire where I left him to finish reading your American Thoreau's "Walden." He enjoyed the book and I hope finished it, for the book was on his lap when I checked on him and immediately sent Thomas for Dr. Guerin.

Ona was beside herself thinking that her supper had killed him, crying hysterically, with me crying with her. She loved your father, his gentle ways, his many kindnesses and courtesies in having a servant to see to his needs. It was something Padraic always found difficult to accept from having worked so hard the early part of his life. I loved to spoil him, and he always gave me wonderful gifts. What fun we had together. What joy! What passion. Pardon me as I weep ...

I will file no complaints with the Lord of Life for allowing me to be with Padraic as my dearly beloved these 35 years. I loved him perhaps even more than my Rory. You need to know that, Maggie, especially after keeping my secrets all these many years. I confessed everything to you and to your father the first year of our marriage. He was incredibly gentle, forgiving of my weaknesses and imperfections. I can think of no other man who made me feel so loved and cherished. Such praise Padraic bestowed upon me. Such blarney! But I loved every word. He was the greatest gift of my entire life.

After all, I am now 75 years and never expected to live so long. I have witnessed much pain and sorrow in Ireland. My greatest joys and happiness were experienced in the loving arms and the life of my Padraic, your wonderful father. We shared many wonderful moments, along with Sean and Mary and their five children before they ran off after gold with no leprechaun to show them the way. Matthew and Heather miss young Matthew, Seamus and Mark, all of them now in San Francisco, the land of sunshine and sunny gold.

At least Matthew's two girls are still close by: Megan in Cork with her Gareth and their precious three youngsters, Brigid and Kenneth in Dublin, closer now with the train, with Kenneth, Jr. three months old already.

I shall miss your father more dearly than life itself. My service is still needed at the poor house and with the sisters of mercy. With Padraic gone, I shall dedicate myself to the work of the Church and the poor. I hope to see you again before I lay down in the ground beside him here upon our Emerald Isle.

I am unable to stop crying. Matthew is coming to take me to their new home. Your old house is rented out to tenant farmers. Matthew is capable in assuming your father's duties. I intend to leave some land to each of you, his children. I doubt I shall ever see Megan and Kevin again and rarely hear from them in their determination to keep their slaves, which concerned your father, who was not at all reserved in venting his displeasure in that respect.

Padraic was proud of you and Darcy for giving 70 slaves freedom, even with some leaving. How long shall it be before the Africans in your land enjoy freedom with this horrid Dred Scott law? It is a shame that your Supreme Court ruled that slaves and free colored cannot be American citizens, a true setback for your cause, and a slap in the face of the millions born there. How are you ever going to reach your goals with such unfair government rulings? Will they ever see the light of justice?

I am happy that your children are doing well in Maryland and California. I receive letters from Liam often. I must write to Megan and Sean to share the sad news regarding your wonderful father, my marvelous husband. I have dreamt of Padraic already, looking as he did at 30, handsome, virile, strong and dashing, my Padraic in the Otherworld, where I shall no doubt join him one day soon.

All my love to you in our mutual sorrow,
Prudence

With tears spilling from her eyes, Maggie walked out of the manor house, initially unaware of the budding trees that had bloomed later than usual that May. The winter was long and cold. Now a profusion of spring colors nearly took her breath away, many clusters of rhododendron and azalea blooming all around the yard. The blossoms moved by a gentle breeze in a brilliant wash of pink, lavender, purple, blush pink and pure white. Dazzling. Spring was among her favorite seasons. Her other favorite involved the radiant colors of a Maryland autumn as leaves fluttered to the ground in having served their purpose for yet another year.

The dogwoods were beginning to bloom in varying shades of pink and white, with the fading blossoms of the fruit trees already scattered on the ground. Most of the fruit trees had minuscule fruit on their many branches, hard kernels with the promise of cherries, apples, peaches, plums and pears by the middle of the summer.

Two robins hopped about on the ground in search of worms, as a bright cardinal snatched seeds from the tall birdhouse and quickly flew away at her slight movement. It was the birdhouse the children loved best, waiting for birds to nest in the *bird hotel,* as Aidan called it. There were different birdhouses all around the plantation to provide shelter and entertainment throughout the seasons. The yard was beautiful on that day in May, a reminder of the changing of the seasons in her life.

Sensing the gentle touch of his hands on her shoulders, Darcy said, "It seems a good day to take a sail in the *Maggie.* Think of all the beautiful blossoms lining the shore, all the shrubs showing off their spring wardrobe as wildflowers dance in the breeze. Before long, the bushes and trees will be green again, their blossoms gone for yet another year."

"Let us do go sailing," Maggie said, gazing into the startling blue of the eyes she loved.

"Let's," Darcy said, pulling her close to him. "You know how sorry I am. I loved your father without knowing him all that well. I know he was a fine man, and Prudence loved him dearly. But surely anyone you love is worthy of my love."

"However did you become so perfect?" she said, kissing him lightly.

"I had an excellent teacher: A perfect wife as my constant example."

Together, they walked through the woods toward the dock on the wide expanse of the Gunpowder River. There they would soon sail upon the *Maggie,* all around the long shoreline toward the ever widening expanse of the Chesapeake Bay.

56

John Brown's Ghost

It was May 8, 1858, when John Brown held his Constitutional Convention against slavery in Chatham, Canada, with both white and black abolitionists in attendance. He had outlined a plan to incite a slave revolt in the State of Virginia to instigate guerrilla warfare by taking slaves into hiding in the Blue Ridge Mountains. It was not until August of 1859 that Brown rented a house outside Harpers Ferry using the name of Isaac Smith. It was the same month that the Richmond *Daily Dispatch* reported ninety blacks arrested for learning how to read and write. That year, Oregon was admitted as the 33rd state, and the Arkansas legislature required free blacks to choose between exile and slavery. Many states in the nation were greatly at odds over the issue of slavery.

Most members of the American Anti-Slavery Society were unaware of John Brown's radical plan to take the Children of Israel to the Promised Land. Darcy considered Brown to be more like Joshua in bringing down the walls of slavery and oppression in the government. Darcy's opinions on the matter had radically changed long ago. In the mind of Frederick Douglass, violence was not the solution in meeting with Brown at Chambersburg in August. Garrison had openly opposed Brown for years. No pacifist, John Brown was convinced that the way to free slaves was a show of power against cruel masters and a corrupt government.

On October 15, 1859, John Brown's plan was set into motion by raiding the federal arsenal at Harpers Ferry. Brown was quickly wounded and captured by soldiers led by Robert E. Lee, and then removed to Charlestown, tried and convicted of treason.

In Brown's address published in the newspaper, Maggie read: "I believe to have interfered as I have done ... in behalf of His despised poor, was not wrong but right. Now, if it be deemed necessary that I should forfeit my life for the furtherance of the ends of justice, and mingle my blood further with the blood of my children, and with the blood of millions in this slave country whose rights are disregarded by the wicked, cruel, and unjust enactments, I submit, so let it be done."

On December 2, 1859, John Brown was hanged.

After that, the remarks of Henry David Thoreau were also published in the newspaper: "He did not recognize unjust human laws, but resisted them as he was bid. No man in America has ever stood up so persistently and effectively for the dignity of human nature ..." with William Lloyd Garrison forced to admit, "In firing his gun, John Brown has merely told what time of day it is. It is high noon, thank God."

That December, Maggie was extremely distressed when the State of South Carolina declared itself as an independent commonwealth, with slavery ending in the Netherland Antilles soon after that.

That March, the clipper ship *Andrew Jackson* arrived in San Francisco only eighty-nine days out of New York. The newspapers also reported that the Pony Express had started its run between St. Joseph, Missouri and Sacramento, California, with the first rider in San Francisco on April 14, 1860.

In Maggie's estimation, the world was rapidly changing. That April, at the Democratic Convention in Charleston, South Carolina, there was enormous division over the matter of slavery. After thinking about making the trip, Darcy and Maggie had decided against it. Luke and Brigid planned to attend the first Republican National Convention in Chicago and were traveling by train.

Back in 1858, Abraham Lincoln had declared: "As I would not be a slave, so would I not be a master. This expresses my idea of democracy. Whatever differs from this, to the extent of the difference, is not democracy."

In 1860, at the Republican National Convention, Abraham Lincoln was chosen as the presidential candidate by a narrow margin. With that news, everyone at Marcus Manor rejoiced. Darcy and Dermot volunteered to work on Lincoln's campaign in Maryland, with Luke and Brigid advocates in New York.

And Prudence was on her way to America.

Sailing on the steamer *Gloria* out of Queenstown, Prudence arrived at the Port of Baltimore in June. The Finnegans held a small reception in their home in town, with the entire family present to welcome Mrs. Padraic O'Reilly to Maryland and the United States of America.

"What an impressive city," Prudence commented.

"It sounds as though you had a lovely stateroom on the *Gloria*," Darcy said.

"Two weeks is a fast crossing, indeed," Cornelius said.

"You arrived far sooner than we did," Maggie said. "Our journey took us six weeks. The steamboats are a true wonder." Maggie closely watched Prudence as she said, "And here we are, both rather mature women now," except that she was astonished by her stepmother's enduring beauty, considering the fact that she was seventy-eight.

"It is the cream you made for me," Prudence said. "I still have Ona make it up for me and I use it daily. It works better than anything else on the market."

"Perhaps I should make some for myself," Maggie said.

"You are still quite beautiful," Prudence said. "And I'm rather fond of your beard, Darcy. It makes you look very much like your dear father. I miss Gareth terribly, along with Aunt Brianna. Padraic really hit it off with your father, and he was enchanted with your beautiful mother, naturally."

"Father wrote to me of his fondness for Padraic," Darcy said, "He thought of him as a fine man."

At Marcus Manor, Prudence quickly became the center of attention, for everyone had heard much of the fine lady for many years. After being introduced to all the former slaves, now good friends, she was grandly wined and dined by one and all. Stories of Africa and slavery were recounted, in addition to stories of Ireland. Music was enjoyed. There were piano duets with Prudence and Maggie. Prudence and Darcy. And Maggie and Darcy. It was great fun for everyone with all entertained and completely enchanted.

In their sloop, the *Maggie,* Prudence sailed with them upon the Chesapeake and the Gunpowder River. Portions of Maryland and Virginia were seen by train, with Washington, the nation's capital, viewed by train, tram, and in a horse drawn carriage. They enjoyed a family picnic on the White House lawn when President Buchanan was off campaigning. Still, a brief tour was taken inside the presidential residence that pleased Prudence immensely.

"Frankly, I don't see how Buchanan can possibly beat Lincoln," Darcy said one evening during supper in the dining room.

"You need a president opposed to slavery," Prudence said. "And even though I would enjoy visiting with Megan and Kevin, after seeing all those slaves in chains in Baltimore, I have no stomach to view thousands more in such a state. That would break my heart. I'm accepting the invitation from Brigid and Luke to visit Philadelphia, with time spent in New York City before my departure. You must be exceedingly proud of Luke and Brigid and their many grand crusades."

"We are proud of them, indeed," Darcy said. "I'm glad you could see this much of America, at least."

"I so wish I had come here with your father," Prudence said to Maggie. "We often discussed making the trip, but you are all so much scattered around this vast nation. I daresay I have done remarkably well on this journey so far. You must all take a steamer to Ireland sometime soon."

"Perhaps," Darcy said, "Our children are scattered as well. Many want us to come to California. Gratefully, Dermot and Priscilla and all their children are still here with us."

"I don't know what I would do without Matthew and Heather," Prudence said. "One day, please do come back to Ireland," and her green eyes lingered on Maggie.

After an extended and sad farewell, the train carried Prudence to Philadelphia, and eventually, New York City at the exact time of the first visit of the Prince of Wales in September. Before long, Prudence was sailing on the *Lady Royal* for Queenstown, with all her children, grand-children and great grandchildren valiantly promising to write to her. Her correspondence was no doubt going to be extensive.

Throughout that entire election year, it seemed to Maggie that John Brown's ghost was everywhere. On November 6, 1860, Abraham Lincoln was elected the 16th president of the United States, but he was not on the ballot in nine Southern states and gained only two counties in the South. The election had confirmed as South Carolina stated, "That the Union now subsisting between South Carolina and other states under the name of the United States of America is now dissolved."

To Maggie, it also seemed that John Brown's ghost had won the brave fight aided by the international acclaim of *Uncle Tom's Cabin* written by Harriet Beecher Stowe.

That December, Megan wrote to her in a letter:

My Dearest Sister,

You and Darcy live by the courage of your convictions and have freed your slaves. Unfortunately, we are now on opposite sides in this great conflict, with South Carolina no longer belonging to the Union. We do not abuse our slaves. Instead, we show them considerable courtesy and kindness.

Kevin fears our nation shall soon be at war. I pray not. I shall write to you again when I am not so troubled by the current events. Georgia shall also soon break away from the Union, so it seems to me that I shall never see Marcus Manor or the State of Maryland.

But I shall always be your sister.

All my love,

Megan Caitlin

57

Civil War

A Nation Divided

On February 9, 1861, the newspapers reported the disparaging news of the founding of the Confederate States of America, with Jefferson Davis as president, to include South Carolina, Mississippi, Florida, Alabama, Georgia, Louisiana and Texas.

On March 4, 1861, the Brosnan family attended the swearing in ceremony of Abraham Lincoln as President of the United States of America in the nation's capital. His campaign slogan: "Government cannot endure half slave, half free."

On April 12, 1861, the Confederates opened fire on Fort Sumter in Charleston Harbor. The war began within the sight and the sounds of the *Dublin Hotel* in South Carolina. Cannon fire awakened their guests, along with Kevin and Megan Gallagher. The South was no longer fighting Great Britain, Maggie despaired, but for the right to own slaves when many nations had already abolished slavery. The Rebel *Stars and Bars* now waved above Fort Sumter. Sadly, the Union had suffered its first defeat.

Early that April, Kevin had written to Darcy about his confusion in "being caught upon the horns of a moral dilemma of unusual proportions involving his slaveholding friends in Charleston." Runaways increased daily. Fear of the slave catchers and the federal marshals in the North erupted into mob violence. Opinions appeared to vary in Charleston, but Kevin found it impossible to leave his community after living there for forty-nine years.

On April 20, 1861, Dermot ran into the parlor waving a newspaper whose headlines read: **WAR! WAR !**

"President Lincoln has issued a blockade against the South," he told his father.

"Is that right? Well, that's not going to make your aunt and uncle very happy, nor your cousins," Darcy said, beginning to cough. "This gol dang cold is hanging on."

In days, Dermot told his father, "Robert E. Lee has resigned from our army."

"There goes Virginia," Darcy said. "I guess Kevin will probably join the Confederacy. I need to shake this cold and get out my uniform. They might not have Federal uniforms any time soon."

Not knowing exactly what to think, Dermot studied his father. "You intend to fight? Wellington's invincible shall rise again to fight the tyrannical Southern slaveholders?"

"You bet," Darcy said, standing, "As one of Lincoln's invincibles. There are millions that need to be freed. Look at the good that came from freeing ours. Every one of them is better off and they make mighty good friends!" Darcy had come around to the opinions of his wife and children years ago.

"You took long enough," Maggie said, hurrying into the parlor to take the newspaper from her son's hand. "Good Law! If it isn't the British trying to conquer the world, I guess grown men need to find something to go to war and fight over. You sit down and get over that croup," she ordered her husband.

Darcy complied. "I could use another cup of that concoction with honey."

"In a minute, darling," she said, quickly reading. "So Robert E. Lee is a traitor!"

"They've taken over the U.S. forts all over the South, since Lincoln said slavery was unlawful back in January," Dermot said.

"We needed a president with some gumption and morality. It was John Brown's ghost whispering in Lincoln's ears in his nightly dreams, with those Southerners forcing our hand. My guess is that Brown is mighty pleased over there in the Otherworld!" Maggie declared.

"You could actually say that John Brown fired the first shot at Robert E. Lee, defector to the South and a dang good general, so I've heard," Darcy said. "It's a shame to lose him."

"Well, at least Kansas is against slavery," Dermot said.

"What about that Louisiana taking over that mint in New Orleans and seizing the one in Georgia! Gol dern crooks confiscating our money," Darcy said, banging the arm of the chair.

"That's yesterday's news, Darcy," Maggie said.

"How about that Russian Tsar, Alexander II, abolishing serfdom in Russia! That should make you mighty happy, Mama," Dermot said.

"Good for the Russians. But they still massacred all those folks in Warsaw for speaking up. The Tsar is following Lincoln's example. But you won't find me in St. Petersburg anytime soon."

"We have us a big enough mess right here," Darcy said, "With men joining the Virginians to fight against us. You can bet that those slave-holders on the eastern shore will hold on to their slaves. Those damn slave catchers kidnapped our free men!"

"With the president calling up troops, I'm thinking artillery and learning about canons," Dermot said in a detached tone, which resulted in momentary silence from both his parents.

Finally, Darcy said, "Maybe cavalry"

"You what?" Maggie flared. "Mercy me, you are seventy-one-years old, Darcy. They don't want old men in this war, do they?" she thoughtfully turned to her son.

Both men just looked at her, neither one knowing how to handle her at that moment.

"They will take anyone who'll serve, Mama," Dermot said, placing his arms fully around his mother.

Relaxing against him, her arms circled Dermot's waist and tears spilled from her eyes. "I hate war," she sniffled, gazing up into her son's eyes before she turned back to her husband. "Poor Megan and Kevin. However will they know if the slaves that become soldiers won't kill them instead of shooting our men?"

"Might give them a moment's pause," Darcy said. "Those colored down in Charleston might not take this sitting down. There's been quite an exodus up here since the Rebels decided to split this country in two."

"We already have 75,000 men enlisted," Dermot said. "And nobody will do any business with the traitors. No commerce whatsoever."

"Losing Virginia is a damn shame," Darcy solemnly said.

"It looks like Arkansas and Texas voted against us, too, Pa," Dermot said.

"How about that West Virginia … splitting off with the Union?" Darcy remarked.

"At least Maryland is with the president," Maggie said. "I'm somewhat concerned about Rebecca being there in New York with her five children. Megan's granddaughter is married to an Irishman who is sure to fight for the Union. She's married to a Yankee."

"It's a strange twist of fate, Mama," Dermot said. "Families divided over this slavery business."

"I just hope the dang Southerners know what they're doing," Maggie said. "It seems to me that men use God to justify their flaws and make their sins sound like something downright righteous… all the time racking up serious debts with all the innocents lost in the shuffle."

By mid-May, Arkansas, Tennessee and North Carolina comprised ten states for the Confederacy, with a population of over nine million, four million slaves, with their national capital located in Richmond, Virginia. The Union still consisted of twenty-one states and a population of over twenty million. Riots broke out between the pro-secessionist and the Union supporters in Knoxville, Tennessee. Kentucky claimed neutrality, the same as Queen Victoria of Great Britain.

The newspapers reported North Carolina as the last to secede. British territorial waters and ports were off-limits for the duration of the war. By the end of the month, Alexandria, Virginia, was occupied by the Federals with the general declaring all slaves "contraband of war" for the Union: Free men. That enormously pleased the Brosnans. But postal service with the South ended, meaning no more correspondence with Megan and her family in South Carolina and Georgia.

The newspapers reported the Union's defeat at Philippi, West Virginia, followed by the Battle of Big Bethel with the Union forced to retreat. The Rebels evacuated Harpers Ferry. Reports of so many battles occurring at the same time proved too much for Maggie and her family to read, with countless battles taking place in South Carolina and all around the nation's capital. Everyone at Marcus Manor was eager to read the newspapers, as some free colored read the news aloud to the rest in the chapel.

In July, President Lincoln requested 400,000 more troops for the Union. Battles continued to rage on all fronts. The President informed the Kentucky militia that Union troops would not enter that state. As the Union Army pressed farther south, thousands of fugitive slaves fled to the North. Everyone at Marcus Manor was doing everything within their power to feed and provide shelter for countless refugees. On some days, the numbers were staggering with supplies unequal to the task.

The government created camps that instantly became overcrowded and poorly staffed. Starvation and disease ran rampant. Maggie organized relief efforts with the neighbors and created a school in the barn where large numbers were now learning how to read and write. Both Ruth and Rebecca taught the frightened, exhausted runaways the basics of cleanliness to rid them of their lice and restore their dignity. Many bathed in the river. A tented community expanded on the banks. Some runaways moved on. But others decided to stay and volunteer their talents and skills within the friendly community of Marcus Manor.

After the Union's defeat at Bull Run, Dermot, forty-three, was soon in uniform, along with his son, young Dermot, twenty, and Frederick, sixteen. Only fourteen, Thomas stayed with his mother and his other young siblings. Priscilla's hands were kept busy helping out with the fugitives.

"It is good you are training men, Pa," Dermot said to his father.

"I am proud that your father was commissioned as a colonel," Maggie said. "He looks handsome in his uniform. The blue goes nicely with his eyes. You all make such handsome soldiers."

Dermot hugged his mother and saluted his father. "I need to tell my youngsters good-bye," he said, hurrying off toward the other farmhouse.

To Maggie's immense annoyance and distress, the war continued. The enlistments increased from three months to two years. Flogging was abolished. Unfortunately, Brazil acknowledged the Confederacy. That September, the Confederate army entered Kentucky and ended its state of neutrality.

The first official school for freedmen was established at Fortress Monroe, Virginia. There was even greater hope for former slaves when the United States Navy authorized enlistment. President Lincoln never expected to come up against such resistance from granting freedom to slaves, and yet, freed men were still being barred from serving in the Federal army.

That December, Dermot was wounded at Dranesville. He returned home to mend. It was the same month that other members of the family arrived on the steamer, *Bound for Glory,* from San Francisco, with the purpose of enlisting in the Union army. All of them were eager to win the brave fight for the United States of America.

The moment that Sean Joseph walked in through the front door on Christmas Day, Maggie nearly swooned. He looked the same as he had in her recent dream. His son, Sean Joseph Jr., twenty-seven, was his father's spitting image, and his younger brother, Padraic, trailed in behind him with his uncle and her eldest son, Aidan. Maggie nearly bowled over her young nephew as she ran by him to throw herself into Aidan's arms.

"Oh, Aidan, I don't really know if I am glad or sad to see you, under such circumstances," she cried, looking at the young man standing right behind him. "Are you Darcy Yuma?" she shrieked, her arms soon encircling her grandson. "I don't know who to kiss first, last, or next. Good Law!"

Darcy was checking out young Darcy Yuma. "Why, you are a handsome young fellow, being my namesake and all," he said, hugging his grandson, now twenty-two.

"You're just as pretty as everyone says, Grandma," young Darcy said to Maggie. "You must have been a honey when you were a girl."

"I'm quite old. Sixty-four in November, you handsome young rascal!"

"I expected to see you in uniform, Grandpa," another young man remarked.

"Patrick!" Maggie shrieked, grabbing him and kissing each cheek.

"Brown Bear," Darcy said. "My stars! You must be eighteen by now!"

"Yes, sir," he said. "But hardly anyone ever calls me Brown Bear anymore. That's my Piscataway name."

"You'll always be our Brown Bear. We loved your mother very much," Maggie said. "You look so much like Mia, except you also look like Aidan. You look like the both of them."

That was when Brigid, Luke and their four children walked through the front doors as a Christmas surprise for their parents. It was the best Christmas ever for Maggie and Darcy with her brother, her nephews, their children and grandchildren there to help bring in 1862—another year of war. Everyone shared in the holiday spirit at Marcus Manor that year, perhaps for the first but hopefully not for the last time.

58

1862 – Antietam

The Angel of Death was kept busy in 1862, claiming the boys in gray and the boys in blue, young men, middle-aged and old men of varying ages and colors, all of them fighting for something they believed in, defending a way of life that was about to change, not just in some ways, but in all ways.

The newspapers reported countless battles. Maggie was eager to read anything of the regiments with Grant and Sherman, for her sons and grandsons were in those units. In February, General Grant captured Fort Henry in Tennessee. Ten days later, Fort Donelson earned him the nickname of 'Unconditional Surrender Grant.' The Confederates were forced to fall back, with Kentucky and portions of Tennessee relinquished. Confederate General Johnston chose Corinth, Mississippi, to take a stand and fight against the Union.

In a letter to his parents, Aidan wrote of the Confederate retrenchment having been quite a surprise, as he, now Captain, and his son, Private Darcy, assisted in launching an offensive along the Tennessee River. The general received orders to await Buell's Army of the Ohio, and instead of fortifying his position, he drilled his men, many of them still raw recruits.

Much to their surprise, on the morning of April 6, General Johnston fiercely attacked the Union, routing many, but some made a strong stand. In the afternoon, a battle line was established at the Hornets' Nest, repeated attacks having failed. And yet, the artillery turned the tide as the Confederates surrounded, captured, wounded, or killed countless Union soldiers. With Johnston himself mortally wounded, his second in command, Beauregard, assumed command.

The Union established another line. Aidan and young Darcy were in the heat of it, covering Pittsburg Landing, with a canon manned by Aidan's brother, Lieutenant Dermot Brosnan, recently recovered and reassigned. Augmented by Buell's arrival, the troops took up key positions, fighting until well after dark. By the next morning, Union forces numbered 40,000, with Beauregard's Army less than 30,000, the Confederate counterattack had failed. Then Beauregard, having suffered many casualties, retired from the field.

On April 8, General Grant sent Brigadier General William T. Sherman with two brigades, along with Brigadier General Thomas J. Wood, in heavy pursuit of Beauregard. Aggressive Confederate tactics forced a retreat to Pittsburg Landing. Then, Grant advanced. The Confederates fell back again. Thankfully, no Brosnan was killed or wounded at the Battle of Shiloh, with an estimated 23,746 casualties by the end of one day on both sides.

Late August, the newspapers reported 22,180 casualties at the Second Battle at Bull Run, among the Union's casualties was young Padraic, the son of Sean Joseph, and Corporal Ronald Rathmore, a Rebel from Atlanta, Megan's grandson. Sadly, cousins had fought on opposite sides. The discovery of Ronald's body was coincidental, with Captain Sean O'Reilly assigned to burial detail. He oversaw the burial of his son and his nephew on the same day, side by side.

War causes great sorrow, Sean wrote to his sister Maggie by candlelight, *for on this day, my son Padraic was buried next to his cousin, Ronald, from Atlanta, Constance's son, our sister Megan's grandson. I fear that this will not be the end of our sorrow in ending slavery in states once a part of our great nation. On yet another day, kin shall no doubt also fight against kin and shall likewise die.*

That June, slavery was abolished in all the United States possessions, as battles continued to rage across the nation. Not knowing exactly where the members of her family might be, Maggie prayed in the small chapel that now overflowed with runaways on most days. Much of their corn was sold to the army for a good price and helped to feed the soldiers. Working equally as hard as all the others, planting and harvesting, Maggie realized that there was barely enough food to feed everyone. Recently arrived fugitives now fished the river, hunted for game, and helped to till the land to feed the ever growing numbers at Marcus Manor.

In helping to organize the fugitives, Priscilla found work for them to do, saying, "You need to stop crying over spilt milk. Everyone here at Marcus Manor earns their keep. Look to the future," she said to a weary old black man whose smile revealed several missing teeth.

"You remind me of old Uncle Billy. I'll bet you can dance and play the harmonica."

"Used to dance, 'ceptin I've been walking so long, I don't think my feet can dance anymore."

"Where did you walk here from?"

"Kentucky. First the Union tried to help us out, and then, the Rebs marched in like they owned the place. That was when I started walkin', and I ain't hardly stopped none since."

"Do you know how to cook?" Maggie inquired.

"Sure 'nuff. Yous be needing a cook around here?"

"Laws, yes!" Priscilla said, handing him a bowl of potatoes. "After you eat something, you peel those potatoes. We could use the help. We'll find a place for you to sleep and you can bathe in the river. I even have some soap for you to use."

Seated on the porch peeling potatoes, tears ran down his old black face. "I ain't got nobody no more," he said, mostly to himself, but Maggie had overheard him.

"Now, you do. People here will make a place for you. What's your name?"

"Uncle Wally," he said, picking up another potato.

"Welcome to Marcus Manor, Uncle Wally. Stay as long as you like," she said, hurrying off to meet yet more refugees, grateful that the army was starting to accept young black laborers. Many young men at Marcus Manor were eager and ready to fight for the Union.

The government collected its first income tax that August, the same month that President Lincoln conferred with the first group of free black men. Gratefully, secretary of war General Rufus Saxton was authorized to arm 5,000 former slaves to fight for the Union.

Early September, Lee invaded the North with 50,000 soldiers, crossing the Potomac into Maryland. Pandemonium broke out at Marcus Manor. Another battle was in progress at Harpers Ferry, where Rebels captured Union weapons. There were prospects of another battle near Sharpsburg where Darcy commanded a brigade under Major General McClellan.

On September 12, Maggie ordered horses saddled up for her to ride to Sharpsburg. It would take three days by horse with any luck at all.

"But Missy," Isaac pleaded, "There's bound to be fighting that way. You're no young woman, and I don't know what we'd ever do without you, Missy Maggie. You're our right arm. You're our courage. We can't lose you. You're our very salvation."

"I've made up my mind, Isaac. Thomas is going with me. Frederick might be there, besides his old fool of a grandpa running around like some young patriot," her voice caught and trembled. "I have to go, Isaac. I have this horrible feeling, and I'll be praying all the way." She applied a slight whip and the horse started. "You listen to Priscilla while I'm gone, you hear me?"

"Yes, ma'am. Yes, Missy Maggie. I hear you."

Four days later, atop a slightly wooded rise at dawn, with the field of battle before them, the sun rose on a massive assault on Lee's left flank. Attacks and counterattacks raged across the cornfields. The Union had penetrated the center of the Confederate stronghold. Union troops crossed the stone bridge over Antietam Creek rolling up on the Confederate right. Though outnumbered two to one, Lee committed all his troops, where the Federals had held back many units of men.

After nightfall, Maggie and Thomas quietly made their way down to the camp where the Union army was entrenched. Tremendous sadness welled up inside her as she heard the anguished cries and screams of the men and witnessed the vast destruction that had taken place on the day. Was freeing slaves really worth the enormous price with so many dying and wounded men and dead horses strewn across the vast field of battle?

The hospital tent was located behind a slight rise not far from an assembled group of Union soldiers. Strangely enough, Maggie had no fear at all. She knew she had to do whatever she was about to do on that particular night in that terribly tragic place.

"Are you a nurse?" an officer asked in a tone of surprise.

"Not exactly. But my family needs me. My husband is Colonel Darcy Brosnan."

A curdling scream was heard in the next tent. The wounded were lined up on a seemingly never-ending number of stretchers. Moaning and groaning, the sounds of death and dying were all around her, as she took note of the ghostly images rising up out of the useless, discarded bodies, their ancestral spirits waiting to take them home.

"Amputations," Maggie inquired, nodding at the tent.

The officer solemnly nodded.

Steeling herself, it seemed to her that she had walked right into the middle of the hell that the fiery preachers described—the ever present hell known as WAR.

Thomas ran up to her with tears rolling down his face. "Terence is dead. He told me to tell his mother and father that he loves them. Then he just died." Her grandson was sobbing. "He was sixteen, a year older than me, Grandma, and now he's dead. Terrence is dead."

"God bless him," she said, sensing the need to stay strong.

"Frederick is wounded. He passed out. I think he's going to be all right," Thomas said, brushing away his tears with the back of his bloody hand.

"Are you hurt?" Maggie inquired in alarm.

Looking down, he said, "No. It's Terence's blood … or Frederick's." He sorrowfully shook his head, momentarily staring at his bloody hand. "I can't believe he's dead, Grandma. I saw Uncle Aidan with some of the wounded soldiers."

"Is he all right?" she asked as her heart started to race.

Nodding, he said, "He had a bandage around his head with blood on it. I'm not even sure if he knew me. He looked dazed … like maybe he was in shock."

The young officer emerged from the tent and said, "Your husband is in there."

Following close behind him, momentarily, Maggie stopped before the large tent. Wounded men were lying on the ground up and down in lines in either direction as she turned to Thomas and said, "Do what you can to help," and she entered the tent.

Inside the large tent were cots with the wounded on both sides. Immediately, she spotted Darcy partway down one row and she hurried to him. There was blood on his face and his jacket was soaked in his blood, and yet, he looked strangely peaceful to her.

"Darcy, its Maggie. I'm here, my darling," she said, suddenly overcome with a peculiar sense of fear.

Looking up at her with his blue eyes glazed, he said, "I never thought my life would end fighting my fellow Americans not that far from our plantation."

"You'll be all right. You know that. Regardless," she said, kneeling and taking his hand. "You should have stayed and helped me ..." she abruptly stopped, choking on her tears.

With a faint nod, Darcy sighed. "I'm a soldier, my love. Surely you know that much about your husband after all these many years."

"One of Lincoln's invincibles," she replied, tears streaming down her face.

"No longer invincible, I fear," he said, closing his eyes and faintly squeezing her hand.

"I want you to know how very much I love you ...more deeply and madly than you ever suspected. We've had a good life, Darcy, a truly good life. You're the man who taught me the real meaning of passion and love."

"What about your smuggler, Aidan, who I shall no doubt be seeing sometime soon? You loved him, too. You could never hide that fact from me, Mary Margaret."

"What I feel for you is much deeper and much stronger. It is everlasting, Darcy. It wells up out of the depths of eternity to fill me with infinite love for you and our wonderful children, those dead and those still living, all forever still alive in my heart. We'll see them again, you and I, in the Otherworld. One day, we shall all be together again. It is something I just know, my love."

Unable to stem her tears, from the look on his face and the touch of a hand on her shoulder, Maggie turned to find Aidan, her son, with his tear-filled eyes fixed on his father.

Rising to her feet, Maggie whispered, "He's bleeding inside in more ways than you might know or be able to see."

"I cannot save him," the nearby doctor remarked.

"I know. The bullets tore through several of his internal organs," Maggie confirmed.

"Yes," the doctor said. "I'm sorry," and he gave her an odd look before he turned and left.

"How do you know that, Mama? Can you see inside him?"

Glancing away, Maggie wondered how much to tell her son. Might Aidan understand her *way of knowing*? "There are things I just know," she said, turning back to Darcy, for she had felt him release her hand.

Darcy had seen her again. He had also seen young Aidan. And now he was gone.

"He's gone," she whispered, seeing the light glowing all around him, thinking others might not be able to see the door opening to the Otherworld for their loved ones as she had for Darcy. She had glimpsed his parents as the light faded and she now turned to her grief-stricken son.

"I'm taking your father and Terence home with me. You will help me, won't you, Aidan?" she inquired, partially collapsing in Aidan's arms.

There were no more tears for her to shed at that moment. Her eyes were dry from the moment she had seen the LIGHT. The light that heals the heart and the soul of everyone in this world and in the next.

"I shall do what I can, Mama. But there is still more fighting to be done here. Maybe you can take Frederick with you, too. I'll ask. But exactly how do you plan to do that, Mama?"

"We'll find a wagon and an undertaker. I'll buy coffins and take them back on the train to Marcus Manor where their bodies can forever rest in peace together in our family cemetery."

By the next morning, there were many more dead men, more dying and wounded men all over the battlefield. General Lee did not retire across the Potomac until after dark. Countless Yankees and Rebels moaned in an unbearable, inconceivable chorus of death, with many already silent and no longer suffering.

Even after purchasing the wagon and the coffins, Maggie continued to hear the anguished cries of the men as she prayed to God that their pain would soon end. She prayed to either save them or take them to the Promised Land where Jesus was likely waiting for them.

That morning, Aidan had found young Darcy Yuma among the other casualties. He was also placed in a pine box on the wagon. Frederick's wounds were too serious for him to be moved. But Maggie was taking her husband and her three grandsons' home to wake and bury, with her heart filled with the deepest, most grievous kind of sorrow.

Among the many sizes, ages, and colors of men and boys on that battlefield were husbands and brothers, fathers and sons, cousins, uncles, nephews, lovers and friends. By nightfall, over 26,000 men were dead, wounded, or missing. It became known as one of the bloodiest battles in U.S. military history. There were kin on either side, with none of them any longer certain of the real reason for the unspeakable carnage on those horrific days in northern Maryland, because of a fierce battle fought and won by some, near a creek that was known as Antietam.

59

The Ravages of War

Letters arrived weekly from her sons and her grandsons scattered across the nation engaged in fighting a presumably never-ending war. Correspondence continued with her brothers and their wives, with only Sean Joseph and his sons in America fighting for the Union, and young Padraic already dead and gone. Two of Sean's son-in-laws had also died near Galveston only months after joining the Union, one left his daughter, Mary Margaret, with five fatherless children. The Union had lost 600 men in Texas, the Confederates' fifty, with the body count higher for the Union in every battle in the "war against the slaveholder's rebellion."

That January, the first all black regiment, the South Carolina Volunteers, were mustered into the U.S. Army, with thousands of other freed men eager to fight for the cause of freedom.

"We've only just learned that Megan's son, Robert, also died at Antietam. If I'd known I would have brought him here, too, even though he may have killed his own kin," Maggie said.

"Terence was just a boy," Priscilla said. "I doubt that Frederick's arm will ever be right again. He's having a truly hard time writing with his left hand. He talks of being useless at the age of eighteen."

"I feel bad for all of us, me losing Darcy, Aidan losing his Darcy. He says his Patrick is a sharpshooter, but he never should have left Shannon and his four youngsters in California."

"Aidan did what he thought was right, Mother, the same as my Dermot. You raised us to be responsible. I hate having two sons in this war. I thought Antietam might have scared Thomas enough to keep him out of it. He's sixteen. I'll die if I lose Dermot or one son. You're so very brave, Mother. You need to know how proud we all are of you."

Self-consciously turning away, she said, "I feel sorry for Megan. I had no idea that Robert had taken up with another woman in San Francisco after his wife died in childbirth. Imagine Megan with a mulatto grandson. It doesn't bother me at all that he's part African. What bothers me is that his name is *Jethro*. That slave driver was a contemptible sort. He never even seemed human to me."

"To think the woman was once a prostitute in the gold camps. Aunt Megan cannot be pleased about that!" Priscilla said. "They had two children and never married. That must be some story!"

"He had two children with his first wife, too. I hope this war is worth all this horror, for the cost of freeing slaves seems to me to be beyond dear," Maggie said.

In March, President Lincoln enacted a draft on men between the ages of twenty and forty-five, exempting those who paid $300, or provided a substitute. "The blood of a poor man is as precious as that of the wealthy," poor northerners were known to complain. It was in the month of May that the Confederacy passed a resolution to slay all black Union soldiers.

Early that month, the Union was defeated by Lee's smaller force at the Battle of Chancellorsville, with Confederate General Jackson mortally wounded by his own men. "I have lost my right arm," Lee was reported to lament. The Union had 17,000 killed, wounded or missing out of 130,000, the Confederate's lost 13,000 out of 60,000. That month the War Department established the Bureau of Colored Troops and former slaves at Marcus Manor began to join up.

In June, former slave Harriet Tubman led Union guerrillas to Maryland's eastern shore to free slaves. She had served as a soldier, spy and nurse throughout the war. After escaping slavery in southern Maryland, Tubman was thought to have taken over 300 slaves to freedom. Often speaking of Tubman's courage to those at Marcus Manor, Maggie still helped runaways, feeding and clothing countless numbers, in addition to trying to mend their broken hearts and lift their spirits.

General Grant's armies had the Confederates under siege at Vicksburg, with 35,825 combined casualties reported in the newspaper before the siege finally ended in July. Lincoln replaced Hooker with Meade, the fifth change in command in less than a year. The tide began to turn as the two opposing forces marched into the farmlands of Gettysburg, Pennsylvania. On July 1, 1863, Lee concentrated his force of 65,000 against Meade's 85,000 and the fiercest of battles began.

In a week, Rebecca, Megan's daughter in New York City, wrote that her father, Kevin Gallagher, had died on the first day of the battle at Gettysburg, the same day that her husband and nephew were wounded. Regrettably, her husband was forced to fight against her father. Another nephew from Savannah had died fighting for the Confederacy on July 2.

On July 3, Brianna and Pilan's son, Corporal Charles (Bright Eagle) Brosnan, nineteen, was wounded at Cemetery Ridge. On July 4, General Lee began to withdraw toward the Potomac. After telling Picket that he planned another fight, Picket had replied, "I have no division." Every man was lost.

On the last day, with young Dermot fatally wounded, he had whispered to his father, "Give Mama my love."

The newspapers had reported that Lee's wounded stretched out over fourteen miles. Over 51,000 men had died in three days. At Gettysburg, the South lost 28,000, the North 23,000, with three former sons of Charleston numbered among the fatalities.

It was always Maggie's hope that Darcy and Kevin would embrace in the Otherworld. She praised God that the two *invincibles* were never forced to come face to face in battle, a secret fear she had from the start. Now, her sincere prayer was for their families to gather together again in the peace and joy of the Otherworld, in order to heal all wounds and release all forms of suffering.

By mid-July, anti-draft riots broke out in New York City, along with arson and the killing of blacks by poor white immigrants: 120 murdered, including children, two million dollars in damages before the returning Union soldiers were able to restore the peace. The war still waged and the fugitives continued to arrive at Marcus Manor.

By August, Frederick Douglass met with President Lincoln to call for equality for the Negro troops. In Lawrence, Kansas, pro-Confederate Quantrill and 450 pro-slavery men raided a town and butchered 182 men and boys. In September, the South scored a victory by placing the Union Army under siege at Chattanooga. By that October, General Grant commanded the operations of the Union in the West.

On November 19, the address of President Abraham Lincoln at Gettysburg was published in the newspapers. Under the direction of Maggie and Priscilla, the children at Marcus Manor memorized every single word and repeated the address together in chorus in the barn seated on bales of hay:

"Four score and seven years ago our forefathers brought forth on this continent a new nation, conceived in liberty and dedicated to the proposition that all men are created equal. Now we are engaged in a great civil war, testing whether that nation or any nation so conceived and so dedicated can long endure..."

The president's speech inspired everyone to remember the valiant soldiers who had died for a just cause. A portion of the battlefield at Gettysburg was dedicated as a National Cemetery.

The work with the fugitive slaves at Marcus Manor seemed a never-ending struggle. Maggie thought it was a good thing that the colored were now allowed to fight, even though segregation made things less than ideal. Could the life of any soldier be easy, she wondered?

The spirit of cooperation stayed its course on the farm, with black and white, former slaves now free, young and old, working together in harmony. Both Ruth and Rebecca had become fine teachers. Some colored children now taught the alphabet and numbers. Little ones counted on their fingers and learned how to write with chalk on a blackboard. Stories were read to many, perhaps treated kindly for the first time, especially by a white haired white woman in a long gown who lived in a fine manor house that was once a tobacco plantation with seventy African slaves.

For the holidays, the ballroom was opened up. Wild turkeys and geese were shot and cooked, along with white tailed deer. A perfect tree was found and set up in the hall. Everyone was caught up in the spirit of season. Musical instruments were tuned. Singing and dancing filled the manor house. The gifts beneath the tree were perhaps small, some handmade, but filled with love. In a trunk in the attic, Maggie had found old toys: dolls, toy soldiers, blocks and trains, which were wrapped and placed under the tree with the names of several children. Without the slightest misgivings, she gave away Triona's old dolls and stuffed animals, wondering why she had kept them so long.

On Christmas Eve, everyone crowded into the ballroom to sing carols near a blazing fire, as small candles burned on the colorful tree. Opening the Bible, Maggie thought that many of the displaced souls present needed to hear words of comfort in facing a future of uncertainty.

Turning to *St. Luke,* the second chapter, Maggie read aloud:

"And it came to pass in those days that there went out a decree from Caesar Augustus that all the world should be taxed ... and all went to be taxed, everyone into his own city ... and so it was, while they were there, the days were accomplished that Mary should be delivered ..."

"And, lo, the angel of the Lord came upon them, and the glory of the Lord shone around about them: and they were sore afraid," Uncle Wally called out in his pronounced southern gospel voice.

Suddenly, all fell silent. Wally was the unofficial preacher at the small chapel near the old slaves quarters now constantly filled with fugitives.

"You're getting ahead of the story, Uncle Wally," Maggie gently said, and the children snickered as he simply nodded and grinned.

"Sorry, Missy," he said. "You jest go on now..."

Picking up from where he had quoted, Maggie read, "And the angel said unto them, Fear not, for behold: I bring you tidings of great joy, which shall be to all people ..."

"For unto you is born this day in the city of David," Uncle Wally called out in his best gospel tone, "a Savior, which is *Christ the Lord.*"

"And this shall be a sign unto you," she continued, smiling through her tears, "Ye shall find the babe wrapped in swaddling clothes, lying in a manger."

Soon, everyone was singing *Silent Night,* written by an Austrian priest the same year that Maggie had arrived in America.

Next, she picked up a book: *A Christmas Carol* by Charles Dickens, and now, the fully literate Uncle Wally helped her to read the story to all gathered together in the ballroom on that Christmas Eve. The story was a favorite among the children.

At the end, everyone called out with Tiny Tim: "God bless you ... everyone!"

In March of 1864, Shannon wrote of the marriage of their daughter, Margaret, twenty-two, to Captain Arthur McGovern, twenty-eight, a Scot-Irish immigrant and Union war hero wounded at the Battle of Chickamauga in Tennessee. Maggie's granddaughter had met the young officer, still recovering from his wounds, at a celebration for returning Union heroes at their church in San Francisco. That same month, General Grant commanded all armies in the United States, with General Sherman assuming the command in the West.

Occasional letters arrived from Aidan or Dermot, both men now with General Sherman, with the letters scribbled at night on a train often expressing their weariness and fear that the war might never end. Aidan was deeply disappointed that he was unable to give away his daughter to a fine war hero. He was also tired of all the killing and all the destruction all these years.

By May, the combined march toward Richmond was underway. It was the beginning of slow yet total destruction, the grinding down and gnawing away of lives, treasures and properties in the South. General Grant's 100,000 men strong marched against General Lee's 64,000, fighting major battles through the Wilderness: U.S. 17,666 losses, Rebels 7,500. Spotsylvania: 10,920 killed and wounded. Cold Harbor was where Grant's mistake lost 7,000 Union soldiers in twenty minutes, with a total loss of 15,500 men. According to newspaper reports, it was the most lopsided of battles.

In the West, General Sherman, with Captains Aidan and Dermot Brosnan in his regiment, advanced toward Atlanta to engage General Johnston's 60,000 Army of Tennessee. There was fierce fighting in Mississippi with the burning of many railroad bridges on the march toward Georgia.

In 1861, *Harper's Weekly* had reported that Charleston, South Carolina, was burned by angry slaves. Maggie feared for the safety of her sister,

Megan, who had already lost Kevin and a few of her children. There had been no correspondence for three years. Maggie thought, surely her sister had come to her senses and seen the injustice of slavery and freed her slaves.

In May of 1864, *Harpers Weekly* displayed Sherman's advance at Buzzard's Roost Pass in Georgia. Maggie was sure that her boys had to be in the drawing, while fearful that her sister would soon be at the mercy of revengeful Union soldiers. Battles raged from Texas to the eastern seaboard and throughout the South. Congress was finally giving black soldiers equal pay.

By that July, General Sherman was fighting near Atlanta, with Lincoln calling for 500,000 more volunteers. More men at Marcus Manor signed on to fight. In August, the Democrats nominated George McClellan to run against Lincoln. The same month the Convention for the Amelioration of the Condition of the Wounded in Armies in the Field was signed by twelve nations in Geneva, establishing the International Red Cross.

Maggie worried for her family in Atlanta. Bread riots were reported in the newspapers. Food was scarce. Her niece, Constance, had four children. In Savannah, Sarah Ann had six youngsters. How were they going to survive? Aidan's son, Patrick, recovered from his wounds sustained at Gettysburg, now helped to supervise the farm. At the age of twenty, Brown Bear had taken a shine to the last Piscataway girl there. Jessica was sixteen, with long dark hair and brown eyes with the thickest eyelashes that Maggie had ever seen. Jessica was also a natural for finding helpful herbs in the woods. Upon seeing the two of them together, it was easy enough for her to see their connections in the Otherworld. Patrick had found his soul mate at Marcus Manor.

That September, Patrick said, "Maybe I should join up with Sherman, take a train South. The president has called for more volunteers. I might find Pa and Uncle Dermot. I pray for them every night, Grandma."

"We all pray for them. General Sherman sent a telegram to President Lincoln, 'Atlanta is ours and fairly won.' Now isn't that something?"

"Pa and Uncle Dermot must be in Atlanta too. I wish they would send us a telegram. In this week's *Harpers Weekly,* Sherman said, 'Gentlemen, I intend to place this army southwest of Atlanta,'" he was mimicking the general.

"I know. How about that corn, Patrick? Do we have a harvest?"

"Yes, ma'am," he replied. "See you at supper, Grandma."

Just thinking about the burning of Atlanta tugged at Maggie's heart. She was fearful of even reading the casualty lists for the citizens. Both Aidan and Dermot had addresses for relatives in the South. She hoped her sons would lend a hand to their blood relations.

The newspapers reported that an outlaw named Jesse James and his gang, along with Bloody Bill Anderson, had attacked a train and killed 150 people in Missouri. Twenty-four unarmed, wounded Union soldiers were dragged from the train and murdered. Over 120 Union troops managed to kill only three of the outlaws. The West seemed as wild as ever to Maggie, with its outlaws and Indians, making her wonder how peace was ever going to be secured across such a vast land?

That November, the National Negro Convention was held in Syracuse, New York, and slavery was abolished in Maryland. President Lincoln established Thanksgiving as a holiday, with a turkey shoot at Marcus Manor to celebrate the end of slavery in the state. That month, Union troops shot Bloody Bill Anderson, his days of killing Union soldiers at an end. Then Lincoln defeated McClellan by carrying fifty-five percent of the popular vote and all but three states.

Lincoln said to his supporters, "I earnestly believe that the consequences of this day's work will be to the lasting advantage, if not the very salvation, of the country."

After the destruction of Atlanta, Sherman and his 62,000 Union troops marched toward Savannah on their March to the Sea. Lincoln approved, with Sherman said to have boasted, "I can make Georgia howl." The Union won battle after battle, the Tennessee Army no longer a unified fighting force. Were Aidan and Dermot still safe, Maggie wondered?

In December, she cringed upon seeing the cover of *Harpers Weekly*: The Rebel Flag of Truce boat with Savannah burning. Trembling inside, she earnestly feared for the safety of her family members in the South.

By December 21, Sherman reached Savannah, leaving a 300 mile path of destruction sixty miles wide all the way from Atlanta. The General telegraphed Lincoln, "I beg to present you, as a Christmas gift, the city of Savannah, with 150 heavy guns and plenty of ammunition, and also about 25,000 bales of cotton."

On the next day, another telegram arrived at Marcus Manor: Words and sentences pasted on a page:

Dear Mother and Priscilla. STOP. The Union has conquered the South. STOP. We are safe. STOP. Trust you are the same. STOP. We are sorry we cannot be home for Christmas. STOP. Wishing you a Happy New Year. STOP. Colonels Aidan and Dermot Brosnan in Savannah with the Unstoppable General Sherman. STOP.

60

The South Surrenders

On January 31, 1865, slavery was finally abolished in the United States of America. It was a time for rejoicing at Marcus Manor and a tremendous relief to Maggie. Her work as a clandestine abolitionist breaking the laws of her nation had finally ended. Slaves were now free throughout the land. For that reason, there were things she felt she needed to say to Darcy.

Early on a February morning, Maggie wrapped herself in a winter cloak and headed for the cemetery. That was even though it looked like it was going to snow and even though she knew his spirit was not in the cold, cold ground of a Maryland winter. Darcy was close to her all the time, as close as her thoughts and secure within her heart. They had shared many memories since they first met in Dingle, Ireland in 1815, nearly fifty years ago.

"Good day to you, my darling," she said aloud, glancing at his tombstone before she sat on a boulder not far away beneath the spreading, bare branches of a large maple tree. Deeply inhaling the crisp winter air, she caught sight of a woodpecker flying off between the barren trees.

"Our Congress has freed all the slaves in this yet divided nation. They call it the 13th Amendment. I fear the war is not yet over, even though

President Lincoln has already met with that Confederate. Those slave-holders are still unable to see the light the way that you finally did.

"Our boys, Aidan and Dermot, are both colonels now. That should make you proud. I certainly am mighty proud of them. They sent me my first telegram, a wonderful Christmas gift that must have cost them a small fortune. I would have sent one back to them, but I wasn't sure where to send it. That Unstoppable Sherman is demanding land for the colored folks down South. Now, isn't that something? Like us sharing our land here. Only, the Southerners might not be so happy with the idea of sharing their land." Maggie smiled at the thought.

"Lee is Commander-in-Chief of the Confederates, with Grant our top man. I hope that Sherman marches north real soon and brings our boys safely home." She thoughtfully paused and glanced all around her to make sure that no one else was listening. "I guess I shouldn't call them boys anymore, should I? Aidan is forty-nine and Dermot forty-seven in June. But they will always be our boys to me. Grown men are always boys to their parents, at least to this mother.

"I expect that you're taking good care of young Darcy and young Dermot. Gareth and Star must have been on your welcoming committee. We lost them both so long ago, along with young Triona. You must have quite a group with Kevin and his kin there now, too. I hope you have forgiven him, Darcy. You both should know something about forgiveness by now. It is important to forgive all who have ever harmed you in any manner. Aunt Brigid taught me that a long time ago. Give Aunt Brigid and Pa my love. Take good care of our grandson, Terence, and tell Robert that we forgive him for being on the wrong side. I just hope he wasn't the one who shot you. I've worried about that for a while now.

"Brian is doing just fine as a dentist out in San Francisco. He and Molly have four children. Timmy and his Juliana have two children already. Timmy is making lots of money as a banker. I told him to help out his mulatto cousins. It's a shame that Robert never married that Fanny. I just hope that she doesn't raise those children in some brothel, for heaven's sake. Now, wouldn't that be something?" and she laughed out loud at the thought.

"I still miss you every single day. I wish I could touch you." Tears filled her eyes. "You have given me such joy over the years. I loved you much more than I ever loved Aidan. I know you never got over thinking of him as your primary competition. What I had with Aidan as a girl seems more like a dream to me now, with you as my dream come true. I tried to tell you that before you left us at Antietam. I saw your spirit leave your body. So many spirits hovered over that battlefield, men who didn't even know that they were dead. It's a sight that I shall no doubt ever forget. I prayed for both the boys in blue and the boys in gray … that they would find peace and forgive each other over there in the Otherworld.

"Thanks for listening to me, my darling. Perhaps I have said this to you more often than you care to hear. Sometimes I just need to talk to you out loud, Darcy, maybe just to keep my sanity. Call in the angels, my darling, sprinkle peace and love over this great land so that harmony may again be restored in a once more united America."

Hearing a sudden stir, Maggie glanced toward the trees in time to see a brilliant pillar of radiating light. Then she gazed up at the sky, for snow was starting to fall. Looking back, the pillar of light was gone. Perhaps it was Yuma, who was often in her dreams, or her father, or Darcy. Or her mother, for the sweet scent of lavender now infused the gentle swirling snowflakes to bring her solace and peace on a cold winter's day.

The winter was fierce that year. The Potomac River froze, which reminded Maggie of 1816 back in Ireland. In the newspapers, she read: "The Mayor of Charleston, South Carolina, surrendered control of the city to Brigadier General Alexander Schimmelfenning at 9 A.M. on Saturday, February 18, 1865. With commanding General William T. Sherman's arrival imminent, evacuation of the city began on February 17 and continued through the early morning hours of February 18. The city had been under siege since July 10, 1863."

Not long after that, a letter told her of Megan's death during the surrender of Charleston. Aidan was excused to check on his aged aunt. He arrived at the fire ravaged house only to discover that she was taken to hospital on the prior day after suffering a stroke. At the age of sixty-four, Megan Caitlin wanted no more of slavery and no more of war. She expired within the hour.

Pictures of the charred ruins of Charleston were sickening. The colored street urchins among the collapse made Maggie wonder how anyone might adjust to the terrible devastation. Rebecca wrote of her mother's burial in a Protestant cemetery. Surely, Maggie thought, the entire South must be overwhelmed with funerals and burials after Sherman's March to the Sea.

On March 4, 1865, many of those at Marcus Manor were eager to attend the second inauguration of President Lincoln, with the colored forced to ride in a separate car on the train. That certainly irked Maggie. Ruth had stayed at home to feed and care for stragglers, mostly Union soldiers walking home.

In the city of Washington, Maggie was reunited with her niece, Rebecca Hoffman, Robert's twin. Thankfully, her husband had recovered from his wounds sustained at Gettysburg. Together, they wept: Over Megan, all their many losses and the sad state of conditions in the South.

"Losing your father must have broken your mother's heart," Maggie said. "I'm so sorry these fine children have lost their dear grandmother." Her grand nieces and nephews stood in respectful silence. "You have a Mary Margaret, too. Why that is mighty flattering, Rebecca."

"I can only hope that she ends up with your passion and principles, Aunt Maggie. Her red hair is like ours." Young Mary Margaret smiled. "You know my parents always said that I look like you. My mother loved you very much."

"And I loved her very much. Your mother cared for young Uncle Sean when our mother was lost with his birth. I know Megan was a good mother to all of you and a wonderful grandmother, as well."

"We stopped seeing her with the war. But she attended Annabelle's wedding."

"I remember your letter."

"Brigid and Luke spent time with Mama. They took her for a carriage ride all over Philadelphia. She enjoyed meeting her nieces and nephews. Cousin Brigid and I are very close, as you know. Luke has done so much good for the cause. Now, he's working hard to integrate the former slaves into our society."

"That may be difficult in the South," Maggie wearily said. "Difficult, indeed."

Early April, the Union *Stars and Stripes* were once again raised over the former Confederate capital in Richmond. President Lincoln entered their White House with a "serious, dreamy expression," it was reported in the newspapers. He sat at the desk of Jefferson Davis in prolonged, respectful silence.

On April 9, Robert E. Lee surrendered to Ulysses S. Grant at Appomattox Court House in Virginia. In a chivalrous gesture, Grant allowed the Rebel officers to keep their sidearms and the soldiers their horses and mules.

The next day there were celebrations in cities all over the North, especially in Washington and at Marcus Manor, with dancing in the lanes, parlors, farmyards and barns. A long, grievous war had finally come to an end, so all their men and boys would soon be home again.

That April 12th was one of the happiest days of Maggie's life, as Aidan and Dermot walked in through the front doors looking none the worse for wear in their dark blue uniforms. They were followed by a limping Sean Joseph and young Sean with his arm in a sling. Next, was Dermot's younger son, Thomas, and Brianna's son, Charles Bright Eagle.

"My Law!" Maggie cried out, kissing Aidan and then Dermot, before she stared at Charles. "Are you Bright Eagle?" she inquired, hugging him before he could even answer her.

"That's right," Charles said. "You must be my Granny. My parents told me all about you. My mother looks quite a bit like you, in fact."

Wiping away her tears, Maggie said, "I am your Granny!" Then she grabbed Thomas and said, "I'm his Granny, too, and he knows it," and she kissed each cheek. "I changed his diapers," she said, taking his face into her hands. "I'm so glad that you're back here in one piece, Thomas."

"Me, too, Grandma. How's Frederick doing?"

"That right arm of his is a bit lame, but he helps Patrick run this place. I just can't get over losing young Dermot, even though he's buried right here. I wish we had Padraic here, too, Sean."

"Me, too," Sean Joseph said, putting both his arms around his sister.

Next, Dermot hugged his mother. "I need to go and see Priscilla and the kids," he said, turning to Thomas. "I hope your mother recognizes me."

Everyone laughed at the beards.

"Oh, she'll recognize you. But she may make you shave. That beard makes you look old, Dermot. You're hiding your handsome face behind a bush!"

Dermot laughed as he hurried out the door, with Thomas right behind him.

"You all need a bath and a shave before supper. Some of your father's old clothes should fit you," she said to Aidan. "You, too, Sean. You're no bigger than Darcy. You might even want his deerskin pants."

"I get dibs on Grandpa's deerskins," Charles blurted out. "I've always wanted a pair."

"Your grandfather had several. No one needs to fight over them. I'll take your measurements and make you some new ones, in fact."

"That would be great," young Sean said. "My uncle was a great soldier. I wouldn't mind just having his old ones, Aunt Maggie."

"I'm sure he would want you both to have them, Bright Eagle."

Aidan wrapped his arms around his mother and held on tight. "I'm mighty sorry about Aunt Megan. It wasn't good what we did to those towns, if the truth be known. But the men had lost far too much over the damn cotton. A bale set fire in the middle of Columbia nearly burned down the whole town, mainly because of the wind. I guess Aunt Megan couldn't take anymore, Mama, losing Uncle Kevin and a few of her children."

Tearing up, Maggie said, "It broke her heart. The way Charleston was for the past two years, it's a wonder she lived as long as she did."

"Maybe she didn't think she was welcome here," Sean Joseph said.

"Oh, Sean, how can you say such a thing? Our sister had to know that we loved her regardless of her slaves. I just wish she'd had the good sense to come on up here."

"It looks like you have more than enough darkies around here," Sean said.

"We've been taking in fugitives since the war began. It's a wonder we could feed and care for them all. Some days I barely had enough strength to go on. It's been much harder on me with Darcy gone, but I've had plenty to keep me busy. And that's a fact."

"Pa is always in my prayers," Aidan said.

"You all lost sons in this war. I'm just grateful that you came home."

"We'll be here for a while, then catch us a clipper ship," Aidan said. "I hear it doesn't take so long through Panama by stagecoach over to the Pacific. We'll stick around to rest up and see some friends before we leave for the West."

"Stay as long as you like. I've got bread pudding, turkey and venison in the icebox." Maggie paused. "You don't know it yet, Aidan, but your Patrick is going to marry Jessica. She's half Piscataway."

"Is that right?" Aidan said, smiling. "I'll bet she's pretty, too!"

"He calls her his bonny half-breed."

"Two bonny half-breeds," Aidan said, chuckling, "A chip off the old block, huh, Mama?"

"He looks like you, Aidan. But Patrick really loves farming here at Marcus Manor."

"Uh oh," Sean Joseph said, grinning.

"Looks like Grandma is trying to keep her grandchildren close," Charles said.

"Are you trying to tell me something, Mama?" Aidan inquired.

"It's mighty pretty around here," young Sean said.

"I can see where some young men might want to farm in Maryland," her brother said. "The rivers here are mighty wide. That Chesapeake is something. It was scary down South. The Savannah was three times as wide this year and made a swamp out of Georgia."

"I read that in *Harpers Weekly*. Horrible flooding in the South. Bad winter here, too, with lots of ice and snow," Maggie said.

"Real wet down South," Sean Joseph said. "But I'll tell you something, sis, the mountains here, or the ones in Ireland, cannot compare with the Rockies or Sierra Nevada. You couldn't get me away from the West." He hugged her. "I found my pot of gold at the end of a California rainbow without having to cope with some ornery leprechaun. However, I've no immediate plans to go back and pan for more gold."

"But you never know," young Sean said, giving his father a nudge.

Everyone laughed.

"I need to get back to California," young Sean said, "to my Peggy. Heck, Sean, III, is almost five. I want to make some more babies. I wish you could meet her. My Peggy is a fine lass."

"There's a letter from her waiting for you in the library."

"There is?" he said, backing off. "Excuse me," and he ran into the library.

"There's a letter for you, too, Sean. And one from Shannon," she said to Aidan. "Young Jeffrey can say the alphabet backwards and forwards and he's only five!"

"Is that right?" Aidan said, following his uncle and cousin, all of them soon opening their letters. Young Sean was in Darcy's favorite chair.

Looking up, Sean Joseph said, "Mary Margaret met a war hero who lost his wife with their fifth child." He frowned and shook his head. "Walter Johnson fought in Texas. Good gracious, ten children between them … and it seems to be a serious courtship!"

"Your daughter will have her hands full," Maggie said.

Scowling, he replied, "Well, she needs to do what makes her happy."

"Matthew and Mark are already in San Francisco," Aidan said, looking up. "I'll bet you Uncle Matthew and Aunt Heather are mighty relieved. No serious wounds for their boys."

"I had a letter from Heather," Maggie said. "Their Seamus got typhus in Texas but he survived. That disease killed a great many men in this war in the North and the South."

"Good for Seamus," young Sean said. "Now we can swap war stories. We get along great and might go into business together."

"His sister, Brigid, has another son in Ireland, Padraic Desmond, named after his grandpa. She has five children now, and her mother says she's not about to stop!" Maggie said.

"Still in Dublin?" Sean Joseph inquired.

"Her husband, Kenneth, is Darcy's cousin. He's active in the Irish Parliament and frequently speaks of Ireland's independence."

"I might help Ireland," Sean Joseph said, his Irish accent still strong. "Plenty of Irishmen talk about helping out their homeland in breaking free of the Crown. We'd all like to free Ireland."

"Thomas Meagher got us to fight for the Union," Aidan said, "With the Irish Brigade."

"Irish fought on both sides, cousin," young Sean said.

"Da always said the Irish fight on all sides the world over," Maggie said.

"Our best war photographer was Irish, Mathew Brady from New York," Aidan said.

"Darcy just barely escaped being in his pictures of Antietam," she said with a sigh. "I opened the newspaper one morning to find pictures of dead men and dead horses, and I nearly lost my breakfast. I guess it made folks more aware of the dear cost of the war!"

"You'll show me Pa and my son's graves," Aidan said, turning somber, "Maybe after supper," he added, looking back to his letter with his eyes filled with tears.

"I'll show you all the graves. We'll take them some spring wildflowers."

Aidan stood and placed the letter in his pocket. "I can't wait to have Shannon in my arms again. The little ones seemed to have grown a mile. I hope to heaven they remember that I'm their Pa."

"We ran into Irish immigrants in Baltimore," Sean Joseph said, "Still leaving Ireland by the boatload ... the same as us." He winked at his sister.

"It may never stop. It's in our blood ... coming to America."

"Bread pudding sounds good and maybe some turkey," Aidan said, pulling his mother up to her feet.

Young Sean smiled. "Dessert before supper. I haven't had any good bread pudding forever."

Everyone started for the kitchen.

With his arm around his mother, Aidan said, "It is good to be home, Mama, really good to be home."

Two days later, the *Stars and Stripes* were once again raised over Fort Sumter in Charleston Harbor. That evening, President Lincoln and his wife, Mary, went to see a play at Ford's Theater. At 10:13 p.m., during the third act, John Wilkes Booth shot the president in the back of the head. President Lincoln died at 7:22 a.m. on April 15, 1865. Shortly thereafter, Vice President Andrew Johnson assumed the presidency.

Secretary of War Stanton was known to have said: "Now he belongs to the ages."

That morning Aidan ran into the house waving a newspaper and calling out, "The bloody bastards have killed our president, Mama. Abraham Lincoln is dead."

"Dear God, what a price he has paid to win freedom for our slaves."

"We will not leave until we pay our respects. Uncle Sean is heartsick."

"I am, too, Aidan! What a waste for a man of his greatness."

"If he's lucky, maybe Pa is talking to Lincoln right now. In spite of holding out for so long about freeing our slaves, Pa loved Abraham Lincoln."

On April 20, many of those at Marcus Manor boarded a train for Washington to attend President Lincoln's funeral. The proud Union soldiers joined the mourners in uniform, prepared to salute a man for whom they had fought four long years to restore the United States of America.

Harpers Weekly reported:

"The fourteenth day of April is a dark day in our country's calendar. On that day four years ago the national flag was for the first time lowered at the bidding of traitors. Upon that day, after a desperate conflict with treason for four long, weary years—a conflict in which the nation had so far triumphed that she breathed again in the prospect of coming peace—her chosen leader was stricken down by the foul hand of the cowardly assassin ..."

And also: "Never was King or Emperor honoured with such obsequies as those with which our Republic has laid to rest its greatest hero. It was not the pomp of the procession, nor the splendour of the funereal rites, that gave character to the touching ceremony, but the infinite tenderness and love of a great people."

Early in the month of May, Aidan and the others from the West boarded a clipper ship, the *Sky Dragon,* for San Francisco. Once again, Maggie bid her loved ones a tearful and sad farewell.

By the end of the month the remaining Confederates surrendered in Texas. The nation was once again united, except for the fact that over 620,000 Americans had died, with disease taking twice the number lost in battle. Over 50,000 amputees returned to their families. By December, the 13th Amendment was ratified and the long struggle finally came to an end.

61

Going Home

On April 2, 1866, President Johnson officially ended the conflict with the last holdouts in the War Between the States. That spring the president also vetoed the Civil Rights Bill. Congress rejected his veto and passed the 14th Amendment, which granted equal rights to all citizens born in the United States of America, regardless of race or religion.

Late April there was a knock at the door and Rebecca answered, "Hello! You look mighty familiar," she said to the black man standing on the porch.

"Yes, ma'am. I'm Johnny. I lived here until that slave catcher hit me over the head and took me away back in '51. I joined the Union when they started taking us ... ran away from that cotton plantation in Alabama as soon as the war started."

"Lordy me! Missy Maggie, come see what the cat's dragged in. Johnny's come home. Johnny Plunkett!"

Upon rushing into the room, Maggie said, "Why, Johnny, is that you?" Walking closer, she adjusted her spectacles. "Darcy and Dermot went looking for you. Moses said they hid you in some cellar and sold you down the river."

"Johnny Brosnan, yes ma'am. Sold me to a mean man from Alabama, but soon as the war started, I run off and signed on to fight against the Rebels. Now I'm finally home."

"Johnny Brosnan?" Maggie said in a tone of amusement.

"I could never call myself Plunkett, ma'am. So I took your name. I hope it's all right. Slaves ... they usually takes the master's name. Seems like it's always been that way."

"It's fine, Johnny. Are you looking for work or a place to stay?"

"No, ma'am. I just wanted to say thank you, 'cause I heard Dermot talking to the man when they got Moses back, paying for him." He frowned. "Yous mighty fine folks. And now, I got me a wife and a child on the way."

"Is that right?" Rebecca said.

"I wanted you to know that I'm fine after being a slave in Alabama and fighting in the war. There were hard times, of course. You look fine, Missy Maggie. I heard you're going back to Ireland."

"Why, yes. Who told you?"

"Ruth. She's such a fine woman. I guess she's been with you for a very long time."

"A very long time indeed, since I came here in 1817, nearly fifty years. In a couple of weeks, I'll be taking a steamer. It only takes weeks, except that I'm nervous since the *Monarch of the Seas* sank off Liverpool with 738 onboard drowned. Lots of steamships seem to blow up or else sink."

"That might make me mighty nervous, too," he said. "But you'll probably be just fine."

"Where are you living now?" Maggie inquired.

"Baltimore. I got me a job working at the docks with some Irish." He grinned. "They don't like us niggers getting the jobs. But they're good fighters, those Irishmen."

"The Irish keep coming," Rebecca said.

His expression sobered. "Ruth told me about you losing the master at Antietam. Terrible battle. Terrible losses in this war. Lots of slaves died, too. They should've let us get into it sooner. I'm awful sorry, Missy Maggie. He was a really fine man, Master Brosnan. A really fine man."

"Yes, he was. He's buried here with his grandsons and our colored friends out in the cemetery. The new preacher doesn't accept colored. Mixing folks together will take time, Johnny. You understand, I hope. Big changes can take quite a long time in coming."

"Yes, ma'am. Some time and some doing." He pensively paused. "Will you be going for good, Missy Maggie, or is you coming back?"

"I'm not sure. My stepmother is unwell. She's now eighty-four-years old."

"My. That's a mighty long life."

"I haven't been in Ireland since 1816. I'm planning to walk through the hills and see all the changes. When you're born in Ireland, Johnny, it stays in your heart forever."

"I guess Maryland will always be in my heart."

"Dermot runs the farm," Rebecca said. "Fair and honest just like his daddy. He's a fine man."

"Dermot, he come looking for me with his Pa." Johnny's moved his hat from one hand to the other. "Well, somebody's waiting for me. We're picking up friends and getting back on the train to Baltimore. It's mighty good to see you, Missy Maggie. You take good care of youself."

"It's mighty good to see you, too, Johnny. I'm truly glad you survived the hard times. You take care and good luck with your child. I suspect you'll have a son."

"Is that right? Why, thank you, kindly," he said, nodding to each of them. "You, too, Miss Rebecca. You all have a fine time in Ireland."

It was hard for Maggie to leave Rebecca and Ruth behind at Marcus Manor. Rebecca had Isaac and her children. But Ruth was alone at the age of sixty-seven. Where had all the years gone, she wondered? It seemed they had all flown by in just a matter of minutes.

"I wish you'd let me come and take care of you, Missy," Ruth said. "I'd like to see Ireland. I've heard about how green it is ... your Emerald Isle. Maybe I'd find me a leprechaun with a pot of gold," she said, sitting on the settee and sipping her tea. Long ago, her mistress had taught her how to be a lady. "Do you have African folks in Ireland?"

"We didn't before. I never saw dark-skinned folks until I arrived in Baltimore. No Indians or Africans. I fear that I stared," she said, sipping tea from her cup, thinking of how she would soon be having tea with Prudence in the cheerful parlor on Goat Street.

"It won't be the same here without you. But I won't live anywhere else. I want to be buried with my kin and the rest of them here. Will that be possible with you in Ireland?"

"Of course, Becky. You are family to me. Stay as long as you like. We will meet again, someday."

The *Silver Swan* was far more luxurious than the *Pegasus* all those years ago. Maggie made many new friends on the long voyage across the sea, mostly Irish, also returning to their roots. They were those who had prospered in America, with many seasick the first week out.

Maggie walked the deck as she had long ago, enjoying the feel of the wind on her face and marveling at the endless vision of the sea before her. There was news of the German Premier Otto von Bismarck being seriously wounded in an assassination attempt. It seemed that he had fared far better than Abraham Lincoln. He survived.

The letters she had brought along with her were reread several times. Aidan tended to write more often than the rest, although she truly enjoyed the letters written by Shannon. It seemed as though they had met and had known each other for years. Young Charles wrote more often than his mother, Brianna. He kept his grandmother informed of the rapid expansion taking place in San Francisco. That was how Maggie learned that Megan's son, Peter Kelly, and his wife, Bethany, had five children between the ages of three and twelve years. Peter never wrote himself. She thought perhaps he was unable to resolve the division caused by the war, with losing both his parents to the Union, at least in his mind. Onboard the clipper ship going home, Charles had met an English girl emigrating from Cornwall. He and Laura were now spending lots of time together.

On the crossing, Maggie had time to read *Alice in Wonderland* by Lewis Carroll, which was primarily purchased for her nieces and nephews in Ireland. The *Poems* of Emerson were her gift for Prudence, whose eyesight had apparently dimmed. She planned to read to Prudence in the parlor or the library, according to her liking.

In Queenstown, Matthew and Heather met her steamer at the dock. Her older brother, now seventy, was still robust with his thick white hair. At sixty-three, Heather, Kevin's first cousin from County Cork, had bright blue eyes and a pretty face framed by light gray hair. After all the kisses and hugs, with the trunks securely tied onto the carriage, Matthew appeared troubled.

"What is it, Matthew?" Maggie inquired, keenly sensing his mood.

After exchanging uneasy glances with his wife, he turned to her with a solemn face and said, "A letter from Antoinette arrived just this morning," he stopped, grimacing. "We've lost our Liam." Tears filled his eyes. "I didn't want to tell you first thing, with you coming home to Ireland after nearly fifty years." He removed a handkerchief from his pocket and wiped his nose.

"We feel terrible having to tell you at all," Heather said. "Liam was seventy-two."

"We'd hoped he might come back home sometime, but those islands are very far from Ireland," Matthew said in a disconsolate tone.

"A very long way," Maggie said, as deep sadness welled up inside her and her eyes filled with tears. "I should have known. He mentioned chest pains in his last letter, and I got this terrible feeling deep down inside."

"Heather gets those feelings," Matthew said. "She dreams of the Otherworld the same as you. You two should get on just fine, since you both talk to spirits and fairies."

"I'm looking forward to getting much better acquainted," Maggie said to Heather.

"Me, too," Heather said. "I'm truly sorry that there is yet no train between Cork and Dingle."

Slowly taking in a deep breath, Maggie glanced all around her and said, "Things have changed a lot in the past forty-nine years."

"Wait until you see the new church and the Christian Brothers' School. You'll be amazed," Matthew said. "This weekend the O'Reilly's are gathering from far and wide to greet the prodigal's return to Erin. I imagine that the fairies and elves will be tickled pink to see you, Maggie, since you're one of the few who doesn't seem to fear them."

"How about me?" Heather chided. "I have no fear of fairies, most of the time."

"Most of the time," Matthew teasingly repeated, helping them both into the carriage. "What do you think of the fine carriage our father gave us?" he inquired, settling in next to Heather.

"It's a fine carriage, Matthew Michael, a very fine carriage, indeed."

"You should take the train through the Lakes of Killarney," Heather said, as the carriage jostled along. "It can be quite frightening. I closed my eyes half way through. But we made it there and back and those lakes are downright beautiful."

"The most hazardous route of any train in Ireland," Matthew said, "And yet, the fastest way. They plan to bring the train to Tralee and Dingle. You truly should see the lakes. As I recall, Darcy wanted to take you there himself."

Gently nodding, Maggie said, "Aye," and she gazed out across the green fields, noting the numerous walls of blackening stones. It was the first time that she had seen the land divided. "Famine walls, I presume."

"Famine walls," Matthew said. "Some lead nowhere or enclose nothing. But it works for some of the sheep and cattle."

"They climb right over," Heather said in a perturbed tone.

"Some." Momentarily, he paused. "Prudence is right fragile. We're starting to fear for the state of her health," Matthew said.

"So dear, Prudence," Heather said. "She's such a gentle soul."

"She always has been," Maggie said, relaxing for a moment before the carriage hit a pothole and jarred her from her reverie.

That happened all the way to Dingle.

It was late evening when the carriage finally pulled up in front of the house on Goat Street. The trunks were taken to an upstairs room with a splendid view of the hills. Immediately, Maggie caught sight of a dapple gray mare prancing in the faint light of a half moon low in the night sky. Ona had greeted her. The servant was still unmarried and in Prudence's services these many years.

Soon, Matthew and Heather excused themselves and headed for home.

"Miss Prudence asked me to awaken her upon your arrival, but she was especially tired this evening. You must be very tired yourself after your long journey from Queenstown."

"I am a bit weary," Maggie said.

"Gareth and Megan Gallagher were with Mrs. O'Reilly this afternoon. They're here to see you," Ona said. "Staying with her parents in

Ballyferriter, they are. Gareth gets along just fine with Matthew. They've brought along all the children to meet their aunt." Ona beamed. "Young Gareth uses his second name, Jonathan. He's almost fourteen now. Sean Joseph is ten, Cathleen eight, Mary Elizabeth not yet seven, and young Matthew Kelly is five. The youngest, Thomas Patrick, is but three-years old. All are beautiful children. You'll see, Mrs. Brosnan. Every one of them is extremely eager to meet you."

The name 'Megan Gallagher' had given Maggie a brief start before she remembered that Matthew had named a daughter Megan Heather, and ultimately, she had married a second cousin of Kevin's. Strange, Maggie thought, having a Megan Gallagher in Ireland, but it also seemed strangely right.

"I thought I heard your voice," Prudence said, pushing open the door and entering the room wearing a robe, her hair covered up by a ruffled nightcap.

"Prudence," Maggie said, rushing over to embrace her. "We didn't mean to wake you." She kissed her cheek and gazed into the bright green eyes she so fondly remembered and had always loved, eyes nearly the same sparkling green as her sister, Megan's, as well as her father's.

"I'm so very glad that you are here. I have missed you so," Prudence said. "I often recall our tea parties and long to repeat them soon." Her face sobered as she turned to Ona and said, "I gave you specific instructions…" in a chastising tone.

Appearing properly reprimanded, Ona said, "You were sleeping soundly, Mrs. O'Reilly, no doubt visiting with Mr. O'Reilly again in the Summerland. I didn't want to disturb you."

With her smiling eyes, Prudence said, "You had best retire now. But first, kindly bring warm milk laced with honey for two with those ginger biscuits newly arrived from London."

"Aye," Ona said, adding a bob, and she gently closed the door behind her.

"You must be quite tired," Prudence said, drawing Maggie to sit beside her on the settee. "She was right. I was with your father in the Summerland, speaking of you, and of how much we both love you."

"And of how much you love one another," Maggie said, taking her frail hand into her hands and noting her sweet lavender scent. "It seems that women important to my father always wear lavender. There is a lavender scent whenever my mother visits me from the Otherworld."

"Eileen wore rose water," Prudence said in a tone of disdain. "I should have stolen him from that woman before she got him to the altar," she said in a sudden rush of strength. "We had the best times. What a man … your father, such passion and such tenderness. He said he loved me and your mother equally. Does that bother you, Maggie?"

"No. Rather, it pleases me that you shared such love. Such feelings are rare. Great love is a great blessing. I have no doubts that my mother blessed your union."

"Now, I am jealous … Them there together," she confessed, bristling slightly.

Amused, but trying not to laugh, Maggie said, "Well, whatever am I to do when my time comes with the two men I've loved over there? Who do I run to in the Summerland first? You have two men there, as well, Rory and my father. I guess angels must decide and arbitrate our happiness."

Smiling and nodding, Prudence said. "I shall be there much sooner than you, my dear."

Again entering the room with a tray with two glasses of warm milk and ginger biscuits, Ona served them and stoked the fire before she silently left.

"You were right about Ona," Prudence said. "She saved my life more than once when I needed Dr. Guerin. He's a handsome young doctor with all his bloodletting and his leeches!"

"Bloody creatures," Maggie quipped, biting into a crisp ginger biscuit and savoring its flavor.

"Heather says that Dr. Sheehan in Ballyferriter is also very good-looking. I guess us old ladies need a few perks, so we might as well have a handsome face on a doctor who holds our hand."

"Amen," Maggie said, and they both giggled.

"I have never had another friend like you, Maggie. Your father was my dearest and most ardent lover, but it was not the same as sharing secrets with a close woman friend."

"Well, here I am. Tomorrow we shall have Earl Grey tea and scones in the parlor, perhaps with blackberry jam?" she inquired.

"We shall," Prudence said. "And upon the piano—we shall play a duet."

Residing in the house on Goat Street was like being awake in a dream for Maggie, with frequent lapses in time that would briefly take her back to when both she and Prudence were much younger. The fragile woman seated across from her in the parlor or at the piano, was failing badly in 1866. But her mind was still sharp, and their conversations were lively. Her spirit was not broken, only her body, the same as the house, which was in a state of disrepair.

Prudence constantly talked about how Padraic had kept everything in perfect order and did the work himself with a measure of joy and enthusiasm. Local men were soon hired to paint and fix, inside and outside, with the curtains and draperies cleaned and restored. The carpets were beaten and a few replaced. Soon, the rooms resembled more of what Maggie fondly remembered from a very long time ago.

Ona helped her plant flowers in the window boxes, which added color and cheer. The two women busied themselves with gardening in the cool Irish sunshine under the clear blue skies, which were much more refreshing than a Maryland summer with its high humidity and balmy nights. In Ireland, the nights were cool, with frequent rain showers and astonishing rainbows that arched high up over the bay and distant mountains.

Gratefully, Mount Brandon remained much the same. Ireland was Ireland. Maggie O'Reilly Brosnan was happy to be home in her native land in a quiet village. Many still spoke Gaelic, which she had nearly forgotten. Slowly, the Irish language returned to her. Some days were like stepping back into the distant past to live her life over again: Visiting fairy rings, St. Michael's Well and the ruins at Dunshean, all the haunts of her childhood now seemed to again be part of a living, breathing, wonderful dream.

"Those Irish Fenians are making trouble in Canada," Prudence said from her rocking chair, "Forced to surrender in a day. Whatever possessed them to undertake such an invasion? Only Irishmen would ever attempt such tomfoolery in a country controlled by Great Britain."

"The Fenians want to free Ireland from the Crown," Maggie said. "Their dream is the dream of all Irishmen." She pensively paused. "It was nice to be there to see Dermot's Cathleen marry Thomas O'Grady. She's expecting come spring, with another child due for Patrick and Jessica in September. Brigid's Shannon is about to marry. It seems to me that I am

about to become a great grandmother," Maggie said, briefly remembering the birth of Aidan, now fifty, in her aunt's stone cottage up the hill
now occupied by tenant farmers.

"Matthew and Heather have twenty-two grandchildren, with Brigid
expecting her fourth child in October. That will make twenty-three. Her
young Brigid seems to follow you around and asks you a great many
questions. I once told her that she reminds me of a fairy princess, and do
you know what she said to me?"

"That she was one," Maggie said. "Besides my red hair, she has amber
eyes ... great grandmother Kelly's amber eyes. Father said that he only had
the chance to meet her once before she passed at the age of seventy-one."

"At times, young Brigid Mary reminds me very much of you. Isn't
her birthday near the time of yours?"

"On November 10th she'll be seven, three days after I turn sixty-
eight, praise God!" Maggie said. "Sometimes looking into her eyes ..."
she abruptly stopped.

"Yes?" Prudence edged forward on her chair.

Still, Maggie hesitated. "I wonder if she might actually be Aunt
Brigid ... back again?"

"Really?" Prudence sat up straighter.

"She is wise beyond her years and amazes me. Yet, young children
are nearer the other side, except for those of us about to return to the
Otherworld."

Suddenly appearing nervous, Prudence said, "Your aunt's birthday
was four days after mine. We often celebrated together on the tenth, with
mine the eighth, hers the twelfth of March. It was Padraic's idea. He was
always very fond of Brigid. So kind and wise, she was, and always there
for him. It took little to persuade me. My affection for her was strong
from the Eve of Beltaine in joining your circle about the great bonfires.
The fertility rites. An evening filled with mystery and wonder in performing sacred Druid rites on the Scorpio full moon. Do you remember
the night?"

Somberly reflecting, Maggie said, "It is a night I shall never forget
for perhaps a different reason," and at once, she clearly envisioned the
double bonfires and remembered the bright moon in the night sky, with
her dressed in a long blue gown as Aidan arrived on a borrowed horse. It
was easy for her to remember his youthful strength and the depth of their

passion on the night that young Aidan was conceived. He was the perfect image of his handsome father, who was lost in a terrible tempest at sea.

"Brigid Mary looks much like you," Prudence said. "Not like Brigid."

"It's just a feeling, an essence. I've no doubt of our connection in the Otherworld."

"Do you feel that we knew each other before?"

"Aye! As you well knew my father before. That much I could see on the night of your fancy ball and my first meeting with the handsome, charming Darcy."

"And did you know Darcy before?" Prudence was watching her closely. "He once said that he felt he had known you forever ... that he loved you from the first moment he looked into your golden eyes so filled with innocence and wonder. The first time you danced together, he said that he wanted to be with you forever." She glanced away, appearing to swallow with difficulty.

"At first, I was jealous of his love for you," she went on, "After all, you had just met, and he was always my favorite. I loved him dearly, though from the night of the ball I did connive to get you two together. Looking back, at first glance I fell in love with your father that night as well. I was thrilled when Padraic came with you to high tea. I didn't want you to just stay for dinner. I wanted you both to stay forever."

"Father didn't feel that he deserved you. I'm so glad you finally won him over, Prudence. Your courtship must have been interesting, knowing how stubborn my father was, how proud he could be."

"I was a shameless hussy," she said, gleefully sitting forward. "I threw myself at him from the day that Eileen died." She shuddered. "What a terrible, pathetic woman, she was."

"Truly," Maggie said. "You threw yourself at my father? How delightful! It must have been great fun for him to have the finest of ladies throwing herself at him."

"I was not about to allow some other pathetic widow to get her hands on Padraic. And they were circling that handsome devil, especially after Mass every Sunday. Like a flock of hungry crows that wanted to gobble him up."

"I see. Quite the catch, my father?"

"The very best. You could say that I courted him."

"He never disclosed your overtures to me. Rest assured. Although I must say that he wouldn't have needed much encouragement. Let's be honest." Maggie settled back, reflecting. "I should think that any young lady who looked into Darcy's beautiful blue eyes would have thought she had known him forever! In Darcy's eyes, I glimpsed eternity, the kind of love that lasts forever and ever. I was lucky indeed that he survived Napoleon and the terrible Battle at Waterloo."

"Darcy wrote the most exuberant of letters after finding you in Baltimore, soon after my letter informed him of Niall's death at sea. I know that your life together was good from the letters you both wrote to me. Your children do love and adore you, Maggie. Your father was so proud. Almost daily he would sing your praises. Perhaps the most painful aspect for Padraic was watching you grow up to look so much the same as your mother, his Mary Margaret." She pensively paused.

"He took me to your mother's grave. Standing at her tombstone, he told her all about me. How I looked, of my green eyes and my hair dark as Megan's. He told her how much he loved me. How fine I was. How grateful he was for her sending me after him with such a vengeance." Prudence laughed and turned to Maggie as she smiled through her tears.

"He did that, my father ... on my mother's very own grave?"

"He did," she said. "It was perhaps the second happiest day of my life. The first was the day he finally agreed to marry me. I thought he would never say yes."

"You proposed?" Maggie laughed.

"Aye! If I'd waited for him, we would both be buried along with your mother. I knew with all my many holdings that Padraic was too intimidated to ask me to marry him. Not that I didn't drop ten thousand hints, mind you!"

"You are an amazing woman, Prudence Elizabeth Pratt O'Reilly. Truly, you are."

"That's what Darcy always said about you. He called you amazing! It seems to me that amazing women run in this family. Do you not think so, Maggie, my dear?"

"Absolutely, Prudence. Most amazing women all around!"

62

An Irish Legacy

There were days when Maggie and Prudence walked about the town and visited some of the small shops. On other days, they went for a carriage ride through the countryside, but not often. Prudence was starting to sleep more and spend more time alone in her room. Nonetheless, their usual afternoon tea was enjoyed in the parlor. And, on occasion, they played a piano duet.

"I see that Tennessee has ratified your 14th Amendment granting civil rights to Negroes. It is a very good thing," Prudence said in July. "A positive result from the terrible bloodshed, the losses for you and me beyond dear."

"On Friday, the *Great Eastern,* the largest ship afloat, is leaving Valentia Island off our coast with 2,730 nautical miles of cable headed for Trinity Bay in Newfoundland."

"Another transatlantic cable," Prudence said in a tone of consternation. "They lost the last one. It broke on the bottom of the sea. I cannot understand why people do not simply sit down and write a letter."

Nevertheless, on August 10, 1866, Queen Victoria sent a telegram to President Buchanan in the United States of America, with rapid communication now possible across the great pond.

Often, Maggie's spent time with Matthew and Heather in Ballyferriter. Sometimes she would ride over the mountain in the carriage. She and Heather became fast friends and often spoke of fairy rings, besides their conversations about the dearly departed.

"Liam appeared to me in a dream," Heather said, gathering vegetables in the garden. "He was smiling and happy with your parents. There was the sacred grove and a blue pond. I saw the twelve elders, the way I usually do, conferring about something important soon to take place. But I'm unsure of what that is. I'm glad that Matthew and I are both still healthy. You never know how long we will keep *Bile* from our door. The god of the underworld is ever on the lookout for more souls."

"How did you learn the ways of the Old Religion? Sometimes *Bel*, the Lord of Light, becomes the Dark Lord of Death. There is no getting round it. As there is day and night, so there is life and death, eternal growth and eternal expansion," Maggie said.

"That's true," Heather said, absently crossing herself, for though raised as a Protestant she embraced many ways of the Catholics. "When I was a lass, my grandmother said that my hands were blessed by *Cian* and *Diancecht*, the Irish gods of medicine and healing. She also believed that I was once a priestess of *Cian*, a high priestess, if you can believe that? I've often healed my children. I can heal Matthew with my touch. Sometimes he holds me and calls me his healing angel."

"He has mentioned that to me," Maggie said.

"I tried it with Prudence, but, in all confidence, she said she has no plans to linger. One great aunt lived to 102, another to ninety-eight. Prudence would hate to stay so long with both men she loved already over there."

"My two men and many of my loved ones are already in the Otherworld, along with the ancient ones, of course. I wouldn't want to linger, either. I can understand how Prudence feels."

"My granddaughter, Brigid Mary, is your *alter spirit*," Heather said, peeling and washing cabbage leaves in the kitchen one day. "She told me that," she said in a serious tone.

"My *alter spirit*? I'm not sure I know what that means."

"After you leave, she shall assume your tasks here in Ireland. Amazing, don't you think, with her being only seven and my grandchild? She says she's an ancient priestess returned to be with my family here on our Blessed Isle." Heather crossed herself again, shaking her head with a look of wonder on her face.

That disclosure gave Maggie a great deal to ponder.

Late on the Eve of Samhain, Maggie awoke in the middle of the night to find the young, radiant Prudence standing at the foot of her bed. She wore a flowing gown and was surrounded by a dazzling golden light. The ancient night of summer's end, a turning point in the Celtic calendar, was the night when the gods drew near and the departed communicated freely with the living.

Suddenly, her father appeared next to Prudence, looking young and radiant. Both of them were smiling and nodding at her, happy to be together again, hand in hand, emanating love and joy.

Sitting up, Maggie stared at the vision before her. Instantly, she understood what she was seeing. Then, after only a few moments, Prudence and her father slowly faded away from view.

From all around the peninsula, hundreds attended the wake. Prudence was an angel of mercy during the many years of the famine and every year since. There was the Mass. And then, her burial next to her father. Padraic Desmond O'Reilly was now eternally at rest between the two women he had loved the most in his life. The Church was filled to capacity with Protestants and Catholics. Flowers were everywhere. Many wanted to thank the wonderful, kind and caring woman they had come to truly love and would long remember. A second service was held at St. James to memorialize a charitable saint in the eyes of the local people.

At the reading of the will, Maggie was to receive the fine house on Goat Street and the O'Reilly family farm occupied by a tenant farmer, his wife and three children, along with a small dairy herd. The family also raised chickens and sold eggs in the marketplace. Two horses and two carriages were also to be part of her legacy, along with four rented tenant farms under Matthew's supervision in various locations around the peninsula. The farm at Ballyferriter was left to Matthew and his descendants, sixty acres of prime land, plus four additional rented tenant farms. Some farmers wanted to buy, which was also to be taken into consideration by the family.

Bonds and monies were left to Sean Joseph and Antoinette, with more divided between Padraic's remaining grandchildren in South Carolina, Georgia, and New York, mainly token bequeaths of a hundred pounds, included Peter Gallagher in California. After learning the truth from Maggie, Prudence had decided against leaving anything to Robert's illegitimate children. But a hundred pounds went to each legitimate child in trust with their Uncle Sean until the child reached the age of twenty. Of late, Sean Joseph had entered into a banking partnership with his son Peter, age forty-two, along with his son's wealthy father-in-law, Bernard Franklin Hamilton of San Francisco. Previously, the man had amassed a fortune with the mining of the Comstock Lode.

Unable to stop her sniffling since finding Prudence dead in her bed on that terrible morning, Ona continued to mope about the house. That was so even though Prudence had left her 300 pounds and the furnishings from her room, which the servant already thought of as hers after so many years of service.

In the library, on the day after the legal proceedings, Maggie said, "I plan to keep you on, unless you would rather not," she added, thinking Ona had to be her age. "I won't be surprised if want to leave. Two young girls have already been interviewed, one hired. My grandson and his family are living in my manor house in America. Patrick Sean Jr. was born only two days ago. Imagine receiving the news in a telegram all the way from Maryland by transatlantic cable! We truly live in modern age, Ona. Fully modern."

"Good news, then," Ona said with a vague smile on her face.

"Won't you please sit down and join me for a cup of tea?"

At first hesitant, Ona sat in the chair opposite her. "Are you sure, ma'am?" she inquired, looking both startled and alarmed.

"It is only tea, Ona, and ginger biscuits might be nice. Are there any left?"

"Aye!" she said, bounding up. "I'll get them, along with another cup, if you please," and she curtsied, blushing as she hurried out of the parlor for the kitchen.

Standing up, Maggie looked all around the library and fondly remembered the wonderful years of her youth. At random, she pulled a book from a shelf. It was the second volume of *The Decline and Fall of the Roman Empire* by Edward Gibbon. She had struggled with the first volume, and years later, she had discussed the book with Yuma while seated on giant boulders near the Gunpowder River. It amazed her to think this was now her library and the library of her children and grandchildren, even her great grandchildren. For a second time, Patrick and Jessica had made her a great grandmother. Mother and child were doing fine at Marcus Manor. There was now another boy to carry on the Brosnan family name.

The generation thrice removed was starting to make her feel old, especially now, considering the many shelves filled with musty old books containing words of wonder and wisdom so important to her and her children, her grandchildren and great grandchildren. Secretly, Maggie planned to do all within her power to bring greater wisdom and understanding to yet others within the green, green shores of Ireland.

Rushing in with a tray with dishes of apple pie, whipped cream, ginger biscuits and a fresh pot of tea, Ona proudly announced, "There's berry pie, too, if you'd like some, ma'am."

"Apple will be fine. Do join me, Ona, won't you?"

In an obvious of state of absolute delight, Ona served two large pieces of apple pie with volumes of whipped cream and two steaming cups of tea as a light snow started to fall outside the windows onto the nearly empty streets of Dingle. The two of them watched the snow falling outside the clean, curtained windows, while enjoying delicious freshly baked apple pie and hot Earl Grey tea in the parlor of the fine house on Goat Street.

Only a short time passed before Maggie began to invite the poorer peasant children in town and from the nearby farms into her home and library to learn how to read and write in English. No books on the shelves were printed in Gaelic. Maggie had never learned how to read German or French. Since 1834, the Christian Brothers had established a school in Dingle that many local children attended. But there were still many children without the means, and still others who simply enjoyed being read to in a fine library near a cozy fire, with the prospects of spicy ginger biscuits and warm tea served with sweet cream.

Everyone in town was friendly toward the new Catholic American war widow who somewhat infrequently attended Mass. It was more for the feeling of being inside the fine Catholic Church than from being in full agreement with the doctrine of the young priest, Father Patrick Mulroney from Ballyferriter. He often inquired after her absence from the confessional.

"I speak with the Lord directly. He listens much better than I do. I have no need to tell any other human being of my mistakes or evil thoughts that may temporarily capture my attention. I am sure that you hear plenty of those, Father, without me adding to burdens on your soul."

It was plain to Maggie that the priest had little or no understanding of her philosophy, or even cared much about what she thought, for that matter. She had no wish to change his ways or to change the ways of anyone, for that matter. She allowed her kin and her children the same privilege of finding their own way in the world of the spirit as she was always given. No one had hindered her quest. She could see no reason to hinder that of anyone else.

In the spring of 1867, during their usual Sunday supper with Maggie in Dingle, Matthew said, "I see that your Africans have been given the vote in America, in spite of your president's constant and hearty objection, I might add."

"America has another state, which makes thirty-seven," Heather said. "It's called Nebraska."

"How about that Jesse James gang?" Maggie remarked, "Robbing trains and banks, murdering folk? They ought to hang him and his lawless group of renegades, shoot the lot of them!"

"It seems that your colored will fare better in time," Matthew said. "And the reconstruction is going on in spite of your bloody president. Kindly excuse my language, but what about him trying to veto all the good things. Whatever is the matter with the man? He's quite daft, if you ask me."

"More chicken?" Maggie inquired. "Dermot says that there's talk of impeaching Johnson. He's certainly no Abraham Lincoln!"

"Don't mind if I do," Matthew said, taking the platter of chicken as Ona was about to get up. "Stay right where you are. I can manage," he said.

Ona sat, frowned and narrowed her eyes. "I'm paid to work here," she said, standing again, "I'm refilling some of these dishes with the hearty appetites around this table, so kindly excuse me," and she went into the kitchen woefully shaking her head all the way.

Amused glances were exchanged all around the table.

"She still complains about having to sit with us," Heather said, "Tells me it isn't right. She was amazed that you had black folk sitting at your fancy dining room table at Marcus Manor, especially after I showed her the pictures. I'm so sorry we never made the trip. Quite a place you had there near that river with over 500 acres."

"She will get used to it," Maggie said. "My former slaves felt strange at first. Lots of runaways sat at that table during the war, especially for holiday meals. We tried to make merry even though there wasn't much to laugh at or sing about, if the truth be told."

"What do you think about your government purchasing Alaska?" Matthew inquired.

"Everyone always seems to want more land," Maggie testily replied. "Like the British sailing over to Asia and taking over island after island. It seems to me that Queen Victoria is as greedy as any other British monarch, if you want my honest opinion."

"I don't know why you're always saying, 'if you want my honest opinion,'" Matthew said in good humor, "Since you're going to give it to us, anyway. You've always been very free with your opinions, Mary Margaret, for as long as I can remember from the time that you could talk. I'm still a bit upset that you wouldn't let me be your footman when you went to the ball and met Darcy ... a lowly footman ... What a shame!" he said, shaking his head and smiling.

"That was Pa, not me. You want another biscuit, Matthew?" she forced a smile.

"Why, thank you," he replied and he helped himself to two.

That fall, the children and grandchildren of Matthew and Heather safely arrived from Cork and Dublin for an extended stay. As usual, Maggie talked them into letting young Brigid Mary stay with her. By then, Brigid and Kenneth Brosnan had six children with yet another on the way.

One evening after supper, young Brigid Mary said, "Tell me again about all your African slaves and how you made Uncle Darcy give them their freedom," and her bright eyes appeared to sparkle.

"Will you never tire of that story?"

"It's a good story, Aunt Maggie. And you tell it so well."

Once more, her grand niece heard all about the African slaves and how her aunt and her cousins had helped runaway slaves escape on the Underground Railroad, which was never really a *railroad*, except in creating a pathway that allowed them to escape from grievous bondage to cruel and heartless masters.

"What's important to understand is that it doesn't matter whether your skin is black or white or brown ... it doesn't matter whether you're Irish, English, Scottish, German, African or some tribe of Indian."

"And it doesn't matter whether you're Protestant or Catholic," young Brigid Mary added.

"Or whether you belong to the religion practiced by our Native American friends."

"The Pis-ca-ta-way," she spoke the word as in a magical chant. "And my cousin Aidan found gold in the river, the same as my Uncle Sean, just lying around waiting to be scooped up."

"You're right. However, it is also important to understand that you have different kinds of blood flowing through your veins, with some skin white, pink, brown, red or even black. And you know what else?"

"What, Aunt Maggie?"

"That all are basically the same in their hearts and their souls. When given a chance, inside people are pretty much the same, though you do need to trust your instincts and stay away from those who don't feel quite right to you. You do understand that?"

Brigid nodded.

"My family is made up of good, bright and beautiful souls just like you, who sometimes ask me to read them stories or tell them about Africans or Indians, Americans, Yankees or Southerners. The latter caused us a whole lot of trouble, I might add. Yet, all of them have strengths and weaknesses, some we like better than others, but members of my family have strong character that I am more proud than ashamed of, and sometimes weaknesses can produce positive results with the passing of time."

"They do?" she replied, widening her beautiful amber eyes.

"There are times when mistakes can turn into great blessings, wonderful situations or relationships. A man may try to invent one thing and invent something just as good or even better. So never be afraid to make mistakes, Brigid Mary. You learn from your mistakes. Promise me."

"I promise."

Her nieces and nephews in Ireland, her children and grandchildren the world over, filled her heart with hope and with great joy. What pleased Maggie the most was that each of them had a smidgen of her blood flowing in their veins. Her blood flowed all around the world. That was a true blessing in her mind. That was what her father had always taught her, as well as her dear Aunt Brigid.

"What's important is being a good human being," Maggie said.

"Yes, ma'am."

"Being kind and caring, doing what you can to help the unfortunate whether you're a Lutheran, Methodist, Episcopalian, Presbyterian, Congregationalist, Quaker or a Catholic."

"Or Druid Pagan?" she said. "I'm like you, remember? I was born with a veil. Mother says it doesn't happen very often, but in olden times, we carried on the tradition of the Druids just like all the Kellys have for centuries and centuries and centuries."

Looking deeply into the young girl's eyes, Maggie remembered the many wonderful conversations with her Aunt Brigid after her mother's death on the night that she first learned of her veil. She and her young niece had also shared many stories of her mother in the Otherworld, and their dreams of her great-great grandmother Kelly. It seemed to Maggie that all the mysteries of her life, past, present and future, were right there before her eyes in the soul of this one special child.

In her bed late at night, Maggie sometimes wondered if her Aunt Brigid had become bored with the solace of the Otherworld and returned early to help Ireland gain its freedom? That might well take place during the young child's life was what she thought concerning the matter. That was something for which she sincerely hoped and prayed.

During the summer of 1868, Aidan and Shannon arrived on the steamship *Rose* all the way from San Francisco. They brought along four of their children: Kelly Sue, fourteen, Aidan McKenna, twelve, Anna Marie, ten, and Jeffrey Jonathan not quite eight. Each child was given an assignment from their school to report back on when school resumed after the summer on the subject of Irish history.

Together, the family toured the Lakes of Killarney by train, an awesome though frightening experience considering the sheer drops. The horse drawn carriage rides were favorites for the children. Maggie now understood Darcy's high praise for the lakes, for she too had heard the *Teezeley Weezeleys* calling back from the mountain. It was much more than an echo, she thought, much more.

It was wonderful to have her family there to take sightseeing all around their fine country, to dance and sing and share meals. All of them visited Killarney, Tralee, Cork and Dublin, where they stood on the high hill of Tara from whence Ireland's once glorious high kings had governed with regal chivalry in times of old.

"You should be pleased with the progress of our colored friends," Aidan said. "There is now a Negro majority in South Carolina, and President Johnson was nearly impeached, with only one vote in his favor. The House was two to one against the man."

"I read that. I wear glasses now, Aidan, but I can still read, praise the Lord."

"How about that Jesse James," young Aidan McKenna inquired. "Do you suppose they'll ever catch him?" He turned to his grandmother and said, "He robs trains and kills people."

"He got $14,000 down in Kentucky," Matthew said. "Read about it in the *Kerryman*. Imagine making a living from robbing banks and a gol dang good living at that!"

"They will catch him and his brother, eventually," Aidan said, "Nasty bunch. Fortunately, they haven't yet hit any banks in San Francisco. Business is brisk. Have you had any word from Antoinette after that volcanic eruption and the tidal waves in Hawaii? I hear the earthquake was horrific. Do we have any family living on the big island?"

"I think so," Maggie said. "Many died from the eruption of Mauna Loa, the last I heard. Antoinette's health is failing her without her Liam." She shook her head. "I see that General Grant is the Republican candidate for president, a wise selection, anything to get rid of that mealy mouth Johnson. He's a spineless sort, if you want my honest opinion. He probably owned slaves."

Chuckling, Aidan said, "I agree with you, Mother. We now have a Memorial Day to honor the men lost in the War. Folk take flowers to the cemetery to honor the fallen on both sides."

"That is a very good thing, a fine and decent thing."

"I see most states have re-entered the Union," Matthew remarked. "A show of unity."

"True. I wonder how the Gallaghers feel about having a colored cabinet member in the government of South Carolina? It must be a serious adjustment for them."

"And all the former slaves are now citizens," Heather said. "How about that, Mother?"

"It's a good thing ... a very good thing, indeed, at long last."

Walking alone with Aidan near the time of his departure for America, Maggie said, "I appreciate your coming with me to the ogham stone so we might speak with our ancient ancestor together."

Aidan smiled, looping his mother's arm through his, as he said, "I'm sorry that we haven't had more time alone together. But with all the relatives we've been pretty busy these weeks. Shannon loves you, as I knew she would, and so do your grandchildren. We all love you dearly, Mama."

"And I love all of you. You have a fine family, Aidan. You should be proud."

"I am proud. With my two hotels and another restaurant, I keep plenty busy these days. Unfortunately, there is no time for me to stop and see Patrick this time. We wanted them to take the train to California, but frankly, besides being married to Jessica, my son is married to Marcus Manor. Patrick is a true farmer, which frankly, amazes me. He misses you and he says that you should come home. It seems everyone misses you at Marcus Manor." Now, Aidan turned to the ogham. "So this is the grave of our ancient ancestor?"

"It is," she said, reaching out to touch the stone. "He is Kelly. They buried the kings, but Druid priests and priestesses were cremated upon an altar of stones. Aunt Brigid taught me that. That is what I want from you, Aidan, to be cremated upon an altar of stones with my ashes scattered on Dingle Bay. You will do that for me, won't you, son?"

For a long moment, he studied her, his dark eyes so much like his father's looking perhaps as the first Aidan might have looked at the age of fifty-two. She was still unsure of how she really felt about his moustache, but the gray streaks in his hair made him look distinguished. He was a handsome man, her eldest son, without question.

"I shall try to do so, Mother," Aidan finally said, his eyes misting over as he placed his arms around her shoulders and she wrapped hers arms around his waist. "Let's hope it is no time soon," he said and he gently kissed her forehead.

All of a sudden, a gentle breeze sprung up, swirling all around them, as a violet mist instantaneously and mysteriously rose up out of the dark blue Irish Sea.

63

The Call of the Otherworld

In America, the war between the races persisted. In 1868, in massacres in Louisiana, white terrorists murdered 200 blacks. The last year of the war, a group of white southerners had gathered in their mutual hatred toward slaves obtaining their freedom. The organization called itself the Ku Klux Klan. Those freed from slavery now faced a new struggle against racism and white terrorism, especially in those states in the South.

In October, John Menard of Louisiana was the first black man elected to Congress, and three days later, Ulysses S. Grant was elected president. That December, the trial of Jefferson Davis commenced with the first blacks serving on a jury. Despite bitter opposition, President Johnson granted unconditional pardons to all involved in the southern rebellion now known as the Civil War.

In February of 1869, charges of treason against Jefferson Davis were dropped, something Maggie had always suspected might happen. In March, Grant was inaugurated as the eighteenth president and Arkansas passed an anti-Klan law. In April, North Carolina did the same. In May, the Golden Spike completed the Transcontinental Railroad and the National Women's Suffrage Association was formed, with Luke and Brigid Plunkett in rapt attendance.

That September, the first westbound train reached San Francisco, with Aidan pleading with his entire family in the east to take a train to the West. Women's suffrage was granted in the Wyoming Territory. That was the best Christmas present ever for Maggie and Brigid. It seemed to her that it was only a matter of time before her daughters and granddaughters would be able to cast a vote in an election in the United States of America.

In 1870, Virginia was re-admitted to the Union. That same month the U.S. Army slaughtered 173 Blackfoot Indian women and children in Montana. That news made Maggie sick at heart. It seemed that the world needed much more time before folks would stop making judgments against the color of someone's skin or difference in culture. Moral blindness appeared to be rampant, with Maggie unable to understand the reason. All that she could do was hope and pray and silently celebrate when the Negroes received the vote in February. The establishment of the Golden Gate Park in San Francisco seemed to please her family immensely.

It was not long after Beltaine when Maggie read in the newspapers that the Fenians had once again raided Canada. The fact that President Grant met with the Sioux Chief, Red Cloud, reminded her of her time with Yuma and Red Bird and all the other Piscataway she had loved.

In June, at the time of the summer solstice, Maggie revisited the ogham stone to mentally perform rituals, calling on *Bel*, the Shining One, and *Dana*, goddess of the moon, and all the other Celtic deities she could remember. She said prayers and performed blessings, mainly for the sake of Ireland and for peace in the world. Then, she blessed America, repeating out loud the name of each of the thirty-seven states.

After that, she walked to the Church to light candles and stuffed a ten pound note into the collection box. Then, she lit one candle for Darcy and another for Aidan. Another candle was lit for Prudence, one for her father, mother, her Aunt Brigid, for Megan and Kevin and Liam, besides all the children on that side of the veil. There was a candle for Triona, another for Gareth and for Star. Maggie also lit candles for Yuma and her old friends, Rebecca and Ruth, her former slaves and soul sisters on the other side now as well. More candles were lit for all the grandchildren who had already passed. Great grandmother Kelly was always in her prayers and blessings, for she had always helped Maggie throughout her long life.

For a brief moment, she apologized for anyone she may have left out, asking all to watch over those in the land of the living and bring peace into the heart of every freed slave. She prayed for sanity for every white man or woman filled with hatred, and solace and forgiveness for the American Indians betrayed by the United States government.

Kneeling in a pew, Maggie prayed, "Please make Queen Victoria free Ireland … and stop harassing the rest of the world. I thank you all for all these many blessings bestowed upon all of us. Amen," she said, crossing herself for added measure, the way her Aunt Brigid had always taught her.

At first the chest pains were mild. After enjoying a quiet supper, Maggie retired to her room. After all, it was the solstice, the longest day and shortest night of the year. All day long, she had experienced a curious sense of otherworldliness, a deep sense of peace such as might be produced by a balmy breeze when sailing upon the Chesapeake Bay with her beloved Darcy.

After climbing into her bed, suddenly there was a brightening all around her. She hardly noticed the chest pains growing stronger, as faint outlines started to take form before her in the light: A man here. A woman there. And children of different sizes and ages. All of a sudden, a deep sense of love filled her, both within and without. Love grander than any words might describe. Then, a sense of unspeakable peace settled over her, as she lay back on her pillows to watch the play of light and forms unfolding, as she breathed in the sweet scent of lavender, knowing her mother was near.

Turning out the lamp, the shimmering lights grew brighter, stronger, starting to take on the faint misty colors of a fading rainbow as she heard Ona gently close the door. Then, there was the faint sound of music. An Irish harp, perhaps the Kelly harp her aunt had often played upon and loved. The harp her mother had played as a girl. It was angelic music with an Irish air, music Maggie loved far more than the piano. At first faint, then richer, deeper, the music and light increased as the forms within the light became clearer and more distinct to her.

Directly to her right was the young, handsome Darcy and he was smiling. His soft blond hair and bright blue eyes appeared to be shining. On her left stood the young, handsome Aidan, with his dark brown eyes and dark curly hair framing his beautiful dimpled smile. There they were, the two men she had loved. Beyond them she could see her father, looking young and very handsome, with a radiant Prudence on one arm and her beautiful mother on the other. Then, she could see young Dermot and young Darcy, Terence, Gareth, Star, Triona and Brigid. All of them looked young and radiant. All around her were the forms of many different people, some she had no memory of at all. But all of them appeared to know who she was. Young Ruth and Rebecca were standing there, along with the other slaves who had died from the cholera or in the war. Even Israel was there, apparently thanking her for saving her children so long ago.

A beautiful woman in a flowing white gown with long red hair and bright shining eyes drifted toward her. She was holding out her arms to her, filling her heart and her entire being with what could only be described as the purest form of LOVE.

"Grandmother Kelly?" Maggie whispered.

Softly smiling, she nodded and beckoned to her.

We have come for you, Mary Margaret, she appeared to say without speaking.

As though floating on the air, Maggie felt herself drawn into the brilliant, pulsating, loving LIGHT, where, all at once, she was embraced by all of them together. Instantaneously, her bedroom walls faded from her sight.

64

Eulogy

The steamer, *Hannibal,* out of Queenstown, crossed the Atlantic Ocean in record's time and arrived early in Baltimore Harbor. For Aidan, it was a relaxing voyage spent with interesting people who seemed to show an interest in the construction of his third hotel. He was spending time with his son, Patrick, and his family at Marcus Manor, along with his brother Dermot and his extended family. But the real reason for him to be there was to scatter the last of his mother's ashes. It was not something she had required of him, but something he planned to do all the same.

The memorial was held in the small, overcrowded chapel. All the members of the family in the east were present: Brigid and Luke with their children and grandchildren, Dermot and Priscilla with their children and grandchildren, Patrick and Jessica and their two children. Plus, the free colored and a few of the neighbors. All of them had gathered together to pay tribute to a woman they truly loved and were unlikely to ever forget. A painting of Mary Margaret by Priscilla bore a remarkable likeness to his mother and was surrounded with huge bouquets of wildflowers and roses.

Many folks simply stood in their place to speak their words of appreciation and love.

"Good-bye Mother," Priscilla tearfully said, with Dermot holding her hand as he added, "We have missed you for a while now. Rest in peace, Mother." They both sat, weeping together.

Many were too shy to say anything. Being the eldest, Aidan was asked to give her eulogy. Reluctantly, he stood at the podium and he began:

"All of you knew and loved my mother, perhaps as much as I did. It always seemed to me that Mama loved every one of you in this chapel that she made Pa build." He paused, smiling, as light laughter rippled through the room.

"Mama made Pa do lots of things he tended to resist, but he usually ended up enjoying those things in spite of himself. Things like freeing his slaves. Darcy Donal Brosnan was a good man and I miss him dearly. I figure those two are together now. Mama said they would be. She was proud to be an American, and she was also proud to be Irish."

Everyone smiled. A few nodded in agreement.

"While Missy Maggie was still living on this plantation, I'm sure you pretty much know how she felt about you. And frankly, I still cannot get over the fact that she is gone from this world. I hope she says 'hello' to Abe Lincoln for me. During the ritual she asked me to perform, I asked her to thank President Lincoln for all he did for this nation before they killed him. But that, of course, is another story." Aidan paused, struggling for self-control and brushing away his tears.

"I returned to Ireland to fulfill my mother's last request. She didn't want to be buried in the ground. She wanted a ritual used for the Druid high priests and priestesses in olden times ... to be cremated on an altar of ancient stone with the smoke rising up to heaven ..."

Gasps erupted from many in the chapel.

"She wanted her ashes scattered in Ireland in Dingle Bay," he went on. "So out of love for my mother as her eldest son and firstborn, I returned to Ireland to dig her up to see that her last wishes were fulfilled," he nodded to his family, already aware of her exhumation and cremation.

"This had to be done in secrecy, mind you, and under cover of darkness. Several of my cousins and my Uncle Matthew helped me out."

The expressions on the faces of many blacks looked uncomfortable, but Aidan continued, "They helped me build an altar of ancient stones near an old ring fort high above the sea, a place special to my mother, where shamrocks grow mixed in with tiny purple violets. The place had a special feeling for me too, strange as that might seem."

He paused and cleared his throat.

"Collecting the ashes of a human body which has burned all night and all day and all night again is no easy task," he said, smiling. "Especially considering the Irish weather, with the peat repeatedly relit to keep it going." Amused, he shook his head and said, "It can be downright amazing what an eldest son might be called upon to do for a Pagan Catholic mother when she has given up the ghost. I understand that's what my father called her long before they married. A Pagan Catholic. He knew a little bit about what he was getting into, but the truth is, due to the bad weather and my lack of experience in such matters, some of Mama seeped into the fertile soil of her beloved Emerald Isle.

"It rained, off and on, especially when I was trying to gather up as much of her as I could from all those rocks and crevices. I want you to know I got most of her into a vase she fancied. Uncle Matthew, Aunt Heather and a young second cousin named Brigid Mary, who insisted on being present, all of us got into a boat and went out onto the bay, where most of Mama was scattered in the sea, according to her last request." He shifted on his feet.

"Then, something not entirely her idea took place. I placed some of her ashes in a leather pouch that Yuma had made for me when I was seven, and I brought it here. Early this morning, I went out to my father's grave and planted some flowers. More instructions from Mama. And in the process, I dug the rest of her into his grave. So maybe a little of what was left of Mama is now with what was left of the man she loved the longest, and I think the most. Although I seriously doubt that any of us really understood the secret thoughts whirling around in her pretty Irish head.

"You know Mama, her spirit was all encompassing. She was everywhere and anywhere she was needed. All of you who loved her need only call her name or think about her to have her near you. That's what she taught me. She's likely to show up in our dreams even when we don't expect her, looking beautiful the same as she did when I was a lad, with her long, flowing red hair and her bright amber eyes filled with love and compassion for a dying child, a dying slave, a dying Indian, or anyone in serious need of her love.

"Our Mama was a woman with a big heart and a great soul who responded to real need whenever called upon. She was a woman of strong opinions, fully incapable of tolerating injustice. It seems that most of all, she was woman of passion and a woman of principle. Anyone knew when she loved them and probably knew when she didn't give a damn, either. She enjoyed life, singing, dancing, playing the piano, reading books and teaching any of us to be knowledgeable, gracious and helpful human beings on this earth.

"She loved and she laughed and she cried. She fought hard for what she believed in. She may still be mad over there in the Otherworld, because she never got to cast her vote in one presidential election in the United States of America.

"Nonetheless, Mary Margaret Kathleen Kelly O'Reilly McKenna Brosnan made this world a better place, by living a fully principled and passionate life, and none of us here are likely to ever forget her. May God rest my mother's soul in peace until we all meet again one day beyond the veil over there in the Otherworld!"

THE END

About the Author

Patricia McLaine is the author of *The Wheel of Destiny – The Tarot Reveals Your Master Plan*, *The Recycling of Rosalie* (novel) and *Cosmic Conspiracy – Psychic to the Rich and Famous* (memoir), and *Bittersweet Summer – Paula's Story* and *Summer of Love – Dana's Story*. She is an international psychic with worldwide clientele and has been featured in newspaper and magazine articles in the U.S. and U.K. as well as appearing on numerous radio and television shows in the U.S., U.K. and Hong Kong, China. Her Blog Talk Radio Show is Exploring the Paranormal with Pattie. Her website: www.patriciamclaine.com .

Patricia resides in Alexandria, Virginia.

You may also connect with the author online at:

http://www.facebook.com/pattiemclaine

http://twitter.com/#!/psychicpattie

http://www.linkedin.com/pub/pattie-mclaine/10/345/898

http://www.pattie-mclaineblog.blogspot.com/

http://www.pattie-tarotblog.blogspot.com/

http://www.blogtalkradio.com/pattiemclaine

www.ingramcontent.com/pod-product-compliance
Lightning Source LLC
Chambersburg PA
CBHW071630260626
47170CB00001B/35